RISKY BUSINESS

LAUREN LANDISH

Edited by
VALORIE CLIFTON
Edited by
STACI ETHERIDGE

CHAPTER 1

CARSON

"*W*hat's your name? I'm going to post this on the internet!"

The shrill, piercing female voice wails in my ear, stabbing its shrieking tones somewhere past my eardrum and directly into my brain. To say it's very angry is an understatement. No, at that decibel, we're beyond Karen and in danger of hitting the banshee-harpy category.

I quicken my footsteps, hustling toward the small crowd of people I can see gathered at the doors of the *Oh Say, Can You See!* souvenir shop. It's the main storefront of Americana Land, the landing point for park guests as they enter and leave the amusement park and where the majority of our souvenir purchases are made. It's supposed to be the first and final good impression the park makes.

An angry guest there is bad news.

I gently slide my way through the people, trying not to push but instead twisting this way and that to create the minimum amount of disruption while watching out for tiny tots and turning on my fake as fuck customer service persona. Nearing the nucleus of the fuckup, I call out, "Excuse me."

As I breach the center of the circle, I see the owner of the angry voice. She's an early-twenties woman with long blonde hair, long black eyelashes, and long bedazzled nails that she's waving around as she speaks. "You messed up, Barbara!" Blondie screeches. "I'll have your job!"

1

The sneered threat is delivered with all the arrogance of 'the customer is always right' ideology that everyone knows is complete and utter bullshit. Except, of course, for the rude customers who pull it out of their back pocket like a 'get out of being an asshole free' card.

"Excuse me!" I announce again, louder and sharper this time to interrupt the next round of verbal warfare. Eyes turn to me from all around the circle. The blonde's are filled with fire, but Barbara looks relieved to see me. I don't know her, but her tag proclaims her name and shows she's a part of the team, and given the way she's patting her gray hair and wringing her gnarled hands, she needs some backup. "What seems to be the issue?"

"Mr. Steen, thank goodness. This *woman* is shoplifting, and when I stopped her, she became belligerent. Security has been notified." Barbara's distaste is obvious as she raises one brow and glares at the woman, who's huffing and glaring back through narrowed eyes.

"Shoplifting? Are you fucking serious?" she screeches. "That's defamation! All these people heard you slander me! I'm going to sue your ass!"

"Please watch your language. There are children," I tell her sternly in the hopes of both stopping her crude language and defusing the situation. Maybe if she realizes the scene she's making, she'll have a shred of embarrassment?

Whirling around, she gives me a quick up-and-down glance and finds a new target. I'm guessing it's because of the white Polo shirt with the embroidered *Americana Land* banner entwined with a flag, a different color from the sky blue of the regular workers' shirts. But I look like what I am . . . a boss. I'm not Barbara's direct boss, of course. There are numerous supervisors, managers, and directors between her and me, but I'm the highest C-level executive most employees working the park grounds will ever see. Not to mention, it's my last name on the sign out front that proudly proclaims, *A Steen Family Legacy*.

The woman continues her rant, aiming it at me now. "I could buy everything in this shitty store twice over without my bank account taking a hit. I've got a black American Express." She flips her hair over her shoulder as if that should explain everything. Part of me is surprised she doesn't whip it out like some credit card form of a dick measuring contest.

"Name dropping a fancy charge card does not excuse rudeness and misbehavior, ma'am. Such as not purchasing items, if that is what happened." I make the statement slowly and directly, just loud enough for everyone in the crowd to hear me, while also giving the woman some wiggle room. I'd prefer to give her an out while making sure she catches every implication. I lower my eyes pointedly to her oversized bag, where I can clearly see our stuffed eagle mascot, Freddy Freebird, peeking out. "Can I see your receipt, please?"

She growls, actually, audibly growls at me like a pissed off tiger or a grumpy racoon, at least considering that she completes the argument with a toddler-esque foot stomp. "Do you know who I am?"

No, what I know is that she does not produce a receipt, instead going for distraction. Too bad for her, I'm well-versed in smoke and mirror techniques from dealing with my take-no-responsibility brother. "Someone who needs to show a receipt for that Freddy Freebird playing hide-and-seek in your purse." I pause dramatically before adding, "Or someone who's about to be led to the security office to await local police officers."

I'm bluffing with that second option, if I'm being honest. Unless she's swiped more than a thirty-five-dollar stuffed animal, we won't press charges. The amount of money the park would shell out over the hassle of paperwork is more than the value of the stolen item. Especially when for the local cops, it's pretty much the same deal. They've got real crime to stop, not piddly shit. But we will escort her off-property and ban her from returning.

I expect her to deflate. Or I expect her to bow up a little more in a final act of defiance. What I don't expect is the sly, knowing grin that blooms across her fake-tanned face, nor the evil delight dancing in her eyes. "You don't know who I am, do you? You really don't?"

Disquiet settles in my stomach, but my course is set. I'm done with this. With this woman, with her disrespecting park employees, and with the still-growing crowd that's starting to take sides. Loudly.

"Leave her alone! You can't prove nothing!"

"The bird's literally in her bag. Just show the receipt."

"Look, Karen—" I start, but she cuts me off.

"Augh! Karen? Did you call me a Karen?" she screams, stepping close enough to get in my face.

I take a deep breath, which doesn't settle my ire but rather helps the growing embers bloom hotter. "I apologize. You're right, you are far too young for that. So . . . McKenzie, McKinley, Brinleigh . . . whatever they call bratty young women who think they can take whatever they want and get away with it—"

I don't get to finish what I'm saying, which would probably be for the best except my words are stolen by the woman slapping me solidly across the face. I feel the inside of my cheek slice against my teeth, and I can taste blood as a collective gasp of shock goes through the people around us.

Before I can react, the circle is broken by security finally arriving. They must've seen the slap during their approach because before I can explain the situation, the two guards grab Shoplifting McKenzie. There's a scuffle, insistent demands of 'get your hands off me!' and 'get on the ground, stop resisting', and I try to stand back and not get in the way.

But it's hard to do nothing. My fists clench at my side, especially as the woman screeches louder and louder, flailing about on the floor like a fish out of water. Her antics become more desperate, her dagger-like nails scratching the guards and her sneakered feet kicking out at the guard trying to take her purse. Freddy Freebird goes flying, as does a stack of souvenir T-shirts, a wallet, and various purse contents. A tube of lipstick rolls along the floor, and for some reason, that feels like my cue.

"Enough!" I bark. The crowd jumps, but the woman ignores me, still fighting as though it's for her life and not a misdemeanor shoplifting accusation with a tacked-on assault charge. Because after this, we're absolutely calling the police. Escorting off-property isn't nearly enough after this.

The guards spin, struggling to corral the woman, and before my brain makes the decision, my body is on top of her. I pin her down, allowing security to focus on handcuffing her.

"Get off me, you pervert!"

"Be still and let them handcuff you. I don't want you to get hurt." It's the complete truth, but even to my ears, it sounds like a heartless lie considering I'm snarling and my voice is hard.

She wiggles beneath me, but the guards are quickly successful. "All clear, Mr. Steen," one of the guards says, panting heavily. "We've got her."

I get up, catching my own breath and in shock at how something as normal as a shoplifting stop turned into something so dramatic. They pull her up by her arms, but she's not what I'd consider 'under control' since she's still shouting and kicking out as the guards walk her away toward the on-site security office.

"Oh, y'all done fucked up now! You just wait! I'm going to own this place!" She flicks wild eyes to the crowd. "You saw that. They assaulted me. This is illegal detainment! If I disappear, tell the police who did it."

I sigh at her dramatics. How in the hell does she think she's the victim here? Barbara's in tears, two security guards are covered in red scratches, and I can taste the blood on my tongue. Hopefully, it's not bad enough that it's showing when I open my mouth. The last thing I need is to say something while looking like Dracula.

And the merchandise she stole is still scattered about, proof of her misdeeds.

Work isn't done, though. Instead of yelling in frustration, I switch back into my fake as fuck customer service voice and address the crowd. "Sorry about that, everyone. Please go back to enjoying your day. Might I suggest a snack at the nearby Boston Tea Party, or a ride on the Founding Fathers carousel?" The options are more orders than suggestions, and I move toward a few people, gently steering them with outstretched arms and a big smile that hurts my face, reminding myself *no teeth, no teeth* and probably looking like a creepy bastard because of it. "We need to clear this area."

Though people do begin moving, I can hear them talking about what just happened. I can't stop that, but I focus on straightening up the mess and making sure Barbara is okay. She's looking a little shocked and appalled at the whole situation. That's not right. "Hey, Barbara, you okay?"

"Yeah, Mr. Steen. I'm fine." Her answer seems automatic because a moment later, her eyes clear and she huffs out, "That was insane. What's wrong with people?"

"Good question," I say agreeably. Quieter, I mutter, "Some people just suck."

She seems to be gathering her wits further, and I leave her smiling at another guest as she tells them how much she appreciates their patience and understanding. I guess that's about the best ending to a shitty situation I could hope for.

CHAPTER 2

JAYME

*O*ne more steadying breath. It's all I'll allow myself before I get out of the car and go inside. After spending all night prepping, I can't be any readier for this meeting. At least concerning information, statistics, and strategy suggestions. But there's a level of nuance to walking into someone else's lion den and taming their shitshow, especially when I'm the surprise guest of honor. Those are the skills I need one last moment to hone until they're razor-sharp.

In . . . two, three, four. Out . . . two, three, four. All right, Jayme. You've got this.

I nod to myself in answer and get out of my Lexus sedan, chosen for equal parts luxury and practicality. I grab my portfolio briefcase, the buttery soft red leather cool in my hand, and smooth my knee-length pencil skirt down my thigh with the other hand. My heels click across the lot for a few steps before being drowned out by screams of delight and a mechanical roar. I glance past the multi-story building I'm approaching to see the sweeping loops of a red, white, and blue roller coaster filled with smiling faces.

The scene would be picture perfect if social media wasn't exploding with vitriol over what happened two days ago at Americana Land. Fixing *that* is why I'm here.

"Hello, can I help you?" the woman at the front desk asks through a polite smile. She looks like she enjoys her job, which is a good sign to me. I've seen too many corporate zombies with plastic smiles in my life. People who don't give a damn about their jobs beyond their paychecks. But if people like this actually like working here, it means there's hope for me to turn this around.

"Yes, thank you . . ." I glance down to the nameplate on the desk. "Ms. Trochin. My name is Jayme Rice. I'm here to see Mr. Steen."

"Oh, I see. Uhm . . . which one?" She cocks her head, giving me a subtle appraisal. I'm not put off by it but rather welcome her doing her job as screener for the company.

"Both of them. I have a nine o'clock meeting on their schedule."

After a quick wait for Ms. Trochin to confirm that I do in fact have an appointment, a man in gray slacks with a silver polka-dotted bowtie emerges from the elevator and comes over. "Ms. Rice? I'm Boston, Mr. Steen's assistant."

"A pleasure, Boston," I reply, noting he doesn't offer a last name, nor which Steen he works for.

He offers a firm handshake and then holds out a hand gesturing back the direction he came. "If you'll come with me. Ben and Carson are . . . ahem, waiting on you."

I adjust mentally even as my feet continue following Boston into the elevator. I thought I'd meet with Ben first, considering I usually don't get shot out of a cannon into the blood and guts meetings. Normally, there's a period of handshaking, sipping coffee, and judging the room. Apparently, not this time. "Wasn't our meeting for nine?"

Boston smiles politely, but there's a glint of laughter in his eyes. "Yes, yes. Of course." He doesn't offer anything further, and before I can question him, the short ride up is over. He leads me down a hallway and into a private office. Two sharp knocks on the inner door as a warning, then Boston opens the door. "Mr. Steen, Ms. Rice is here."

I walk into the office, my eyes quietly evaluating *everything* that I see. Too often, it's the unspoken details that are the clue to any situation, a lesson I learned long, long ago as a little girl. My eyes eventually lock on the older man behind the desk, Ben Steen, from my research. His hair is a blend of salt and pepper shades that are echoed in his trimmed mustache and beard, which surround a deep frown. His tie is a classic red showcase of power, especially paired with his pale blue shirt. It's a very on-brand look for an Americana Land CEO.

I approve.

"Mr. Steen, I'm Jayme Rice. Nice to meet you." I hold my hand out, stepping forward. But as soon as Mr. Steen stands and takes my hand, we're interrupted.

"Dad, we're in the middle of something. Can you do whatever *this* is later?" The other man in the room sounds bored and put out by my presence. I cut my eyes to him, recognizing Carson Steen, the middle child of Ben Steen and his heir apparent. Unbidden, it occurs to me that the online photos, while showing an attractive man, did him zero justice. Online, he's handsome, but in a relatively normal way.

In person, with thunder storming in his blue eyes and the hard set of his jaw, he's absolutely magnetic. If I met him at a club or saw him from across a crowded room, I'd be instantly intrigued. But we're not out at a meat market with EDM music providing a backdrop, and given the way he's dismissing me to focus on the senior Steen, I think he'd probably ignore me to go get another drink from the bar in any case.

"Mr. Steen," I greet Carson, offering a handshake to him in order to say I will not be denied, "nice to meet you as well."

He looks at my outstretched hand a beat too long but does stand to shake.

"Ms. Rice?" he questions, letting me know he didn't even listen to my name. I don't know if it's a power move or if he genuinely didn't listen, but I play it level.

"Yes. Jayme Rice, from Compass Public Relations. Nice to meet—"

I'm cut off once again when Carson whirls on his father. "An outside public relations firm? Are you fucking serious? I'm handling this."

Ben Steen sighs as he leans back in his leather chair. Pulling his reading glasses off, he closes his eyes for a moment and rubs the bridge of his nose.

Though he requested help from our company, there's always an outside chance that he'll dismiss me before even hearing me out. But I know my value and the skills I bring to the table, so I hold my tongue and don't give away my plan to help Americana Land recover from the social media shitstorm Carson stirred up with 'shoplifting McKenzie', as he called her.

Three million shares across social media have divided the Twitter and TikTok-verse. And the Steens don't want to alienate their customer base any more than things have already gotten.

"Please sit down, Ms. Rice," Ben Steen says, obviously feeling the same way I do. I lower myself gracefully to one of the chairs in front of Ben's desk. Much harsher, he says, "You too, Carson."

Carson doesn't want to. It's obvious that he wants to either stomp out the door or argue with his father. But he's got a lot at stake here, and with a witness, he's unwilling to publicly engage in a family battle. That tells me there's hope for him and a possibility of fixing this situation.

If he'll listen to me.

Satisfied that his son isn't going to create another incident, Ben looks at me, effectively giving me the floor. Only then do I begin my pitch, knowing who I need to sell to since Ben contacted Compass in the first place. He's on board. Now I need to bring Carson into the fold.

"Carson, in the short time that you've been with the company, you've quickly become an effective Chief Marketing Officer," I start, knowing a man like Carson is probably used to compliments. But at the same time, he can't help but notice that I sort of damned him with faint praise. 'Effective' is not a word normally used for someone like him. "However, the situation Americana Land finds itself in now is quite different from a successful summer ad campaign. Would you agree?"

It's a test of his honesty and a test of him as someone I can work with. I need to know if he's willing to actually listen.

Reluctantly, a growl vibrates in his throat, surprising me with its sexiness. He nods once. "Yes."

His agreement is hard-won, but still given, so I'm taking the win.

"Good. And that's why I'm here. While you specialize in marketing, and I'd never try and tell you how to do that part of your job, my specialty is quite different. Public relations. In particular, I work with people or companies that need crisis intervention after a PR mishap."

"PR mishap?" Carson questions. "You say that like I did something wrong." His eyes coldly pin me in place as he accuses me of blaming him.

"Much like Americana Land is going through right now," I continue as if he didn't just try and defend himself. "Self-inflicted or a result of outside forces beyond your control. And at last check, the video had been watched 17.4 million times in less than forty-eight hours."

The reminder is purposeful, a trigger point to further test his reaction. He grits his teeth but dips his chin. I'm getting to him, I can tell. But damn if his gruff grumpiness isn't getting to me in unexpected ways too. He's like a tiger, sexier even as he looks more dangerous and unpredictable.

I uncross and cross my legs the other way, and his eyes drop to my calves before flicking back to my eyes. The unprofessional side of me notes it, and that he sees me as a potential conquest, a woman, not just a PR consultant. But I stay focused on my mission.

"Time is priority. We need to address this, now."

Ben claps his hands, a small smile starting to bloom on his face. "Excellent. Ms. Rice, Carson can see you to his office and the two of you can get to work fixing this."

Knowing when we've been dismissed, I stand with a reassuring smile. Sensing the same, Carson does too, though he gives his father a harsh sideways glance that says this is hardly over between father and son. I wonder what he'd say if I weren't here?

I follow Carson out of the office door and through the outer office area, where Boston gives me a thumbs-up as we pass, either in a 'good job' motion or a 'good luck', I'm not sure which. But given Carson's reaction to my presence, I'll take either.

As Carson leads me down the hall, I take stock of him. He's tall, a few inches over six feet, with dark hair that's in finger-tousled waves, likely from his running his hands through it in stress, his broad shoulders framing a strong back that tapers to a black leather belted waist, and his slacks hug his ass as he walks. Again, he's an attractive man.

How can I use that to our advantage?

My brain stays mostly in PR mode, even as I personally assess Carson's sex appeal. As a woman, I can feel my body reacting, the warmth in my belly, the tightness in my chest. But the only thing I'm here to focus on is how to use his looks as a weapon to help in this situation, and definitely *not* the yummy set of slack-clad cinnamon buns tempting me to give him a good smack.

He opens a door with his name on the gold-plated plaque. I step past him, but I swear I hear him take a deep breath. *Is he sniffing me? Or taking one of those calming breaths to keep from ripping into me?* Either is unacceptable and counter to my goal.

Our goal.

In his office, I see a desk with two chairs in front and also a couch area off to the side.

I choose to take a seat on the couch, not wanting to be on literal opposite sides of the desk when I need Carson Steen to work with me. For his own good, because I saw the way his father looked at him when he said something. Carson may not know it, but he's playing with very, very little rope before his father decides that the company comes before DNA.

Carson grabs one of the chairs from his desk and turns it around to sit across from me, less intimate than sharing the couch but allowing me to read his face directly. And at least there's no monolith to corporate authority desk in between us. "Mr. Steen—"

He holds up a hand. "You can save the lecture. Dad's already handled that, and I'm not listening to it again." Carson's frustration looks remarkably similar to his father's at this moment, and I suspect if he had glasses and were about twenty pounds heavier, he'd be rubbing the bridge of his nose too because he closes his eyes and sighs. "I don't need to hear that I fucked up."

"Good. Because that's not what I'm here for," I reassure him. "I'm here to help you find a way *out* of the predicament you're in. Actually, it's a good thing that you said that, because we're only able to move forward if we start from a common ground."

"So we agree it's a fucking mess," he scoffs bitterly.

I nod. "It is, but now let's not waste time. Let's instead start with the basics. Tell me about you. Not the *Wikipedia* page notes or the press release blurb from the Americana Land website. I need to know the nitty, gritty stuff you don't tell anyone."

Carson's mouth twists into a sexy scowl, and for a moment I think he's flirting with me. But the fire in his eyes makes me unsure. "Want my deepest, darkest secrets, do you?" he taunts, one dark brow lifting in challenge as he glares at me icily. "No drink or dinner first?"

"Want and need are different things, Mr. Steen. It's not that I want to know the things you hide, it's that I need to so I can effectively circumvent any potential pitfalls for our PR recovery operation," I explain, pivoting quickly to try and keep this man on my side. It's not purely professional interest, I have to admit inside myself. I'm quite interested in whatever deep, dark secrets Carson Steen holds.

Maybe they'll help me stop noting the nuances of his expressions . . . anger . . . disappointment . . . interest . . . attraction?

Carson inhales deeply through his nose, his nostrils flaring as he gets his emotions under control. "Carson," he says after he exhales. "At least call me Carson if you're cleaning up my clusterfuck."

I smile warmly, knowing it's an olive branch, or at least as much of a submission as he can offer. "Carson," I say agreeably, "and you can call me Jayme. If it helps, from what I know, you were in a near impossible situation and you did the right thing sticking up for your employee. But in a world where people jump to conclusions, it's a PR situation nevertheless. If it's easier, we can start with the incident rather than your secrets?"

Carson nods and leans back in his chair to tell me his version of what happened, starting with his noticing a disruption as he was merely doing a walk around of the park, to his defense of Barbara the clerk and the assistance of the security guards, to the entitled hissy fit 'McKenzie' had thrown.

"I was trying to defuse the situation as quickly and effectively as possible. At the time, I thought we'd done that." He shakes his head, continuing. "It wasn't until that evening, when I got a Google alert, that I found out that this time, the 'do you know who I am' stuff wasn't empty bullshit."

"As in realizing that 'shoplifting McKenzie' is really Abby Burks, the social media darling behind *Abby's Adventures*," I fill in. "Her 'Abby's Army' has gone foamy-mouthed rabid, and video of the incident has been posted and shared millions of times. Not to mention the pages of comments calling for your head . . . s." There's an awkward pause as I add the -s to the end of 'head' because Abby's fans are quite literally suggesting that Carson be doubly beheaded.

He frowns but nods as he bites out, "And that she wasn't shoplifting but had been given permission by my own damn department to visit Americana Land and was gifted a souvenir pack."

"You didn't know at the time, but you knew about the approval for her visit?" I clarify, and Carson shakes his head in frustration.

"No idea. That isn't something that requires my approval." He shrugs noncommittally. "She wanted approval to film, which people do every day here, and a Freddy Freebird and a T-shirt isn't exactly a big money loss. But there was *nobody* from Park Operations around, who should have been there to make sure something like this didn't happen, that we knew she was a VIP. And how was I to know that she's some media darling who'd have people boycotting us and sending me death threats?"

"Death threats?" I repeat, sitting up straighter and glancing around as though ninja assassins might burst through the windows at any moment. "Anything we need to take action over? If so, we need to get the legal department on it. There are too many people who don't stop at sending nasty emails."

"No, Legal's already been made aware," Carson says, remarkably chill for someone discussing death threats. "And they're just mouthy cowards behind keyboards. Besides, I can defend myself."

He curls his hands into tight fists, the knuckles cracking like snapping mouse traps at the force, before purposefully relaxing them to lay them flat on his thighs. I can't help but note the strength in them and the way his fingers taper to blunt ends, calloused and rough from whatever he does in his spare time.

Some people have naturally graceful, pianist hands. Carson Steen has hands made for gripping or pounding flesh. He's got the hands of a warrior, and I could easily see those hands grasping a battle-axe as he goes to cleave into his enemies. Or probing the flesh of his lover, rough but at the same time thrilling as he . . .

"On that note, tell me about you," I continue, forcing myself to close the incident subject for now. There's no other immediate option. However uncomfortable it may be, we need to do this so I can get on to fixing this situation for Americana Land and focus my brain on the issue at hand.

Damn it . . . no more thoughts of hands!

"Short version? Middle son of Ben Steen. My mother's not important. My older brother, Archer, is a lost cause and a total fuckup of a human being. But I'm close to my younger sister, Toni, anyway. Her mom is my dad's second wife, Izzy. I'm the CMO of Steen Amusements, the company and park my grandfather started, dad inherited and grew, and the one I'll take over someday. Favorite color, green. Drink, coffee, or bourbon if it's after six o'clock. Food, Korean barbecue."

He smiles like he answered my question, even though we both know he gave me about as much depth as a *Tinder* profile. All he's missing is some dumb 'meaningful' quote from a movie or a song lyric.

"Noted," I say sarcastically, acting as though I'm scribbling in a note-book despite already knowing all of that except for his personal feel-ings about his big brother. "What else? You mentioned defending yourself. Are you a fighter?"

His jaw goes tight and his eyes narrow.

"I'm not trying to offend you, Carson. But you did throw yourself into the middle of a situation when most people would've stepped back and let the professionals handle it." I take a deep breath. "I need to know if any other altercations are out there, even if you think it was insignificant or was a long time ago."

Mirroring me, Carson takes another breath before answering. "I've been in a few fights. When I was younger, just stupid kid stuff," he spits out begrudgingly. I nod, not wanting to make a big deal out of it when even that small detail was like pulling teeth. "I'm not a hothead, though, if that's what you're getting at. I took a calculated risk to help security secure McKenzie . . . I mean, Abby . . . so that nobody would be hurt and the situation could be resolved as fast as possible."

I don't argue with that. What's done is done, and if everyone made good choices all the time, I'd be out of a job. Instead, I push forward, changing the subject. "Okay, what else? Hobbies, crazy exes, family drama, sex tapes, vengeful former employees. What's in your skeleton closet?"

Carson gives me a look that again, I can't fully read.

CHAPTER 3

CARSON

"*W*hat? Why?" I demand, though I understand why she's asking me. She doesn't really want to know the inside of me. She wants to know how to save my ass. But still, I'm stalling, wishing I'd wake up from this nightmare. A nightmare of my own creation.

Jayme looks at me expectantly, not deeming my question worthy of an answer.

"Fine," I grunt, running my hands through my hair and tugging at the strands in frustration, a move I've perfected in the last forty-eight hours. "No crazy exes or drama, beyond what my own family creates, and no sex tapes. Dad thinks I'm a potential liability not because I don't know my shit but because I prefer to live my life in a way that he doesn't approve of. But just because he's all oatmeal for breakfast, out of the office by five, and quiet evenings at home before 10 o'clock bedtime, doesn't mean I need to be."

"What do you mean?"

"I mean I want to *live* life," I exclaim, feeling anger and maybe a bit of excitement start to build inside me. "Motorcycles, the occasional bet on a game, travel, and yes, roller coasters. I like having some excitement in my life. But I'm not a mess who requires a full-blown media campaign to fix."

Her lips quirk at my assessment, but she says, "Agree to disagree."

"Really?" I snap, my anger at myself and this fucking McKenzie-Abby person finding a new target. Who is she to come in here, all high and mighty, making me feel like a loser who failed my family's legacy? Does she think she'll throw me off or something and that'll somehow lead me to open up to her?

What does she know about the pressure I live under to be the best, to make up for my older brother, to represent myself and the Steen name? She's sitting in my office in a designer black pencil skirt and silk blouse, with perfectly highlighted and curled blonde hair, looking like she's never seen a day of struggle in her life.

Jayme leans forward, staring unblinkingly into my eyes with her chocolate brown ones. They're beautiful, deep doe eyes that at the same time sparkle with fire like the deepest, most precious amber in the world.

The fierceness of the fire there stops me in my tracks as she informs me, "In normal times, I would be happy to let your secrets remain yours. A little bike riding that's never resulted in a speeding ticket, a weekend boat trip with a woman of consenting age, and some gambling on basketball wouldn't be a big deal."

Okay, I didn't expect that. She's almost understanding. And also . . . damn, she knows more about me than I thought. But she's clearly not done raking me over the coals.

"Carson, right now, your entire image is under fire as the representative of not only Americana Land, but of the Steen family. So yeah . . . you're a problem." She points at me with a perfectly manicured, blush pink nail. "Or maybe better put, you *have* a problem."

I don't usually give much thought to my image because I'm not someone most people recognize or care about. Until now, apparently. "So, what now? What's your big fix-it plan?"

She pulls a red leather notebook from her matching bag, opens it, and then holds it out to me. "First, motorcycles say danger, risk. Especially something as non-ecologically friendly as a Kawasaki Ninja H2/R that's been tweaked to race specs while sacrificing on the fuel economy. Is it even street legal if someone takes a look at it?"

She pauses, letting it sink in that she not only knows that I ride but what I ride. I press my lips together, not willing to appreciate her attention to detail when they're *my* details. Continuing with a self-satisfied smirk, she says, "Bikes create a bad boy image, if you will, something we need to move you away from."

I hold up a finger, stopping her before she can roll on. "Correction. Motorcycle, not bike. I'm not riding in the Tour de France. And I'm not going to stop riding my motorcycle."

"For the next three months, yes, you will." Her glare pins me in place, and I am once again in slight awe of her brown eyes that are shot through with flecks of gold fire.

"Bossy looks good on you." My charm doesn't sway her in the slightest. If anything, her eyes go darker and her lips turn down. "What do you want me to do? Park my motorcycle and buy a damn sedan? Start listening to classical music as I drive in at a respectable fifty-five miles per hour every morning? If so, not just no, but hell no. You might as well tell me to neuter myself."

Okay, I'm mad, and maybe my volume is a little high, but she can't seriously think I'm going to turn into some real-life version of a Ken doll, all bland and boring. And dickless.

"On that subject, we need to address your social activities. No more boat trips to Catalina with random women," she says, her finger underlining something written down in her notebook. I look closer and see that she's written '*be discreet with acquaintances,*' underlining it in green. "And we'll need to vet anyone you're, uhm . . . *spending time* with."

"You're making it sound like I'm picking up prostitutes," I growl. "That weekend on the boat was with Nora, a woman I've been friends with for years."

Why am I defending myself to her? Why is it important what she thinks of me? I try to tell myself that it's because she's a snapshot of what the general public is saying and thinking about me, but I'm not sure that's true.

Jayme hums before reciting from memory. "Mmm-hmm. Nora Wilson, college classmate whom you dated years ago. She had since married and was recently divorced. Thankfully, before the trip." She rolls her eyes heavenward in appreciation for that small gift.

"The trip was because she was upset about her divorce," I grind out. "We weren't intimate at all. I wasn't taking advantage of her. I was being a good friend."

"I'm sure," Jayme says cynically, clearly figuring we put some motion in the ocean during our trip. "But you can see how it looks from the outside. Your old sweetheart, with a freshly broken marriage, running off for a beautiful, scantily-clad weekend with you. It looks like you're either the cause of the marriage break-up or the rebound fling."

"Or a good friend."

Jayme lets out a sigh of defeat. "Carson . . . look, I'm not trying to piss you off. I'm telling you how you're perceived. It doesn't mean that's how you actually are. You could be an angel, you could be a demon. I don't care. My job is to deal with how the public sees you. My job is to fix perceptions. Your family comes with baggage. Your grandfather had a questionable history of how he got the money together to start your precious Americana Land. Your father had a long-running affair with an Americana Land employee while still married to your mother, and then he left her to marry the mistress, making her your stepmother. Your older brother has been divorced twice and is a playboy. So when you go out with a woman while the ink is barely dry on her divorce decree, it looks . . . bad. Birds of a feather and all. The motorcycle riding and gambling add to your image as a bad boy with more money than sense, and that image is being dinged left and right by this whole Abby Burks situation. She's basically America's sweetheart on YouTube and you practically tackled her to the ground."

Her voice has gotten louder and higher, more and more strident as she reads me up and down. She's uncomfortably spot on. I do come from a line of men with a deep bastard streak. I wake up every morning and look at myself in the mirror, reminding myself that I'm not the culmination of my genetics.

But somewhere in the midst of her tirade, I began to notice the flush of pink on her cheeks, the rise and fall of her chest as she breathes heavily, and the way her skirt inched up when she scooted to the edge of the couch to yell at me.

Something about the way she's holding her own, going toe to toe with me, lights me on fire. In both good and bad ways.

I sit back, stunned. She's beautiful, intelligent, and has obviously done her homework on me. It's not often that I'm at this much of a disadvantage. I know almost *nothing* about her.

"Fine. If you want me to listen to your *suggestions*," I concede, giving the word extra weight to make sure she remembers that I haven't agreed to her ridiculous rules yet, "I want to know who I'm working with too. Why should I listen to you?"

She swallows thickly. "I'm not telling you my deepest, darkest secrets if that's what you're after. That's not what I'm here for."

The very idea that she has secrets is exciting, a dangling carrot for me to chase. What tang to her sweetness, what spice is there to her beyond her intelligence and sass? She has to have some. You don't get to this level of backbone without having at least a few scars inside. "Give me something, at least."

"I've been a PR representative with Compass for six years. I started there straight out of college after completing my internship and was officially offered a spot with them one week after they turned in my grade on the internship course. I started with smaller cases but found my niche in image consultations, specifically image repair. I've handled cases for high-profile clients and tend to be who's sent in for crisis management."

"That's very nonspecific of you. No details? Hobbies, crazy exes, family drama, sex tapes?" I throw her own question back at her. "Boat trips to Catalina?"

"My image isn't the one in need of help," she reminds me dryly, completely unaffected by me. "Those things are irrelevant."

I nod but silently note that she doesn't deny any of the things I questioned her with. Maybe she does have some kind of wild side.

"Care to know what I see when I look at you? What Jayme Rice's image is?" I ask. I'm trying to get my footing back, but she kicks it out from under me at every turn, leaving me off-kilter. It's thrilling and equally disconcerting. It's been a long time since I've been challenged this much. Part of me wants to see if I've still got the sauce.

She leans back again, mirroring my position, and waves her hand in a 'get on with it' gesture.

"I may not be a PR specialist, but I can read people. You create façades for others, but I suspect the reason you're good at it is that you live behind a created front yourself. There's a mask to you, and while I don't know *what* you're hiding behind this mask, I know *why* you wear it. You're afraid to let people see the real you, the grumpy mess eating chips in bed at two in the morning, the happy goofball dancing around when there's no music, the sexy woman I'm sure you keep locked under professional knee-length skirts and buttoned-up blouses. I don't know which, or if you're all of them. But you want to be what everyone expects you to be, and you want me to

21

take the same advice. Problem is, I'm a hell of a lot deeper than that. And I suspect you are too."

She flinches, giving me an instant of insight before her mask shuts down again over her expression. But her eyes hold the hurt my words caused. "Deeper? You could've fooled me," she lashes out. "What you're showing me is about as deep as a kiddie pool."

"Then open your damn eyes," I growl, my frustration driving me forward again. I'm on the edge of my chair, leaning into her as I challenge. "Or are you too afraid to do that? To be real?"

Jayme uncrosses her legs, scooting forward to meet my challenge on equal ground. "I'm not afraid of anything. But if you got to know the 'real me', as you call it, I'd scare the hell out of you. You're in over your head, with me and with this situation. And this is the one and only time I'm going to throw you a life preserver. Take it or don't, your call. Americana Land or your pride, what's it going to be?"

We're both standing now, dangerously close to each other over the small table between us. Our panting breaths mingle, and the anger between us ignites.

"You smug bitch."

"Arrogant asshole."

The door opens, startling us both, and I watch as Jayme realizes what she's just said. Her cheeks flush, and her eyes and mouth widen in shock as she mentally backpedals. "Carson, I'm—"

"Everything okay in here?" Xavier asks in concern. He's one of the marketing analysts in my department, and if he's poking his head in without knocking, we must've been getting louder than I thought.

"Yeah, we're fine," I tell him, but he looks back and forth from Jayme to me, trying to read the situation. To Jayme, I say, "I'm sorry. That was unprofessional of me. I deserved that."

I'm giving her an out and taking the blame, one hundred percent. She's here to help, and I acted exactly like the arrogant asshole she called me. Hell, like the devil everyone online is calling me, for that matter.

She takes a breath and steps back. "Thank you, but I apologize too. It seems we got off on the wrong foot. Maybe we can reconvene after lunch and start over?"

Decided, Jayme picks up her leather bag and marches out. I definitely watch her hair swing left and right above her ass, which is swishing the opposite way.

After she's for sure gone, Xavier whistles softly, giving me a look. "Damn, man. What'd you do to her? She looked ready to kill you or kiss you. Maybe both."

I purse my lips, wondering about that myself. "Probably the former."

"I don't know," Xavier muses, making my ears perk up. He's a smart man, one of my best analysts precisely because he does have a way of reading people, so I can't dismiss what he has to say. "Sometimes the best kisses are after wanting to kill each other. At least that's the way it is with me and Alicia."

I chuckle, knowing that he's been married to his high school sweetheart for twenty years. "Don't you have like five kids? Alicia must want to kill you often."

"Shoot, if it wasn't for my getting the snip-snip years ago, I'd probably have my own basketball team by now," he jokes. "You could bet on me every time."

"Well, I don't think that's going to be an issue with Jayme." I look at the empty doorway, wondering what the hell just happened. "Hell, she may not even come back."

He shrugs doubtfully. "If you say so."

CHAPTER 4

JAYME

I take a sip of my warm tea, my traditional reward for a long and taxing day. It's better than whiskey, although I feel like today, of all days, I could make an exception.

After lunch, Carson was downright civil, blander than plain white toast, and I'm not sure if he was actually listening to me or letting me talk so as not to rock the boat further. He did answer my questions, robotically and concisely, without any of the emotional context that would let me know how he actually felt about his answers, which is almost as important as the facts themselves.

But at least I got more information about Steen Amusements and Carson Steen, which was my goal, anyway.

Reading over the email on my laptop, I double- and triple-check my response to the firm . . .

Hi, Patrick. Today went as well as expected. There was the typical initial pushback, but I think Carson Steen is salvageable, and the repair of Steen Amusements is completely doable. I'll be in touch with any concerns or significant progress. -Jayme

Fortunately, my boss at Compass is pretty hands-off on the day to day, but he does like to be kept in the loop, especially when I first make contact on a new assignment. Even as I hit *Send*, I'm replaying the day. I sometimes have to be crude and rough with clients who aren't ready to hear hard truths about the consequences of their actions, but today was different and I know it. I didn't resort to name-calling with Carson for his own good but because I lost all sense of professionalism. He got to me.

And that can't happen again.

I try to put myself in Carson Steen's place. What would my reaction be to someone coming into my family's business, calling me to task, and attempting to muzzle me? I probably would've reacted poorly too. His chest-beating, alpha-hole, territorial-style anger makes sense from that perspective.

My thoughts continue as I let the stress leave me with each sip of my herbal tea. But with that come worried thoughts. What is Carson doing? Is he out riding his motorcycle too fast or sitting on the sidelines at a game he's wagered on?

Shit. I know what he's doing. Hell, I know where he is.

I set my laptop down and don't bother with the last of my tea before stomping off to my bedroom. Grabbing a fresh skirt, I scan my blouses. This calls for something a bit different from my daily work wear, but I still want to be professional. I need to draw those boundaries with Carson . . . and myself.

When I see it, I can't help but talk out loud to myself. "Perfect!"

First up? A black silk blouse with a hint of lace at the shoulder that gives it a cap sleeve effect. Sexy but modest and goes perfectly with my cocoa-colored skirt that matches my eyes. A pair of black strappy pumps that make my legs look a mile long, and I'm out the door, thankful I hadn't gotten as far as washing my face or pulling my hair up for bed.

A few minutes later, I walk into Verdux, Carson's bar of choice. This is where he goes after a rough day. And I'm right, he's clearly visible perched on a barstool as soon as I walk in.

He doesn't look toward the door when I enter, his gaze focused on the glass of bourbon in front of him, and I take the opportunity to sit at a booth where he can't see me to do a little recon.

The bar isn't quite what I expected Carson's favorite haunt to be. It's not a sports bar, nor is it a dark-wooded, old money place. It's more of a businessman's place, with a few suited professionals taking up space here and there, working last-minute deals over drinks rather than a boardroom table.

The old-fashioned teak bar is long, with a considerable selection on the wall behind it, and the lighting is dim and warm, no sign of neon or disco flashes. The bartender is an older man in a black polo, and the lone waitress I see dashing about is wearing a matching polo with slim black pants. They're dressed to disappear and be discreet, well paid to not see or hear anything.

Verdux is a good choice for a person looking to be invisible. I can give Carson that much, at least.

Turning my attention to him, I look him up and down. He looks lost, almost vulnerable compared to earlier. He's removed his tie, the top two buttons of his shirt are undone, and his sleeves are rolled up to reveal muscular forearms that go along with those sexy hands. His eyes aren't hazy as though he's been drinking too much, but rather, it seems he's thinking deeply about something.

About me? Today?

There's a woman at the end of the bar giving Carson openly appreciative looks, and a sense of ugliness blooms in my belly when I consider that he might send her a drink, slip her hair behind her ear, and walk out of the bar with her on his arm.

He has every right to do so, but it's not the image he needs right now.

Is that the only reason you don't like that idea?

I don't get a chance to evaluate the question further when the woman makes a move of her own.

She gets up, sliding down the bar to sit at Carson's side. She knows what she's doing, her hair shiny and gorgeous, her eyes smoky and sexy, and her outfit remarkably similar to mine, except her skirt is a few inches shorter. She's looking for someone, for the night or forever, I'm not sure which.

Carson Steen ain't it, honey, I want to tell her. But part of me worries he might be.

I watch as she smiles at Carson and his gaze flicks up to her. He says something I can't hear, but he raises his empty glass toward the bartender who nods. The woman waves as well, ordering a drink of her own.

I need to stop this. Not examining my reasons, I get up and cross the room, positioning myself at Carson's other side.

"Carson?" I let my voice drop, deep and deadly in warning.

He glances over his shoulder, the surprise in his eyes quickly replaced by humor at whatever he thinks he sees when he looks at me.

"Hey, babe," he drawls, as if that's a perfectly normal way to greet me.

The woman on his other side leans forward, looking around Carson to consider her apparent rival. She's gorgeous, a vixen who would haunt any man's dreams, but when she looks at me, she sees competition.

As if we're in one.

"You know her?" she purrs to Carson.

Carson's eyes don't leave mine for a moment as he dryly answers, "Yeah, crazy ex. She's stalking me, probably has a whiteboard with photos of me plastered all over it."

I narrow my eyes, playing along but upping the ante because two can play at this game. "Yep, except I sliced out all the eyes so he doesn't see me following him and sneaking into his apartment at night. And lots of red yarn to connect the conspiracy." I reach up to cup his face, letting the pad of my thumb skate over the tender skin beneath his eyes affectionately. "I'll save you from those lizard people, baby. Before they replace you."

In my peripheral vision, I see the woman shift back in shock, but my attention stays focused on Carson to see what he's going to do next. Privately, his eyes sparkle in good humor, and he turns to the other woman, shrugging. "You'd better go."

She looks uncertain, quietly asking, "Are you okay? Blink twice if you want help." She stares at him unblinking, carefully looking for a sign of distress. She must not get one because she stands up, muttering, "People are crazy as fuck."

When Carson turns back to me, his lips are twitching as though he's fighting a smile. "Couldn't stay away from me?"

I help myself to the seat beside him. "More like I wasn't sure I trusted you to behave."

He turns back to his drink, picking up the tumbler and swirling the clinking ice cubes around. "I've been a good boy."

"Doubt it," I reply as the bartender sets down a fresh bourbon in front of Carson. He holds the wine the other woman ordered for a moment, seeming confused about the abrupt change in Carson's companion situation. "I'll take it. She had to leave suddenly."

The bartender shrugs and sets it down for me. I take a sip and find it's a rich and fruity merlot. "Not bad," I tell Carson, who's watching me closely. "I'm more of a margarita person myself. I like something with a little bite."

I clack my teeth together, letting my lip curl slightly, and he chuckles, a hint of a smile on his lips. "Is that one of those deep, dark, highly guarded secrets of yours?"

The alcohol or the change in scenery seems to have relaxed him from this afternoon's cold shoulder. Or maybe it's my sudden appearance?

"One of many," I answer coyly, as though intrigue and mystery are my best friends when the truth is, my besties are lightly salted popcorn and *The Ultimatum: Marry or Move On.*

Carson waves at the bartender. "Can you get the lady a margarita instead, please?"

The bartender looks at me for approval and I smile. "Teremana margarita with double lime?" He nods and slips down the bar to make my new drink, leaving me and Carson alone once more. "I can definitely use one of those after the day I had."

I smile brightly, making sure Carson knows I'm kidding. Thankfully, he plays along. "Rough one?" he asks. "New client's an asshole?"

"I've had worse. But some clients just don't like to admit they need help."

Carson runs his finger along the rim of his glass, looking thoughtful but staying silent.

I press on. "It's hard. I get that. But if I needed heart surgery, I'd go to a cardiologist. If I needed my car worked on, I'd consult a mechanic. So when you need PR work, you get a PR person."

The metaphor is one I've used before with a decent amount of success. Companies and clients aren't always overjoyed to see me, especially when I come in and start bossing people around mid-crisis, but that's my job.

"I should be able to fix this myself," Carson mutters so quietly I almost don't hear it.

It's my first look at the real Carson Steen. The man with high expectations, not only of everyone around him but of himself. This whole clusterfuck, as he called it, is weighing on him heavily, despite his broad shoulders and bold confidence.

"You ever see a barber cut their own hair?" I ask. "I have. It's a mess. Even the best barber has to get a haircut from someone else. There's no shame in getting outside help from a specialist. This is what I do, and I'm damn good at it. You can trust me, Carson."

He turns to me, not only his eyes, but his entire body. He's either going to tell me to fuck off or that he's in. There's no middle ground. I can sense it. I turn too, my knees going between his widespread ones as I look him directly in his eyes. "What's it going to be?"

My breath pauses in my chest, awaiting his verdict. This assignment is a big deal for me, a big trust from Patrick, but more importantly, I find that I want to help Carson. He's not this monster the media, and Abby Burks, especially, are making him out to be. He's a dedicated worker who believes in his family business and thought he was doing what was best for people he considers to be part of the Steen Amusement family.

"I'm in."

Two little words, but it's a huge concession on his part. He's giving me control and cooperation, two things I think he rarely offers anyone. Even in his tone, I can tell that this is a major, major effort on his part.

"Good," I answer softly, even as inside I'm doing excited backflips. "I'm glad, because I can help you. I can help Americana Land. But I'm not going to lie, this is going to be rough. I'm going to ask you a lot of personal questions, and I need your honesty. And I'm going to make suggestions you're going to hate, disagree with, and want to veto. We can discuss them, and I can explain my reasonings, but you're going to have to work with me."

His eyes fall to his lap where his hands rest on his thighs, and my gaze follows. The tan skin of his fingers is inches away from the paler expanse of my thigh. Beneath my skirt, my core clenches, but I fight the urge to spread my knees to give him access.

"What do you want?" he asks, his voice husky.

Well, isn't that a loaded question? Be professional, Jayme. You're making progress here.

"I want people to understand who you are and that what happened was a big mix-up, but you acted with the best of intentions. Moreover, I want people to think fun, family outing when they hear the words Americana Land. Your brand and Americana Land's brand are what I want."

His sigh is heavy with the weight of the tarnished crown he wears. "Okay, where do we start?"

Holy shit! I did it!

Not that I doubted my skills, exactly, but I was worried Carson wouldn't be able to get out of his own way. It's still a dangerous road, though, so I don't want to go at him too hard. Instead, I start with an easy one.

"Did you really ride a jet ski off a ramp?" I whisper, a 'surely not' smirk on my lips.

He laughs, breaking the serious mood between us. There's a sparkle in his eyes as he argues, "There was a shark!" I give him a dubious look and he shrugs. "Fine, it was a mechanical shark, but it was a race for charity. They were raising funds for the Ocean Life Foundation, and the ramp was *right there*. I mean, I kinda had to. Everyone loved it."

I laugh too, having seen the pictures and video on *You Tube*. "It was pretty awesome," I admit. "But we need to keep the crazy stunts to a minimum for a bit."

"Can I still ride my motorcycle?" he asks hopefully, his puppy dog eyes begging for permission.

I roll my eyes. "Fine, but you have to stay under the speed limit and wear a helmet."

He holds his hand out. "Done."

I shake his hand, and sparks fly between us. His thumb traces over my knuckles gently, and even that small touch sends fire through my veins. I don't want to let go, but after a moment, though I'm not sure whether it's me or him, our hands slowly separate. I instantly feel the loss of his heat.

"What else? It sounds like you want me to turn into a monk. No-fun Carson," he suggests.

"No. You can have fun, but we need to work on the types of fun you have and the visibility of them while we do some damage control."

"Types. Of. Fun?" he repeats. "Do you know how boring that sounds? I feel like you're going to suggest I take up knitting or collecting Sci-Fi action figures."

"Hey!" I protest, smacking his shoulder. "I'm a Sci-Fi nerd. My *Expanse* knowledge is only secondary to my *Dr. Who* trivia."

His brows screw together. "Am I supposed to know what those are?"

I gape. "Seriously?"

His laugh is loud and bright as he points a finger at me. "Gotcha!"

I shake my head, grinning at his delight. "Can't blame me for believing you really didn't know. You don't exactly strike me as the *Star Trek* versus *Star Wars* opinion type."

"*Trek* all the way. Nobody beats Picard."

"Them's fighting words," I drawl, holding up my fists like I'm ready to throw down. "Put 'em up, put 'em up."

Carson holds his hands out wide, warning loudly, "Uh-oh, we got a badass over here."

And somehow, we end up talking the evening away. From his love of all things sport and my competitive swimming pseudo-career as a teen, to our polite but spirited disagreements on what sort of food best chases away the blues, to our mutual desire to be the best, always needing to prove ourselves.

With each shift in the conversation, I feel like he and I connect on another deeper level. Drinks become dinner at the bar, the two of us talking over delicious meals we order from the kitchen. Eventually, chastise him good-naturedly . "You know, Carson, you really could have shown me all this from the start."

"And miss seeing you go all Alpha-female on me?" Carson retorts with a grin. "Please. Your calling me an asshole was almost worth all the other trouble."

I laugh at what he obviously means to be a high compliment . "I'll admit, I do have a temper sometimes."

"That we seem to have in common," Carson says, taking the last bite of his burger. He groans and pats his stomach. "Tell me again why I got two free refills on the waffle fries before even touching my burger? Ugh, you're going to have to roll me out of here."

I hold my hand out toward my plate of salmon and asparagus, a decidedly lighter choice that wasn't half bad given that Verdux is more bar than restaurant. "Every choice has a consequence. That's the lesson of the day, I think."

Carson's answering grin is mischievous. "You're right."

Before I can worry what he means by that, he takes my hand and pulls me to my feet. For a split second, I think he's dragging me toward the door.

Not that he'd have to drag you, girl.

But instead, he leads me to an empty area near one of the tables and pulls me into him. "Dance with me."

"What are you doing?" I ask, though I'm not stopping him or moving back in any discernible way.

"Paying the consequences of my dinner choice," he says as if it's a completely reasonable thing for us to dance together after the day we had. "Need to burn that burger off."

He's a respectable distance from me, his hand light on my back and letting mine rest in his outstretched one. We'd be appropriate at a middle school dance with PE teacher chaperones keeping a close watch. But this feels intimate, especially as the song works its way into my body.

Rita Ora's smoky, sexy voice surrounds us, making conversation unneeded as we sway. He turns me in a circle, putting his back toward the door, which feels protective and lets me know that he has been listening to me, to my suggestions about being aware of his surroundings. No one is going to get a candid shot of Carson Steen dancing with an unnamed woman in a dimly lit bar tonight. There will be no headlines, no amplification of the image issue he's already battling. It's a small victory but one I'll take gladly.

He doesn't speak, at least not with words, but his body is doing plenty of communicating while we move as one. Before I know it, the air between us is charged and disappearing by the inch.

"Jayme," he whispers, his breath hot on the shell of my ear. Unconsciously, I tilt my cheek toward him, but when I feel the slight scruff of his five o'clock shadow against my soft skin, it's the wake-up call I need.

"Shit. Carson . . ." I step back and hear a small sound of disapproval deep in his throat. I want him to growl at me like that again . . . against my skin . . . or against my pussy.

No. I can't do that. I can't want that.

"I need to go," I tell him quietly, sounding unsure even to my own ears.

"I'll see you tomorrow." It's not a question but a demand. Even with the chemistry between us tonight, he still wants my help. Or at least I hope that's why he wants to see me again.

"Yes. We'll get started on a plan for branding you and Americana Land. Carson Steen, nice guy. Has a good ring to it, don't you think?" I smile gently, hoping he hears that I'm trying to get us back on track. Back to a professional level, because heaven and hell know that I'm feeling anything but professional right now.

His smirk and the heat in his blue eyes make filthy, bad promises. "Sure, I'm such a *nice guy*."

He's anything but. He's dangerous—to my career, to my body, to my heart.

CHAPTER 5

CARSON

*T*apping on the conference room table we commandeered for this morning's meeting, I look at the screen of Jayme's laptop, where she's got the conclusion of her PR proposal campaign. "You've been busy," I tell her.

She looks at me sharply, one brow arching high. "Why do you sound surprised?"

I shake my head, trying to backpedal. "Not surprised. I guess I was thinking that after last night, I went home and crashed . . . though I did have some *sweet* dreams. But this? I've seen whole teams put together much less in twice as much time. I don't know whether to be insulted or impressed."

My charm works its magic this time, and her pressed lips soften into a smile. "I did some of this before I went to Verdux last night," she explains. "Some of it even before I met with you. What do you think?"

"Honestly?"

She blinks, forcing a doe-eyed Bambi look that doesn't suit her in the slightest. "No, please lie to me."

Licking my lips, I admit, "I like it. All of it. But can you walk me through it one more time?"

It's not an easy confession for me to make. I like to be the best and am used to meeting the needs of Americana Land myself, either by deciding the team's direction or approving ideas from my skilled team. Either way, the responsibility lies with me.

This situation is different, though. And maybe, I thought as I shaved in the shower this morning, maybe a set of eyes that aren't as close to the situation could be useful. And Jayme's ideas are solid, well researched, and innovative. Much like the woman.

"Sure," she replies, clicking back to slide one. "We've addressed your image as Carson Steen, nice guy."

I nod, knowing that was a hard-won discussion last night with considerations given on both our parts. The motorcycle concession on her part was counterbalanced with no betting on mine. I easily agreed to no public dates, no social media posting, and no appearances in the park while we repair my image.

"Good. So we need to move on to brand repair for Americana Land. The ultimate failure of the Abby Burks incident is in the bad press, so we need to combat that with fierce and focused positive press. But not local, prime time commercials and Facebook ads. Those demographics are already your loyal customers, right?" She waits for me to agree.

"Yes. Repeat customers are our largest win, with over sixty percent stating they'll return for another visit in post-surveys. Age-wise, same goes for adults over the age of thirty-five. Some of those are families, but the large bulk are over fifty-five." I have that information off the top of my head because it's been one of my biggest accomplishments since taking over the marketing department.

"Exactly. And you worked for that. We need to focus on a younger audience, the ones who are creating a viral impact from the Abby Burks video. We need them to want to come to Americana Land, and honestly, right now . . . they don't. Americana Land's reputation isn't fresh and fun. It's not a destination for kids out on a weekend adventure or a vacation activity."

"Ouch," I deadpan. "You make it sound like this is a place for old fogey people."

Jayme gives me a sorrowful look. "It is. But we can fix that perception. It's all about image, Carson. Our aim is to reach the thirteen to twenty-five age brackets. The ones who follow social media, who skip commercials when they're streaming but listen to influencers, who create trends and move on to another hot thing with the next breath. Those are our targets."

Her words are fast, her cheeks pink, and her smile wide. Her excitement is infectious and gives me hope that she can do what she's suggesting. I sincerely hope she can because it sounds like an amazing direction for Americana Land to move toward, Abby Burks incident or not. But reaching out to the social media generation to fix a social media gaffe is also risky as hell.

"You think this is doable? We're not going to step into a bear trap we're unprepared for?"

Jayme's eyes light up. She knows she's got me. Better yet, she's got *this*.

"It's completely doable. We can do it together."

The words hang heavily, sounding like she's talking about much more than a PR campaign. I lean forward, covering the inches between us, and let my eyes fall to her pink lips. Her smile melts as her lips part, letting out a tiny sigh.

Right as I'm about to taste her, she disappears. I open my eyes to find she's pushed her chair back from the table, away from me. "Carson, I can't. We can't," she whispers, looking as though the words pain her.

But I'm not one to give up easily. "Why not?"

She licks her lips, giving them a glossy sheen, and I follow the movement with my eyes, feeling hungry for her. "This is an important assignment for me and a make-or-break moment for you. I think we should stay professional." Under her breath, so quiet I almost miss it, she adds, "Or at least try to be."

"Professional?" I echo darkly.

"Yes," she says, sounding less certain by the moment. It's a small salve on my feelings.

I want her. She wants me. But she doesn't want to want me. At least not right now.

I can wait for her, though. We can handle this PR nightmare and then explore these fireworks between us. I like danger and risk, but I can be calculated and tactical when the situation calls for it. And Jayme Rice is going to need every bit of strategy I possess.

I don't let the promise of a kiss die in my eyes, but I sit back in my chair, giving her breathing room. "Okay, so what do we do?"

The question seems to throw her, and I secretly take a small delight in setting her off balance after the way she's done me since first walking into Dad's office. It's a full three seconds of silence before she blinks and refocuses.

Pacing along the conference table, she explains her plan once more. "A multifaceted approach using social media. One, we need to create a hashtag storm with photos of Americana Land, the experience, the people, the rides, all of it. We can use professional photos and on-brand user candids, especially young adult visitors. People need to see the photos everywhere online, as YouTube ads, in tweets, and 'Gram posts. Two, we need a fun activity that's viral worthy, a daily 'Find Freddy Freebird', perhaps. Like a *Where's Waldo* deal . . . something people can do at home, and when they visit, taking a picture with a Freddy Freebird mascot is a big deal. The ultimate find. And three, which is the most important one, we need to show not only acceptance of the social media generation, but celebration of it."

Her pause is full of promise.

"How are we going to do that?" I'm already using 'we' for this project, knowing that Jayme has a brilliant idea in that gorgeous head of hers. It's a bold change from my attitude only twenty-four hours ago where marketing was my baby and no one could touch it or tell me anything.

"An influencer extravaganza." She swipes her hands through the air, looking vacantly into thin air. "This will be a branched initiative. First, we need to invite a few select influencers for sponsored trips. In exchange, they'll post content on their feeds highlighting Americana Land. And best of all" —she claps her hands, excited as she finishes — "a summer concert series."

I want to be over the moon with her idea. I really do. Especially given how happy she seems, but as she looks at me expectantly, what comes out of my mouth is, "We already do that every year."

That's the truth, and I'm honestly a little surprised that she doesn't know that. Her research has been impeccable, maybe even too much so in some areas, so how did she miss that we do a multi-show series every summer? The headliners are usually bands from decades past trying to make a little cash by singing classics to the gray-haired set, but they're always sold out.

Jayme rolls her eyes at my confusion and laughingly pushes at my shoulder as though I said something funny. "Not the boy band redux concerts. Aren't you listening? A series directed at the social media generation."

Nope, I'm not listening now. Not when I'm distracted by her touch, however fleeting. I want to take her hand and press it to my shoulder again, move it to my chest and down my abs to my cock.

"Carson?"

My name on her lips rouses me from my fantasy. "So . . . uh, another concert series?" I sound like an idiot, but my brain is not receiving the majority of the blood flow in my body at the moment so I'm lucky I can form actual words and not just make gibberish sounds. I fight adjusting myself in my slacks, but do shift in my chair a bit to make room. Thankfully, Jayme doesn't notice.

"Yes. We'll contact Spotify, TikTok, and Instagram artists—DJs, bands, indie singers—and have them perform. Again, using their followings as market targets, and live streaming the shows on various platforms to emphasize the brand recognition. We'll finish the season with a big show. I don't know who yet, but we'll get someone right on the cusp of making the jump to mainstream and make it an interactive set, with the live stream moderated by someone doing engagement activities like prize giveaways and Americana Land trivia."

That is different from what we typically do. Very different, but interesting. My brain's already going a million miles per minute, in a hundred different directions as I work out the logistics of putting Jayme's idea into play.

When I'm silent for too long, she asks, "What do you think?"

"I like it," I tell her honestly. "It's going to be a lot of work, but we already have an on-staff production team that does planning and set-ups, the graphics department can get on flyers, and the IT crew can source a small group to do the livestream prep and management. Our biggest issue is going to be the timing. We've got a lot on the calendar, so putting these concerts around the other ones, our shows and parades, and the annual charity event, will be no easy feat."

I go quiet as I think about everything we'll need to tackle because this will be no small undertaking if we do it right. A campaign like this will affect every department from the on-the-ground teams to administration, but it'll be worth it if it works.

Jayme snaps her fingers in front of my eyes, which are seeing a to-do list instead of her beaming smile. "Guess that means you approve?"

When I focus on her once more, I find her fighting back laughter as she watches my brain work. "I approve," I growl, though I'm covering laughter of my own. "As long as you're promising to work with me, side by side, through all the late nights."

Every bit of that sounds as though I'm proposing sex, sex, and more sex. She said we needed to stay professional, and I can do that, but a project of this scale in this timeframe is going to require a lot of close work, and flirting with danger sounds right up my alley.

And make no mistake, Jayme Rice is danger in a stunningly sexy package.

"I think I can fit you into my busy schedule," she teases, looking up at me through her long lashes, unsuccessfully fighting back a small smile.

"Then let's do it."

CHAPTER 6

CARSON

I should have left hours ago. Jayme did, after a long day of working together to brainstorm ways to make this new campaign come to life. I wonder what she's doing now? Is she curled up on her couch in comfy pajamas or getting dressed up for a night on the town again?

Not liking that second idea at all, I stare out the window. The sun has long since gone down, and the sky is black with sparkles of white stars, but the real light show is closer. Americana Land is alive beneath me, people walking around hand in hand, rides whirling, children screaming in delight. All of it's lit up in LEDs and neon, almost every color of the rainbow.

It's home to me, a home I dedicated myself to years ago. A home I won't let down.

I turn back to my computer, trying to focus on the day's work I missed while plotting and planning with Jayme. I thought I'd get a lot done tonight with a quiet office, but the truth is, I've gotten exactly two things accomplished . . . Jack and Shit. And Jack left the office an hour ago.

Okay, I've read my emails, approved a few expense reports, and made notes on some proposals. But that's all rubber stamp stuff, nothing that my assistant couldn't do if I were out of the office. It's nothing in the big scheme of things, especially compared to what I want to finish.

I'm excited by Jayme's idea of a fresh, new take on our summer concert series, and I can't wait to really bring it to life. It's brilliant in its simplicity, and I should've come up with it on my own. But more interestingly, I'm excited by her.

She's calm, cool, and collected but went toe to toe with me in a flash. Her mind is sexy and quick, challenging me to up my game. And her confidence makes me question my own worthiness. She's a fucking queen.

And I'm a king.

A king who's not going to get any more work done tonight while my brain is filled with obsessive thoughts of Jayme.

I push back from my desk, striding across the room to lock my office door. Not to do anything scandalous, but so I can change clothes without being interrupted. Though it's not likely anyone else is still here, I won't take a chance at being caught by a janitor in my underwear in the office. That'd definitely go against the 'good guy' image Jayme has in mind for me.

I hang up my slacks and shirt, making a mental note to send them to the dry cleaners, and trade them for black jeans and a long-sleeved gray Henley and my leather jacket. I swap my Oxfords for short but sturdy cap-toed boots and grab my helmet.

I'm ready to go.

There's just one problem. I don't know where Jayme lives.

We talked about a lot last night, but she didn't tell me her home address.

A secret smile curls my lips as I realize that she tracked me down at Verdux, and I'll do the same to her. I just have to use my big brain and not so much my little brain. Not that anything on me could be described as little, of course.

In the elevator going downstairs, I figure out how I'm going to work this magic. As soon as I emerge, I put my plan into action.

"Hey, Ellie!" I say to the night security guard.

She jumps in surprise, looking up from the bank of monitor screens in front of her with one hand pressed to her chest and one on her hip where her Taser sits. "Oh, my gracious! Mr. Steen! I didn't realize you were still here. Your floor's been quiet for hours."

I smile warmly, especially when she relaxes her hands and is no longer considering shocking me with ten thousand plus volts of electric piss-yourself juice. "No worries. I've been locked up in my office all day. Didn't even get out for lunch. Had to watch all the fun below through my window."

"Poor, poor you," she banters back in a scolding tone, which makes me laugh. "Off for a late-night ride?" She gestures to my helmet, which I've set on the counter.

"You know me too well," I answer. "I do have a question before I head out, though."

"Yeah, of course. What can I do for you?" Ellie looks eager to help. I hope that's still the case after she hears what I want.

"When visitors come in, they have to sign in with security, correct?"

Her nod is slow as her brows draw together. "Yeah."

"And you make a copy of their driver's license for your records?" She doesn't answer this time, but her brows have basically become one united unibrow of suspicion above her glasses. "I need to see Jayme Rice's driver's license. She's the new PR consultant we're working with." The words rush out in the hope that she won't examine them too closely.

Ellie gives me a wary look, leaning back in her ergonomic chair with her arms crossed over her chest. "And why would I do that? No offense, Mr. Steen, but this sounds like the sort of thing that ends up with me talking to police and looking like a damn fool. I've seen it happen on *Law & Order*. I believe they call that an accomplice, and I ain't one of those for no one. Not even you."

"Nothing sketchy, Ellie. I promise. Cross my heart even." I make the motion on my chest, but Ellie's doubt-filled face doesn't change. If anything, she looks more dubious at my intentions so I decide to put my cards on the table. It's a gamble, but I think Ellie will respond to the truth better than any cover story I could cook up.

"Look, I'm gonna be honest with you here. I'm a nice guy, a good one . . . you know that. She's giving me shit about my motorcycle riding being dangerous, so I want to show her what it's all about. Nothing more, I swear. She tracked me down at Verdux last night, so I'm returning the favor."

Hopefully, honesty really is the best policy with Ellie because she narrows her eyes, scanning me like a human lie detector. Crazy thing is, I believe she can actually tell whether I'm lying or not, so it's a good thing I'm telling the truth. Mostly.

Oh, I do want to show Jayme what riding is like, but I also want to feel her thighs wrapped around my hips, her chest pressed to my back, and her arms squeezing my torso. I don't let any of that show to Ellie, but I'm pretty sure she still knows.

After a long minute when I'm not sure she's going to help me, Ellie looks at her watch. "Well, would you look at that? It's my bathroom break time. I'll be gone for less than five minutes, right down that hall." She points toward the closest restroom. "So if anyone happened to take a quick peek in that binder over there, I wouldn't know about it and certainly wouldn't be responsible in any way, shape, form, or fashion."

I grin at her clever workaround. "Thanks, Ellie. I promise it'll be fine."

"Just know that I'll sell you out in a heartbeat if anyone comes a'questioning."

"Won't happen," I vow, hoping I'm right. "But if it does, I'll buy you a whole case of those Fireworks cookies you like." I've noticed her eating the Pop Rock candy-covered cookies from the souvenir shop in the park from time to time. "Hell, I'll buy you a case for this."

"For what?" she asks, playing dumb. She stretches exaggeratedly and then gets up and slow walks down the hall, whistling a tune to herself. I don't waste any time, lunging for the binder she indicated and flipping to the page for yesterday.

I find Jayme's address and quickly memorize it. "Ten thirty-four Everton," I repeat to myself a few times.

I damn near speed walk to the parking lot, throwing a leg over my motorcycle. Though I'm itching to peel out, I take a moment to program the address into my phone to get directions. The preview shows it's taking me to a nice area, and as I head that way, I smile behind the face shield of my helmet. "I'm coming for you, Jayme."

A short ride later, I pull up to the curb of a far beyond 'nice' apartment building. Either Jayme is making serious bank at her job or she's got a secret revenue stream from somewhere because this place is swanky with a capital 'who'd you wank to get a place here' vibe.

The first obstacle? The beast of a doorman who looks like he moonlights as a bouncer at a heavy metal thrasher club. With his bald head and dead stare and a body that's stuffed into a suit that he looks like he's about to burst out of, he basically dares me to come his way and be his evening's entertainment. But I'm not scared. In fact, I can understand why Jayme would appreciate a building with security masked as concierge service.

I turn off my motorcycle and confidently stride to the doorman. "Hey, man! How're you doing tonight?" I greet him.

"Fine. Can I help you?" His question is polite, but the tone is more 'fuck off' than 'let me be of service'.

"Yeah, I'm here to see a friend."

"Name?"

"Jayme Rice."

He looks at me as though contemplating stabbing me or breaking my neck, and it's a hard decision because he'd enjoy them both.

"Your name," he explains, his face void of all expression.

"Carson Steen," I say with a smile, knowing that the last name has enough weight to open typically unopened doors.

Not this time. He blinks once, giving the impression that he's checking a mental list, before stating formally, "You're not on the list of visitors this evening, Mr. Steen. Perhaps another night."

The suggestion is a complete dismissal if ever I've heard one. I'll admit that I'm surprised. I didn't expect it to be this hard to get in the door of an apartment building, even one with a doorman. I consider doing something dubious like shimmying up the fire escape or distracting the doorman-slash-guard and rushing past him, but something tells me he's got me in his sights, and nothing short of a bomb going off will tear his threatening glare from me now.

Holding up my hands in a classic 'no harm, no foul' move, I step back. Slowly, I reach into my pocket for my phone. One press and it starts ringing.

"What's wrong?" Jayme answers.

"Hello to you too. Why do you assume something's wrong?" I say, narrowing my eyes at the way the guard's lips are twitching. Is he laughing at me?

"Carson, it's nearly eleven thirty at night, so either this is a booty call —*which it had better not be*—or something's wrong." She sounds fearful that I might've forgotten my promise to be good already, and I contemplate telling her some crazy story like I saved a rabid racoon from a forest fire, but it bit my nose, causing a bulbous red clown look, and it'll be on the morning news complete with an interview with Carson 'Bozo' Steen.

Or maybe go with something believable like I got arrested for a bar fight, but that's considerably more boring. But honesty worked with Ellie, so I take my chances again, this time with Jayme.

"Neither. But I am downstairs, and your bouncer won't let me in since I'm not on *The List*. So come downstairs, okay? Wear jeans and a jacket." The doorman flicks his eyes from me to the motorcycle behind me and grinds his teeth. Unconsciously, I take a step back to give me a fighting chance if he throws down.

Or to get a head start. I might be quicker than him.

She's quiet for so long I look at my phone to see if she's hung up, but the call timer is still counting up. Is she thinking about doing it or trying to figure out how to get out of it? Or worse, how to talk me out of riding again?

"Give me ten minutes," she says breathlessly.

One look at Deadly Doorman has me suggesting, "Make it five or you might have to call in a missing person's case. Remember, the doorman did it."

Her laugh is bright and light. "Myron? He's a softie, wouldn't hurt a fly."

I look at the Myron she's talking about, who's scowling and blocking the doorway as though he really wishes I'd make a move for it so he can tackle me. I can see the 'come on, try it' plea in his eyes. And this guy's name is Myron? That sounds like a computer tech guy, not a deadly machine of a man.

"If you say so. Just remember, Yronmay idday tiay." I wait a moment, double-checking my Pig Latin in my mind. "Shit, I think I said that wrong, but you know what I meant."

She hangs up still laughing and promising to hurry. Myron breaks his silence as I put the phone back into my pocket. "You didn't say it wrong," he declares flatly.

Awkward! And vaguely threatening.

Luckily, Jayme seems to hustle, and only a few moments later, she appears, walking toward the door. Without looking back, Myron opens the door right on cue.

Does he have eyes in the back of his head or something?

Somehow, that seems possible. But the idea disappears when Jayme steps through the door. She's stunning in her professional pencil skirts and blouses, but dressed down, Jayme is all badass babe. Her light-wash jeans have rips that show small slivers of thigh and knee and expertly highlight her curves. Her booties are black with a small, stacked heel that gives her legs the illusion of extra length. And her simple black T-shirt is cropped and loose-fitting, making me imagine ways to get a peek at the soft skin of her belly. Or better yet, get my hands there.

And in just another twist of fate, she's wearing a classic leather flight jacket. On Tom Cruise it looks pretty sweet. On Jayme Rice? Absolutely sexy. I greet her with a smile, running an appreciative hand down her leather sleeve. "You look gorgeous."

She says thank you, but the nervous smile says she's uncertain about my sudden appearance at her apartment tonight. I want to allay those fears immediately. "You tracked me down last night, so I'm returning the favor. Full disclosure, I got your address from the visitor log."

Myron grunts. "Ma'am?"

She holds a hand up to Myron, and though he's not happy about it, he honors her wishes. To me, she asks, "Why?"

I step closer, wishing it were only the two of us to hear this confession. "Because even though we spent all day together, within minutes of your leaving, all I wanted was to see you again. And tomorrow seemed so far away. So I thought we could go for a ride."

One of her arched brows lifts. "A ride? That's it?" I repeat the crossed heart motion and charming smile that got Ellie on my side, hoping they work on Jayme too. She points her finger into my chest as she tells me, "You are *bad*, Carson. We talked about that, remember?"

I take her pointed finger in my hand, pressing her palm to my chest though I know she'll feel my heart pounding. "I'll be good. You have my word."

Her eyes drop to her hand beneath mine, and I swear I feel her press into me, her fingertips branding me through my shirt. I want to guide her back through the door she just exited and up to her apartment, but instead, I fight my instincts and pull her toward my motorcycle. I help her onto the back of my bike, where it's a squished seat, and carefully adjust the zipper on her jacket. Her breath catches, turning the moment into something intimate.

"I know I said I'd wear my helmet, but I only have one," I say softly. Lifting it up, I carefully place it on her head as her eyes search mine. I buckle the chin strap, and though I want to touch her smile with my fingertips, or my lips, I lower the face shield, giving us the slightest buffer.

I am fucking losing it for this woman. And that's dangerous as hell. Not only because she's the one person who might save me and Americana Land, but because I've never had anyone get under my skin like this. So fast, so deep, without even trying. Shit, without even wanting to.

But I've never been one to back away from a risky move. And I'm not going to start now.

I throw a leg over my motorcycle, giving Jayme a head tilt. "Hang on."

There's no hesitation on her part. She wraps her arms around me and presses her chest to my back as if it's the most natural thing in the world, and my body responds like she's always supposed to have been there.

Before she can change her mind or give me any more rules to follow, I turn on the motorcycle, the rumble drowning out everything the way it always does. This is why I love riding, not some so-called bad boy image as Jayme suggested, but the way that it requires total focus while somehow allowing me to go completely mindless. Work deadlines don't matter when I'm riding. Neither does family drama or anything else.

Except this time.

Nothing can distract me from Jayme and the whoop of joyful surprise she makes as I pull off into the dark of the night.

CHAPTER 7

JAYME

*C*lutching Carson's torso, with my ass threatening to pop out on the shallow saddle created by his motorcycle's seat, I'm trying hard not to scream. There's a level of trust in letting him be in control like this, following his moves as he leans left and right, making turns through the nearly deserted streets. I don't know where he's taking me, but I know I want to go.

This is so much more than a bad idea. It's potentially self-destructive on a nuclear level. Not because I can't get close to a client. Sometimes, that's the best way to do my job. One of my best friends, Taya, is actually a former client I helped when she needed to soften some rough edges on her public personality. We go shopping and have lunch and tell each other outrageous stories that make us laugh until we're crying and rolling on the floor. I know more about her than most people do, and vice versa, so we're definitely close.

But this is different.

I don't want to laugh with Carson. I want to dig deep under his skin and explore what really makes him tick. Scarier still, I want to let him into my own closely-guarded world. I boldly told him that I wanted all his secrets and let him think I don't have any of my own. But that's not true. Everyone does, including me.

I let the wind whipping past us take those worries away with every mile of road we cover. I want to enjoy this, however fleeting this moment and experience might be. Curling into Carson's back, I can pretend we're just two people out for a night ride with nothing keeping us from going as far as we want.

He drives us past the city limit sign, heading toward the western mountainous bluffs that are crisscrossed with trails and campsites. I've been out here before, when I thought hiking might be a good stress relief from my busy life that's ninety-eight percent work. Instead, I discovered that 'hiking' is shorthand for walking in the heat and dirt, with annoyingly buzzy bugs as escorts, while panting for air and trying not to die, only to make it to your destination and have to turn around to do it again to get home.

In other words, not my favorite thing to do.

We roll back and forth along a winding road, moving in sync. I know this isn't nearly as fast as Carson can push his bike. To him it probably feels like puttering, but it feels exhilarating to me. And it's infinitely better than hiking.

We get higher and higher along the bluffs until he slows to pull off the road onto the shoulder. He rolls another twenty feet or so before coming to a stop and shutting off the engine. He plants his feet on either side of the motorcycle and then reaches down to tap my leg as a signal to get off.

Being as careful as possible, I put one foot on the ground and do a weirdly awkward hop to get my other leg up and over the seat without kicking Carson in the back because that'd be the type of graceful oopsie I'd make. I manage that part successfully, at least, but my hopping leg feels a little tingly and asleep, and my knee buckles.

"Whoo!" I screech, the sound echoing through the night as my fists grab handfuls of air. Carson somehow dives to catch me, never letting the motorcycle wiggle an inch. Wrapped in the fierce cage of one of his arms, I feel even more unsteady, though.

"You okay?" he asks, not letting go. If anything, he holds me tighter. "I should've warned you that the vibration can make you feel a little numb."

"Numb?" I echo. That is not what I feel. I feel alive, like every nerve in my body is buzzing on the same high-voltage frequency. He looks at me, concern in his eyes, and I realize that he can't see my face through the helmet's darkened face shield, especially when there's only moonlight surrounding us. I nod, the heavy helmet making the move jerky. "I'm good."

He relaxes slightly, still looking uncertain, but releases me to adjust the handlebars and put down the kickstand. I fidget with the chin-strap, finally managing to take the helmet off myself once I find the little buckle. Blinking several times to adjust to the change in dark-ness, I look around to see where we are.

"Cutthroat Curve?" I ask, reasonably sure of my surroundings though I haven't been here at night.

Carson smiles in surprise. "You've been here before?"

I shake my head. "Not like this. Just driving through during the day." Cutthroat Curve is a bit of a misnomer because it sounds like the sort of place people go accidentally flying off the edge into the blue abyss to crash to the bluffs below. And maybe it would be if it weren't for the ten different curves in the road before this final one at the top of the mountain. No one speeds up here. It's not *vehicularly* possible to gun it through these switchbacks. And there is a guardrail, though it's worn and misshapen from years of protecting stupid drivers who push the pedal a bit too far.

Luckily, that's not Carson.

I expected him to be a good rider, but he was exceedingly conscien-tious. Maybe because he had me on the back of the motorcycle? Or perhaps he wanted to show me how well he can keep a promise?

"Come here," he says, taking the helmet to set it on the bike and then taking my hand. He leads me over to a large boulder set nearly on the edge of the bluff. "Careful. There's a rock here you can step on, and then up you go."

I look down to where he's pointing and carefully place my boot on the small rock, stepping up to the large, flat boulder. Carson's hands are tight on my waist as he ensures my footing is steady and my balance solid. Slowly, I lower myself down to sit and find the rock still warm from a day in the sun.

Once I'm settled, Carson follows me and makes himself comfortable with one long leg outstretched in front of him and the other bent. He rests his elbow on the raised knee, turning slightly to look at me.

"Thank you for coming with me tonight."

I want to say 'of course' or maybe 'I wouldn't have missed this for the world', but we both know that's not true. His coming over tonight was a gamble for him. He didn't know I would agree. In fact, he probably figured I'd shoot him down after the shit I gave him for riding. Not to mention, this is still inappropriate as hell. But I'm caring less and less about that by the moment. Because when I'm with Carson, I feel like . . . me.

Just Jayme Rice. Not Jayme Rice, the PR magician.

I can't explain that to him, but I stick with the truth. "Thank you for asking me. It's beautiful here." I look out over the cliff, the black sky dotted with stars and the city below a speckled area surrounded by the darkness of the mountains. You can't help but feel insignificant when you see how small things are, and that's just one city, in one state, in one country, on one planet.

When I consider that, what I do seems almost silly. Who cares what one person, or even a group of people, think when it's all a trivial percentage of a whole that's inconceivable to most?

"Yes, it is."

I feel Carson's eyes on me and realize that however cheesy it might be, he's complimenting me instead of the spectacular view. A small laugh tries to bubble up. "Does that usually work for you?"

"I don't know. You'll have to tell me because I've never used this one before." He reaches over, his fingers making slow, torturous trails over my own as though asking to hold my hand. My focus zeroes in on the sensitive skin there, and my fingers search for his. We intertwine our hands, his thumb still drawing shapes over my skin that make me hyperaware of his touch.

"I guess that answers that, huh?" I whisper, the laugh finally popping free.

Instead of laughing back with me, he frowns. "Why do you do that sometimes? Play things off as a joke instead of facing them head-on?"

I don't do that. Do I?

I think back, from our first not exactly friendly meeting to now, and realize he's right. But . . . "I think I do that with you. I guess coming into this, I expected you to be . . . different."

I think back to my research and the pre-conceived perceptions I had after seeing Carson on the viral video and reading what information was available online. I thought he'd be a grown-up version of a spoiled rich kid with no regard for anyone but himself.

But he's not. He's something else entirely. Demanding and exacting, yes, but of himself as well as everyone around him. Blunt and confident too, in a charming, sexy way that makes me think he's used to getting what he wants, even if he has to work for it.

"You think I'm playing games, fucking with you?" he asks, sounding hurt.

Wanting to explain, I say, "When I meet people, it's usually because something catastrophic has happened. They're not at their best, and I give a lot of grace for that. But also, to work with a variety of people, I have to figure out how to help them help themselves. Some people need a bossy bitch, others a sweet, cajoling, grandma type, others still a bestie to cheer them on. I become who my clients need me to be so they can get to the next level."

Gentler, he says, "Then who's the real Jayme? I've met the bossy bitch, the excited cheerleader, and the brilliant idea generator. But who are you when it's not about the client?"

The air is heavy with his meaning. He doesn't want to be another line-item on my list of successful campaigns. But can he be more?

"That question is harder to answer than it sounds," I confess.

His thumb begins its slow strokes again. "Start at the basics. Your *Wikipedia* page." I haven't forgotten that's what I called his basic story. He's using my own tricks on me.

"I already told you some of this to convince you to work with me, but . . . I have four brothers, and I'm the youngest." I'm not sure why that's where I start, but it seems safest.

He winces but immediately grins. "No wonder you're tough as hell. You had to be."

"You're not wrong," I agree, remembering the trouble my brothers gave me. "One summer, my brothers convinced me that girls did not burp. Only boys, and that any boy who heard me would never want me as a girlfriend. Never mind that I was only eight and had zero interest in boys then, but I decided I wasn't going to burp ever again."

His chest is jumping as he fights back laughter. "How'd that go for you?" he chokes out.

"Not well. I damn near exploded, trying to keep it in or run off to burp where no one could hear me." I think back to the crazy antics I went through to not let anyone hear me, including climbing a tree in the garden out back and telling Mom that I only wanted chicken noodle soup to eat because for some reason, my childlike mind thought it wouldn't give me any gas.

"So then my brothers got more creative. They started drinking sodas in front of me, guzzling them and burping so loudly it rumbled their chests. And then they'd offer me a sip. I tried to say no, knowing I wouldn't be able to hold it in, but they'd get fancy new soda flavors at the store that I couldn't resist when they were all talking about how delicious they were. I mean, who can turn down green apple soda? Not eight-year-old me, for sure, so I'd take a drink and they'd hold me there, waiting for me to give in and burp. If I didn't, they'd tickle me until my laughter would bubble up and bring the burp with it."

I laugh now, almost the way I did then, but thankfully, I don't have a soda-filled belly tonight.

"It sounds like you're close," Carson says.

I nod, thinking that I need to call my brothers, each and every one of them. We're scattered about with busy lives, but I'd like to think we're still close. I know they'd do anything for me and me for them.

"What about your parents?" Carson asks.

Reflexively, I flinch. "They're good. I mean, great," I stammer.

"Well, that's complete bullshit."

Even in the dark, I can see his frown at my non-answer. He's asking for more than he knows.

"You know that movie *Fight Club*?"

"*The first rule of fight club is we don't talk about fight club*?" he quotes, his back going rigid and his jaw tight as he comes to a different conclusion than I intended.

"Yeah, that one. But *not* like that. My parents really are great, but I don't talk about them. Ever." It's my line in the sand. It always has been. With friends, with boyfriends, with anyone. And I hope, now more than ever, that Carson can respect that.

"I get it. I'm not exactly running around talking about my family either. We put the fun in dysfunctional."

He's trying to make me feel better and lessen the awkward vibe my declaration created. And selfishly, I let him. "They're not that bad," I say, but when he gives me a dubious look, I agree. "Okay, they kinda are. Your dad's bio reads like a tabloid. At least, it did years ago."

Carson lets me throw the spotlight back on him, thankfully not digging into my family story any further. "I know. Esmerelda, or *Izzy* as she prefers . . ." He throws his voice high, imitating who I assume to be his stepmother. "She was a dancer in one of the Americana Land shows. I'm not sure how Dad and her even crossed paths because he doesn't go into the park very often." He pauses, tilting his head. "Actually, maybe that's why he doesn't go out there? I bet Izzy doesn't want him to."

He shakes his head, seeming to let that speculation go. "But they met, fell in love, and she got pregnant. Dad was living two lives, one with us and the other in secret with Izzy and Toni. I guess he had it all under control, and then Mom found out. Understandably, she didn't take it well, to say the least, even though they'd been unhappy forever and were barely roommates long before Izzy came into the picture. She basically went ballistic, saying she was going to take Dad for every penny, take the park, take Archer and me. I was old enough to understand what she was doing. She didn't want us, or even the money, really. She wanted to embarrass Dad the way he'd embarrassed her."

He goes quiet, thoughts swirling behind his eyes in the dark as he stares off into the night. He's shared way more than he did that first day when he gave me his 'short version' of his life, and this feels way more intimate than any Google search results.

"It's okay, you don't have to say anything else," I offer.

His eyes clear when he looks at me, and he shakes his head. "I want to. I want to tell you. Not Jayme Rice, PR consultant, but you, Jayme."

It's like he plucked the phrase right from my head. No, from my heart. I lick my lips, wanting more . . . of him, of his story, of his heart. I think he's going to kiss me, but then he speaks again, softer this time, sounding more broken and less confident than I've ever heard him.

"She took the money. In the end, she thought that's what would hurt Dad the most, so that's what she took. She left us with him as punishment, for him, and took as much as she could get her hands on and disappeared to live on an island somewhere. I haven't heard from her in years. Dad barely saved Americana Land, and when he married Izzy, his lawyers demanded that he get a prenup. Izzy was furious, but eventually, she was willing to sign anything that would make Dad hers officially. Dad was all she ever wanted. And Archer and I walked into this ready-made family of three—Dad, Izzy, and Toni—as outsiders. Dad tried his best, I know he did, but I was so mad at him. In my mind, it was all his fault, or sometimes I blamed Izzy. But I get it now. He was lonely, and Mom was . . . who she was, and Dad fell in love. He should've handled it better, for sure, but I can't blame him for doing what he needed to so he could be happy with the person he loves."

"That's really . . . mature," I say, not sure what to call his conclusion. "And very different from what the media portrayed back then."

His sneer communicates clearly exactly what he thinks of that. "They raked Dad over the coals. Like he couldn't own a family destination unless he was without flaw. I know that I have that to look forward to, especially after this Abby Burks incident put me front and center on their radar."

I wish I could disagree with him, but he's right, especially given how specific and ugly Abby's Army have been with their cutting remarks about Carson. Comments have ranged from 'little dick energy' and 'fragile male ego' all the way to calling for Carson's resignation and threatening daily protests at the Americana Land gates until his head —either one—is on a pike out front. "What about your siblings?" I ask carefully.

His shrug is heavy. "Archer, we've talked about. He's broken, but he never had any desire to put his pieces back together. He just slashes out at everyone around him with the jagged bits and then blames them for getting hurt. Toni is . . . amazing. She's young, but so fucking smart. I'm protective of her because she's gotten some shit over being Dad's 'love child' or worse, but she's old enough, and ballsy enough for sure, to handle herself."

I examine the smile he's wearing. It's different, and I realize what it is. "You're proud of her."

"Hell yeah, I am. She's earned it."

"She's a lucky girl," I tell him, thinking of my own brothers. They might drive me crazy sometimes, but I wouldn't trade them for anything.

His eyes bore into mine. "I think I'm the lucky one."

We are not talking about our families anymore, but moving into talking about us is even more dangerous territory. "Carson," I start quietly, "I don't know if—"

He cuts me off with a press of his finger to my lips. When I go quiet, he traces my bottom lip slowly, relishing the texture of my lips. "I want to kiss you. I understand if you don't or if the risk is too much for you. But I want you to know that I want to taste you, explore you. I want to see if this could be something."

His words terrify me because they're echoed in my body. My head is screaming 'danger, danger, danger', but even so, I'm considering it. I'm not impulsive, not with what I do day in, day out. Yet, I find myself covering the small space between us to press my lips into his. He must sense my hesitancy because he simply sips at me gently, continuing to build the heat that's been burning since I walked through the door of his father's office and laid eyes on him.

His hand weaves into my hair, tugging the strands gently. I gasp, the sound igniting us. He slips his tongue past my lips, and I meet him eagerly, but he takes his time learning me, teasing and nipping my lip to discover what I like. I'm not sure I even know anymore. I just know that I like him.

The shock of bright lights shines through my closed eyelids, and I jump in surprise, breaking the kiss. I cover my squinting eyes as Carson looks over his shoulder, hissing at the brightness. The car passes us, returning us once again to the quiet of the night as the engine's roar is hidden by the next curve in the road.

Our eyes meet, mere inches separating us, but where only moments ago, we'd been on a path to something hotter, now there's an intimacy that feels good. Comfortable and hot, but not insistent and urgent.

"Hi," I whisper.

In response, Carson traces my bottom lip with his thumb once more. "Will you watch the sunrise with me?"

That's not what I expected him to say. I don't know if I thought we'd go right back to kissing or talking or if he'd offer to take me home. But we let the quiet of the night envelop us as I snuggle into Carson's side, his arm wrapped around me.

We stay like that for hours, not saying much as we stay in our thoughts. And together, we watch the sun rise. I decide that maybe walking mountain trails sucks, but being on the edge of a cliff, both literally and figuratively, with Carson is a stress relief I didn't know I needed.

CHAPTER 8

JAYME

*I*t's way too early for my phone to be ringing, so I ignore the ridiculously loud *beep-beep-beep* completely. For three rings I let it just buzz, and then I remember who I am and that avoiding a call isn't something I can do. Shit hits the fan for my clients at all hours.

Fumbling, I reach for my phone. "Mello," I mumble without looking at the caller ID.

"What the actual fuck, bitch? Were you gonna send *me* to voicemail? I don't think so." Taya's voice is sharp and accusing, and even through the phone, I can sense her head swiveling as she reads me down. "That is not what best friends do."

She's right, and thankfully, giving me shit as a friend and not as a client. Or former client, I guess, because though I met Taya when I was helping her professionally, she's been my best friend for a lot longer at this point. She's the wild to my structure, the free-wheeling to my safe and sound, and the wrecker of my best laid plans. Like going to the Americana Land offices today.

Getting home after sunrise is something I haven't done since college, but this morning, I feel blissfully buzzy after the late night with Carson. I told myself, and Carson, that I'd take a catnap and be in for a day's work as usual.

This call will likely change that.

"I know, Taya. I wouldn't dream of skipping a call from you. I'd be too afraid it was your one call from jail and you'd end up stuck there without bail. All because I was sleeping in for once." I let my voice go deep and sad, as though imagining her imprisoned overnight and it being my fault.

There's a long beat of silence and then we both burst out laughing.

"I take it you're not in jail, then?" I venture.

Taya makes a clicking sound with her tongue. "No, not this time, which you'd better be thanking your lucky stars for. But what's with the sleeping in late? That's not like you."

Before I can answer, she squeals. "Ooh, were you out late working? Who fucked up so bad they've got you pulling an all-nighter? Let me pull up Twitter."

I hear her long nails clacking away, likely on her laptop, as she searches for dirt that she would never find if I'd done my job correctly.

"Why do you assume it was work?" I tease. She snorts, her laughter growing to the point where it's almost offensive. "Hey, it's not *always* work."

"Stop. Stop. You're killing me, bitch." She sobers, or tries to, at least. "Okay, okay." She breaks down in a small fit of giggles again. "It wasn't work. It was . . . book club? A charity gala? Something bougie like that with finger sandwiches or some shit?"

I pause, the words right on the tip of my tongue. I shouldn't say anything about Carson to anyone, even my best friend. Especially since this is a convoluted mix of professional and personal. But if anyone would understand, it's Taya.

I first met her three years ago when she burst onto the music scene virtually overnight. And suddenly, her coming-up story was something she needed to overcome. Her music agent called it 'rough edges'. The truth is, Taya grew up nearly feral, scraping for every cent and fighting for every day she got, sometimes doing some shady things just to get by. I helped her face her history head-on, creating a narrative that she controlled so that she wasn't blindsided by interviewers trying to shock her into a reaction they could label as 'rage' or 'fury'. And if there's one thing Taya is good at, it's surviving, whatever it takes. And somewhere in that process, we became thick as thieves and both shared way more than we typically do with people.

"It wasn't anything like that. It was . . . something else." She knows me well enough to hear the telling weight in that pause.

"*Errk.* Do not say another word on the phone, Jayme. I'm calling because I need to see you today, so you can tell me in person when we're sure there are no bonus listening ears." The warning is threaded through the words, a sign of how far she's come since those early days when she said what she wanted and everyone who didn't like it could go to hell on a speeding super slide of lava, right up their ass. And yes, that's a literal quote from Taya to one interviewer she didn't like.

But while I'm proud of her progress, I can't see her today. I have to go to the Americana Land offices to help Carson with our planned approach to fixing things. "Taya, I can't."

"Did I ask? No, I did not. Because it wasn't a question." Her biting tone softens slightly, which is honestly more concerning. "I need to see you today. I need your help with something."

Shit. Professional or personal, I can't tell her no.

"Are you in town? Or close, at least?" I say hopefully. Maybe I can do a quick visit with her, help with her drama, and then hustle to the office to help Carson? I'm already replanning my day and resetting my goals I hoped to accomplish before crashing into bed tonight.

There's a knock on my apartment door. "Taya?"

"Open up, bitch." She starts laughing, knowing she's got me by the short hairs. Not that I have any. My waxing appointments are pre-scheduled on a routine, the same as my nails, hair, and lashes.

I scramble out of bed, tripping over the blankets and stumbling heavily. Somehow, I manage to stay vertical as I run through the living room. Right as I'm about to open the door, I catch a glimpse of myself in the mirror.

"Shit," I hiss, realizing I'm nearly naked in just my bra and panties. Matching ones, of course. Not that I planned that just in case when Carson showed up last night. I grab a blanket off the couch, wrapping it around myself like a towel and tucking the tail in between my breasts.

Taya knocks again, more of a bang this time. "Now, Jayme. Before someone sees me out here and decides that we're having a lover's spat and contacts *TMZ.*"

I yank open the door. "Shut up! You can't say things like that!" I snap, horrified that Taya's going to ruin all the hard work we've put into making her seem like a stable, normal person even though she's totally not. I pull her inside, her feet shuffling in her furry slides and her smile wide. "What the hell?"

"Chill. Ain't no one to hear me on this floor."

Frowning, I glance out into the hallway in confusion before asking her, "How do you know that?"

She's regained her composure and is enjoying having information that I don't. "Myron told me," she says airily, waving a hand as though it's no big deal.

But it definitely is.

"Myron is paid very well to *not* share things like that," I argue as I shut the door.

"And I'm Taya," she counters, knowing the power her name carries. "And your best friend, which he's well aware of. Don't worry, he's not telling tales to any Joe on the street. He knows I'd kill him . . . if you or your dad didn't get to him first."

I can't argue that, and sensing that she's won, Taya struts to the kitchen, helping herself to my coffee maker. As she passes me, I realize she's wearing the infamous TikTok leggings that make her butt look especially fabulous and a matching tie-dye, neon yellow crop top. I need to check her accounts and make sure she's not posting anything too risqué, though that line for her is pretty far out.

"Be right back," I tell her, hustling down the hall to get dressed. Slipping on soft cashmere joggers and a short-sleeved top, I take a quick minute to call Carson.

"Good morning, beautiful," he answers, and I can hear his smile.

"Hey, Carson. I had something come up this morning and won't be able to make it in until later this afternoon," I tell him sadly.

"Oh." It's the smallest syllable but contains as much disappointment as I feel.

"I know."

From the kitchen, Taya calls out, "Snap-snap, Jayme, or I'mma start helping myself to whatever I want."

Shit. I need to hurry. Taya quite literally means she'll pocket whatever she finds interesting. She'll give it back—she always does—but in the meantime, I won't have a salt shaker, the candle holder on the coffee table, or my car keys.

"I have to go, Carson. I'll come as soon as I can, but in the meantime—"

He cuts me off. "Don't worry, I've got things here. I am a marketing genius, despite recent evidence to the contrary. I'll work on the bullet points we laid out."

I sigh in relief. "Thanks."

"Hang up the phone, bitch. Your ass is mine now," Taya sings from the doorway, two cups of steaming coffee in her hands.

"You good?" Carson growls, not used to Taya's style.

I laugh at the protective streak that pops in him as Taya sets one mug on the nightstand. "Yeah, I'm fine. I'll see you later."

He still sounds hesitant but says goodbye before hanging up, and I do the same.

"Okay, first my crisis and then I want all the deets on . . . that," Taya tells me, waving a long-nailed finger toward my phone. She kicks her slides off and climbs into my bed, making herself at home. "Your coffee is sweet and creamy, just the way you like it. Mine is black with a shot of Fireball."

I make a face of disgust. "How do you drink that? Especially at this time of day."

She sips it easily and shrugs. "You do you, I'll do me—bitter, hot, and spicy."

Not awake or rested enough to argue effectively, I pick up the coffee she made for me and climb back into bed, wishing I could sleep for another hour or two but knowing that's not going to happen. Not with Taya already gearing up.

"Hit me."

Taya smiles, enjoying making me wait. "Do you remember the time we went to lunch and that guy came up and touched my hair?"

I choke on my coffee. "Oh no, please tell me you didn't."

The story she's reminding me of was one of those very public spectacle rough edges we dealt with. Taya and I were out to lunch, minding our own business, when a guy came up and started gushing over Taya's long, bright blue braided hair, saying she'd make a gorgeous model. Without asking, he reached out and petted her hair, wrapping a lock around his finger. Taya had flinched back, shouting in shock and anger. The guy hadn't expected her loud 'don't touch me, asshole' and had balked as if he'd had some right to touch her. He'd stammered, trying to explain that he was complimenting her, and before I knew what was happening, Taya had ripped her wig off, exposing her natural short hair, and started smacking the guy with it, the blue braid becoming a whip. His high-pitched screams could've been used for a horror movie soundtrack, and it wasn't until I'd threatened to call the cops that I'd gotten either of their attention. The guy had wanted me to call the cops at first, thinking I was calling on Taya, but he'd changed his tune really fast when I mentioned that he'd assaulted her first and she had every right to defend herself. "That's right, asshole. Keep your hands to your muthafuckin' self," she'd said.

The video had gone viral, and while there'd been plenty of people on Taya's side, she still came out looking like an aggressive, fists first, questions later sort.

Hopefully, nothing that drastic has happened. Again.

"Yeah," I say warily. "I remember."

"You are not gonna believe this shit, girl. That dick-weasel had the audacity to send me a DM on Insta! Talking 'bout how he's some bigshot photographer now and would love to do a shoot with me. Like I didn't tell his crazy ass to leave me alone last time and he didn't try to get my record company to pay him off for his 'pain and suffering'. Ooh, I could make him suffer through some pain . . ." she growls, her eyes bright and her fist punching air as though the guy is right in front of her in my bedroom. Somehow, she doesn't even spill a drop of coffee as she fights the imaginary guy.

"Are you serious? What'd you say?" I demand. I'm already cycling through options on how to spin this because I have no doubt that Taya ripped the guy a new one and pissed in the old one. It's her style.

She pins me with a look, smug arrogance nearly wafting off her in waves. "I told him to fuck off and that if he contacted me again, I'd have legal after him so fast he'd wish I only beat him with my wig."

I blink. That's . . . not what I expected. Actually . . . "Taya! That's great progress, girl! You didn't threaten him with bodily injury or use rude insults. Or put him on blast. You used your resources . . . namely, legal ones. I'm so proud!"

She preens, flipping her hair, silver and black curls today, over her shoulder. "I knew you would be."

I can't believe it! But wait . . . "You said you needed my help with something. What else is there?"

She digs her toe into my thigh, punishing me for something but I don't know what. "You broke me, Jayme. All my piss and vinegar is gone, replaced with some snotty 'call my lawyer' bitch. I'm mad at you."

But she doesn't sound mad. She seems proud, if not a bit confused, by her reaction to the wannabe photographer's message.

"Taya, you're not some snotty 'lawyer' type bitch. You're a woman who's well aware of what requires her attention and what doesn't. Delegating out the shit to the people you pay to handle it is what you're supposed to do. You are Taya-*clap*-Fucking-*clap*-Simmons-*clap*. You don't need to waste one second of your day on some pissant like Elliott Jones. You have better and more important things to do." This is a Taya-brand pep talk, a specialty I developed when working with her that later became how we communicate as friends.

She stares at me for a minute, taking in my words before looking into the depths of her nearly empty coffee mug. She mulls it over and then nods to herself. "You're right. I can pawn him off and not give him another thought. Hell, I didn't even remember his name or I wouldn't have clicked on the DM."

I smile at her conclusion, amazed at how far Taya has come. There were days when I truly thought I wouldn't be able to save her from herself. She wanted to fight everyone and everything, as though the whole world was out to get her, even when people wanted to help her. But she's different now. Not in the way she worries about, but in a more mature way, but still one hundred percent Taya.

"Speaking of other things I need to do . . ." She sits up in the bed, crisscrossing her legs in front of her as she sets her mug on the night-stand. "I need to pump you for information about whoever's keeping you out till all hours of the night and that you have to call in the morning like he's your keeper. But mostly, who the hell is making you smile like you were doing on the phone earlier?"

Before I can start to argue, she holds up a finger, her long nail threateningly sharp. "And don't you dare try to tell me it's nothing or I will slay you like one of RuPaul's drag queen walkways."

She undoubtedly will, and honestly, I could use someone to help me sort the mess of thoughts swirling in my head. "This goes without saying, but this is just between us."

Taya gives me a wry look, as though whatever I'm about to tell her is nowhere near as juicy as the other secrets we've shared and waves her hand to tell me to get on with it.

"Right. Okay. So . . . I'm on a new assignment, and the client is *interesting*. He got a raw deal—"

"Don't we all?" Taya adds.

"Right? He was helping employees who were dealing with an unruly guest and ended up being blasted for it." After a moment, I end up telling Taya everything about the incident at Americana Land, trusting that she can keep it quiet because she's proven herself to me.

As I finish the story, she hums thoughtfully. "That fucking sucks. But what about you and him? That's the tea I want."

"I kissed him," I blurt out.

Taya pushes me, nearly knocking me over and definitely spilling my now-cold coffee over my hand. "Get out! You?"

I can feel the hot blush taking over my face as I lick the sweet but cold coffee from my finger. "He picked me up last night, and we went for a ride on his motorcycle."

I drop that tidbit, knowing that Taya will be as shocked by that as the fact that I kissed Carson, and her mouth dropping open in an O reaffirms that.

"You. On a motorcycle. Hang on, let me imagine that." She closes her eyes, one fingertip pressed to her temple. "Nope, can't do it."

It's my turn to send a friendly kick her way. "It's not that crazy." Taya opens one eye, her perfectly drawn eyebrow lifting to tell me what she thinks of that. "It's not!"

But if I'm honest, she's right. I'm not the type to get close with a client, not the girl who hops on the back of a motorcycle to ride off into the night, and I'm definitely not the sort to kiss as the sun rises. But with Carson, maybe I am. Or could be?

"Well, look at you!" Taya shouts in surprise. "I don't know what's on your mind right now, but I like it. You look like you're thinking about fucking."

"Taya!"

"Bitch doth protest too mucheth," she says in an awful British accent, butchering the Shakespearean quote. In her own voice, she adds, "You can't tell me you're not thinking of riding this man the way you rode his bike."

"Motorcycle," I correct automatically, the way Carson did to me.

It sets us off laughing because while I might've corrected what she called Carson's motorcycle, I did not argue that I want to ride him, and we're both fully aware of it.

"Have you told him yet?" Taya asks after we manage to fight off the giggles and settle down once more.

That's a big question. Because she's not asking about whether I've told him that I'm attracted to him or want to 'ride him', as Taya calls it. She's asking the one question that only she would, because she knows more about me than anyone outside my family.

Because she knows my biggest secret.

"No. It's not that serious yet. It came up and I sidestepped." I do the same thing again with Taya, moving away from that potential land-mine. "And I feel like we need to focus on the PR blitz we're running. Actually, a brilliant thought just occurred to me. You can maybe help me with that. Do you know any up-and-coming artists who would love a chance to perform in a summer concert series?"

"How big we talking?" she asks, "because I've always got my eyes on kids trying to come up and steal my crown." She adjusts her invisible crown, haughty as hell and well aware that they'll pry her crown from her cold, dead hands.

"Big enough to draw a crowd in person and through live streaming, good with promos, and young enough to counter Abby's army of rabid followers." I'm laying my cards on the table with Taya, knowing she's my best shot at a musical fairy godmother.

"Oh, I gotchu," she says, snapping her fingers. "Jazmyn Starr is your girl. Make sure you spell it right when you search her up because her momma uses the alphabet with zero fucks." Instead of letting me Google, Taya grabs her own phone and pulls up Jazmyn's Instagram feed. "Look at this shit," she tells me with a smile as she clicks a video thumbnail. "Perfect for you."

The video that fills her screen is one of pure pop propaganda, a fusion of Madonna, Miley Cyrus, Britney Spears, and Taylor Swift. Jazmyn pays tribute to all the greats, but with a dark twist all her own. She shakes her head, her shaggy mullet flopping around her smoky eyes as she scream-sings.

Taya's right. Jazmyn Starr is perfect. "Oh, my God, she's it! You're the best!"

Taya grins, a hand pressed to her chest as she soaks in the praise. "Of course I know what I'm doing. I can even get you an inside track with her agent. He brought her to the label and is looking for opportunities."

"Really? Thank you!" I lean her way, giving her a side-hug squeeze.

"No biggie," she says casually, but Taya doesn't do favors for just anyone. She believes in not owing anyone for anything, so it's a huge deal for her to do this for me. "So, what else are we doing today?" Taya asks.

I need to work, especially on contacting Jazmyn Starr's agent, and with whatever progress Carson and his team have made this morning. I want to see Carson too. But what I say is . . .

"Anything you want, Taya. I'm yours."

"That's what I thou-ou-ought," she sings, grinning as she presses her finger to her ear like she has an earpiece in. "Let's go shopping. I'll call ahead."

With that decided, I hop from bed to get dressed in public-appropriate clothes because being out with Taya means eyes will follow, even when the store agrees to close down for an hour while Taya has free reign to browse. But I take a quick second to text Carson.

Me: Won't be in today after all. Working on a lead for our concert series headliner.

Carson: Sounds good.

A minute later, though, as I'm pulling a curling iron through my hair, my phone dings again.

Carson: I miss you.

I smile, reading it again. Before I can answer in kind, Taya barges into the bathroom to steal my phone. "Nope, lover boy can wait. Your ass is mine today."

I sigh, knowing she'll stand by that and keep my phone. She's able to hold onto things tighter than a bank if she wants to. It's usually so I don't work while we hang out, and it's honestly for my own good. But today, I really want to grab my phone back and talk to Carson. Which means I probably need today to get my head on semi-straight and let some logic rule over my . . .

"That man can have your pussy tomorrow," Taya says, finishing my own thought as well as setting her boundary for today.

CHAPTER 9

CARSON

"*Hey*, Boston, is Dad in?" I say, already walking to his office door. If he isn't, I'm still going in.

Boston hops up, intercepting me. "Yes, but—"

I only hear the 'yes' before I open the door.

I should've waited Boston out, listened to him, or maybe called Dad before showing up because I will never get the image that greets me out of my head. Izzy is sitting crossways in Dad's lap, her arms around his neck. Dad has one arm around her back and one hand resting on her inner thigh as they kiss deeply. Thank God Izzy is wearing pants today because if she'd been wearing a skirt, I think I'd have to scoop my eyeballs out with a spoon to make the image disappear.

"Carson!" Dad shouts at the interruption. "What the hell? Haven't you ever heard of knocking?"

"Sorry, Mr. Steen. I tried to tell him," Boston says deferentially.

I snort derisively, pointedly directing my vision to the ceiling so I don't have to see any more than I already have. "And this is definitely against the corporate handbook's guidance on appropriate office behavior. Sorry, I was hoping to meet with you about the PR campaign."

I know that's a topic he won't let lie, and even better that it is my true intention in wanting to see him.

"Oh! Of course," he mutters, gently pushing Izzy out of his lap. She stands, straightening her slacks and then her hair. "Sorry, dear."

Izzy smiles warmly at Dad, but her smile is more of a grimace when she whirls my way. She's a beautiful woman, and I can see what Dad saw in her all those years ago. I don't begrudge her place in his life over Mom. He deserves to be happy. But that doesn't mean Izzy's my favorite, nor am I hers.

"Hi, Izzy. How are you doing?" We agreed on polite civility long ago, neither of us wanting to step on the other's toes too much.

"Fine. And you, Carson?" she says in return.

"Fine."

And that's about the extent of that. We're good for another month or so, or at least until Dad invites me over for dinner and I have to make small talk with her for an entire meal. There's only so much one can say about the weather.

"Have you talked to Toni lately? I know how much she misses you when you get busy."

That's the other topic we can find common ground on—my half-sister, Toni. There was every chance in the world that Archer and I would hate Toni and vice-versa. We grew up with Dad claiming us proudly while Toni was hidden away. And trying to blend into one big, happy family when we were teens and Toni was in elementary school certainly didn't seem likely.

But I've loved Toni from about five minutes after we met for the first time. She's the absolutely epic little sister that anyone who has half a heart would want, bright and bubbly as champagne, with enough bite to keep things interesting.

I cringe, regret flashing sourly in my gut. "Shit, I've been so caught up with this whole Abby Burks thing that I haven't called or texted her. I'll do that today," I promise Izzy.

"Thank you. She's having a rough time at school with something, but she's not talking to me about it," Izzy says worriedly. She and Toni are close, but there are things that a teenage girl doesn't want to discuss with her mother. Of course, she might not want to talk about them with her brother either.

And there are probably things I don't want to hear about too. *La-la-la-la-la* . . . I sing to myself, blocking out any thoughts of Toni being a grown woman.

I nod, silently promising to see what I can do.

"You two get to work," Izzy orders us good-naturedly. Dad starts to argue, but she holds up a hand to stop him. "It's okay, Ben. I'll go wander about my old stomping grounds for a bit. It's nice to see how far everything's come but know the history is still there too." Izzy pats her heart as though the foundation of Americana Land resides in her chest.

Dad watches her go with a sly smile, and I'm pretty sure he's staring at her ass as she slides out the door. Once she's out of sight, Dad turns his attention to me.

"What's going on? Is Miss Rice figuring out how to right our ship? I hope you're not giving her trouble." Dad's frown says clearly that he's afraid that's why I'm here—to bitch and moan about Jayme.

Why does he automatically assume that? It's not as though I'm some entitled brat who feels like I deserve my corporate role by birthright. I worked my way into it with blood, sweat, and tear-stained textbooks I pored over during late-night study sessions to get through school. But he's treating me like a placeholder who fucks up on the regular.

Or my brother.

That's what irks me. Yes, I fucked up with the Abby Burks thing, but I'm not Archer.

"We're working together well, actually," I tell him through gritted teeth. "She's had some good ideas, and I've got the team working on putting them in place while I work with her on the cornerstone of the campaign."

Dad leans back in his chair, looking at me closely. "Well, holy shit, Son." Slowly, a smile blooms in the center of his silver beard and mustache and light fills his eyes.

"What?" I say, my brows knit.

"I think you met your match in that one." He sounds rather pleased with himself.

Helping myself to one of his chairs, I get comfortable while I enjoy making him wait for the details he's hungry for. "Jayme's good. I don't know where you found her, but she came in with some fresh ideas. She's helping with a hell of a lot more than just this Burks situation."

73

Dad frowns thoughtfully, and I realize that I walked right into a trap of my own making.

"Like what? Did she find something else wrong?"

It sounds like an accusation to my ears, even though Dad's tone is merely curious.

"Not *wrong*. More like opportunities we can take advantage of, especially in the social media arena since that's where things went awry."

I explain the full scope of the campaign Jayme's planned and the progress my team is already making on implementing it since the urgent meeting I called this morning. "Xavier has a small team starting to scour for candid shots of younger guests for that demographic, and then they'll use them to create buzz. I've got Stephanie working on sourcing a few travel-specific vloggers in that age range for sponsored vacations in return for directed marketing. And Jin is going to coordinate with the graphic arts team to design a *Find Freddy Freebird* visual."

I'm proud of what we're accomplishing, of what we've done in a short time. There's still a lot to do, but this is a solid start.

"And what about you? What are you doing, specifically?" Dad crosses his arms over his chest, considering me.

An immature side of me wants to take offense, to get angry with him. But I'm no longer a child and instead rise to the challenge with my words and thoughts rather than grunts and growls.

"Overseeing all that I just mentioned," I reply tersely. I'm not letting him get away with casting shade, but I'm not going to lose it either. "And I'm working with Jayme on a new summer concert series."

Boom. Mic drop. I'm planning a whole handful of concerts.

He pulls his glasses off, pinching the bridge of his nose as he sighs. "I meant what are you doing to repair your reputation? We can't have everyone thinking you're a hot-headed asshole who gets rough with guests." So quiet I barely hear it, he mutters, "Even if that's what the video makes it look like."

"I thought I was helping," I declare, my jaw clenching as I hold onto my temper. Leaning forward, I jab a finger into the surface of Dad's desk. "I'm sure if you asked Barbara or the security guards, they don't regret my getting involved on their behalf."

Dad holds his hands up in a calming gesture despite his clear frustration. "You misunderstood me, Carson. I merely meant that the video makes it seem that way. Even now, I know you well enough to recognize you're trying to stay calm, but every vibe emanating from you says *fuck off, asshole*. You've got a severe case of resting asshole face."

His laugh is hollow and does nothing to relieve the sting of his words.

But maybe he has a point. He's able to see past my outer defenses better than most, and I do have a chip on my shoulder where he's concerned. Especially about Americana Land. I work my ass off for him, for this place, with the weight of the future resting on my shoulders. I want it, I want to do a good job, and I'll admit, I want to make him proud.

Somehow, it's never enough.

"Jayme's helping to fix me too, if that's what you're worried about. She's got me on a short leash, playing the part of the *sweet little lap dog* you want." The fact that he expects that of me is laughable considering he doesn't even meet that bar. Nor would a meek Shih Tzu type be a good leader for Americana Land.

"That's not what I want and you know it!" Dad growls.

At least I know where I get my passion . . . and righteous anger. "What do you want, then?"

Dad takes a heavy breath, and I watch exhaustion wash over his expression. "Carson, I don't . . ."

I'm not sure what he was going to say because he resorts to simply shaking his head in disappointment.

I'm done. Not with fixing things, because I always handle my shit, but this conversation is over.

I get up, looming over Dad for a split second until he rises too. Eyes locked, we stand with only the desk between us, but the truth is, there's so much more keeping us apart.

"Jayme and I will continue working to repair the damage I've apparently done to our brand and myself," I proclaim with all the finality I can muster.

He only hears one thing. "Jayme? You mean Miss Rice?" He tilts his head in warning, and I realize that I've played more cards than I intended.

It's not that I called Jayme by her first name. That's usual for our family-themed company despite the mess of our own family. But something in my tone must've shown that I'm not thinking merely professional thoughts about Jayme. Either that, or Dad is particularly in tune to workplace romance.

Bitterly, I wonder if it's the latter.

"I've got it under control," I bite out, spinning on my heel and striding toward the door.

"Carson," Dad calls out. I ignore him and Boston's questioning look as I pass by him.

Back in my office, I flop into my chair. I wanted to fill Dad in on the progress I'd made and maybe make him proud. Instead, we both got our hackles up, something that happens too often.

My gut instinct is to call Jayme and see what she's doing, but she said she was busy and I want to respect that she's putting out someone else's fire today. I also don't want her to think I can't manage a simple project implementation, something I've done hundreds of times with zero issues. It's not that, anyway. It's my dad. And Jayme doesn't need to play therapist to my family drama.

But with my phone in hand, there is someone else I need to check in with.

I push a few buttons and wait as it rings.

Toni answers. "It's about time, butt-munch."

"Butt. Munch? What the hell is that supposed to mean?" I ask, fighting a laugh.

Calling Toni was the right move to make. She always makes me feel better, no matter what's going on. Even that first day of viral mess, when she called me and I tried to get off the phone to deal with everything, she'd somehow brought a hint of sanity to my craziness. I was refreshing my web browser and shouting, 'no, no, no', and she was giving me shit over not knowing who Abby Burks was because I'm such an old boomer. It could've been a case of kicking me when I was down, but it wasn't. It was Toni showing me that in the darkest moment, there was humor to be found . . . if you know where to look. She does, and she'll show you if you're unsure.

Her teeth snap together on the other end of the line. *Clack-clack-clack.* "Eating ass. It's all the rage, man. You should try it or your *Yelp* reviews are going to tank."

"There's a lot to address there. Let's start with, I don't have *Yelp* reviews. I'm not some hot new restaurant in town. And I'm not talking about butt stuff with you."

"Well, I'm here if you need tips or tricks. I'm a wealth of knowledge on a wide variety of topics, you know," Toni offers sweetly. I can almost picture her, curled up in the chair in her room, her school laptop in front of her and her phone pressed to her ear. By now, she'll have kicked off her favorite boots, pulled her long, dark hair into some magical self-supporting twist on top of her head that shows off huge earrings, and be sipping on flavored water from her favorite insulated cup that's covered with stickers from whatever she's decided is a must-have this week.

"I'm sure," I tell her dryly. "And if you don't know, you've got Siri on demand."

"Shh, I'll never tell my secrets." She laughs, the sound replacing the bitter pit in my stomach after my conversation with Dad.

It's not long before I'm laughing along. "Thanks, Toni. I think I needed that."

"Don't tell me . . . I'm getting an image . . ." She's impersonating a late-night infomercial fortuneteller, and without seeing her, I know she's pressing her hand to her forehead. "Mom and Dad are giving you shit."

It's not a question. She knows as well as I do that Izzy and Dad are one of the things that pull us together. But there's more too. Despite whatever drama made us family, I care for Toni and truly like her, both as a person and as my sister.

"You know it. But I'm supposed to ask you what's up? Izzy says there's something going on with you." There's no reason to sidestep or tiptoe up to it with her.

She huffs a sigh, somehow eye rolling audibly. "Of course she did."

"Yeah, moms can be so annoying. Oh, wait," I joke darkly, thinking of my own absentee one. "And I noticed you didn't deny that something is going on. Out with it."

"Not comparing moms. Just bitching about mine," she explains. "And I'm fine."

I let the silence drag, waiting her out.

"You suck," she snaps. "Fine. It's nothing, just some guy . . ."

She trails off, and I want to give her the same lightness she gives me, but I'm more violence and glowering brooding than Chuckles the Clown. "Is he munching your butt? I'll kill him, so start pulling bail money together."

She sniffles, and I realize she's started to cry about whoever this guy is. I was kidding, but I might actually kill him if he's hurt Toni.

"No, he's just stupid," she confesses.

"Stupid like . . . doesn't appreciate how amazing you are and is a normal teenage expression of male testosterone fueled ignorance, or stupid like . . . he hurt you?" My voice is even and careful, but the distinction is important. One means he lives and I talk Toni through ditching the dead wood over ice cream. The other means I really might need that bail money if I get caught beating the shit out of this guy.

"You can stop with the protective brother act. Topper doesn't need to be 'taught a lesson' or whatever you're contemplating. I've got it handled, but I'm allowed to be bitchy about it while I cope and don't need Mom or you trying to sort my shit for me."

She's a force to be reckoned with. At only eighteen, she is more world weary, independent, and bold than most adults with years of life under their belt. You never doubt where you stand with her, which is probably what this guy couldn't handle. Toni calls it like she sees it, whether you want to hear it or not.

I stare out the window, watching the roller coasters go up, down, and around, with everyone screaming at the twists and turns. It feels a lot like life, and I wish I could do something to help Toni, figure out some way to make her path a little straighter and easier. But I understand wanting to solve your own problems. It's my preference too. But someone recently told me that it's okay to reach out for help when you need it.

"I'm here if you need me, okay? To listen, to plot revenge, to provide an alibi, or to drive the getaway car. I'll even buy the eggs and toilet paper or pay the hitman through an untraceable Caribbean account. You just let me know and I'll make it happen."

It works the way I hoped it would, and Toni lets out a muffled laugh at my list of possible ways to handle things. "You're the worst, Carson."

"You mispronounced 'best brother ever'. And for no reason in particular, what's Topper's first name?" I ask.

"Topper is his first name, and I'm not stupid enough to give you his last name."

I feign choking, tapping my chest with a palm for good measure as I repeat, "Topper is his *first* name? Holy shit, Toni. That's a bad enough last name, or a God-awful and questionable nickname, but who names their kid 'Topper'? I don't even know him and I know you can do better . . . way better. Topper. What the fuck?"

Another laugh.

I feel like I'm helping even though she wants to deal with Topper on her own. If she won't let me stand in front of her or beside her, at least I can help bolster her up and offer support.

"Thanks, Carson. You really are the best."

"See, I knew you could say it right," I praise, still giving her shit about calling me the worst when I'm obviously an amazing brother.

"Shut up," she sighs, but it sounds much better now.

We talk a bit more, and when we hang up, she seems more like her usual perky-with-a-touch-of-crazy self. I feel a bit more centered too, even though we didn't talk about my issue with Dad. There's no need to, really. It's happened before and it'll happen again. Today's just one more instance of my not being what he wants but what he's stuck with.

CHAPTER 10

JAYME

"We did it!" I shout, rereading the email on my laptop. My eyes flick to Carson. He's sitting at the head of the table, working on his own laptop. His black tie is loose, and he undid the button at his collar and rolled up his sleeves hours ago. When he looks up, there's a blankness in his eyes as though he didn't hear me or maybe didn't process what I said.

"We. Did. It!" I repeat, this time louder and with the addition of a shoulder shimmy shake.

Excitement rushes through me and I can't contain it. I stand up from the chair I've been poured into for hours and dance around the conference room I took over days ago as my work zone. My feet are bare, my heels long forgotten, and the carpet is stiff beneath my toes, letting me twirl and tap dance, though both are awful considering I'm neither a ballerina nor a tap dancer. But I am an excited, happy, successful woman. And that requires a victory dance.

Carson leans back in his chair to watch me, and a smile blooms across his face, flashing his white teeth amid the dark scruff of a beard he's grown this week as we've worked round the clock to do damage repair.

"Did you hear me?" I ask, rushing for him. I spin his chair around and he lets out a whoop of surprise. "Get up and celebrate with me!"

I grab both of his hands, pulling one then the other, forcing his body to move back and forth. It's not quite a dance, but it'll do.

Carson grunts in good humor. "What are we celebrating? What'd we do?"

I freeze, wanting to see his expression when I tell him. "We, and by we, I mean *me*, but I'm a team player like that, so I'll say we . . . got Jazmyn Starr to sign on for the summer concert series. Ahh!" I let loose a playful screech of joy, glad there's no one in the office this late because they surely would've already come busting in to make sure everything's okay with the racket I'm making. "And she wants to meet with us! Just a formality for signing, so effectively . . . We. Did. It!"

I realize I'm jumping up and down by myself while Carson looks at me like I've lost my ever-loving mind. It's possible that I have, given the long days of back and forth I've had to go through to get to Jazmyn Starr's agent's assistant, and then the agent himself, and then for him to present the opportunity to Jazmyn. She was one hundred percent *not* on board at first, and getting her to listen to what we're doing with the summer series was a process itself. I had to drop Taya's name just to get Jazmyn's attention.

Annoying, frustrating, and ridiculous . . . but I did it and it worked!

I make a mental note to send Taya a thank you basket of her favorite candy bars, 100 Grand bars. She could have fancy truffles and Swiss chocolate at the drop of a hat, but I know the one candy that reminds her of how far she's come. She told me once that she'd see those bars at the bodega by her apartment and try to figure out how much money that was, but she couldn't conceive of it. Now, she could spend that in a day without her bank account feeling a pinch. Plus, chocolate, caramel, and crunch? Who could turn that down? Not Taya, for sure. Though my favorite has always been Toblerone.

"Was there ever any doubt?" Carson asks. "I knew you could do it." He tilts my chin up with his finger, his eyes tracing my smile. He's wearing that same look he had when he talked about his sister . . . pride. He's proud of what we've done. Of what I've done for him and Americana Land.

"Oh, yeah, never any doubt," I say sarcastically, feeling warm now that I've stopped dancing all over the place. Or maybe it's because I'm so close to Carson.

"I didn't doubt you for a second. Only wondered if Jazmyn Starr was going to see the brilliance in your idea." His thumb glances over my jawline, up to where his fingers thread into my hair, and while my body goes utterly still, inside I feel like I'm vibrating. Holding me there, he lowers slowly, giving me time to stop him.

I should. I know it.

Stop. Don't. The words are right there on the tip of my tongue but turn into 'don't stop' in my mind.

We've spent the last few days together, talking and laughing and planning. We've flirted, for sure, and I haven't forgotten that moonlit kiss on the rock, but we've been so busy with actually working that we haven't taken it further.

Until now, when Carson is looking at me with want in his dark eyes and possession in his touch. His breath is ragged, and I can feel the tenuous restraint he has as he holds himself inches from me.

"Jayme, I know you want me to be a good guy, and I've been trying so fucking hard. Trying to stay away from you even as we work side by side. But I'm reaching the end of my rope here." His voice is hushed, rumbling in his chest as if the confession of weakness pains him.

I don't decide, the words just come forth . . .

"Carson, kiss me."

The demand unleashes him, and he attacks my mouth with a hunger I didn't know he was hiding. I've been struggling to stay professional too, fighting the urge to touch his hand or scoot my chair too close just to smell his earthy, woodsy cologne.

But this is something else. He's consuming me with just a kiss.

Asking a man like him to be 'good' is like asking the wind not to blow or fire not to burn. It's simply not in his nature. He's exciting and raw, chases not butterflies but fireworks, while still doing his best for others like Barbara, Toni, and even his dad.

He's a heady blend of good and bad, dangerous and protective.

And I'm lost in his intensity, matching it with a need all my own. Our tongues tangle. I wrap my arms around his waist to press my palms to his back, and his grip on my hair tightens, pulling the strands delightfully. I want to melt into him or absorb him into my body. Is there a way to do both at the same time?

I hear my own whimper, and while I'd normally be mortified at the needy noise, I find that I don't care. I want Carson to know how much I want him because he's not hiding his desire from me either. I can feel his cock, hard and thick, pressed against my belly, and I grind against it.

"Fuck, Jayme," he groans, breaking our kiss to press his forehead to mine to simply enjoy the sensation of our bodies rubbing together. "You're gonna make me blow in my pants like a damn teenager."

He grabs my hips, holding me still to buck against me. I can't help but smile at the thought of making a man like Carson lose control. I feel powerful and sexy.

Seeing my smile, Carson growls, "You like that? You want me to use you? Rub my cock against you until I cover you with cum?"

His hips find a rhythm that's driving us both crazy. Oh, shit. Carson Steen is a dirty talker, my one secret weakness.

Too breathless to speak, I nod eagerly.

Carson backs me up to the conference table, lifting me to sit on the edge. My skirt rides up my thighs as he steps between my knees and pulls my core to meet his cock. Even through the layers of fabric between us, the pressure against my clit feels good and I grind reflexively.

"Yes," I moan. "Right there."

"Take what you need. Tell me what you want. You know I like it when you're bossy," Carson whispers into my ear. A shiver works through my body, from both his hot breath and the way he celebrates all of me. He appreciates my strength and boldness and isn't too fragile to let me shine, all the while wanting to give me pleasure.

Brrring—brrring—brrring.

The loud sound of the phone ringing is jarring, but Carson doesn't let it interrupt us. He's guiding my hips, keeping rhythm with my movements with his own hips as he thrusts against me. I want there to be nothing between us so he can slip inside and I can feel him stretch me, but I can't stop moving long enough to take off our clothes. Not when I'm this close.

Brrring—brrring—brrring.

The phone rings again, and this time it breaks through our focus.

"Motherfucker," Carson snaps, taking the two steps away to grab the phone from the credenza at the back of the room.

Instantly, I feel raw and vulnerable, on the edge of the table and of an orgasm. I wiggle around, getting more of my ass onto the table's surface and pushing my skirt down so I don't seem like the sort of wanton woman to fuck a client on the edge of a conference table. Despite having almost done so two seconds ago and considering picking up right where we left off.

Carson's back suddenly goes ramrod straight, and his eyes pin me in place. "Yes, I know. I appreciate it. Thank you, Ellie."

He hangs up the phone and then turns back around. His jaw is clenched tight and his lips are pressed into a thin line. Instead of looking at me, he scans the room. "That was Ellie, our night security guard for the admin building, reminding me that conference rooms are considered public spaces, and as such, they have security cameras that she's unable to turn off."

"What?" I yelp, hopping from the table and straightening my clothes. "Oh, my God. No!"

I look around wildly, searching for a camera. Maybe I can destroy it? I bet a good hit with the heel of my shoe would do it. I spy the small globe in the corner of the room and rush to move a chair over, climbing up with my shoe in hand. But Carson is there to stop me.

"What are you doing?" he asks, concern etching his brows as he holds me steady in the wobbly, rolling chair. Okay, so maybe I should've thought this through a little more, but desperate times call for fast and decisive measures. And if risking a broken neck is what I have to do, then so be it.

"Destroying it. You of all people know how much damage a video can do."

"We didn't do anything wrong," Carson says evenly.

"It doesn't matter. You know that. You didn't do anything wrong with Abby either, but look what happened!"

Okay, not my best moment. I might be losing it a little. But I'm having mental flashes of our almost-sex tape getting out and going viral just like the Abby Burks video did. I can't be a PR consultant if I can't manage my own image.

"Get down from there," Carson orders, his tone no-nonsense and hard. Even if I wanted to disagree, he picks me up and lowers me to the floor like I weigh nothing.

"Carson," I argue.

He puts his hands on my shoulders, stilling me. "Jayme, we didn't do anything wrong. And destroying the camera now won't fix it. There's no way to undo what Ellie saw." He lets that sink in, having to wait an embarrassingly long time for his logic and rationality to sink into my panicking brain.

I sag, finally admitting that he's right. "Shit."

"Wave to Ellie?" he jokes, waving at the small camera globe I just tried to destroy. His smile is easy, as if nothing potentially reputation-ruining happened.

"Are you serious?" I say, shaking my head at his craziness. "This is why you need me." I soften the dig with a teasing smile.

"Oh, I could fuck up a lot worse if that's what it takes to keep you around," he offers. "But I'm hoping I can find some other way to keep you *coming* back for more."

How is he flirting with me at a time like this?

Brrring—brrring—brrring.

The phone rings once again, and I look at it with irritation. I think Ellie is concerned we're about to hop back on the table and give her a show. Not that I haven't considered continuing what we were doing, but I'd at least have the decency—and brains—to go somewhere camera-free.

But I wave at the camera above me. "Hi, Ellie. Thank you," I tell the camera, and I imagine that somewhere in the Steen building, Ellie waves back.

CHAPTER 11

CARSON

"*T*hank you so much for coming in for a status update meeting, everyone," I tell my team as they shift around in their seats, filling the conference room. "Although I hate that I caused all of this, I do think we've found the silver lining in this particular situation. I do want to say again . . . thank you for saving my ass."

Jayme scowls. "I think Carson meant to say 'reputation', not 'ass', because one is the truth and the other warrants a call to HR."

I can read the warning she's basically shouting at me with her face and offer her a teasing wink in response.

"Right. My reputation . . . and Americana Land's reputation," I correct myself. "That's what's at stake. Who'd like to go first with updates?"

Stephanie, one of my analysts, raises her hand. I've told her she doesn't need to do that. We're not an elementary class, after all, but old habits die hard and it's sort of become her 'thing' now. When she holds her hand up, it's because she's got something important to say, and we all listen carefully. I nod, giving her the floor.

"I've been working on recruiting vloggers for directed marking. Timing has proven to be an issue for some of my prime targets, but I found two locals who highlight regional attractions who are on board. One already did his visit and sent me his videos for approval. Jayme, would you like to see them before they go live?"

87

Jayme, who was taking notes in her red leather notebook, stops writing to tell Stephanie yes.

I raise my hand too, a nod to Stephanie's habit, to add, "I'd like to see them as well."

"Will do. I'm also working with some out of area vloggers. I've got one coming in this weekend. If it's okay, I'll likely do a walk-about with them. Full disclosure, I'm a fan, but I promise not to fangirl," Stephanie vows. "I'll just take them through the park to really high-light the experience and make sure they have a great time."

"That sounds good. I like the personal touch." Giving Stephanie approval is easy because she would never do anything to jeopardize Americana Land.

Unlike me, apparently.

Jin leans forward, looking down the table to Stephanie. "Make sure you show them the new Find Freddy Freebird site online so you can hunt for the hidden Freddy Freebirds in the park. I'll send you the locations so you have a heads-up and the Freddy Freebird visiting hours for photos."

Xavier jumps in. "I'd like the pictures too. We can use them for the social media blitz."

It's a good segue, and Xavier takes the floor once Stephanie indicates she's done.

"The photo offensive line has been a pretty easy process. People are excited about their visits to Americana Land, so a few keyword searches led to plenty of options. We did media release forms with a bunch of them to be safe and have already uploaded a gallery onto the park's website and changed our focus on our social media pages to target the teen to twenties demographic."

"What's the response been?" I ask.

"Good engagement, actually," Xavier answers. "We're not seeing the follow-through with ticket sales at the gate yet, but the online responses have been mostly positive."

Jayme's head jerks up. "Mostly? Show me."

Xavier clicks around on his laptop and then throws the image to the screen behind me. It's a picture of a young, pretty woman holding up an Americana Land bag with a big smile on her face. She's decked out in full gear, including a Freddy Freebird shirt, red tie-dye shorts,

AL flip flops, and an Abraham Lincoln mini top-hat headband. It looks like a photo ad for our merchandise.

"We thought this was a great variety of available items, but the comments went a bit off-kilter." He moves our attention to the list of comments. "This one in particular." He reads from the screen, "Make sure you keep your receipts for all that or they'll accuse you of shoplifting, throw you to the ground, and assault you. Just ask Abby Burks."

I grit my teeth, my vision narrowing to the point the words on the screen become black squiggles on a white background. "What the hell?"

"Delete it. Now," Jayme orders.

Xavier looks from her to me, gauging who's in charge, but on this, we're in full agreement. "Do it."

"Before I do," Xavier continues carefully, "you need to see the rest of the thread." He points at a link to a video of the Abby Burks incident and then highlights the other comments.

Why'd Abby play Grandma Barb like that? Should've just said it was a souvenir pack. Boom! Zero problem.

Junior Steen can tackle me anytime. #shootingmyshot

Abby's a dramatic bitch. Never liked her.

Grandma Barb! She's a fixture. Love her!

Who's the hottie? Heyyy Daddy!

#ManagerGoals. Back your people no matter what.

This is not the improved image we're chasing, but I look to Jayme, judging her take on the thread. Xavier notices and follows my gaze for further instruction. Jayme studies the screen quietly for a moment. "What are the analytics on that photo versus others in the same time frame?"

One of Xavier's team, Padma, pulls that information from the file cabinet in her mind and gives Jayme a run-through of rapid-fire statistics. Jayme doesn't seem flustered by her pace. In fact, there seems to be a computer running behind her eyes as she evaluates both the numbers and the psychological impact of the thread.

"Leave it," Jayme decrees finally. To Padma, she specifically requests, "Keep a close watch on the analytics and thread for this one. If there's anything . . . and I mean anything, good or bad, that you think I need to see, don't hesitate to contact me. Anytime, day or night."

"Same. I want to hear about anything like this sooner rather than later. Don't wait for an update meeting," I add to the entire team.

"One more thing on this," Jayme says to Xavier. "Can we add some shots of team members to the photo stream? I've never seen or heard anything about Barbara being affectionately known as 'Grandma Barb'. For the target demographic, that's an emotional hit. Lots of them never had grandparents, especially not warm, accepting, unconditional love types." She pats her chest emotionally. Her eyes going hazy, she stares off into the distance, and I wonder if she's thinking of her own family, given the way she doesn't like to talk about them. "Get a shot of Barbara with a group of teen or twenty-ager guests. Close, arms around each other, big smiles. One big, happy family. Tag it with the Grandma Barb hashtag and caption. Let's see how that does for statistical engagement."

Xavier is scribbling notes onto his iPad. "I'll have it by end of day, live online within twenty-four hours."

"Excellent. Thanks, Xavier. Anything else we need to address or ideas we can supplement our current strategies with?" I ask the table. I value their input and knowledge and am happy to consider their offerings even though Jayme seems to have things well in-hand with her experience in reputation rescue.

"Okay, let's keep at it, then. Jayme and I are working on the summer concerts. We've got our big headliner, Jazmyn Starr, prepped to close out the series."

There's a gasp, and like everyone else, I turn to see an unfamiliar face in the corner of the room. The young woman there is bright pink, her hands pressed over her mouth and her eyes wide. "Sorry, sorry," she mumbles from behind her fingers. "Just excited."

Jayme gets up to go over to the woman. "I don't think we've met. I'm Jayme." She offers a handshake, which the woman takes reluctantly.

"I'm Kyleigh, an intern. I didn't mean to interrupt. Sorry."

"No need to apologize. Actually, I'd love to know what's got you so excited. Is it Jazmyn Starr?" Jayme asks, leading her as she sits down next to Kyleigh in an empty chair.

Kyleigh's nod is as quick and fast as the words gushing past her lips. "Oh, my God, yes. She's awesome! I love her style. And her music. And her."

Kyleigh is fangirling big-time, her voice spiraling higher and higher. But the instant she realizes everyone is looking at her, she clams up.

"No, no. I need this sort of feedback. You're our target audience, after all," Jayme tells Kyleigh, smiling warmly. "Do you mind if I pick your brain?"

"Mine?" Kyleigh echoes. "Uh, okay."

"Tell me everything you know about Jazmyn Starr. The info only a true fan would know."

That seems to be something Kyleigh can talk about easily because she instantly starts reeling off facts about Jazmyn's childhood, musical styles, influences, and more. "She's friends with DJ Amalfo too. He started out as a Starr-light—that's what she calls her fans— and adds her bass lines to his mixes."

"DJ Amalfo?" I repeat.

Kyleigh smiles wide. "Yeah, he's this great mix of classics and fresh beats. He'll seamlessly blend Jazmyn Starr with something old like Blink-182."

Todd sputters, choking on his coffee. "Did you just call Blink-182 *old*?" Todd's creeping up on forty, though I bet he'd definitely insist he's mid-thirties.

Kyleigh shrinks again. "I think that's what they're called. They've got a song called *I Miss You* or something like that? I'm not sure, it's a guy with a weird accent, like he's trying to sing in cursive but not very good at it."

"What's singing in cursive?" Todd asks, looking even more confused.

Kyleigh sings, adopting a drawling, mumbled sound. "*Dond waste yore toime yon me, yorall redii the voice insoide moye yedd.*" She shrugs. "Kinda like that, but I'm very good at it either."

Todd looks like he might explode.

"Focus," I remind everyone, hoping to bring us back to the topic at hand—the summer concerts—before a generational skirmish breaks out.

Kyleigh looks grateful for the help and finishes with, "Yeah, DJ Amalfo does stuff like that because he likes Jazmyn's music too."

"Where do you see him live?" Jayme asks.

"Live streaming, usually. He does pop-ups at clubs or venues. Sometimes, even warehouse raves. And people dance along at home with the show."

I don't consider myself old by any means, but I simply can't relate to what Kyleigh is talking about. I'm somewhere between EDM raves and the concerts by the old bands that we usually host in the summer. Hell, the last concert I went to was a BTS show that I got tickets to for Toni. I didn't know a single word of any of the songs, but the dancing, costumes, and energy were amazing. And I'd gotten the title of Best Brother Ever from Toni when I tried to copy the choreography, so it was a definite win.

"Oh, my God," Jayme gushes suddenly. "I've got it!"

She snaps her fingers and gets up, pacing with wild eyes that definitely aren't seeing the conference room or team right now, but rather an idea taking shape in her mind. Talking to herself, she mutters, "I can't believe I didn't think of this before! It's perfect. Quick implementation, instant publicity, a sense of community . . ."

She trails off, and my team looks to me for a reaction. *Are we really listening to this crazy woman? This is the 'fixer'?*

"Care to share?" I tease with a grin, excited to hear what her brilliant mind has come up with now.

"We're going about the concerts all wrong. It seemed logical to implement them in a similar fashion to what Americana Land has already done successfully. Build on your strengths, especially when we're trying to move quickly." She shakes her head, talking aloud but also seeming to talk to herself as she fiercely proclaims, "But *no*. That's not good enough. Not nearly good enough."

The slight to our programming cuts deeply. I know how hard everyone in this room has worked on those concerts and don't take kindly to it being dismissed so callously. Not even by her. "Excuse me?"

My tone brings Jayme out of her reverie, and she holds her hands up apologetically. "No, it's perfect for *that* series. But it's not what we should do for *this* one. We're trying to reach the Kyleighs out there, want them to see Americana Land as a fresh, current vacation destination that they can support."

She's pointing at Kyleigh as though she's the representative for an entire generation.

"And?" I prompt, willing to see where she's going but impatient for her to get there when she's talking poorly about my own department's work. "End state, please."

"A festival. A weekend-long festival."

Jayme's statement should mean something. Or at least she says it as though it does. But I don't get it. Pivoting for more insight, I try for a softer approach. "Please explain."

Xavier flinches next to me, so I guess I was a bit sharp. Especially given the arched brow glare Jayme is shooting my way.

"We've been reaching out to artists, trying to organize them to come weekly. But guests are going to pick and choose who they want to see from the line-up. It's not like students can get out early every Friday for a concert or ask for time off work. They'll have to prioritize, probably pick one at most. But what if they didn't?"

Jayme makes a loop around the table, meeting the eyes of every member of my team, ending with Kyleigh, who looks like she might throw up. I get the feeling she thinks she started this firestorm, but I'm hoping it's going to be a beneficial burn by the time Jayme's finished.

"We'll have a festival . . . music, special food and drinks, merchandise, activities. It'll be like Coachella or Electric Daisy Carnival, but right here at Americana Land. We'll do an all-access·pass so people can see every show and ride every ride. With it all happening at once, people can come for a long weekend. It'll be the event of the summer."

I'm starting to get it, or at least understand her excitement. But productions on this scale don't happen overnight.

Being the logical, reasonable one isn't usually my area of expertise, but thinking out loud, I say, "With the concerts spread out, we have a renewable stream of photos, advertising, and posts for social media. It's one thing if one concert doesn't go well" —I hold up one finger, and then a second— "and we have another to fall back on. But a festival? It'll be do or die, all our eggs in one potentially fucked-up basket. The social media blasts from attendees will have to match the narrative or it's going to be a huge failure. Like Fyre Festival-level catastrophic."

"It's dangerous, I'll give you that," Jayme concedes. "But aren't you a gambling man? One who likes risks?" She bats her eyelashes, well aware that she's using my own habits against me.

I answer her with a wry glare.

"Gamble on yourself, your team, on me."

The soft plea in her tone surprises me. She could easily boss this thing into fruition and no one would give it a second thought. They trust her because I trust her.

But that's not what she's doing. She's letting the decision be mine. At the end of the day—or the festival, I guess—it will be my redemption or my failure. She'll stand beside me either way, but it'll be mine to own.

In a way, this is the repair of my reputation as well.

"All right, people. This is a lot to do in a short period of time. Is it even possible?"

Scanning for feedback, I see Spencer talking in hushed tones with Kyleigh. Spencer has been on the marketing team since before I was here. She's in her fifties, with a closely cropped sharp hairdo that she keeps a soft shade of blue to match her boldly oversized glasses.

"You sure?" she asks Kyleigh. The beaming smile is answer enough. Spencer holds up her hand. "Carson?"

"Yes?"

"Kyleigh and I would like to take this on. We'll be project managers and get everything rolling. I'll need everyone's full cooperation—both marketing and the broader AL team—but I think we can do it." Spencer looks certain, and she is not one to do things halfway.

I look to the rest of the team. "Anyone opposed? This is going to be a major time crunch, so if you need to step away from this, now's the time."

No one says a word.

"Well, I guess we've got a festival to plan."

CHAPTER 12

JAYME

*C*arson's team files out, excitement and nerves leading them to chatter about the various things they need to work on. This is going to be an epic undertaking of massive proportions on the tightest time crunch.

This is bigger than any other reputation rehab I've ever tackled, by far. But I feel compelled to do it. For Carson. He deserves the best.

He deserves *my* best.

And I didn't give it the first round.

I'm mad at myself for not coming up with this idea sooner. Admittedly, the multi-faceted approach we've been using has been working, building traffic to the social media, creating a positive buzz around the Americana Land name, and restoring Carson's reputation.

But I pride myself on seeing beyond the standard approach. My innovation and creativity are what make me uniquely good at what I do. And this rehab needed a swing for the fences knockout, which is what I should've brought to the table from the get-go but am only now offering.

Was I too blinded by Carson, the man, to help Carson, the client?

I follow him down the hallway to his office. His strides are quick and long, leaving me behind several paces as I struggle to keep up. He holds the door open for me to enter but then shuts it behind me with a sound of finality. He sits down on the couch, and I sit beside him, scanning for hints of his thoughts.

Given the hard line of his jaw right now, I think he's disappointed that I didn't come up with this idea sooner too.

Straightening my back and ready to take my lumps, I say, "I'm sorry."

For some reason, at the same time, he mutters, "I'm sorry."

We look at each other, matching confusion in our eyes. "What?" we say in unison again.

"Ladies first." Carson holds his hand out, giving me the floor to speak.

I scoot several inches closer to him. This is going to be hard enough to admit. I don't need to shout it from the rooftops too. I notice that I'm twisting my hands and force myself to still them, laying them in my lap, one over the other.

"Jayme?"

"Hang on . . . I owe you an apology, but I'm working up my guts." I glance up from my hands to find him fighting a smirk. "I don't do this often, so I want to do it right."

"Of course, you definitely want to do it justice," he says agreeably.

Frustrating man, trying to make it easy for me to admit that I fucked up.

I take a fortifying breath, meet his eyes directly, and begin. "I'm the best at what I do for a reason, and I bring my A-game to every assignment. Every client deserves that—"

"Especially me," Carson adds.

"Especially you," I echo. "But I got us halfway down a path that was more about easy than innovation, and it wasn't my best. To make matters worse, I brought up the festival idea with the whole team instead of doing it privately. You deserved the opportunity to hear the idea first, have time to tweak it with me and then present as a united front. Instead, I got overly excited and ran with it in the moment, and that was unprofessional of me. I'm sorry, Carson."

It all comes out in one long breath, leaving my chest aching and my lungs burning as I run out of oxygen. Carson's stoic reaction, or non-reaction, I should say, doesn't make me feel any better.

"You done?" he asks.

I'm ready for anything. At this point, he has every right to yell, to be disappointed in me, or even to fire me and hire another PR representative to help him and Americana Land. It'd serve me right for being blinded by him to the point of distraction. "Yes. Let me have it."

A shudder works its way through his shoulders, and he pins me with the fire in his gaze. "I would very much like to. However, about the matter at hand . . ."

Wait, what did he just say? Is he flirting at a time like this? Whiplash shoots through my nerves. Maybe he's not mad?

But no, the snapped responses during that meeting made his feelings explicitly clear.

"The festival idea is . . ." He's searching for words, never a good sign. "Brilliant. I do wish we'd thought of it sooner, but every new idea comes from a spark, and that spark happened in real time today. We got to see it develop into a flame, and it was beautiful to watch. *You* were beautiful to watch as your mind raced, considering and rejecting ideas on the spot, planning possible ways to make it work and getting everyone in the room dedicated to this crazy idea of yours in a matter of seconds. It was stunning."

"I'm . . . you're . . . uhm, what?" I'm stumbling over my words because my brain isn't able to make the least bit of sense from what he's said. I feel like I've got puzzle pieces from a *Sesame Street* ten-piece and a thousand-piece Impressionist painting puzzle and I'm trying to slide them together. But they do not go . . . at all.

Carson softens before my eyes, his eyes brightening, his shoulders dropping, and a low chuckle rumbling in his chest.

"You're not mad at me?" I ask, still trying to find some logical connection between his earlier reaction and his current one.

"For the festival idea? No." He runs his fingers through his hair, one of his few tells that he's got something heavy weighing on his mind. "But you did hit one of my sore spots, and it pissed me off. That's why I said 'I'm sorry' to you—for my rudeness when you're only trying to help us."

"I didn't mean to press your buttons. Can you tell me what it was so I don't do it again?" I ask carefully.

"Not good enough. Not nearly good enough," Carson grits out as though the words get stuck in his throat.

At first, I think he's talking about me, but when he gives me a pained look, I realize that he's quoting me. I said that . . . about my concert series idea. And then it dawns on me . . . he thought I was talking about him.

"Oh, Carson! No. That's not what I meant. I meant what I gave you —*my* ideas—weren't good enough." I reach out to cover his hand with my own, needing to comfort him. I don't know why that phrasing hit so hard, but I certainly didn't mean to hurt him in any way.

He shrugs, the movement an obvious attempt at downplaying his reaction. "I know. But like I said . . . it's a trigger point for me."

The meeting comes into a sharper focus as I replay his reactions in my mind with this new lens. He wasn't mad at me or disappointed in my ideas. It was something deeper and personal, something I can relate to. Because I said those words to myself.

"Families are tricky things, shaping who we are in ways both good and bad. My family is full of high-achieving perfectionists who have it all, do it all, and crush any goal they set," I admit. "It's hard to shine in a family like mine. I usually feel . . . invisible? Or maybe not on their level?"

I tilt my head, trying to put my feelings into words, but this isn't something I share with people. It's not even something I think about, but with everything I'm asking of Carson, the least I can do is offer my own truth.

"I'm a behind-the-scenes person, Carson. If I'm doing my best work, nobody sees it or realizes they're seeing it. It can make it hard to feel like I matter because it's not tangible. I can't say 'I increased profits by ten percent' or 'decreased expenses by one million dollars'. I can't even tell my family that I prevented a PR catastrophe because that would defeat the purpose of doing it. So, realizing that what I'd set in motion here, for you and Americana Land, wasn't good enough, wasn't my best . . . disappointed me. And since I'm the only barometer I have, the expectations are higher than high."

Probing delicately, I ask, "Did what I say trigger you because of your family?"

His growl is one of frustration and long-held anger, and I don't think he's going to answer, but after a moment, he says, "Did you know Archer was the chosen son when I was younger? That he even worked here for a short while?"

"What? That wasn't in any of my research." I'm surprised. My deep dive into projects borders on obsessive, to the point I often find info my clients wish I didn't know. But nothing in my investigation of Americana Land, Carson, or the Steen family showed Archer as anything other than a playboy who flits around from woman to woman, living off a trust fund. Certainly, nothing hinted that he'd actually worked, much less at the family business.

Carson nods. "One of my first jobs as Chief Marketing Officer was to wipe everything I could, and to be honest, there wasn't much out there on Archer, the professional, because he wasn't. But here, in the office, I had to prove myself over and over again because people figured I'd be like him. And I worked my ass off to show that I wasn't. But no matter how hard I work or how much I do, I can't wipe that assumption from one person's mind. My dad's."

I hear the sharp grind of his teeth as he closes his eyes and wonder what voice is playing in his head right now . . . his father's or his own? I suspect they're one and the same at times.

"There's no way your dad thinks you're like Archer," I refute bluntly. "I've seen what you do here, how much you care. Hell, the whole reason I'm here is because you stepped in to help an employee. You could've walked on by, said it was her job, not yours, but you didn't because you care about people. And now you're the one paying the price for it."

"But it's still just one more fuck-up to dear old Dad. If I'd kept my head down, the situation would've still been handled but there wouldn't have been all this drama and dragging Americana Land and the Steen name through the mud again."

"Again. The key word there is *again*. Nobody's perfect, least of all Ben Steen. Fuck knows, he messed up, and his personal choices definitely affected his professional image. Back then, things were different, though. Gossipy grapevines were forgetful, not instantly and perpetually searchable with the click of a button. And you don't have to be some perfect robot son to be worthy of your role as CMO or as his son."

"If only that were true," he scoffs.

"Are you sure it's not you who expects you to be perfect? Because obviously, I've got my own issues with that." I offer a small smile with the self-deprecating sense of camaraderie. "Maybe we're two peas in a pod?"

Carson looks up at me through thick lashes and finally offers a hint of a smile. "Not sure that's a good thing. This pea pod is pretty fucked up."

"Nobody wants pristine, organic pea pods anyway. I had to do image rehab once because an actress went all Mother Earth-granola-crunchy to the extreme, telling interviewers about her detox shits because 'Everyone poops and it's perfectly natural.'"

I laugh at the memory and how hard I had to fight to keep a straight face during that conversation, especially when my client wanted to discuss my own bowel habits. No, thank you, not interested in that convo.

"You'd think that wouldn't be controversial, but you'd be *so* very wrong. She went from beloved to most hated overnight because everyone thought she was being all holier-than-thou about it, and honestly, she was. I had to help her find a balance between her personal self and the image she needed to be hirable. Point being—perfect is boring, and people hate it even though they think they want it."

"You might want to repeat that to yourself," Carson quips pointedly. "I think you're being too hard on yourself about not coming up with the festival idea sooner."

"Hey!" I protest, pointing my finger at him accusingly, "Don't use my own mental mojo on me. I'm working my magic on you." I mean as a client, because sometimes my job requires me to be more like a therapist than anything else.

Carson grabs my hand, encircling it with his own until our fingers interlace. "Yes, you are." He brings our hands to his lips and presses a gentle kiss to the back of mine. The scratch of the scruff along his chin against the sensitive skin of my hand sends a jolt straight to my core. "There's one more person you've got to bewitch, though."

He kisses my knuckle.

"Huh?" Okay, so intelligent wordsmithing isn't my forte when all the blood in my body has gone south.

"We need to tell Dad about the festival." His tongue dips into the valley between my index and middle fingers. "It's going to take funding and coordination between all departments. I need to grease the way for Spencer and Kyleigh." Another kiss, this one wetter and promising similar attention elsewhere on my body.

His dad. Ben Steen. Carson's own devil.

Well, that's one way to splash cold water on the heat that was building. I think my pussy just went drier than the Sahara.

"Could we not talk about him while I'm imagining you kissing me like that somewhere else?"

Carson's evil grin is diabolical. He releases my hand so that our fingers aren't interlocked any longer but then takes my index finger into his mouth, his tongue swirling over the pad. He nibbles the plump flesh there gently. "Where do you want my mouth, Jayme?"

He lays kisses along each fingertip, leaving me fascinated by the pucker of his lips, the pink fullness surrounded by dark scruff, so soft and yet coarse, both sensations driving me crazy. "Everywhere."

"Tell me . . . do you want me to kiss your neck?"

My head lolls over, giving him access, but he simply takes my middle finger into his mouth, sucking gently. I whimper in disappointment, but it's because I want more. More of what he's promising—with words and actions.

"Your breasts?"

I nod, arching my back to lift my chest encouragingly for him.

"What about your pussy? You want me to lick and suck you there, lapping up your cream until you come for me?" He turns my hand over, laying a soft kiss to the palm before licking a long line down the center to show me exactly what he'd do to my core, which is pulsing in time with my racing heartbeat. I scissor my legs, looking for relief.

"Yes," I moan.

He flicks his tongue along the sensitive skin between my thumb and index finger, and it's easy to imagine it's what he'd do to my clit. This has been building between us over weeks, and I'm weak with desire, on the edge without so much as a touch to my pussy.

"Fuck, I can't wait to taste you, drink you down. I bet you taste delicious," he groans before teasing my hand again.

"Touch me, Carson." I don't beg or plead, it's a demand. If he doesn't touch me, I'm going to do it myself, right here on his couch. At least I know there's no camera in his private office and the day shift security isn't getting an eyeful.

There's no slow progression up my thigh to my center, and Carson doesn't let go of my hand. But with his other, he dives up my skirt and under my soaked panties, finding my core easily. "Oh, fuck," he murmurs when he feels how wet I am. "For me?"

"For you," I confirm. "You drive me crazy. I shouldn't be doing this, but I can't stop."

He taps my clit, a slight punishment for saying I shouldn't do this when it feels so good, but the sting sends a shiver of pleasure through me. He circles my clit, tapping it again as he presses our interwoven hands over my head. I could get away, but I don't want to. Not at all. I want more.

I buck my hips, and he slips two fingers inside me instantly, curling them. "Right there? I can feel your walls clenching me tight, wanting me inside you. Is that what you want?"

I make some sort of unintelligible noise that sounds like, "Uhhuhmmm."

Carson must understand, though, because all at once, he grinds the heel of his hand against my clit, curls his fingers against my inner walls, and squeezes my hand tight. The pressure of it all sends me flying into space, shattering into pieces that will never fit back together the same way.

"Beautiful," I think I hear his whisper, but maybe I imagine it.

The waves slow, my body and my consciousness crashing back together. "Oh, my God," I pant.

"You can call me Carson, not God," he jokes.

I laugh lightly at the stupid joke, unconsciously pushing his fingers out of me. He lifts them to his mouth, licking each one slowly and deliberately. "Delicious. I knew you would be," he growls, acting like my juices are the most luxurious delicacy he's ever tasted. "I want more."

Heat burns my cheeks, and I'd bet I'm turning seven shades of red from his dirty compliment. "I'm never gonna get you to be a 'good guy', am I?" I tease back, making sure he knows I'm kidding. Because Carson Steen is a good man, he just has some rough edges that I do not want to file down. At least not for real, because I'm finding I rather enjoy them. "Just a tamed beast?"

"Barely tamed," he declares shamelessly, stretching his arms out along the back of the couch and spreading his knees wide. I can see the hard ridge of his thick cock in his slacks, but it's the shit-eating grin on his face that makes my heart stutter. He looks relaxed, confident, and calmer than I think I've ever seen him.

"Is this the part where you offer me a ride on your *motorcycle*?" I drop my eyes to his lap to indicate what I expect him to want me to ride.

He cups himself, shifting his cock to a more comfortable position in his slacks. "No, this is the part where we bask in the afterglow of that glorious orgasm of yours. And once we've done that justice, we'll get back to work."

I blink, surprised at his answer. "That actually sounds like a great plan," I confess, not ready to move yet. "Reluctantly."

I curl into Carson's side, my head on his shoulder. It feels good to just *be* for a moment, still and steady as we relax and catch our breaths. I try to close my eyes, but the blood rushing through my body is now redirecting to my brain and ideas are sparking like crazy.

"What if we do a laser light show? With those smell machines like they have on 4d rides where we pump out citrus scents with orange lights, fresh mowed grass with green, or ocean with blue? We could make each musical set have its own vibe with sensory additions beyond the music. And sell LED necklaces and bracelets to add to the rave effect? We need one of those drinks where the cotton candy melts into it—alcoholic and non-alcoholic versions for the younger crowd. And special edition Freddy Freebirds."

My mouth is running at warp speed, but my brain is going even faster.

Carson sighs, and I look up, expecting him to be annoyed with my overzealousness. But he's smiling happily. "Guess our afterglow moment is over? You know the first thing we have to do, though, right?"

I furrow my brows. "Write up a bullet point list to go over with Spencer and Kyleigh?"

He shakes his head. "Talk to my father."

"Shit," I say.

"My feeling exactly," he answers, laughing at my concise summary.

Ben Steen leans back in his chair, his elbows on the armrests and his hands steepled in front of his mouth as he considers Carson. "A party? This is your grand idea to fix the Americana Land image?"

He sounds uncertain, but not harsh. To me, at least. Carson seems to feel differently.

"Yes. A 'party', as you called it, otherwise known as a festival, that will be a social media buzz loud enough to drown out any other storylines while creating an improved image for Americana Land as a vacation destination for not only families with young children or older people but targeting a different demographic in an innovative manner."

It's nearly verbatim what Carson and I discussed before approaching his dad, delivered with considerably more bite. Ben's eyes go hard, returning Carson's determined glare. Two bulls preparing to charge one another without realizing they could get so much more done if they worked together.

Using a soothing tone, I echo Carson's pitch. "This will be a way to reach a new demographic, which happens to be the Abby Burks generation. A festival will be a direct rebuttal to her drama, creating a positive social media presence around the Americana Land name."

"Hmm," Ben says thoughtfully, his gaze turning to me. It's my job to read people and situations, but Ben Steen is not only a closed book, but rather, one with a lock securely fastening any thoughts or emotions inside. I don't know if he's going to laugh at me or agree. Or maybe yell? There's no telling. "And you want carte blanche to run with this?"

That definitely does not sound promising.

"Yes," Carson answers immediately, taking Ben's attention back.

"What about the timing? We have the charity event coming up soon too, you know. It's a big deal for the local children's hospital. We can't interfere with that."

The annual charity event at Americana Land has been a staple on the philanthropy social calendar for over ten years. The funds go to a local hospital to help pay for uninsured children's care so that their families aren't wiped out during an already difficult time. I would never suggest anything that would compromise that. But before I can tell Ben that, Carson jumps in.

"I'm aware," Carson grits out, his frustration with his father's reminder apparent. "This would actually be completed before the charity event and the concert series kick off. There's no timing conflict, and that project has its own dedicated team, as it has since it began. Mike was already aware of the proposed dates of the new concert series, and since we're consolidating to a single date, it actually makes things less congested on the calendar."

Tense silence stretches between the two men, and though I'm in the middle of this whole thing, I feel on the outside of whatever quiet conversation is happening in their posturing and mental games. This has been going on for a long time and won't be solved in one conversation. Especially one had during a professional and personal crisis.

"Done." Ben Steen's decision is as easy as that. One word.

There's still more to unravel here, but I can take that one step at a time. First, I need to fix the image issues, then I can help Carson figure out how to communicate with his dad. For now? The focus has to be on this massive undertaking of a project. I have faith that Carson and I can do it together. With his team, of course. And maybe then I can work on helping the two men find some common ground to settle their shit.

CHAPTER 13

CARSON

"*L*os Angeles," I note, looking out the window of the chartered private plane. "Or Van Nuys, technically, I guess."

Dad would never have approved anything other than flying business class, but after Jayme worked some of her negotiation magic with a local pilot for hire, we proved that it was actually more cost effective for us to fly out on a private plane this morning for our meeting with Jazmyn Starr and then fly back tonight. If we'd flown one of the major airlines, the next flight home would've required an overnight stay, and while I would've been more than okay with a night alone with Jayme, the hotels are expensive and booked solid for some convention plus an award ceremony that's in town.

"Same difference," Jayme quips, glancing out her own window.

She's had her nose buried in her notebook since we left, not impressed with the sunrise from our vantage point or the view of the Hollywood Hills as we fly in. But it's given me time to study her covertly.

When she stepped out of her sleek black Lexus this morning, my eyes nearly popped out of my skull like one of those cartoon cats when they see a sexy kitten strutting by. Her white suit is pristine and fits her as though it were custom-tailored for her body, and the red high heels are the perfect touch of badass boss. I'd honestly developed an instant fantasy of joining the Mile High Club and writing our names in the sky, but Jayme was all business.

After reviewing our strategy for this meeting, she retreated into her planning and plotting, and I logged onto my laptop to get some work done too. But still, I couldn't help but glance over as she'd cross and uncross her legs, lick her lips as she read silently to herself, and do a giddy wiggle as she received an email from another social media artist hungry to participate in the festival.

"Have you flown in here before?" I ask.

"Huh?" Jayme says, her finger marking her place on the page. "Oh, yeah. Bunches of times. Anytime I've had to come to LA, this is where I fly in if I can. Van Nuys is better for private planes, but you can still get where you need to go with relative ease, or what constitutes as ease in LA." She laughs at her own joke, but LA's traffic is truly no laughing matter.

"How long do you think it'll take us to get to the record label's office?"

"Well, it's roughly five miles away, so probably . . . an hour?"

"Perfect," I answer dryly, "so nothing crazy."

The plane touches down, and we roll to a smooth stop. The ding lets us know we can unbuckle and prepare to deplane. Before we get very far, the flight attendant comes out from her area near the cockpit. "Do you need anything for your ride? Coffee, water, a snack?"

"No, thank you, Lisa," Jayme tells the woman. "We appreciate the easy flight. See you this afternoon?"

Her camaraderie with the woman is natural, much like with everyone. Jayme puts people at ease within moments of meeting them, Lisa included, and then works her magic.

"Yes ma'am. Have a lovely day, Jayme . . . Mr. Steen."

See? Lisa is calling me by my last name, but she and Jayme could probably go out for drinks tonight and be besties before morning. She's amazing that way, and I'm glad she's with me for this meeting with Jazmyn Starr.

Today has to go right. There's no other option.

I take the steps down first, offering Jayme a steadying hand, but she alights the stairs to the tarmac below as though she's floating, not balancing in precariously sexy heels. Damn . . . those heels!

We climb into a waiting Mercedes, and the driver begins expertly navigating through the airport traffic.

"Let me send a text to Steve confirming our arrival," Jayme says, clicking on her phone.

Steve Capetti is Jazmyn Starr's manager, and a surprisingly slick one considering Jazmyn is still relatively new to the scene. But her star is rising fast, and Steve is a big part of why that's happening. It was a process just to get his personal cell number, and now Jayme is texting him as though it's no big deal.

This festival is going to happen. We're going to make it happen, and Americana Land will be not just recovered from the bad press but the feature of tons of good publicity. All at my hand, with Jayme's guidance. For once, I'll be the best I can be.

I think it over and over, letting it become a mantra, never considering that anything but this will be true.

"Shit!" Jayme hisses.

"What's wrong?" My fight or flight instinct flips on instantly, and I'm ready to fight . . . for the festival, for Americana Land, for myself.

"Steve says Jazmyn is hungry. She wants to meet at a restaurant instead of his office." Jayme looks thoughtful, her fingers poised to respond but not until she considers every angle.

"What do you think? It feels spontaneous, but I'd bet it's not," I suggest.

Jayme looks up at me, smiling. "Oh, it's a total power play. But I think it'll actually work in our favor. A fun mimosa-filled brunch instead of a dry office meeting? Done. Plus, I think we might be able to get some fake-sneaky shots and plant some gossip about 'why is upcoming sensation Jazmyn Starr meeting with Americana Land's bad boy?' That would get some buzz started before we even promote the festival."

"Impressive."

She preens at the compliment dramatically, slipping her hair behind her ear. "I know."

I wait while she types out a response to Steve and then clarify, "I thought we wanted to show me as a good guy?"

Jayme throws me a sassy wink. "We do, but people love a bad boy too. It's all about the nuances." She frowns at her phone. "Uhm, excuse me, Carlo?" The driver looks up into the rearview mirror.

"Change of plans. Can you take us to . . . Green Goddess? It's on Victory Boulevard."

Carlo nods in answer, then carefully types on the large screen on the dash. "About a twenty-five minute ETA."

Jayme types on her phone once more and then sets it down to give me her full attention. "Do we need to go over things again?"

We don't. We've talked about this meeting, the contract we had legal prepare, Jazmyn Starr herself, and dissected the whole thing from every angle. Still, I'm nervous. Or excited. Or both?

I've got a lot riding on this—my reputation, my team, Americana Land, and maybe most of all, my relationship with my dad. If I can pull this off, I'll be proud of myself, and surely, he'll see how far I'm willing to go for our name and legacy. If it implodes, I don't know if I'll recover from it. This failure would be a hundred times worse than the Abby Burks incident.

But I answer, "Yes, let's do it one more time."

We roll through everything in Jayme's notebook once more, and before I know it, Carlo is stopping the car at the curb in front of a building with so many windows that it looks like a greenhouse. Vines drape across the front, ivy climbs the sides, there are plants shoved into every nook and cranny of various brass plant stands, and there's a huge stone statue of a nude woman by an arched wooden door.

"Green Goddess," Carlo proclaims needlessly.

I open my door, offering Jayme a helping hand to exit the car. "Are we eating brunch or planting a garden?" I question quietly where only she can hear me.

"Both?"

"Just don't check the types of greenery too carefully. I don't think those are all garden-variety ferns."

Jayme chuckles, and her heels click-clack on the brick sidewalk as we make our way to the door. "We've got this, Carson. I promised you and I meant it."

Her quick vow as I open the door and we step inside means more than she'll ever know.

At the hostess stand, we're greeted by a young woman with thick blonde dreadlocks interwoven with metallic beads, huge round-framed glasses, and oversized linen overalls. She presses her hands together in a prayer motion and bows her head. "Welcome. Thank you for including us on your journey today."

Uh, what? I suddenly feel like Alice entering Wonderland. I was kidding, but maybe there is something 'special' in the greenery planted outside.

"Hi, we are meeting Steve Capetti here. I'm not sure if he's arrived yet?" I look past the hostess to scan the restaurant, but there are so many plants, I can't see much.

"Right this way." The hostess takes a few steps deeper into the forest of greenery and I realize she's barefoot beneath her linen overalls.

"Is that legal?" I whisper to Jayme. "Seems like it'd be a health violation."

She shrugs. "It's LA."

I know she's right, but I prefer Jayme's sexy heels to dirty, naked feet.

At the table, Steve and Jazmyn have their heads bent together in deep conversation, but they part and smile warmly as we approach. Well, Steve does. Jazmyn gives me an up and down and then does the same to Jayme. She's plainly sizing us up. Steve is too, but he's more discrete about it.

I do the same, getting to know who and what I'm up against for today's meeting. Surprisingly, Jazmyn Starr looks exactly like her filtered photos and TikToks. She's wearing bold, smokey eye makeup with a thick streak of lime green eyeliner that matches the shoe-strings laced through the holes along the sleeves of her black and white striped shirt. There's also a gathering of lime and gold safety pins in her left ear and a stack of rings on every finger. Except . . . I think the constellation of dots around her eyes are tattoos, not makeup as I'd thought.

Though I've never seen Steve, he's exactly what I expected—a pro. Dressed in what can best be called California executive, he's got on designer jeans, an open-throated dress shirt, and a sport coat that I can tell is deceptively casual. It looks off the rack . . . but probably costs more than some people's monthly rent.

He likely found Jazmyn online and, seeing talent, hitched his wagon to her star. I imagine talent managers, like department managers, are sometimes excellent and sometimes useless. I hope Steve is as quality as his thousand-dollar sunglasses.

"Jayme! Carson! Nice to finally meet you in person," Steve greets us, standing to offer his hand. Jazmyn doesn't move, simply staring at us straight-faced. She looks bored already. On one hand, maybe she's already made up her mind about the concert and wants to sign and be done. On the other hand, maybe she wants to be anywhere but here. At home, the beach, or maybe Dunkin Donuts?

Jayme shakes Steve's hand, then offers hers to Jazmyn. After a long beat where I consider that she might not follow through, Jazmyn does finally shake Jayme's hand. I take the cue and shake both their hands as well.

Sitting down, a waiter appears. His curls are standing up wildly, and his slouchy jeans and band T-shirt look vintage or at least well-worn, possibly slept in, but he's thankfully wearing shoes. I'd estimate his most recent shower at four days ago. "Can I get you something to drink?"

"Water for now, please," I answer.

"Spring, sparkling, or electrolyte?"

I must make a face of surprise because Jazmyn barks out a laugh, but I manage to answer, "Spring is fine. Unless you've got a bourbon?"

Jayme knocks my knee with hers under the table, but I see interest blooming in Jazmyn's eyes. I'm not opposed to a bit of self-deprecation if it gets us what we want—Jazmyn signing on the dotted line.

"Would've thought they'd serve water from the hose in a plant-heavy place like this," I joke, and Jazmyn smiles vacantly. Is she on something, perhaps? If so, what, and should I be concerned about it?

"Can you imagine?" Jazmyn intones. "Tap water? Gross. I'd rather drink piss straight from a stranger."

I can tell she's waiting for a reaction, testing us, so I fake a shiver of disgust at the very thought. And I must pass her test because the mood at the table becomes much more comfortable.

Score one for me. But LA is a strange place.

"Steve says you want me to perform at Americana Land." It's a flat statement, no excitement or interest, which is especially concerning considering this is supposed to be an easy meet-and-sign deal. If anything, the money alone would make all but the most jaded performers sit up and take notice, and Jazmyn is too young and too new to be that careless about the bankroll we're offering. "That's where Abby Burks was assaulted."

Jayme stiffens beside me.

"No," I growl. Jayme places a light touch to my hand on the tabletop, not intimate but it's enough to stop the rage bubbling up at Jazmyn's accusation. "I mean, yes, we want you to perform. No, Abby Burks was not assaulted."

"That's not what she said."

Jazmyn's digging for a story, but I don't have one to give her. I've said my piece and am moving on with Jayme's help. That's what we're here for. So I give the barest-bones, detail-free, calmly practiced answer. "Ms. Burks created a scene where it looked as though she was shoplifting and then was intentionally unhelpful in getting the confusion straightened out. Including resisting being escorted to a more private space by our onsite security guards."

"So she was asking for it?" Jazmyn follows up with a taunting smirk of her black-painted lips.

"Of course not," I snap. "Not in the way you mean. I would never, and my staff would never, behave in an objectionable manner like that."

Jazmyn flashes a 'gotcha' smile. "Touchy."

Fuck. I walked right into that one. But those unfounded accusations have been hard to hear, and defending myself and my team is my first instinct. Especially when I know we didn't do anything wrong.

In a stern voice, Steve says, "Jazmyn, could we not?"

She rolls her eyes before schooling her face back to blank disinterest. "Whatever."

Great, things are going just great.

Jayme clears her throat then plasters a bright smile on her face. "Why don't we order some food and then discuss the exciting plans we have?"

As if summoned, the waiter reappears. "Our special today is oat grain hoecakes with goat milk crème fraise, kale salad with home-grown bean sprouts, feta, and a raspberry vinaigrette, and chef-designed quiche. Served with fresh-squeezed orange juice mimosas." He cuts his eyes around the table. "Or I can get you a menu?"

I get the sense that no one takes that option but rather orders the special regardless of what it contains. I glance at Jayme, then Steve and Jazmyn, and seeing no arguments, I say, "Four specials would be great. Thank you."

And on the way out of here, I'm getting some real food. There's got to be a decent taco truck somewhere between here and the airport.

"Great, shall we get to it, then?" Steve suggests as the waiter slips away. "We've had our lawyer review the contract, and everything seems to be in order, but I understand there are some updates?"

I nod confidently. "Yes, some exciting ones. During our initial conversations, we were aiming to present a series of concerts, topped off with a Jazmyn Starr special." I offer her a smile, hoping to intrigue her with this next bit. "But I think we've come up with something much better."

"Better than a Jazmyn Starr concert?" Jazmyn says doubtfully, examining her nails. "Good luck with that."

For a newly signed artist whose primary audience is through Spotify and YouTube, she's beyond confident. I hope her show stands up to that confidence.

"How about a one-day, jam-packed festival of music from a list of up-and-coming artists? We've already got quite a few on board, but we need our headliner act." I expect that to be a dangling carrot Jazmyn can't resist. I mean, isn't that the point . . . all teens and young adults are into this festival set-up? Instead, her eyes narrow.

"Like who? I'm not playing with just anyone. I'm very *selective*." She almost purrs the word but somehow makes it sound like a threat at the same time.

Meow. Retract those claws, kitten!

"Of course not," Jayme rushes in. "But we've done our homework. We've already talked to Marquis, Alien Babies, DJ Swizzle, Saint Sabotino, and best of all . . . DJ Amalfo."

Jazmyn leans forward, her hands slapping on the table. "Amalfie is going to be there? Why didn't you say so?"

"The festival is only one day," I continue. "If you wanted to visit Americana Land as a VIP guest the day after, I could arrange a tour. Walk onto rides, all the food treats you want, front row seats for the parade."

I'm selling the Americana Land experience as best I can, but what I'm really thinking about is squeezing as much good PR as I can get out of this particular stone. Unfortunately, it seems that Jazmyn is still not quite on board as she twists her lips and rolls her eyes.

"And a personal tackle by yours truly? The full Abby Burks experience?"

I thought we were solid on a concert, but she's pulling no punches, and I'm concerned that she might be backing out of the whole thing. Even with the promise of DJ Amalfo.

"You don't like Abby Burks, do you?" Jayme says, moving into the line of fire of the bullets Jazmyn is shooting at me with her eyes. I'm not sure what she's getting that. Everything I'm getting is saying that Jazmyn is trying to stand in solidarity with her influencer sister. But I trust Jayme's assessment. She's either seeing something I don't or her background research revealed something I missed.

Jazmyn crosses her arms, glaring at Jayme. "She's whatever."

"You've brought her up twice and our food isn't even here yet. She got a lot of publicity at the cost of Americana Land and Carson Steen. But this festival is going to be big—every blog, Instagram, Twitch, Discord, even mainstream media—all with your name as the headliner. *Potentially* . . ." Jayme's voice trails off as though she's the one considering whether Jazmyn is worthy of leading this festival.

Damn, that's good. She's a pro at turning the tables, especially when people think they're running them.

"Wait." Jazmyn says sharply.

Steve leans forward, his elbows on the table, putting himself between Jayme and Jazmyn. It's like we're all hungry hippos going after the same marble in the middle of the table—in and out, back and forth. "We want to do the concert. I'll put that out there."

Narrowing my eyes, I ask Steve, "So, what do you want?"

It's just the right amount of take no shit Alpha to push Steve and Jazmyn into talking. For the rest of our meal, we talk through our visions for the festival, and though she denies it, I can see the excitement growing in Jazmyn's eyes. She even makes a couple of suggestions that Jayme writes down in her leather notebook.

By the time we finish our brunch, which is surprisingly good, the thread of an idea has grown, knitting into something greater. "We'll share this with our project leads and make sure it's all in place for the festival."

"Even the dancers?" Jazmyn says, her hands pressed together in a pleading move that doesn't seem like her, but rather a much younger, sweeter, and more innocent version of her. In a surprise move I'm still reeling over, Jazmyn's main request is that we fly in a group of kids who did the TikTok famous dance to her biggest song. They're a dance troupe from an inner-city studio who've never had a chance to perform on a stage like this. And she wants them to get a VIP treatment park visit too.

"I can't make promises that they'll be there yet, but I will contact them and see what I can do."

"I think that's everything," Steve says, a broad smile on his face. He knows as well as I do that this meeting will lead to big things for all of us. This festival is truly a win-win situation for Americana Land, me, Jazmyn, the other performers, and even the dancing kids. Though I'd bet Steve is happiest about the financial gains Jazmyn, and therefore he, will get from their percentage of profits.

"I misjudged you," Jazmyn says suddenly, garnering our attention. "My bad."

She's looking me boldly in the eye, offering her ring-covered hand for a shake. "Uhm, thank you?" I stutter, confused at the semi-apology. But I shake her hand. "I hope to keep that up."

"Fuck knows, people judge the hell out of me. I get a kick out of it most of the time, you know? Even fuck around with them for shits and giggles. But you seem like an okay person, Carson. And not the type to enjoy being center stage. I bet this whole thing has had you clenching your tighty whities so hard that they're nearly a butt plug at this point." There's a small delay of shock and then Jazmyn laughs heartily.

"I'll say that if I never see my name in the press again, I'd be completely fine with that," I offer. "Not going to discuss my underwear situation, though."

"Jazmyn," Steve says in warning. I bet he has a hell of a time keeping her wrangled in, but he seems to be managing okay with it. For now. I just hope he can keep her on target for the festival.

As the waiter returns with the check, he sets down four small glasses of green liquid so bright it almost matches Jazmyn's eyeliner.

"What's that? It looks like antifreeze," I ask in slight disgust. My stomach's already revolting at the idea of anything that color being edible.

"Plant shots. Pureed seaweed, lemongrass, phytonutrients, B12, CBD, turmeric, maca, and basil. It helps with digestion." Jazmyn picks hers up, holding it high. "Cheers, bitches." And without clinking against anyone's glass, she downs it in one go. "Ahh."

I blink, not believing what I'm seeing. "You did not just drink that," I murmur.

"It's good for you, old man. Keeps the pipes clean. Definitely better than bourbon if that's really what you drink," she answers, showing that she was listening earlier. Plus, there's a dare laced through her words.

Steve picks his up, apparently used to these ground-up weed smoothies, and then Jayme does the same. They look at me, waiting, but I just look at Jazmyn in amused shock. "Did you just call me . . . *old?*" I ask, trying not to be offended.

She shrugs.

"Well, in that case," I say, raising my glass. Feeling the pressure, I pick it up and take a sniff. It smells like . . . a freshly mowed lawn. Not exactly a scent that makes me think 'yum.'

"Chug, chug, chug," Jazmyn chants, getting into it.

Just do it, man. It can't be that bad.

Without warning, Jayme and Steve both turn it back on cue, leaving me the lone holdout.

Jayme's tongue slips out to lick her lip and then she smiles. "It's not as bad as I thought it'd be."

It gives me the courage I need, and I tilt my head back and pour the stuff down as quickly as I can.

"Ugh! Ma gawd, thut's aw-ful," I gasp, smacking my lips to try and get my throat to open up again.

Wiping my mouth with my napkin, I swallow thickly again, trying to lose the taste but no dice. Coughing deeply, I look over at Jazmyn, who's giggling. "Not bad."

"Sir, are you okay? Do you need some seltzer, perhaps?" the waiter asks, popping up at my side out of nowhere. All I can see in my mind is something out of an old slapstick comedy movie, with the waiter spraying me in the face with a seltzer bottle, which makes me laugh. That makes me cough anew.

"Shit," I hiss, reaching for my mimosa. I take a swig of that, but orange juice, champagne, and yard clippings don't taste good together either, so I resort to chugging what's left of my water. Somehow, I manage to choke on that too. I thought spring water was supposed to be all smooth and natural?

"I think he's going to die," Jazmyn stage-whispers.

"You said it wasn't that bad," I accuse Jayme.

She shakes her head. "No, I said it wasn't as bad as I thought it was going to be. It was worse."

I'm reeling from that gross taste and the betrayal, but her vibrant laugh helps me relax a bit. "I'll get you for that," I warn, not meaning it in the slightest.

"I'm not sure LA is right for you, Carson," Steve taunts.

"I think I'm ready to eat delivery pizza and drink a bourbon in my plant-free home," I answer. Though when I glance to Jayme, there are several other things I'd like to do at home too.

CHAPTER 14

JAYME

"*I* have a surprise for you," I tease as we walk out of Green Goddess into the sunshine of an LA afternoon. I can't believe how that meeting went, careening from disaster to success to comedy seemingly minute by minute, but I'm glad Jazmyn is completely sold on the festival idea. The signed contract in my bag is a relief of epic proportions.

There's still more to today, though.

"A surprise?" Carson repeats hotly, his gentlemanly hand on my back moving to my hip and squeezing suggestively.

I slip him a coy smile. "I think you'll like it."

A groan rumbles in his chest as he pushes me toward the waiting car. "I need to kiss you after that amazing performance in there, but I know I can't do that here. Get in."

I nod at Carlo as I dip into the car, and Carson follows me, closing the door behind himself. Pressed up against me, thigh to thigh, he cups my jaw. Before a single word can be said or the car gets started, his lips find mine as he kisses the hell out of me.

Which is amazing until . . .

"Ugh . . . you taste awful," he mutters. "Grass clippings."

I stick my tongue out, running it on my teeth in a failed attempt to get the grossness off. "Plant shot."

We look at each other, noses screwed up in distaste, but at the same time, it's funny in a gross sort of way. Somehow, the kiss seems to have reactivated the *blech* of the Green Goddess's lawn drink. I reach for the bottled water in the door and Carson does the same. I guzzle the liquid down until I have to gasp for air. The water dribbles down my chin, and I swipe at it with my hand but realize Carson is continuing to chug even though water is running down his chin in rivulets, dripping to his shirt.

I laugh. "God, that shot was awful."

Carson's bottle is empty, and I think he'd drink mine too if I weren't clutching it tightly. "Fucking disgusting," he agrees. "I'm all for eating healthy and all that, but . . . damn."

We collapse back against the seat, panting and laughing.

"Ms. Rice?" Carlo says carefully. I meet his eyes in the rearview mirror. "Stop two?"

"Yes, please," I answer.

When I turn back, Carson is assessing me with interest. "You really do have a surprise for me? You didn't mean making out in the car on the way back to the airport?"

I try to decipher the look on his face. There's surprise, but something deeper layered beneath it that I can't define. "I do. I knew the meeting with Jazmyn and Steve would take a bit, but I planned a little something extra for us when I arranged everything."

"Thank you. Nobody's ever done anything like this," Carson says quietly, his eyes boring into mine.

I grin. "You don't even know what it is yet. What if it's another plant shot? Or something worse?"

He shrugs, totally relaxed. "I trust you."

It's then that I realize what I'm seeing . . . the little boy who just wanted to feel loved and wanted. For someone to love him enough to do something just for his enjoyment. My heart breaks a little for Teen Carson and what he went through with his parents and Izzy. In a divorce situation, a lot of siblings turn to each other for comfort, but Carson couldn't even do that with his brother. He was alone and an afterthought, or worse, a pawn.

"Do you want me to tell you where we're going?" I offer.

Carson shakes his head vehemently. "No, I like the surprise."

He relaxes back into the seat, his arm outstretched in welcome for me to snuggle into his side. It feels nice to slow down for a moment and enjoy the victory of today. We're going to make the festival happen and it's going to be amazing. We deserve a small break to recharge.

Carlo pulls up to the gated entry and types in the code Taya gave me. The black metal gates swing open slowly.

Carson looks around, confusion knitting his brows. "Where are we?"

"A friend's place," I answer, teasing him with a wink that says I've got secrets.

As the house comes into view, Carson whistles. "You've got some fancy friends."

I do, but Taya isn't one of them. Her house, however, is one of her flashiest expenses, with white rope columns, tiled archways, and lush green grass, even in California. Inside, there are more bedrooms and bathrooms than she could ever need or use, but to Taya, it's a reaffirming sign that she's made it and will never be the struggling artist dreaming of her big break she once was.

Carlo parks in front of the huge double doors and we get out. But we're not going in the house, even though the warm wood and black iron scrollwork seem welcoming. "The kitchen's inside to the left, Carlo. Help yourself to anything. If I had to guess, the fridge is stocked with sodas and the pantry with sweets."

He dips his chin gratefully and then taps his watch to remind me that we are on a schedule, which I appreciate.

Slipping my hand into Carson's, I pull him away from the front door toward a pathway leading around the side of the house. "Come on."

He smiles eagerly, still looking around in shock. "Where are you taking me?"

"You'll see." I'm excited too. I haven't been here in a long time with Taya's touring schedule being as crazy busy as it is, but I spent many days and nights here when I was on assignment with her. It's quiet and peaceful, something I think Carson could benefit from.

Behind the house is a large pool and deck area, but I bypass those too.

"Nice," Carson deadpans, one brow raised in appreciation for the area.

I stop at another gate at the back of the property, making practiced work of the lock there. Stepping through, I reveal the reason for our being here, the private beach stretching out in front of us, the Pacific Ocean crashing on the sand a hundred feet away.

"Maybe I do want to know what friend," Carson says in curious awe. "Is this a male or female friend? Or someone I need to be concerned about either way?"

I laugh at the streak of jealousy. "Female, and absolutely worthy of worry. But not in the way you mean. She's my best friend, and if ever there were a reason I'd end up needing bail money . . . it's her. You talk about liking danger and risk, like motorcycles and gambling. Her version of a Tuesday is tequila, tacos, and taking a bitch down a peg or two."

Carson chuckles, thinking I'm kidding, but Taya did once throw hands at a Mexican food taco truck with some woman who thought she was gonna do something. She didn't realize that Taya stays ready and her 'supposed life story of growing up rough' was the fairytale version we told the press. The truth was worse, much worse, and Taya's read of a situation and reflexes are always on point.

On the other side of the gate, I bend down and slip off my heels. Wiggling my toes in the soft sand, I sigh in relief. These shoes are my good luck heels, but they are not my most comfortable pair for sure. "I figured we could use a break, at least for a few minutes."

"I didn't exactly wear my clam-digging gear today," Carson grunts as he gestures to his business attire. But he slips off his shoes and socks, tucking them carefully next to the fence beside mine. He left his jacket in the car, so it's easy for him to roll his sleeves up a few turns too, showing off his ropey forearms. After a moment, he bends and does the same to his slacks. He looks ridiculous and sexy as hell at the same time.

Of course, I'm also wearing a silk blouse and a white skirt, not exactly a beach outfit either, but there's only so much planning I could do. If I'd told Carson to bring a change of clothes, he would've thought it was for something else entirely.

"Now what?" he demands.

"Now, we walk. And breathe. And relax." Carson's eyes widen as though I suggested riding dolphins like water skis or something equally outrageous. "It'll be good for you."

"Sounds awful." His grumble of disagreement is ruined by the smile that flashes immediately after, and I know how he really feels about it.

We hit the beach, walking slowly, hand in hand. The sand is soft and giving beneath our feet, and the waves run in, getting closer and closer. Wind whips through my hair, and after a moment of trying to wrangle it, I let it fly on the breeze. Knots be damned.

Staring at the water, I remember the first time I swam here. "I've always been a swimmer. I told you how competitive I was as a teen. So I'm comfortable in the water. But when I came here, I was drowning. Not literally in the water, but in my head. I had a client I couldn't reach, but she really needed my help, and I couldn't figure out how to get her to listen to me." The desperate frustration of those days comes back to me as fresh as it was then.

Quietly, Carson asks, "What did you do?"

"I came out here to swim and bawled my eyes out," I confess. "I figured the salt water and my tears would mix and no one would be the wiser. But she was smarter than I gave her credit for, and when I came back to the beach, she was sitting here waiting on me. She asked, 'You done with me yet?' and I wanted to say yes so fucking badly. I could go back to the office and have a new assignment by the next morning, someone who actually wanted my help. But she . . . needed it. So I said no."

Carson smiles sadly, understanding my reasoning as well as I do. "You couldn't admit defeat, least of all to yourself."

"That day, we talked about everything and nothing. It started slow, with stupid stuff and silly stories, and then finally, she told me why she was sabotaging herself. She cuts people off before they can get close enough to hurt her, a response she developed from being disappointed in people time after time. That was when we started actually working together and when we became friends. More importantly, it's when I became me. I learned a lot in school and had a fantastic mentor who trained me. But right here on this beach is where I left behind my could'a, should'a, would'a thoughts, expectations, and comparisons. I decided to be . . ."

"A badass?" he suggests when I search for the right word.

I grin. "A badass," I repeat. I wouldn't have put it that way, but it feels right. In helping Taya, she helped me find myself, and that was when I started doing my best work, though I'm still a work in progress. "I thought walking here might . . . I don't know . . . maybe help you find yourself too."

I hadn't even realized that's what I was doing, but it's plain as day now that we're here.

Carson is a man who wants the best of himself at all times. And there's nothing wrong with that if it's to satisfy your own sense of self. But he worries about his father too much, pushing himself to meet an ideal that doesn't even exist. He deserves better than that. He deserves happiness on his own terms.

"I'm not sure I can just decide to do that. Finding myself is a bit more complex than finding a shell." He kneels down, picking up a small, flat scrap of a scalloped shell to demonstrate how easy that is.

I do the same, picking up a spiraled brown and white shell. "Or maybe it is that easy," I suggest. "You're already doing it. You're an amazing CMO, a good son, and a great man. You just need to be reminded of that sometimes."

"You're like the asshole whisperer," he praises.

I laugh at the odd compliment, the sound carrying on the wind. "No, I've just dealt with a lot . . . for myself, for clients, and for friends."

Carson steps in front of me, stopping us. Looking down at me, he says seriously, "I don't want to be your friend, Jayme."

"I . . . I . . ." Stuttered sounds are all that come from my mouth. I'm conflicted because I'm feeling a hell of a lot more than professional or friendly about Carson, and I want to explore this. But as much as I say I'm a badass, there's some level of me that worries about jumping into the water too. Carson is in a vulnerable period and needs my help, and I don't want to take advantage. And there's so much he doesn't know about me.

A soft smile curls my lips, but before I can say anything, Carson sweeps me off my feet and runs toward the water.

"Carson! What are you doing?" I screech, my fingers scrabbling for purchase on his broad shoulders as my laughter echoes across the wind. He high-knees it into the ocean, the waves getting higher and higher until he loses his footing in the soggy sand and we tumble into them, him spinning so he holds me higher in the shallow depths. I go under for a second, barely remembering to hold my breath before swallowing the salty water, and search wildly for the surface. I pop through, immediately sputtering, to see Carson flinging his hair out of his eyes, which are staring at me with dark desire.

"What? Why?" I ask, still laughing as my feet scramble to find the bottom.

He lounges back in the water, floating and kicking lazily. "You said swimming helped you think, and the way your eyes were jumping left and right, like you had an angel and a devil on your shoulders, it seemed like you needed a minute to think. Or maybe think less?"

It's ridiculous . . . or it should be. But he seems perfectly at ease swimming in the ocean in slacks, a button-up shirt, and tie. And with giving me a moment of reflection about this thing building quickly between us.

I can at least confess one thing. I lie back next to him to float on the waves. My blouse bubbles up from the water, and I press the air bubbles out, leaving the silk stuck to my skin. "I don't want to take advantage of you."

Carson moves faster than I expect as he stands upright. "What?" he scoffs. Confusion mars his brows as he searches my face for some deeper explanation. "Take advantage of *me?*"

I keep my eyes on the sky, watching the birds soar in circles as they look for food along the beach. "I've seen this before. When people are struggling or lost, sometimes they feel like the person helping them is some sort of savior. And that can be . . . attractive. Or they're vulnerable, and being professionally vulnerable can be confused with personal emotions. I don't want to go too far and then you regret . . . me. When all this is over and you don't need me anymore, I don't want you to feel like you don't want to be around the person who saw you at your worst."

"I think it's sweet that you think this is my worst," he jokes, his voice deep with emotion. "But unless you make it a habit of getting close to your clients, I'm not seeing the problem. I'm telling you flat-out, I want you, Jayme. And it has nothing to do with this situation we're in but with the fact that you're an amazing, beautiful, intelligent woman."

"Two." I look from the sky to Carson. "Two clients I've gotten close to. One owns that house. The other is here in the water with me."

CHAPTER 15

CARSON

*J*ayme's admission does something to me, unleashing a tight rein I didn't know I was holding back. But now that it's untethered, I can't hold back. Reaching out through the water, I bring her to me, pulling her lush curves against mine.

With our mouths close together, I quietly admit, "I don't think anyone has ever seen me as vulnerable or been the least fucking concerned about taking advantage of me. Hear this . . . you're not, Jayme. I want you, I want this."

I kiss her lips softly, gently sipping at her. She tastes of salt, and a hint of that grass smoothie still, but I don't care anymore. I'd drink a hundred of those things if I could kiss her. When our lips part, she sighs, a sound not of resignation but of happiness . . . of acceptance. "I want you too," she whispers. "I want this, Carson."

I think I dream it for a second, but when I open my eyes, I see her bright ones shining into mine with joy. And freedom.

It makes me realize, as much as this is an unleashing for me, Jayme just let herself off the chain too. And she attacks me with passion, her arms going around my neck and her legs wrapping around my waist. Her skirt must slip up her thighs, or hell, maybe it rips? I don't know for sure, but I grip her smooth skin in my hands, kneading the flesh beneath the water.

"Fuck yes," I growl, pulling her core against my rigid cock. Considering how goddamn cold the Pacific is here, it's a testament to how sexy and beautiful and intense Jayme is. Her hips buck as she rubs herself on me, driving us both wild.

I guide her hips, using the buoyancy of the water to lift and lower her as I stride to shore. As the water fades away, I feel her clutching me tighter, her bucks becoming smaller as she holds on.

"Climb down," I order, tapping her hip.

Pouting, she does so, her eyes boring into me. I rip my shirt off and lay it on the sand, holding it in place with my foot as a makeshift blanket. Her eyes scour over my chest and then dip lower as I unbuckle my belt and undo my slacks. I shimmy my hips to let my pants drop, then lower my underwear. I stand back a step, letting her drink me in with her eyes. "I don't want to touch myself and risk getting sandy."

I splay my hands, fighting the urge to do it anyway. I'm pulsing, harder than I've been in years. My desire for this woman is that rampant. What I don't tell her is that in addition to getting sandy, if I touch myself, I'm probably going to come so hard Greenpeace will try to drag me back into the sea as a sperm whale.

"Let me help," Jayme says. She drops to her knees in the sand in front of me, my cock bobbing mere inches from her cheek. With her hands on my hips, she looks up at me and whispers, "You're beautiful."

I'm not. My cock is a raging, purple monster at this point, desperate for any contact and already leaking along the head. But Jayme looks at me as if I'm the most delicious thing she's ever seen. She laps at the fluid, her moan more vibration than sound, and lays tiny licks along the underside and then along my shaft. I groan in desperation, pleading, "Jayme . . ."

She swallows me, and my back arches in pure pleasure, giving her even more. But she takes it gratefully, moving up and down my cock and covering me with her saliva.

She finds a rhythm that drives me to the edge, and sand be damned, I thread my hands into her hair, holding her still so I can fuck her mouth. "Are you okay?" I ask, and though her lashes are slightly damp, she nods and swallows, her throat reflexively working me. "Fuck, your mouth feels good."

Throwing my head back, I fight to stay on the verge of coming, not wanting to fall over yet. "No," I hiss, pulling free from the warm wetness of her mouth. "Not yet."

She grins like the Cheshire Cat, knowing she almost got me. I step back and pivot, sitting down on my shirt so my bare ass isn't on the sand and then motion for her to climb onto me. Jayme slips her skirt higher up around her waist and lifts one knee, then the other, to get her panties off. Straddling my lap, she lines up her pussy with my cock.

I grip her hips tightly, not letting her impale herself onto me yet.

"Jayme?" I grit out, my voice rough. I'm not sure exactly what I'm asking . . . Does this mean something to you? Are you going to regret this later? Do you want me half as much as I want you?

But she understands and nods slowly. With a single smooth, sinuous motion of her hips, she rolls herself over and down, engulfing me all the way to the hilt. She groans, obviously stretched more than she anticipated. "*Fuck*."

"You can take it," I growl into her ear, holding her still again. "That tight, silky pussy of yours can take every inch of me."

"It's . . . big," she grunts back, clenching around me without moving. She grins, looking down at me with the sexiest expression I've ever seen. "And I'm going to ride this big cock until you explode inside me, flood me with your cream, and call *me* your goddess."

She's a dirty talker too? I nearly come instantly because I think I've found perfection.

She bucks harder, both of us shuddering at the feeling of her ass slamming down on my thighs. I run my hands up inside Jayme's blouse to cup her breasts, and finding the stiff nubs of her nipples, I pinch them between my fingers until she cries out.

"Later, these are *mine*," I vow as her hips lose rhythm in favor of arching her back, lifting her breasts for more of my touch. "I'm going to suck, fuck, and pound you into full submission to me."

She smiles suggestively, her hands going to my shoulders for leverage. Then she tenses her thighs and bounces up and down on my cock quickly. "Or else I'm going to get you hooked on this pussy."

Our eyes lock, and even though we're not saying it, I can read her thoughts.

We're both fine with either situation.

I want to roll Jayme over, press her into the sand, and pound her hard and fast with deep, savage strokes. But I won't hurt her and instead keep myself still, letting Jayme ride me and take her pleasure from me. My hands leave her breasts to stroke and feel her body, my fingertips memorizing every perfect curve that I've only been able to see until this point.

Jayme pauses her riding to undo her blouse and cast it aside, shrugging her bra off and leaving my brain overloaded as the supple handfuls of her breasts bounce as she goes faster and faster.

"Fuck, Carson . . ." she whimpers, bending forward. I reach down, grabbing the cheeks of her ass and squeezing them as I buck up into her, thrusting to meet her hips. She pitches forward just enough that I can kiss her silken lips.

I wish I could make this last forever. But the newness of our desire and passion combined with the weeks of flirting and intimacy leaves us both on the edge.

"Jayme—"

"Yes!" she answers, grinding her clit down onto the base of my cock. I growl, and with a powerful thrust, drive every bit of myself inside her. Her cries match mine, and I can feel her spasming, clenching and shaking on top of me as I fill her with a deep explosion that comes not from my balls but from deep in my gut. Or maybe from within my soul.

My arms tighten around her back, pulling her close as I empty myself into her, my cock aching as I spurt again and again. Jayme kisses me, our lips bruising each other with out of control hunger, both of us totally in the throes of our release.

The rhythm of the crashing waves is the first sound I hear afterward, Jayme still on top of me and my arms still wrapped around her. I look up, worried that I'll see concern or upset.

But instead, she smiles down at me, a dreamy, satisfied, happy look in her eyes as she kisses me softly, the urgency of our passion sated. I'm still inside her, and I can feel the aftershocks of our bodies, but as she quivers around my cock, I'm slowly becoming aware of something else.

"Jayme?"

She moans luxuriously. "Yes, I did, and yes, you were more than satisfying."

"Uh, thank you," I murmur, not immune to an ego stroke. "But I think I have sand burn on my ass."

Carefully, I try to shift but end up hissing in discomfort. Yup, I definitely moved my ass up and off my shirt during our beachfront activities, and now I've got sand so far up my ass I might end up making a pearl in a few weeks if I don't do something about it.

Jayme looks down at her own legs, her knees dug down into the sand for leverage. "We definitely have sand in places it shouldn't be." She lifts delicately, my cock slipping out of her as she rises fully to her knees. "Definitely gonna be some chafing. Gonna need lotion or baby oil or something."

"Movies make sex on the beach look way easier and sexier," I complain, still trying to shift without flinching too much.

Standing, we shake out our legs and arms a bit in the hopes the sand will magically fall off. But it's stuck to us like . . . sand in sweat and, *ahem*, other *stuff*. Carefully, we try to pull bits of clothing on and head back toward the house. But a few steps later, we're both wincing and end up walking back considerably more bow-legged than when we first arrived.

"Ooh . . . ouch . . ." Jayme complains, wiggling her hips.

I'd offer to carry her or help in some way, but I'm holding back some whimpers of my own. Yeah, I'm definitely going to need a shower . . . and maybe an enema. Never thought that thought would be in my head right after sex, but here we are.

On the back porch, Jayme slides open the door, and we see Carlo inside. He's made himself at home, his feet on the coffee table and a game on the television over the fireplace. He takes one look at us over his shoulder and grins. "I'll call the pilot and tell him we'll be late. An hour?"

Jayme points an admonishing finger at him. She's at least got her blouse on over her breasts, and her skirt's semi-tugged down. My dick's still flapping in the breeze behind her. "Not a word. And yeah, an hour's fine. Let us wash off and find some clothes."

"And maybe some ointment?" I whisper quiet enough for only Jayme to hear.

But Carlo laughs, so I guess it wasn't quiet enough.

Jayme leads me into a large bedroom that's bathed in sunlight coming through the bank of windows along one wall. The king bed has more pillows than your average TJMaxx on restock day and looks inviting as hell. But with only an hour until take-off, plus more than a little bit of chafing, there's no time to throw Jayme to the bed for round two.

The bathroom is equally expansive, with warm charcoal tiles on the floors and shower walls and a wall of mirrors above the double vanity sinks. Jayme reaches into the shower, turning the water to lukewarm. "Usually, I prefer hotter than lava, melt your skin off temperature," she says as she sheds the soppy bits of clothing she's pulled on, "but I think that'd make me cry right now, and it's just my knees. I can't imagine what it'd feel like on your dick."

She looks down at my groin and her eyes go wide. I'd love to say it's because she's once again impressed with my size or considering dropping to her knees for me again, but I'm betting it's because my cock is looking red and irritated.

"Maybe a cool shower, then?" she suggests, turning the knob back to the right.

We step into the shower, both writhing in discomfort when the water slides over us. "I would love to wash you," I tell her, "but if I touch you, I'm going to get hard again, and I'm not sure I can handle that delicate skin stretching right now. Raincheck?"

"Probably for the best since we need to hurry," she agrees quickly. "But I'm looking forward to it."

Thankfully, the shower has both overhead and handheld sprayers, and with a little bit of squirming and total abandonment of my self respect, I'm able to get myself clean. Though Jayme unsuccessfully tries to hide a giggle as I spray out my butt crack, and she looks me up and down. "Careful there, stud, I might want you to do that on pulse mode."

"Very funny," I grumble as I use my slippery free hand, which is well coated with coconut scented body wash, to sweep out more grains of sand. "Keep talking and I'll pin you to the wall and return the favor."

"Promise?" she asks, biting her lip.

"You're giving me ideas . . . for next time," I promise.

With that setting the current tone, we make quick work of finishing up our shower.

"Let me grab us some clothes. She always keeps merch for guests," Jayme says, leaving me standing in the bathroom with a towel wrapped around my waist.

I meet my own eyes in the mirror. Today has been one big roller coaster. Not one of the completely safe, but intentionally designed to feel wild ones like at Americana Land, but more like one verging on the edge of insanity. It's been amazing and dangerous in a way my motorcycle has never been. Jayme herself is better than the wind whipping through my hair at one hundred miles an hour. She blows through my soul, a tornado of possibilities.

"I don't know if these are going to fit you?" she calls out from the bedroom. I step into the room, finding her digging through the dresser and already wearing sweats and a T-shirt. She holds up a pair of gray sweatpants with a stylized T and a geometric design on the left thigh that match the ones she has on.

"And there's no underwear for you, so commando it is." A coy smile teases at her lips, and she feigns being dramatic with a hand to her thrown-back head, "Gray sweats and a bouncing dick, you'll be the talk of every woman online. Exactly what you don't need."

"All I'm hearing is ouch-ouch-ouch with every step," I say deadpan.

"Oh, I'm sure there's lotion in the bathroom. And these look baggy enough, you can probably flop back and forth without ever touching cotton."

Jayme disappears back into the bathroom, and I grab the sweats from the bed where she tossed them. Slipping them on, they're a little short, but she's right, the hips and crotch are very baggy. And thankfully, the inside of the cotton is fluffy and soft, so it's not too rough on my sensitive dick or butt crack.

A picture frame on the dresser catches my attention, and I move closer to check it out. It's Jayme . . . with someone I never would've expected. Taya. She's an artist major enough to only need one name. The T on the sweats suddenly makes more sense.

Taya is Jayme's friend? Her best friend? I never would've guessed that in a million years. Jayme is such a professional, analytical and strategic, and Taya has a reputation for being a wild child who does whatever she wants, when she wants. She's earned her nickname of La Loca. It seems an odd pairing, but from what Jayme has said about her best friend, it seems like a close, happy friendship.

I feel a little closer to Jayme, privy to one of her secrets, even if it's not directly from her. I understand that she has to maintain a degree of privacy, especially if their friendship is rooted in a professional client-PR relationship. But she felt safe enough with me to bring me here, and I appreciate the peek behind the curtain of her heart.

"Found it!" she exclaims from the doorway.

I take the offered lotion and shake it up. Dropping the waistband of the sweats below my balls, I squirt a bit of it directly to my cock. Feeling Jayme's eyes on me as I work it into the skin, I look up to find her focusing intently on my movements. "You like watching me?"

She offers a smile full of dirty thoughts, nodding slowly.

I feel myself growing hard and groan . . . in pain.

"Oh! Sorry!" she squeaks, turning around. "I'll grab our clothes, though I think they're beyond saving. My skirt ripped, and your shirt is completely stained. It has sandy ass prints ground into it."

"Just toss them," I say.

"Consider it done," Jayme answers. "And there's a shirt in the top drawer."

I open it to grab the shirt and find that we're totally matching. I guess we're flying home as Taya super fans.

CHAPTER 16

JAYME

*W*alking around the grounds for the festival, I look for any potential issues or concerns, along with any last-minute things we could add to make it even more spectacular. We've gotten so much done in the weeks since our trip to LA, but it's taken around-the-clock work by the entire team. I've enjoyed working side-by-side with them all, especially Carson. We've gotten to know each other better over spreadsheets and checklists, as well as late-night dinners and conversations.

"What do you think about the lights in the trees? Do we need more?" I mumble, eyeing the strands of LED lights critically. They're electronically controlled and can be programmed to switch colors with the beat of the music, dance randomly, or light sequentially.

Spencer does the same, lifting her glasses to her forehead and then lowering them again as if she'll see something different with and without the lenses. The experienced marketing executive has been essential in all of the planning for the festival, and I've been happy to work with her, especially today. "What about disco balls? They're fun and would reflect the light."

"That's brilliant!" I exclaim. "Do you think we can buy some and get them hung in time?"

She gives me a sly look. "At this point, I just toss out Carson's name and things get done. People here are willing to help him because he's willing to help them."

It's working. All of my hard work at repairing Carson's reputation is having the desired effect.

The social media around 'Grandma Barbara' has grown to the point that park visitors want pictures with her as much as they do Freddy Freebird. And with the video showing Carson saving the beloved Grandma Barb, the Abby Burks effect is diminishing greatly. Carson is basically considered a hero at this point who stood up to an entitled brat who was creating drama for clout.

We just need this festival to be perfect too, and then the Americana Land reputation will be restored.

"What else?" Carson asks.

Spencer turns to Kyleigh in a silent 'show 'em what you got' move. They seem like a great team, with Kyleigh willing to jump in and get her hands dirty and Spencer willing to share her experience and mentor the young intern. Kyleigh checks her iPad, confidently rattling off the details of her list. "Stage preparation – electrical cords run and taped down, amps in position and sound checked, instrument spots marked, pyrotechnics being triple verified tonight and rechecked in the morning before the opening act. Effects – laser lights have been checked, and we'll get on adding disco balls." She dips her head at Spencer. "The bubble machine and fog machine are ready, and the glitter bombs are in place, though we have to trust those to work because there's no pre-check without it looking like a glitter explosion."

Kyleigh pauses, her eyes flicking to Spencer, who mumbles, "Glitter is the herpes of the craft world."

It seems like it's an ongoing joke between them because they both quirk their lips at that. Kyleigh continues the read-through of her list. "Musicians – at local hotels, all confirmed and prepped. They'll be arriving in the morning for sound check before the park opens. Food and drinks – kiosks placed and stocked. Vendors – stocked with glow and blacklight merch, commemorative T-shirts, and special edition Freddy Freebird stuffies. Did I miss anything?"

She looks at Spencer, who smiles back proudly, and then to Carson and me.

"I think you two make an amazing team," Carson praises.

Kyleigh beams, but Spencer narrows her eyes. "Carson, more than just us two have worked on this."

"Oh, I know this has been a huge undertaking, involving every department. And tomorrow is going to be a busy day of craziness, but I want you to know how much I appreciate you." Carson looks from Spencer to Kyleigh. "It wouldn't have happened without you two at the helm of this ship."

"I appreciate that," Spencer says, still not assuaged, "but what I meant was you're the captain of this ship. You've done a lot too, and when tomorrow goes off without a hitch and makes Americana Land the talk of the internet, you get the credit for that." She pauses and then adds, "And you too, Jayme."

I shake my head. "I don't need credit. It's all this guy," I correct, gesturing to Carson. This is his doing, the grand resurrection of his reputation. He'll be the one standing on the stage tomorrow, and I'll be behind the curtains where I belong.

"Thank you," Carson says quietly, obviously unaccustomed to praise and taking the compliments to heart. "That means a lot, Spencer."

She leans in closer, her voice hard, to add, "Don't let the old man take credit either. You tell him, loud and proud, what *you* did."

Hmm. It seems the tension between father and son has caught the attention of more of the home office staff than I realized. I'll need to help address that before this assignment is over because that can fester and grow, strangling the good progress we've made here.

Spencer looks pointedly over Carson's shoulder, and we instinctively turn to look. Ben Steen is walking across the Great Garden area straight toward us, with Izzy and Toni Steen flanking him.

Carson turns fully, a bland smile on his face. "Dad. Coming to check up on me?"

Ben's face is equally impassive, no doubt hiding the concerns he has on the eve of an undertaking of this scope. They really are the spitting image of each other. "Just seeing how things are going. Felt like I should show my face, considering this is such a big deal and I am the CEO."

Carson stiffens, but I don't think Ben notices as he scans the area, taking in the completed setup and workers moving about. Meanwhile, Izzy smiles politely. "It looks lovely, Carson. I'm sure it'll be a great event."

I gotta give her props, she is doing everything she's supposed to do —the warm smile, the supportive hand casually woven through her husband's, the kind compliment. But it feels forced, the awkwardness between her and Carson obvious.

"Are you kidding, Mom? It's gonna be dope, bigger and better than Electric Forest. I can't wait, already got my costume ready," Toni gushes. "Don't worry, Dad. I've got pasties to cover my nips . . . this time." She smirks, barely shaking her head and making a flashing headlight motion with her hands in front of her chest.

But that gets Ben and Carson's attention. Simultaneously, they snap, "Toni."

Toni rolls her eyes. "So easy, these two. One little mention of potential nudity, and boom, they're united in battle." She laughs easily, and both men relax . . . a little. "Don't worry, guys. I'll be wearing so much blacklight body paint that no one will see an inch of bare skin. Think it's okay if I paint *Smack Here* on the ass of my bootie shorts, though?"

She tilts her head, tapping her chin as though considering it.

"No." I'm not sure if it was Carson or Ben who spoke because at this point, they sound remarkably alike.

"Are you really wearing a costume?" a small voice whispers.

Toni looks at Kyleigh and asks, "Who're you? And yes."

Kyleigh looks horrified that she actually spoke, but after making a visual check-in with Spencer, she quickly says, "I'm Kyleigh, an intern working on the festival."

Despite Kyleigh's nerves, Toni seems delighted at the conversation with a potential new friend. "You and me, girl. We're gonna be like this tomorrow." She crosses her fingers, pointing them back and forth between the two of them.

"Uh, sure. I'm escorting Jazmyn Starr around mostly, but . . ."

"The hell you are, *we* are doing that now," Toni corrects. Quieter, she whispers, "Did I hear that she's got the kids from King's Krossing dancing with her?"

Kyleigh screams silently, her hands curled up by her face as she nods wildly. "I know, right! I can't believe it! This is like my dream come true!"

I think we just witnessed the two young women truly becoming best friends.

"Yours and mine both, girl," Toni agrees. "I've got that whole routine down, perfection from one to done."

Carson clears his throat, garnering everyone's attention again. "Everything's fine, Dad. We've got it all under control."

Spencer leans forward, breaking in before tension can possibly rise again. "Yep, as we said in our status update, we've got it all ready, Mr. Steen." Her confirmation is directed solely to Carson and high-lights that we were in the middle of something important when Ben walked up.

I think Spencer is my new favorite person. Not that I'll tell Carson . . . or Taya . . . that. Carson is the orgasm dealer, and Taya . . . is Taya.

"Thank you, Spencer," Carson answers firmly, dipping his chin toward her.

Ben tries a different tact, addressing me. "Ms. Rice, I understand we have you to thank for this festival idea?"

"Actually, it was born from a team meeting. Everyone was doing such a great job implementing the strategies I suggested that we were able to brainstorm even more innovative ideas to bring Ameri-cana Land into the Twenty-First Century." I'm walking a fine line, wanting to highlight Carson and his teams' strengths while reminding Ben that he might be the CEO, but Americana Land wasn't perfect before this incident.

Ben makes a *harrumph* noise, catching the slight dig. "Traditions create a foundation upon which Americana Land is built."

"Yes, but every foundation cracks eventually and has to brought up to current codes." I smile gently, softening the blow by degrees. "But that's why you brought me in. It's exactly what I specialize in—reframing reputations and images for the now, and more impor-tantly, for the future. I think you'd agree that it seems to be working quite well."

I incline my head, my eyes questioning. He can't disagree, and we all know it. Not when the daily Find Freddy Freebird is trending, analytics show searches for the park are up by eighty percent, photo engagement is rising with every post, and presale tickets for the festival are sold out.

"It does seem to be," Ben allows.

Carson grins victoriously. "Was it that hard to admit, Dad?"

"No," he says, looking at Carson in frustration. "I'm truly happy things are going so well." If he stopped there, I think things would be okay, but he adds, "If only we hadn't needed to recover from that unfortunate incident."

Enough of this. I swear, these two are so used to their battle of wills, of coming from opposite sides of every issue, that they don't even recognize that they're hurting themselves and the company.

And I'm done with it. I'm well aware of the nuances of these difficult relationships, both personally and most definitely professionally, especially with clients. But at some point, it's worth the pain to rip the Band-Aid off. It's necessary to get to a place of healing.

And that's what Americana Land needs, as well as Ben and Carson. But it's risky, jumping in the middle of their relationship. It has the potential to blow up in a major way, especially on the eve of an event.

Even riskier, I have a vested interest in Carson's feelings, and interfering in his relationship with his father is not my place. Except it is. Their relationship is key to their reputations, and that's my responsibility.

"Spencer, Kyleigh, could you give us a moment, please?" I tell them stiffly, knowing that this is *not* a conversation to be had in front of others. If I do that, Ben and Carson are both going to be defensive and likely tune me out. Not on my watch.

Spencer gathers Kyleigh and leads her away, while Izzy apparently senses an impending 'business conversation' and leads Toni away too. Just the three of us now. I turn on them, prepared to put them on blast. "That was . . . unprofessional at best, and damaging to the reputations I'm working my ass off to save for certain," I begin, holding up a hand when they both open their mouths. "Uh-uh. Not now, not until I've said my piece. Ben, Carson, both of you need to stow this dick measuring contest you've got going on. Especially here, in the middle of the park. Your interpersonal issues are hurting your company, your family, and yourselves."

"I . . ." Carson starts, but I shake my head.

"No, you've both had your chance. It's mine turn now. I'll start here, in the park. You both need to recognize the basics. Americana Land was a dying park stuck in the eighties, dependent on seniors and families for a falling profit margin and out of touch with the disposable income of a huge segment of the population, which it desperately needed. Moving into the future, using the resources and ideas of staff to be more relevant, innovative, and profitable will be key. It's going to hurt." I count out one on my finger, then add a second. "It's going to be awkward, and it's going to require the two of you to work together." Holding up my three fingers, I focus on Carson. "I'm here to fix your professional stuff, but if it requires fixing your personal relationship, I'll do my best, though I'm not a therapist."

"Excuse me?" Ben sneers, clearly not used to being spoken to quite so bluntly.

"Jayme." Carson's tone is cold and flat, and he's obviously not ready to listen either.

I need to work on him first. I hate that I even think this, but I know him better and can get past his shields more easily. It's using what he's shared with me in confidence against him, but for his own good. I start off by giving him a look, hoping he understands. *This is for you.*

To Ben, I say, "You called me here. What did you expect to happen when I came? Did you think I was going to tell Carson that he'd messed up his reputation and that Americana Land's beyond repair?" He tries to answer, but I keep rolling. "I don't think so. I think you truly wanted me to help. Which I'm doing, but be aware that the biggest change that's happened since my arrival is Carson doing what his gut says without worrying whether you're going to approve of it. Or be proud of him."

Carson's jaw is clenched so hard I can hear his teeth grind. He's furious with me. I'm overstepping, but this is part of what I do. It's not always about the façade, not when I can repair the foundation, as Ben called it. And I think Carson and his dad are closer to a better relationship than they think.

"Ben, what your son wants is to show you that he's got the goods. And guess what? He does. But you two butt heads so much, you might as well be goats playing King of the Mountain."

I throw my hands up, but I'm not done. I've barely started. "Frankly, the best thing you two could do for the company is sit down and learn to talk to each other, not snip and snipe, undercutting each other at every turn. Because your employees, your executives? Every time you two go off like this, they lose faith in *you.* But more importantly, you two need to talk as a family. As father and son. Because I can see and hear the love you two have for each other. You just both *suck balls* at communicating it."

At some point, Izzy and Toni have come back with popsicles, and Ben looks around helplessly, hoping for support. But his wife is no shelter this time, glaring at him as if to say *you fucked it up. Now do something about it.*

Finally, Ben clears his throat. "Carson," he says slowly, as if unknotting a particularly hard lump in his throat, "I am proud of you. I always have been."

He makes the compliment sound as if it should be obvious. It's definitely not. But it's a step in the right direction.

Carson's shoulders are stiff, his back straight. "Thank you."

You ever see someone who's obviously having the worst day of their life, like they're crying ugly, snotty tears, folded in on themselves, disheveled and out of sorts, but when you ask them how they're doing, they say 'fine' in that flat, auto-tone of an expected, but entirely untrue, answer? That's the vibe of Carson's 'thank you'.

I twitch my hand, barely brushing my pinkie against his in a subtle show of support. He takes a big breath, his lips pressed together, but finally adds, "You've built something special here at Americana Land, kept it going through difficult times. Including this one. I hope we can work together as we move toward a better future."

Okay, still robotic as hell and sounding like a couple of fake-ass politicians reaching across the aisle temporarily because of some national emergency, but it's a start, some acknowledgement of the other from them both.

"Okay, good job for today," I declare with a coach-worthy clap of my hands. "Next time, you two do this in private, away from the park. Now if you'll excuse us, we do need to get back to our check-ins so that everything is perfect tomorrow." I don't want to push them any further when this small set of admissions was as difficult as it was. And we really do have a major event in less than twenty-four hours.

Ben looks shocked at being dismissed, as if it's never happened to him before. Maybe it hasn't? He is the boss, after all. But he blinks away the wrinkle in his brow and takes Izzy's hand. "See you later, Son."

Carson nods. "Yeah, Dad."

With that, Izzy and Ben walk off. Toni leans toward Carson, holding her hand up to speak behind though she whispers loud enough for me to hear, "I like her. You should see what she thinks about butt-munches."

Carson sighs as he closes his eyes and pinches the bridge of his nose. "Toni, please. Not now."

She shrugs, smiling easily as if the uncomfortable situation between her brother and father didn't just happen. Though I guess she might be used to it by now? "I'm going to go find Kyleigh and see if I can help her at all. Jazmyn Starr and King's Krossing . . . you did good, Bro."

She skips off . . . literally skipping and waving at various people here and there, who smile and wave back. She's comfortable here, I realize. She'll probably end up on the Americana Land team too some-day. Alone, Carson looks at me with thunderous fury in his eyes. I can feel it coming, bubbling up inside him and ready to be unleashed on me. He licks his lips, the words right on the tip of his tongue.

I'm ready, my defenses solidly in place. I know what comes next—lashing out at the person who's trying to help. I've had other clients do it more than once. It's painful and ugly, but I can take it. No one can get past my walls.

Except Carson already has.

But he doesn't say a word. He simply . . . walks away.

CHAPTER 17

CARSON

I hold the hurtful words back behind an iron-set jaw and pressed together lips. How dare Jayme light the fuse on my relationship with my dad and then stand back and wait for the fireworks to start? What's she playing at?

Having years of practice of stuffing words down is the only thing that saves me. Saves her.

I spin on my heel and stalk off, destination unknown. I simply need to get away from Jayme until I can get a handle on myself, my thoughts, and most importantly, my mouth. Unfortunately, I hear the click of her heels behind me, chasing as she calls out, "Carson, wait."

I want to whirl on Jayme, push her up against the nearest wall, and demand that she explain herself. But I force my feet to keep moving and grit my teeth so hard that sharp pain shoots through my entire skull. I can't do this . . . not now and not here. If anything, I've learned that the hard way through the Abby Burks incident.

Awareness of my surroundings, and of the eyes watching Jayme chase after me right now, keep me moving. This is bad enough, but if I speak to her now, with the way I'm feeling, it'll be even worse. I snort, the realization that she's changed me for the good bitter in contrast to what she just did. I need to be alone, and I know one place I can do that.

I beeline for the From Sea to Shining Sea Ferris Wheel. It was one of my favorites when I was a kid, allowing me to feel free and floating, but in reality, be safe and secure. Sometimes, I would ride with

Archer and we would come up with these fantastical stories of how we were superheroes scanning the people below for villains who needed to be taken out, or pilots fighting against the wind to make a smooth landing. Other times, especially later, after Mom left and I was in a tense situation with Dad and Izzy, I would ride alone as a way to get away from everything and everyone. It gave me space to process, to rage, and once or twice, to cry where no one would see me.

It's exactly what I need right now.

"Hey, James, I need a minute. Will you hold me at the top until I call down?"

The ride operator dips his head. It's been a long time since I've made this request, but he knows how important it is when I do. Thankfully, there's no one in line so my ride won't cause anyone to wait unnecessarily. That'd be another image problem I can't afford.

Entitled brat, Carson Steen, makes people wait indefinitely while chilling on the Ferris Wheel.

But no matter, the Ferris Wheel isn't cool any longer . . . kind of like how Americana Land was, I suppose.

"Thanks, man." He's stopped the ride, which spins even when empty as an enticement to get riders, and opens the door of one of the cars. The cars are painted to look like big hot air balloons, with brown wicker baskets below and red, white, and blue flag balloons above. Of course, it's all metal, but the painted illusion gives it that sense of floating.

I sit down on one section of the round bench, spreading my arms along the back and letting my head fall back against the metal railing. Closing my eyes, I wait out the short ride to the top and then the slight swinging as James pushes the stop button below.

Only then do I let my guard fall.

"What the fuck?" I mutter to myself. I wish there were an answer on the wind, but none comes. Jayme had no right to get into the quagmire of my relationship with my dad. She's here for image repair, not as some sort of family therapist. What was she thinking?

I've only been here in the silence of my whirling mind for a few minutes when the car starts moving again. I look around in confusion and then call out, "Hey, James, a few more minutes?"

He doesn't answer and the car keeps moving.

As I get low enough to see James, I throw my hands out. "What the hell, man?"

He shrugs sheepishly. "The lady pays."

"What—" I start to ask what he means, but as I go a little lower, I can see for myself. Jayme is standing on a step near the operator's area, her arms crossed over her chest as she shoots a hostile glare my way.

What the hell is she mad about? I'm the one who's mad. She should be apologizing to me!

As I come even with the platform, she steps forward, and I realize she intends to get into the car with me. I stand in preparation to exit, but when James unlatches the door, he blocks my way, allowing Jayme to duck under his arm and climb in. He quickly slams the door shut again, latching it from the outside.

"James!" I shout.

"Sorry, man. I need my job, you know I do, but she promised me VIP passes for the festival tomorrow, and my wife is going to go crazy when I tell her. I'm looking forward to her 'thank you, honey.'" He grins like a total hound dog, one who loves his wife.

He steps back and pushes the button to start the wheel spinning again. I lose my balance for a second at the sudden jolt but grab onto the railing to steady myself. Jayme doesn't fare as well and stumbles in her heels.

"Whoooaah!" she yells. Tumbling to the floor, she hisses. "Shit! That hurt."

I look down to see her legs askew and her head against the hard metal. I can't leave her on the ground, no matter how furious I am.

"Dammit!" I carefully step forward and offer my hand. Jayme takes it gratefully and I help her stand. Once she gets to a low squat, she sits back onto the bench, rubbing her head. "You okay?"

She scowls at me like it's my fault she bumped her head. "Fine."

I fall back to the bench myself, sitting opposite Jayme. We sit in silence as the cart lifts higher into the air. James must hit the button because we stop at the top, still glaring at each other.

"Well?" I prompt finally.

"What do you mean, 'well?'" Her brows drop down low in confusion.

A sour smile curls my lips. "Aren't you going to apologize for that shitshow? That's the play, right? Fuck things up, apologize with feigned regret so everyone forgives you, then move on as if it never happened?"

She recoils as if I've slapped her. "Is that what you think I do? What I was doing back there?" She snaps as she points toward the garden below. "I was doing that for *you.*"

Incredulous, I demand, "That's what you consider *help*?"

"Yes!" She nods vehemently. "I was trying to get Ben to see that he's not this perfect god who created this flawless park. I literally said that Americana Land is outdated, and he has you to thank for pulling it, kicking and screaming, into the Twenty-First Century."

She did say that. And reluctantly, I have to admit she was right. But that's not all she said.

"You're conveniently forgetting the part where you forced him into begrudgingly admitting that he's proud of me." I huff out a sigh of disbelief. Dad isn't proud of me, but he knows when he's cornered. If a few simple words let him walk away with his pride, he'd sound off like an auctioneer. It doesn't mean that he meant a bit of it.

"Or maybe he is!" she shouts loudly enough for James to hear.

"You two okay up there?" comes from below.

"No. Bring us down," I answer.

At the same time, Jayme yells, "Yes, we're fine."

The car doesn't move. Fucking James and this fucking Ferris Wheel.

Quieter, she repeats, "Maybe he is proud of you but is just shitty at communicating it. You two have this big *thing* in between you that neither of you knows how to get around. I'd say it's your mom, or the divorce, but maybe your brother? I don't know, but it seems like both of you are coming from a place of insecurity. You ever think of that?"

I don't respond. After a moment, Jayme continues.

"I mean, for fuck's sake, you're a grown ass, functional, independent adult who handles his own shit, who went to extremes to help his own people. Who shows up to work every day to carry on the family legacy. Who also has balls big enough to go up against me, and to be clear, not many do. Did you think of any of that?"

I'm reminded of that first day, when we were arguing, when she was so passionate and fiery. Her cheeks are flushed, her eyes bright, her breath fast enough to cause her breasts to rise and fall rapidly. Except then, she called me an arrogant asshole. Now, though she's spitting fire, it's . . . with compliments?

Confusion wars with the anger I've been stoking. I try to form a coherent thought, but what comes out of my mouth is, "What?"

Gentler, she repeats, "You're a good guy, Carson. I keep telling you that. I don't care about this whole image your dad thinks you've got that he doesn't approve of. I mean, seriously . . . a motorcycle? *Ooh* . . ." She holds her hands out, wobbling them and her head to show how ridiculous she thinks that is. "I know dentists and priests who ride motorcycles, gambling on sports with discretional money while maintaining good credit. Unbelievable!" She throws her hand to her head, as if that's catastrophic, and then rolls her eyes. "Hell, I wouldn't care if you'd been fucking your friend on the deck of that boat. People have done worse."

Before I can correct that one, she keeps ranting.

"You show up, do your best, are a good leader, have creative ideas, and listen to others, and as evidenced by the sand burns on my knees, you're willing to take risks when warranted. I see all that and more in you. But you have to see it in yourself."

I've never been put in my place quite so well, especially with praise.

"Is that how you see me?" I ask cautiously. There's something beginning to bloom inside me that's much more powerful than a desire to make my dad proud. A desire to make Jayme proud. And a pride in myself.

If asked a few weeks ago, I would've confessed to a bit of an ego. I'm more than satisfied with myself and my work, happy to brag about the good things my department has accomplished under my leadership, and smugly assume that I'm better than my dad, given that I've never had a relationship fail as spectacularly as he did.

But the truth is, maybe I'm not as confident as I'd like to portray. On some level, deep under a lot of layers, I'm still that teen who felt like he wasn't enough, whose dad had to go out and get another family to be happy. And I'm holding a grudge, punishing him for it, but also, punishing myself.

Jayme scoots over to my side, taking my hand and holding it firmly between both of hers. "I see an amazing man who's accomplished so much and is set to do even more. You are a success . . ."

I look up from our hands to her, finding her looking at me earnestly. She's talking my language and she knows it.

"Of both your father's making, and your own," she finishes.

I take a big breath, her words settling into cracks I thought I'd long ago sealed over. "You're kind of amazing yourself," I admit. My feathers are still ruffled, but she's steadily soothing them.

"And a bitch. I know," she offers with a smile, bumping my shoulder with hers. "Therapy is a side gig of this job, an uncomfortable one since I'm not a trained shrink. Though maybe that's what makes me so effective," she humbly brags. She pauses for a second as if trying to decide whether she should say more. Tentatively, she adds, "I truly think you and your dad could be better if you'd talk a little. I think what you take as judgment from him is more than likely his way of tiptoeing around you. Or whatever this thing between you is. For years, he's been putting one foot in front of the other, never knowing when he's going to step on a landmine."

"You think we're salvageable?" I ask, feeling better despite things not being perfect with Dad.

Her laugh is a surprise, bright and infectious. "Hell, you're not even on my top twenty of worst clients. You two just need a couple of beers and a manly ugly cry or two." She throws her voice, mimicking a drunk frat boy, "I luv you, man!" She finishes with a fake hiccup and a smug grin.

"A manly ugly cry?" I repeat incredulously. "Do you realize that we don't even have tear ducts?"

The tease is easy and good-natured, an olive branch after our argument. I lay my arm around her shoulders and she curls into me.

"Not even in your top twenty worst clients?" I question. "Guess we'll have to up our game."

"You'd be surprised at what happens behind the scenes," she hints without offering any details. "But I am sorry I shared things you told me in confidence. Secrets shared are secrets risked. And telling your dad what you'd said was wrong, even though I did it with the best of intentions."

On the surface, her apology feels genuine, but there's an undercurrent I don't understand. I know she has secrets of her own, like being best friends with Taya, but her job requires that. I can understand the need for an NDA with clients like hers.

"Someone once told me to gamble on her, and I did. So far, it's been a damn good risk." It's more than an acceptance of her apology. It's an admission that despite my initial reaction, maybe she did the right thing by me.

I feel Jayme smile against my shoulder. "She sounds like a smart cookie."

She's quiet for a moment and then suddenly sits upright. "Cookies! We should sell cookies tomorrow. How did I not think of that sooner? *Shit*."

She stands up, leaning into the metal railing. "Hey, James? Can we come down now?"

"Sure thing, Jayme!" comes the quick response, making me wonder how much James could hear of the louder portions of our argument. The cart jolts back into movement, and Jayme stumbles a little, but I'm right here to steady her this time.

"Do you think we could get cookies by tomorrow morning?" she mutters, her mind working behind her eyes. "Something fun like iced ones with sprinkles? Or Dunkaroos? Oh! I know! Rainbow swirl ones!"

Her rambling spiel turns to delight with the idea. I can't help but grin at her excitement, but realistically, there's no way.

"Will you go for a ride with me tonight?" I ask.

She stops in the middle of a list of possible bakeries that would pull an all-nighter for a custom order. "What?"

I cup her face in my hands, my nose mere inches from her. "We've done everything we can. The team has done everything they can. We're ready, the park is ready. Let's go for a night ride, take a minute to relax and breathe so we can tackle tomorrow together."

I can feel her energy centering as I speak slowly and hypnotically. She starts to speak, and I can feel her need to argue. She's as much a perfectionist as I am, and she wants to spend this last evening going over every list, every possible thing that could go wrong to either prevent it or pre-plan a solution.

I press a hard kiss to her lips, prying my way into her mouth to taste her deeply. Every stroke of my tongue against hers is a counter argument.

We're ready. The festival is going to be great.

I need you. I want tonight to just be us.

I feel the moment she falls into me, under my spell. Mid-kiss, she murmurs her agreement.

And just in time because James opens the door. "Oh! Uh, sorry . . . you said . . ." he stutters.

"All good, man. Thanks for the ride."

Holding Jayme's hand, I help her to the platform. She pins James with a look. "Remember our deal?"

"I didn't see nothing, hear nothing, and don't know nothing," he quotes.

"Good man," she praises him with a wink. "I'll have your tickets at the front gate in the morning."

Fuck, she's slick as hell and thinks of everything, and that is so damn sexy.

CHAPTER 18

CARSON

*A*fter a quick stop in my office to grab my helmet, I rush us downstairs.

"Have a good night, you two," Ellie calls out as we scurry through the lobby. I toss a conspiratorial smile her way, and she makes a lip-zipping motion.

I'm sure Jayme would prefer to stay here, working on preparations for tomorrow and obsessing over every little detail until her eyeballs burn and she's pulled every blonde strand from her head in stress. But we've done what we can and I trust my team. I'll still text Spencer to check in before crashing tonight, but for now, we can leave guilt-free.

I slip the helmet onto her head, memorizing her hopeful smile as it disappears beneath the face shield. I climb onto the motorcycle and hold it steady while Jayme climbs on behind me. I'm glad that she's wearing slim-fit slacks today, though the sand burns on her knees are long healed.

"Ready?" I ask, looking over my shoulder.

She nods, the helmet bobbing on her head slightly. I remind myself that I need to get a helmet for her, not only because of helmet laws but because her head is so much smaller than mine.

I start the motorcycle, the roar breaking the quiet of the night, and once I feel her arms wrap around me tightly, I pull off. The parking lot gives way to the road, and I accelerate into the night, free for the time being. The wind whipping past us washes away any last bits of worry about the festival.

It's the two of us. Not Jayme, the fixer, and Carson, the fuck-up. I'm not Carson, the amusement park heir, either. She doesn't care about any of that. She just cares about me, enough to risk this thing growing between us in an effort to improve my relationship with my dad and make my future better.

She sees things in me that I don't, but I see her too. Her generosity and kindness, even when they're packaged in hard words and tough to acknowledge, spot-on observations.

We ride for what seems to be hours, leaning into curves together and flying through straightaways, no destination in mind. But we end up back at Cutthroat Curve as if it's our place. Maybe it is? The place where things changed and we began.

I want to start over, though—or maybe it's a continuation—from this new, deeper place of understanding between us. Jayme squeezes me tightly with both her arms and thighs, and it feels as though she can read my mind.

I pull over on the shoulder and move a few feet deeper into the soft dirt before stopping. I can see for miles, over the cliff and all along the road in front of us and behind us. When I shut off the motorcycle, it goes dark, only the moon high above and the distant glow of the town below lighting the night.

I hold the motorcycle steady as Jayme climbs off and begins to take off the helmet. I pop the kickstand down and throw my leg over the back, coming to help her undo the clasp. Once she's freed, I hook the strap over the handlebar and look at her face in the moonlight, feeling something inside me move deeply.

"How're you doing?" It's a loaded question, meaning more than just how she feels after the ride. I mean with the festival, with us, with the argument . . . with *everything*.

"I think I understand why you like riding so much," she answers, adding a huge 'gotcha' smile.

I'm already chuckling, though I don't know why. I lift my brows questioningly.

"All that vibration." She shimmies her whole body as if the motorcycle's rumbling is still working its way through her.

With that little statement, everything else is forgotten and my focus zeroes in on her. "You like that?" I ask, dropping my voice deeper and huskier.

Taking a step toward her, I force her to look up slightly, though in her heels, she's not much shorter than I am.

"Carson . . ." she whispers with a needy sigh. The touch of my lips to hers seems to flip a switch inside her. Whatever was holding her back on the ride has evaporated into the scant air between us. She kisses me back passionately, wrapping her arms around my neck and pulling me in tight. Our bodies slam into each other, trying to occupy the same space, and she gasps when I grab her ass, gripping it hard in my hands.

I knead her flesh through her tight slacks, and she arches her back into my touch, groaning in pleasure with each squeezing hold. I test her more, surprising her with a sharp smack to her left ass cheek.

"Oh!" she cries out, but not in pain. "Was that for tonight?" she asks coyly, "or for fun?"

"Do you want to talk more right now?" I challenge.

She shakes her head with a sexy tilt of her lips as she tells me boldly, "No, I want you to make me come. The motorcycle ride has me on edge." I smack her ass again, a dark brow lifted. She corrects herself. "You have me on edge."

I offer her a satisfied nod. "Turn around and bend over the motorcycle." Even as I tell her what to do, I don't wait for her to obey. I spin her myself, pressing gently on her upper back to guide her to the seat where she can safely lean forward for support.

Running my hands down her back, I reach her waistband and tug at her tucked-in blouse until it's hanging free. Standing behind her, I grind my cock against her ass, wanting her to feel how much I want her. And then I slip my hands under her shirt to cup her full breasts. Through the silk of her bra, I can feel the hard nubs of her nipples, and I pinch them between my fingers, drawing a hiss of pleasure from her.

Using my nose, I brush her hair out of the way and lay a line of sweet kisses along her neck. She smells like night air, perfume, and a hint of salt from work today. Whispering hotly, I ask, "You want me to fuck you right here on the side of the road?"

She moans but shakes her head. "Lick me . . . oh, God, please . . . lick me."

I love that she's confident and openly tells me what she wants. Hearing her plead is sexy. Hearing her make a demand is erotic. I make quick work of the button of her slacks, and she helps wiggle them down until the waistband locks her feet from spreading any further. Her round ass is pale in the moonlight, split by the string of her thong. Any fingerprints or handprints from my earlier play have faded, and I long to replace them.

I drop to my knees behind her, grabbing the taut flesh once again and kneading her. Slowly, I trace a fingertip along the line of her thong, pulling the string from between her cheeks and continuing down until I feel how wet she is. Her folds are soaked and slippery, and I can smell the scent of her desire. "Fuck, Jayme," I groan.

My balls are heavy with need, and I imagine that's how she feels too. On edge. Unwilling to deal with the hassle of her panties, I pull the string further to the side, desperate for every drop of her desire. Without warning, I bury myself in her, my nose in her ass and my tongue dipping into her pussy.

"*Shit*," she gasps as she arches her back to give me more access to every inch of her.

I let her sounds guide me as I taste her sweetness with my hungry mouth and eager tongue. Coating my finger in her juices, I circle it on the tightness of her ass, teasing the sensitive flesh there too. "Can I touch you here?"

"Fuck, yes. You can touch me anywhere, Carson," she whines, her hips bucking. "I'm so close."

Her encouraging, needy words crank the throttle on my efforts, my fingers, tongue, lips, and more squeezing, licking, pressing, sucking, and grabbing her everywhere I can reach.

"I can't wait to taste your cum," I confess, the words mumbled against her flesh, but she must understand because she cries out. It's all the warning I get before she convulses, her hips bucking as she loses herself. I hang on to her as best I can, shoving my tongue deeper into her, savoring the deep, tangy sweetness. The pulses of her orgasm let my finger slip into her ass the tiniest bit, and she arches hard. It gives me the room I need to suck her clit into my mouth and flick my tongue over it as fast as possible.

She flies again, or maybe it's the same orgasm? All I know is that she's soaking me and I want to drink every drop, swallow her essence until she can't come any more.

Her fist bangs on the seat of my motorcycle, and I think she might even be biting the leather. Usually, I treat my ride with kid gloves, never risking anything that might damage it. But Jayme could gnaw a damn hole through the seat right now like a rabid raccoon and I'd look at that spot fondly, remembering this moment.

When she sags, panting and shuddering, I stand up. Letting my hands trace up her thighs, I grab her ass again, using my thumbs to part her folds. I ask her again, "Do you want me to fuck you right here on the side of the road?"

We're barely out of sight, not by much, but there are still no headlights for miles. We're utterly alone here, but there is something dangerous about fucking on the side of the road. She knows it and I know it. This is definitely something she would've warned me about, or even yelled about, a few weeks ago. But I know her answer before she speaks. Still, I wait, wanting her to say it.

"Yes. Carson, fuck me hard and fast," she gasps. "Fill me up."

I rip my pants and underwear down, letting my painfully hard cock free to the night air. Slowly, I give myself a stroke, squeezing tightly at the base so I don't come as soon as I feel her velvety walls gripping me. Still bent over, she looks back over her shoulder at me, watching as I line up with her core.

I grip her hips hard, secretly hoping the fingerprints stay this time, and slam into her. Her back arches so hard that I hear a faint crackle in her vertebra, and she throws her head back, her face lifting to the moon. Her moan is broken by the hitch in her breathing.

I grunt at the feeling of her silky tightness surrounding me and press in again, going even deeper. I think I bottom out inside her, but the primal sounds coming from her throat guide me to do it again.

Each stroke is deep and hard, and gradually, I pick up speed until I'm pounding into her. My thighs slap hers with every thrust, and I pull her hips back until her ass hits my hips each time. We're wild and powerful, raw and animalistic.

I'd be worried I'm being too rough with her, but she's there with me every hammering stroke of the way. "Yes, yes, yes," she grunts in time with our movements, encouraging me to give her more.

I slide a hand up to her hair, weaving my fingers in near the root to tug sharply. She hisses, which I take as a good sign. Letting go of her hip momentarily, I lay two quick smacks to her ass, and I feel a quivering spasm grip my cock.

"Can you come again?" I demand.

She nods, moaning. "With you."

"Get there. Make your pussy suck me dry." The order is gruff and crude, but I feel a fresh gush of Jayme's juices coat us. And then I feel her fingers slipping around my cock, gathering the wetness before centering over her clit. She is so fucking sexy, taking her pleasure on my cock and getting herself off again. "That's it. Fucking perfect."

I grip her hips again and find a punishing rhythm, slamming balls deep with each drive. I fuck her as hard as I can, lifting to my toes with each stroke to get as much of her as possible. I can feel my cock swelling, getting harder and harder inside her as I feel like my whole body is going to explode.

She hovers on the edge, her breath caught in her throat. I smack her ass one time, and she clamps down on me, crying out into the night. "*Fuck . . . Carson . . . yes!*"

My balls churn hot and then explode, cream pumping into her in pulses. I throw my head back, coming harder than I think I ever have in my life. I swear I feel my soul leave my body and then snap back into place.

Her pussy is still shuddering, the spasms demanding more from me. I told her to suck me dry, and fuck if she's not doing it. I thrust deep inside her and hold her still in my grip, grinding myself against her.

My legs are shaking with exertion, but I want to stay buried in her a little while longer. Gentling my touch, I trace over the skin of her lower back and hips. "Fuck, that was . . ."

My vocabulary fails me, and Jayme laughs lightly, both of us moaning softly as her laughter makes her squeeze around me.

"Yes, it was," she agrees, apparently unable to find words either.

We've fucked ourselves stupid.

Slowly, I pull out of her, wishing I didn't have to. But I see headlights way down below. They're still several minutes out, but I don't want to risk someone seeing Jayme half-naked. I'm protective of her and her reputation too.

As we adjust our clothing as best we can, I tell her, "At some point, we need to do this in a bed where we can take our time, fuck in every different position, and then just lie there afterward until we fall asleep."

Her smile is full of danger. "Where's the risk in that?"

I take her in my arms, grinning in joy. "Ooh, you're naughtier than I thought. I love it."

She giggles happily, and I feel ten feet tall and bulletproof. I grab the helmet and help her slip it back on, and then we ride off into the night again. But it feels different now.

Something shifted in that Ferris Wheel car, but it shifted even more on that deserted cliff. My jumbled mess and Jayme's organized chaos are twining together into something greater than the sum of its parts. Or at least that's how it feels to me.

She didn't say where to go, but we end up outside her apartment building. I pull over to the curb, giving the doorman a cocky smirk. Turning the motorcycle off, I tell her, "Myron isn't happy to see me again."

So much of our time together has been spent at the office, I realize. It's my second home, and I spend most of my days and nights there anyway, so I hadn't noticed that though it's been weeks, I've never been inside Jayme's place, nor has she been to mine. It feels inordinately weird that someone so close to me hasn't sat on my couch, slept in my bed, and padded barefoot into the kitchen for a morning cup of coffee.

I want that with Jayme's place too. To mark her space with my presence, see her living room, make some memories in her bedroom. Hell, I want to have a space in her toothbrush cup for one of mine and a towel on her rack. I want things that are . . . downright domestic.

The thought's not as scary as it would have been a short while ago.

"Myron's fine. He looks out for me is all," Jayme says, throwing a wave Myron's way. He lifts his chin, and I'm certain that greeting is all for her and none for me.

"Can I come up?" I ask, suddenly nervous. This means something to me.

She smiles in surprise. "Yeah, of course. But we have an early morning," she reminds me.

"I'll set an early alarm to give me time to go home and change." That'll also give her time to get ready because tomorrow is a big day for both of us.

She takes my hand and leads me toward the door. "Hey, Myron! How're you tonight?" she greets the stony-faced man.

He gives me a very protective warning look and then gives Jayme a friendly smile. "Doing well, ma'am. Can I help with anything this evening? Take out the trash, maybe?"

His face is light and kind, but it's obvious he means me.

Jayme laughs. "Har-har, Mr. Comedian. No, I'm good for tonight. But . . . uh, can you set up a car to take me in the morning? Seven o'clock?" She cringes as she asks, as though she's unaccustomed to asking for help. Or realizing that she just told her doorman that the guy who gave her a ride home will be gone before sunrise.

"Of course," he answers easily. But when Jayme walks through the door he's holding open, he glares at me. "Don't hurt her," he says menacingly.

I pause. "Is this the part where you threaten me?"

He shakes his head, his eyes dark but full of something deeper than a warning. "Don't need to. Just don't do it."

I blink. I wasn't expecting that. He sounds . . . concerned for Jayme. I get it, she's amazing and has people falling into line to do her bidding. Me included. But I guess I expected the monster of a man to resort to fists and death threats, not polite orders.

"Carson?" Jayme says from a few feet inside the lobby where she's stopped after realizing I wasn't behind her.

"Coming," I answer. I dip my chin at Myron, acknowledging his request and silently letting him know that I have no intention of hurting Jayme.

We take the elevator up to the fifth floor, and I look down the hallway as she leads me to her door. There are only two doors on this side of the building. I'd expected there to be several apartments along each side.

She unlocks her door with her thumb and then shrugs at my questioning look. "Fingerprint scanner. The landlord had them installed for security."

"They'd have to get past Myron first. Does he sleep or is he like one of those robots that goes for weeks on a single electric charge?" I joke.

Jayme laughs. "He's the night guard. Brad is the day guard, and Javier is the weekend man. Though they live on the first floor, so we can call any of them if we need to."

They're not simply doormen but full-service, on-site caretakers.

Damn. I'm feeling much better about Jayme's safety and security. And I realize that her comfort is well taken care of too.

Her apartment is warm and cozy, but also large by any city standard. The living room has a fluffy sectional couch turned toward an electric fireplace with a television on the wall above it. There are a bunch of pillows, but they're sorted into groups of three, and the blanket thrown over the back looks casual, but I'm sure it was perfectly arranged. The coffee table is brass and glass with a vintage feel and holds a stack of books, a candle, and a single coaster.

To the left is the dining area and kitchen, which I can see into. The cabinets are light wood, classic and traditional but modernized with sleek white countertops. The dining room has dark green geometric wallpaper and a gathering of brass candlesticks in the middle of the table.

Everything I can see are beautiful, simple quality pieces that are timeless. In a way, if I'd been told this was a model home unit, I'd have easily believed that. But knowing Jayme as well as I do, I can see the little touches of her personality here. She is classic and well put together too, but with a twist, like the apothecary jar of seashells by the fireplace, which could be a generic staged piece, but I bet they're from the beach by Taya's house. And the fresh white tea towel hanging from the stove handle that reads *Eat a Bag of Dicks*. I'm not sure where that came from, or if I want to know.

"Nice place," I tell Jayme, who seems to be waiting for a comment from me.

"Thanks. Come on, let's take a quick shower before we crash." She takes my hand and leads me down a hallway.

We pass a set of glass doors closing off a small office with a library's worth of books on the shelves along one wall. There are a couple of other regular doors that are closed, so I don't know what's behind them.

Then I'm in Jayme's bedroom. It feels like a dream come true, or at least the start of a particularly hot fantasy. But after our earlier adventure, I might need a little persuading before I'm ready for a full round two. I chuckle to myself, knowing that simply seeing Jayme feel pleasure would have me rock hard and raring to go in seconds.

Her bed is neatly made with layers of fluffiness—a comforter, folded blanket at the foot, and a throw, plus a few decorative pillows. It looks like a cozy nest where she can curl up. And honestly, I could lie on top of all that stuff and fall asleep in seconds at this point. It's been a long day and an energy-filled night.

But she keeps leading me further into her sanctuary, into a huge main bathroom that is clearly intended just for her. The space is bright, with white tile and wood cabinets that match the ones I saw in the kitchen. The large soaking tub looks inviting, but instead, Jayme turns on the shower.

I follow her lead and strip down, laying my clothes neatly over the edge of the tub since I'll have to put them back on in the morning to get home. Jayme tosses hers into a bag with a dry-cleaning chain's logo on it.

She hangs two fluffy towels up by the shower and then steps inside. I pause, watching the water slide over her skin, droplets running from her breasts, down her belly, to the cleft of her pussy.

"Come on." She welcomes me in with a wave of her hand and an inviting smile.

The warm water sluices over my skin too, relaxing tension throughout my muscles that I didn't know was there. She hands me a bottle of shampoo, and unlike before when we were trying to make a flight, we do have time now. Sleep is the only time restraint we have and not nearly a strong enough enticement for me to miss this opportunity to worship Jayme.

I pour out a healthy amount of the shampoo and then work it into my hands. "Lean back," I tell her. She looks uncertain but does as I say. I lather the shampoo into suds through her strands, massaging her scalp with strong fingers. "Feel good?"

"Mmhmm," she moans. Her eyes are closed, but her lips are falling open as she relaxes into my touch.

I help her rinse her hair, then add conditioner with the same attentive detail. While that soaks in, I turn my attention to her body. I find a bottle of body wash and a pouf and use it to wash every inch of her . . . twice. Only when she starts giggling at my work do I stop.

"I don't think my boobs have ever been this clean," she teases. "Right arm, boobs, left arm, boobs, belly, boobs, leg, boobs."

Okay, so maybe I'm a little obsessed, but her breasts are right there in my face with proud little hard nipples begging to be touched. Or licked or sucked, but with the abundance of soap, I went for hands so that I don't end up blowing soap bubbles later.

"Just making sure they know they're appreciated," I tease with a serious face, looking her right in the chest. "I acknowledge you, I appreciate you, you are perfect just the way you are."

She laughs softly and steps away from me, letting the water wash away my hard work. I use the pouf to make quick work of washing myself, not paying half as much attention to myself because nothing is as attention-grabbing as Jayme's bare breasts. And then when I'm rinsed, she grabs the towels, handing me one.

I go to dry her off with it, but she laughs and pushes me away. "I got it. You do you so we can curl up naked in my bed."

That sounds like a fantastic idea, and I start quickly rubbing my skin to dry off. After a moment, she clarifies, "To sleep."

I throw a playful glare her way. "You play dirty."

"Sometimes," she admits. "And another night, you may find out *how* dirty I can be."

It's a little thrill to think about, but when we do finally curl up in her bed, her ass cradling my cock and my arms wrapped around her, exhaustion hits me hard and fast. She was right, we do need to sleep a little bit before the big day.

I don't want anything to interfere with things going perfectly, least of all a sleep-deprived brain that forgets something basic like my own name. Or worse. Instead, I drift off to sleep, where strange dreams of a sign declaring *Welcome to Amerijuanica Land* greets me instead of Americana Land, and the festival turns into a smoke-filled fiasco that ends up all over social media.

Nope, definitely can't have that happening. Luckily, even in my dream, Jayme comes in to save the day, riding in on a hot air balloon with a huge fan that blows away all the smoke as she yells into a megaphone. "Put that shit out and eat a cookie instead!"

I laugh in my dream, but maybe in my sleep too.

CHAPTER 19

JAYME

*S*aturday arrives full of sunshine and blue skies, promising an amazing backdrop for the festival. I arrive at Americana Land bright and early, ready to work. My outfit for the day definitely isn't my normal dress of professional business wear, but today, I'm going to need to run here there and everywhere, so jeans, sneakers, and a special staff edition neon-yellow shirt are warranted.

As the driver drops me off at the park gate, he looks at the huge balloon arches being assembled out front and asks, "What's going on here today?" He reads the big banner stating, *Americana Land Freedom Fest* and *harrumphs*. "Attention whoring."

I don't let it worry me. He's not the target demographic by at least four decades. Hell, if he's irritated by it, that's a sign we're on the right path.

If it's too loud, you're too old, man!

I laugh to myself at the saying, hoping it doesn't come back to bite me in the ass later when I'm shoving ear plugs in my ears to block the loud music. At the front gate, I add James, the ride operator's, name to the VIP list as I told him I would and head inside.

Every step of the way, I'm evaluating the visuals for social media opportunities. What will make a good video or photo? How will guests interact with the environment? Can anything be improved?

Inside, I see Spencer and Kyleigh talking with Carson and head that way. They're wearing matching neon shirts too, an effort to make staff stand out from the crowd.

"Good morning," I greet them. "How's everything going?"

Three pairs of eyes meet mine. Carson and Spencer seem pretty calm, but Kyleigh looks on the verge of spontaneously combusting. She doesn't say anything, but the way her body is vibrating is answer enough. Actually, on second glance, Spencer could probably use a cup of coffee to perk up. She's eerily serene, especially in contrast to Kyleigh.

"Good," Spencer says, not giving anything away. She continues talking to Carson, and I pick up on where they are in their checklist. "Artists are all being picked up at the hotel now. They'll be shuttled over for sound check and then taken back. I have someone on hand at the hotel to cater to them just in case anyone pulls a Mariah." She gives Kyleigh a subtle head tilt and then mouths, "Jazmyn."

I'm not surprised, but I hope our headliner can keep it together long enough to perform the way we need her to. "If you have any issues come up, I can deal with her," I offer, and Spencer nods gratefully.

"What? Who?" Kyleigh says, looking from me to Spencer in confusion.

Spencer pats Kyleigh's hands in a motherly move. "It's fine. Let's continue down the list."

We get to work, confirming that bubble machines, fog machines, laser light shows, and glitter cannons are prepared. We check in with the engineers who are prepping for the sound check and promise to follow up with Spencer about any concerns. The vendors have everything they need to sell food, drinks, and merchandise. Freddy Freebird costumed employees are stationed around the park, each in Freedom Fest special gear for the day. There's special signage on displays throughout the area, all with #AmericanaLand and #FreedomFest hashtags to encourage people to tag their selfies and group photos.

By the end of Spencer and Kyleigh's run-through, it's clear that Freedom Fest is going to be a planned-to-the-smallest-detail success. It has to be.

"Wow, I'm truly impressed and grateful for all your hard work," Carson tells Spencer and Kyleigh sincerely. "I can tell how much ownership you put into making this event happen."

Kyleigh beams like a puppy getting its first head pats as a reward for sitting on command. "You're welcome, sir."

Spencer is a harder sell. She knows what's up and what this festival means. "I appreciate the opportunity to show what I can do and how much I can handle. I look forward to this becoming a regular thing, whether with a repeat of this festival or other events. Also, if you can finagle it, Kyleigh here needs to be brought on full-time. She's a great asset."

Damn. I think I love Spencer. She's got no qualms with saying exactly what she thinks and what she wants, and she backs it up with solid work. Plus, she's willing to mentor others, a sign that she's got a good heart. Carson would do well to keep her on his team, right at his side. Good leaders surround themselves with other good people, and together, they all grow. Plus, I don't think Spencer would put up with any shit from Carson. He needs that too.

Carson grins at her. "Heard. Noted." To Kyleigh, he says, "Done."

Kyleigh squeals, jumping up and down exuberantly. One sideways glance from Spencer, though, and she reigns herself in. Her voice still high-pitched, she says, "Thank you, Mr. Steen. Thank you, Spencer."

"Call me Carson," he corrects her. "Everyone on the team calls me Carson."

Her squeak of agreement is kind of adorable, actually, and I can understand how thrilled she is to get the job of her dreams with a mentor she respects.

"Okay, where do you need us?" I ask Spencer, letting her leadership shine.

She points over to the right, off toward some of the rides. "Check in with Xavier and Padma. They're going to be with the photographer, getting opening shots and spamming our pages to build excitement. Should be . . ." She looks at her watch, noting that it's almost ten, and says, "In the Thirteen Colonies area."

"On it."

Spencer hands me a small map and a radio. "Keep it in your pocket so you can find your way around without stopping at the park directories." To Carson, she asks, "Where's your sister? I have something I need to talk to her about."

"Toni?" he echoes, as if he has another sister she'd be talking about.

167

I laugh and excuse myself, sending Carson a sexy wink as I head off on my mission.

HOLY FUCKING FIRECRACKERS AND HOT DOGS ON THE FOURTH OF JULY!

To say that the festival is a hit would be an understatement of the century. We're only on the third musical act to hit the stage and the entire park is full of visitors. People are packed in the Great Garden area, most of them wearing themed outfits of some sort, from classic red, white, and blue regalia to outrageous party costumes.

I think I just saw a glitter unicorn skip by. *A glitter-corn? Or a uni-glit?*

I shake my head, forgetting the conundrum when I see a guy dressed as Abe Lincoln, complete with a neon painted beard and top hat with streamers running down his back. He's sipping from a Freddy Free-bird kid's cup, an actual bald eagle figure with a straw coming out of its white head.

Closer to the stage, I can see an opening in the crowd, and a woman is twirling some sort of LED-lit balls on strings. More than yo-yos, they make wild shapes in the air as she flicks and spins them, and the crowd surrounding her cheers her every move, entranced with her skill.

Through the mass, I see another neon shirt and duck left and right to get a better look. Realizing it's Carson, I bob and weave my way his direction.

"Hey!" I yell, bumping his arm.

He looks down, a polite smile on his face, but when he sees me, it becomes something deeper. "Hey yourself."

Or at least I think he does, but I'm mostly reading his lips. Honestly, I can barely hear a damn thing.

I pull him lower to speak into his ear, still needing to shout. "This is amazing!"

He nods his head enthusiastically.

The group on stage, Alien Babies, judging by the abundance of *Area 51* signs in the audience, reaches a loud crescendo and then goes silent. I panic, thinking the sound went out, but when I look to the stage, I see the singer with her arms held up high, hands shaking so hard that her whole body is vibrating as if lightning is washing through her. Then in one powerful jolt, she swings her arms down, her headbang sending her lime green braids flying. Right in time with the move, green glitter shoots out over the crowd, and everyone tilts their faces up into the shower as if the sparkly confetti is a gift from God herself. The crowd goes wild, headbanging and bumping into each other.

The glitter rains down over us, and though I try to keep my mouth closed, I swallow some and then ungracefully spit a bit out. Someone grabs my hand and quickly twirls me, but before I can react or Carson can intervene, they let go to spin the next person as they work through the crowd.

It's chaos. It's wild.

It's beautiful. It's perfect.

Everyone is smiling and happy, dancing and enjoying themselves.

Carson pulls me back to his side, and I look up at him.

"You're covered!" I exclaim with a bit of a laugh, but I clamp my mouth shut so I don't swallow even more of the tiny sparkles. I once drank too much dyed beer at a St. Patrick's Day celebration and peed green for two days. I wonder what the pass-through speed of glitter is. Two days? Five? I don't know, but I'm going to find out firsthand, experimental style.

His brow furrows, not understanding over the loud music. Instead of repeating myself, I reach up and brush my thumb over his cheekbone where a bunch of glitter has stuck to his skin. He lets me brush off as much as I can, neither of us caring who's around or who might be watching.

But that's a dangerous risk to take when the whole point of this festival is that it's beaming out to social media. I can see phones held in the air as people film themselves and the stage or livestream the festival. It's exactly what Carson and Americana Land need, but not what we need personally.

"We should see if Spencer needs anything," I suggest. Carson points at his ear and shakes his head. Rolling my eyes, I grab his hand and start pulling him out of the throng of people.

Once we get further away from the stage's speakers, I hear someone yelling my name and look, expecting to see another neon shirted staff member. But what I see doesn't make any sense at all. It's a woman in a holographic jumpsuit. The knotted turban on her head and the silvery geometric shapes painted on her face match the super-short outfit. She's a walking, yelling, smiling disco ball.

She gets closer, her smile growing. "There you are, I've been looking for you," she shouts.

That voice . . . I know her. I grab her arm and spin her around. That ass . . . I know that ass. Back facing me, I get closer, trying to see her eyes through the dotted designs covering her skin. I know those dark eyes that are laughing at me right now.

"Oh, my God! What are you doing here?" I hiss, looking around to see if anyone else has figured out what I just have.

Taya is here. At Freedom Fest.

I realize there's a guy beside her in an equally outrageous outfit and recognize her bodyguard, Captain. I don't think he's actually a captain, of either a boat or in the military, but that's what he goes by, and he's not the sort of person you question. Especially about his origin story. That's how movie villains start their monologue and end up going off the deep end.

Oddly enough, they don't particularly stand out in the crowd. Taya is probably safer here than walking around the streets of LA where people would expect to see her. And as outrageous as her outfit is, it's not nearly as wild as most of the other ones here.

I rush her for a hug, and she squeezes me tightly but yells, "Don't fuck up my makeup, bitch."

Her smile makes me laugh. "I can't believe you're here."

"Wouldn't have missed your shindig." She sees Carson standing next to me and lifts a questioning silver-painted brow my way. She's asking so many questions with that one arched curve of skin and hair.

Does he know about me? Does he know about you? Are you fucking him yet? What does he mean to you?

It's friendship shorthand, and I answer with my eyes, knowing she'll understand.

No. No. Yes. Everything.

Taya offers her hand to Carson, and he shakes it politely. But she pulls him in, using a hand on his shoulder to force him lower so she can speak directly into his ear.

She doesn't yell, but I'm close enough that I can hear.

"I'm the bestie. Don't fuck her over or I'll kill you, and that's not an exaggeration."

Carson grins as though she's kidding but then sobers when he sees her hard expression. I love her, she's an amazing friend, but I don't need her threatening people over me.

"Tay—" I say, but stop myself short. Carson doesn't know who she is, nor do the people dancing around completely unaware that one of the most famous artists in music is mere feet from them. I look at Carson with wide eyes, hoping he didn't catch that. It's not my place to share.

And yes, I did overshare his information with his dad, but that was for therapeutic reasons. Sharing Taya's identity and whereabouts is a safety risk, a completely different thing.

But there's no surprise in Carson's eyes, and Taya notices as well. "You know who I am?"

He dips his chin once. "You have a beautiful home," he shouts.

He's known all along and never said anything, keeping the secret to himself and not even letting me know that he knew whose house I'd taken him to.

He passed a test I'm not sure I even consciously realized I was giving him.

WE NEVER FIND SPENCER OR KYLEIGH, BUT THE FOUR OF US MAKE OUR way through the crowd in a chain—Carson holding my hand, me holding Taya's, and her holding Captain's. I look around to make sure everyone is enjoying themselves, partying responsibly, and sharing hashtags with their photos as we go.

After a while, we're simply four more people in a sea of neon body paint, bass lines, and lighting effects—including the disco balls, which look amazing with the tree's LED lights and the stage's laser lights reflecting off them. We're jumping along with the beats, dancing with the people around us. It feels like we're part of one huge family.

The Americana Land Freedom Fest family.

I make a mental note to do some posts with that hashtag and caption. Especially if the photographer got some good shots of the festival-goers with Grandma Barb.

Generations of fun.

It's basically writing itself in my mind. I want to tell Carson, but knowing that he can't hear me that well right now releases me to simply enjoy the craziness and leave the work until later.

DJ Amalfo's set finishes, entirely as amazing as Kyleigh promised. You can feel everyone catching their breaths, recovering from the steady dancing as they rave about the show and share excitement for the upcoming headliner. Slowly, anticipation fills air, building steadily. The crowd begins to chant, "Jazmyn! Jazmyn! Jazmyn!"

As though the chant were music itself, people are jumping up and down and skipping around. It's not out of control, but the plan-for-every-situation part of me is beginning to freak out a bit. "We need to get this calmed down."

Carson grabs my hand, pulling me away from the crowd, and I grab Taya's too. Our chain all together again, we make our way to the edge of the crowd. With our neon shirts and Carson being easily recognizable by staff, we're able to get backstage fairly quickly. Carson sees Spencer, Kyleigh, Toni, and Jazmyn talking and guides us that way. "Over there."

The Americana Land crew, including Toni, are wearing matching neon shirts. But not Jazmyn. She looks ready for the stage, wearing three-inch platform boots, red leggings which have been ripped to shreds along the front of the thighs, a black T-shirt with a cut neckline hanging off one shoulder, and so much jewelry and chains, I'm surprised she can move. Her makeup is dramatic black and white eyeshadow accented by false lashes and a literal smear of red lipstick across the lower half of her face. And her mullet is teased high at the top. She looks like a vampiric anime dream girlfriend.

"What's going on?" Carson demands.

Spencer steps forward. "Minor issues. Being resolved as we speak."

Jazmyn is near hyperventilating, though. "Minor?!" she screeches. She's nothing like the flat, sarcastic, unaffected starlet we had brunch with. She's freaking the fuck out.

Toni and Kyleigh gather on either side of her. "It's gonna be fine, Jazzy. We got you."

Jazmyn's wide eyes flick between the two supportive women, but she shakes her head. "This isn't meant to be. King's Krossing is down a member, that crowd is insane, and Steve can't find my lucky rabbit's foot. I can't perform without it."

She's shrinking back right before our eyes, and I seriously consider whether she might make a run for it. Luckily, I don't think those boots were made for walking, much less running. Hell, I'd break an ankle just standing up in them, so hopefully Jazmyn can perform in them. Because she's going to. She's got to.

Spencer speaks calmly and clearly, sounding equally in charge and motherly. "Steve will find it. We've got three people looking."

That's at least one issue addressed.

"What happened with King's Krossing?" I ask.

Toni answers, "One of the kids is grounded."

"From performing?" I look at her wide-eyed, hoping she's kidding. "That seems a little extreme, right?"

Toni shrugs. "His mom isn't budging. Said he knew he had to pass Geometry if he wanted to perform, and it was his choice to not study for the exam. You gotta admire her dedication to education . . ." She trails off, not looking sure whether the punishment fits the crime. "I do have an idea, though."

"What?" Jazmyn grabs Toni's shoulders, getting right up in her face. I vaguely wonder if she's going to bite her. Maybe that's how she got that smudged lipstick? Has anyone actually seen Steve? Or this rabbit?

"It's crazy, but . . ." Jazmyn gives Toni a little shake, but Toni laughs. "I could do it. I know the whole routine, have done it roughly a thousand times, and have experience on stage." It's a small brag, but right now, it seems to reassure Jazmyn a little, given the way her eyes brighten.

"No." Carson's refusal is instant and final.

Except . . .

"Where have you been on stage?" Spencer asks Toni directly, not letting Carson's 'no' bother her in the slightest.

"I've been in dance classes since I was a kid. My mom's a dancer, you know?" Toni smirks because everyone knows that about Izzy. "Look."

Toni pulls her phone out of her pocket and clicks around until her social media comes up. Turning the phone around, we all watch as Toni perfectly does the King's Krossing dance to Jazmyn's song . . . in her bedroom.

"That's not quite the same thing," Spencer says carefully. "How many takes did you have to do?"

But Jazmyn's nodding her head. "That's okay. It'll be good to have a familiar face up there."

I guess Jazmyn, Toni, and Kyleigh have become faster friends than I thought because the three of them are having one of those eyes-only three-way conversations now.

"Toni?" Carson meets Toni's eyes. "Are you sure? This is risky. If something goes wrong, you'll get slayed with this many eyes. And if it goes right, they'll still say you got the gig because you're family. There's no winning here."

Toni rushes to Carson, slamming into him in a fierce hug. "Thank you for looking out for me, Bro, but I got this." She pats him on the chest and praises, "And good job on slang usage. You even used 'slayed' correctly."

"What? I just meant they'll kill you," he mutters, confused.

Issues handled, all eyes turn to Jazmyn. She's quiet for a minute, listening. The crowd out there isn't chanting her name any longer. Instead, they've started singing her songs without her. It's . . . moving, actually.

"My rabbit foot?" she says in a small voice.

"Fuck it," I hear from behind me, and then Taya shoves me out of the way. She's in boss mode now and gets right up in Jazmyn's face. "Look here, girl. You don't need no dead animal bits for luck."

"But—"

Taya's look of disgust is obvious even with the heavy silver face paint. "Your so-called luck?" She makes air quotes with her ridiculously long nails, which I now realize are also silver, with little bits of mirror glued all over them. Gotta give her credit, she really knows how to embrace a full look.

"It's inside you. It's called work. You're the one who stayed up all night practicing songs, pouring your energy into lyrics, and learning how to play piano so you could be better. That ain't luck. You earned that" —she points behind her to the crowd behind the stage curtains — "with work. So get your shit straight and get out there! Do what you've always dreamed of. This right here is your moment, and you damn well better take advantage of it. Because if you don't go out there, I sure as fuck will."

Taya swings her hair behind her back, except it's all up in her turban. It doesn't matter, though. The invisible hair flip is still impactful.

Everyone is frozen, mouths hanging open. Not just us, either. Taya was reading Jazmyn loud enough that even the backstage crew has stopped to stare, especially given that Taya's voice is quite recognizable.

Captain moves closer to Taya's side, and she pats his chest. "It's all good. We're not gonna have a problem." She looks around, meeting the eyes of everyone staring at her in a challenge. "Because nobody saw nothing and they ain't heard nothing either. Right? We're all just out to have a good time tonight with zero drama."

People nod their heads, hearing the threat in her words. Some even scamper back to work.

"Wow," Jazmyn sighs. "You're . . ."

"Yes, I am. But that doesn't matter." She clicks her nails together in Jazmyn's face. "Who are you? You think I recommended you for this shit because I thought you'd fail? No, I did not. I thought it was your time. Don't make me be wrong." Her head is swiveling so much that I worry her turban might unwind, but it seems to be secure . . . for now.

I step forward, worried for Taya. I'll need to pre-emptively spin a story on this little stunt of hers because there's no way all these people are going to keep their mouths shut. But I also deeply appreciate her willingness to help, not only me, but Jazmyn. "That's true, Jazmyn. When we came up with this idea, Taya is who suggested you. She's why we reached out."

If I'd told Jazmyn that God herself had recommended her, I think she'd be less surprised. But it doesn't matter if she doesn't go out on the stage.

It takes a minute, but slowly, we can see Jazmyn's confidence returning, her eyes brightening and back going straighter. "Let's do this!"

She gives a few hops, somehow not breaking an ankle in those boots. Maybe she's got steel ankles or something?

Taya claps her hands. "There ya go, bitch. You better show up, show off, and show out because I'm here for it!"

She claps her hands, emphasizing each word. Energy building, Jazmyn shakes her whole body like she's spasming. It's similar to what Taya does before she goes onstage, except she'll usually give her cheeks a fierce pat. Both sets of cheeks—one for a little color and one to start the jiggle, she says.

Steve rushes up, looking harried. "I found it!" he shouts, shoving a black and red rabbit foot toward Jazmyn.

Jazmyn meets Taya's eyes and then tells Steve, "It's okay. I don't need it."

With that, she runs on stage to grab the microphone. "Helloooo, Starr-lights!"

CHAPTER 20

CARSON

*F*rom backstage, we can see the faces of all the guests light up when Jazmyn hits the stage. The scream of joy is so loud it's a literal, palpable thing I can feel along the tiny hairs on my arms.

"Helloooo, Starr-lights!" Jazmyn yells. With a crash of electronic music following that declaration, the show starts. She rolls straight into one of her lesser-known songs, but the crowd sings along with every word. Jazmyn is surprised a bit at first, but by the end of the song, I think she's near tears.

She takes the microphone from the stand and walks back and forth across the stage. "Starr-lights, I was so nervous coming out here tonight. I'm just a girl who likes to sing in her bedroom and started posting stuff online. I got a few followers—"

"I love you, Jazmyn!" a voice calls out from the crowd, and she blushes.

I swear, she actually turns pink above that red lipstick. I don't think it's a trick of the lighting.

"I love you too," she calls back, laughing. "And then a few more people followed me. But I never dreamed that there were so many of you who felt like I do—like this whole world is so big and there was no way that one person could be that important. That's where I was when I wrote this next song, staring up at the stars and feeling small. But I want you to know . . . each and every one of you is important. To me."

She sings a song called *Constellations*, which reminds me of the tattooed stars on her face that I mistook for freckles. It starts out a little slower, and I watch as the crowd locks arms around each other, swaying back and forth in waves. I hope the videographer is getting this and the live streaming is working because this is magic in action.

Magic that Jayme helped start.

I catch her eye and then subtly step closer, touching her hand with mine. It's a question. I want to hold her hand, right here in front of everyone, but I know it's a big risk, for me and for her. I don't want to be seen as similar to my dad, who had a workplace romance. And Jayme told me that client relationships are strongly frowned upon, especially mid-assignment.

Fuck it.

I've done enough worrying about image and reputation and what everyone else thinks, especially Dad. I'm doing what I want. She told me to trust my gut, and that's what I'm doing. I take her hand, squeezing it tightly. She answers with a side-eyed grin that I can only see in my peripheral vision because I'm trying not to draw attention to what's happening between us. But I can feel her giving in to us.

Jazmyn hits the chorus, which is a forceful combination of screaming and singing. I'm honestly not sure where she's getting that much power from. She's relatively small, but I think her voice could fill the whole park, even without a microphone. She's got the audience in the palm of her hand.

The lights on the stage shoot out over the Great Garden in flashing patterns, creating energy and movement and showcasing the crowd. It's a sea of neon glowsticks, light-up hula hoops, glow in the dark costumes, and signs with Jazmyn's name.

Fireworks go off overhead, and there's a collective gasp from the crowd before everyone oohs and ahhs. It's beautiful, and totally unexpected, to be honest.

"I didn't know about that," I yell to Spencer, who's smiling bigger than I've ever seen before.

"I like to go above and beyond," she shouts with a no-biggie shrug. But we both know this is a huge deal and a sign of what she's capable of when given free rein. Maybe strictly following the traditions that Dad put in place decades ago hasn't only been holding me back, but others as well.

"In budget? Permits?" I clarify.

She dips her glasses down her nose to scowl at me. "Of course."

I can't help but smile, and with a flashed thumbs-up, I say, "Great job, then."

Smugly, she goes back to watching the fireworks, which are spectacular. Bright streamers of light shoot up into the sky en masse, a finale, but the show's not over. Jazmyn finishes the song, and then, breathing heavily, she sits down on the edge of the stage. Her heavy boots swing as though she's a child in a too-big chair as she talks to the audience again.

"You know, Starr-Lights, back when I was posting stuff online and praying I'd get a single like, there was a special group of people who heard something in one of my songs that made them want to dance." The crowd cheers loudly, knowing that she's talking about King's Krossing. "They created choreography to the song, and when they posted it, their dance went viral, taking my song along for the ride. So when I got the invitation to come to hashtag-AmericanaLandFreedomFest, I wanted to bring them along on this ride."

Damn, I could hug Jazmyn right now! She just threw out our whole hashtag in the middle of her speech about the most anticipated song of her set. I know that live streamed. I meet Jayme's eyes, which reflect the victory I'm feeling too, and feel her shaking our entwined hands in delight.

"So . . . welcome to the stage, King's Krossing!"

The dance group takes the stage, running in from the other side. A few of them do tumbling passes, and I worry about the stage setup, not wanting them to run into an amp or guitar. But they land safely and take their places, waving at the crowd, who's going mad and shouting individual dancers' names.

"I also want to welcome a special friend, Toni Steen, daughter of Ben Steen, CEO of Americana Land." Toni runs out too, her smile wide and both hands waving in the air. She looks completely at ease, and a knot in my chest slowly starts to unwind. "Sometimes when you meet someone, you automatically know that they're going to be a ride-or-die friend. That's Toni. I met her yesterday and we're already besties!" Jazmyn laughs and hugs Toni before they stand together, posing for a quick picture by the front-row photographer.

The audience cheers. I even hear a few people shout, "Hi, Toni!"

"Okay, let's do this!"

The music starts with a heavy bass drop, and Jazmyn skips around the stage. Toni takes her place in the line-up, and King's Krossing starts clapping, hyping everyone up. Jazmyn's too active, singing too close to the microphone to make every word crystal clear, but the crowd knows them by heart and sings along. As King's Krossing and Toni start doing the dance steps, I can see the audience doing them too. It's like a massive flash mob scene.

"Wow!" I shout.

"I know," Jayme yells. She lets go of my hand, but it's only to clap along. And though we don't know the song, the words, or the moves, we party along with everyone. Even Spencer sways back and forth a little bit. Kyleigh is doing a watered down, and slightly off-beat, version of the dance, but she's having fun too.

Pyrotechnics go off on stage, and Jazmyn throws her hands wide, letting them frame her, and then she joins the dance too as the band plays a repeat of the verse and chorus.

It's amazing. And I have Jayme to thank for it.

Other people too, obviously, but she's the one who came up with this idea, and it is absolutely going to be the savior of Americana Land's image. I'm watching as we become relevant to a whole new generation right before my eyes. Even our existing line-up of concerts will benefit from what we've learned doing this festival. And it's all because Jayme had a crazy idea and the guts to push me out of my comfort zone.

Gamble on yourself, your team, on me.

I did, and it's paying off in more ways than I could've dreamed.

Jazmyn plays a few more songs, the lights, fog machine, and effects accompanying her, but I've honestly stopped paying attention. All I can focus on is the woman at my side. I step in front of Jayme, blocking her view of the show, and she looks up at me with a question in her eyes.

"Thank you," I say, trusting that she'll hear me before I cup her jaw in my hands and kiss her. She gasps in surprise, and I take the kiss deeper, wanting to tell her through my actions how much I appreciate her and what I'm feeling. Her hands press to my chest as she lifts to her toes and leans into me for more.

"Ooh, bitch. Yes ma'am, getcha sum," Taya calls from somewhere to my left. She's been dancing along with Jazmyn's show too, though her dancing is more stomping and attitude than complicated footwork.

I'm not sure if she's talking to Jazmyn onstage or to Jayme about me. Either way, I press one more kiss to Jayme's soft lips. When I pull back, she's smiling happily.

"You're welcome," she answers. "And I liked that. A lot."

The show finishes, and Jazmyn runs off stage, panting and beaming. She hugs Toni and Kyleigh, the three of them chattering over one another.

"You were amazing!"

"So were you!"

"Oh, my God!"

I honestly don't know who said what. It blends together into one high-pitched squeal that makes me inordinately happy. Finally, I'm able to get their attention.

"Thank you, Jazmyn. That was a great show. And Toni, that was awesome! I haven't seen you dance in a while. In my head, I guess you're always the Sugar Plum Fairy, but you slayed that." The reminder of one of her most hated roles from her childhood ballet days is a brotherly tease, and she flips me off before laughing. "I told you that you could do better than some dude named Topper. You're a certifiable backup dancer now, on tour with *The* Jazmyn Starr."

I give her a silly wink, thinking she'll keep laughing. But instead, she grimaces.

"Who's Topper?" Jazmyn asks, scenting gossip.

"Uh, the guy I'm dating," Toni answers shyly.

My eyes nearly bug out of my head. "What? I thought you broke up? You said he was stupid."

Toni gives me a withering death glare and a healthy dose of attitude. "Because he hadn't realized that he liked me yet. But now he has, and we're dating."

I am so confused. It must show on my face because Jayme pats my arm comfortingly. "She's a teenager, Carson. Take it from me, a teen girl's heart is like the autumn wind."

"What the fuck does that mean?" Taya asks, giving voice to the same thing I'm thinking, but when Jayme gives her an eyebrow, she nods. "*Oh* . . . yeah. Autumn wind . . . pumpkin spice . . . changing minds."

Before I can get clarification, Spencer interrupts, done with the foolishness. "Everyone, the roadies need to begin the teardown or we'll be here till sunrise, and I, for one, have plans tomorrow, so let's get to it. Snap, snap."

She claps her hands, and around us, people start moving. She's definitely the boss right now.

"What are you doing tomorrow? Or, uh, today, I guess?" I ask her curiously. It's late, well after midnight, and the whole park is closed except for the Great Garden. It'd been a perfect way to corral everyone toward the front gates for the last big show and then funnel them out.

"Sleeping," is Spencer's dry reply. "And drinking a bottle of white wine by myself on the back porch with a delivered dinner of carbs and cheese."

That actually sounds amazing.

"You deserve it. Hell, take Monday off if you need to," I tell her. "Both you and Kyleigh."

"Not sure that's a good idea," a flat voice behind me says. Dad.

I turn, already on edge. "I'm fine managing my people's work schedules and approving PTO without your input, Dad."

Dad's eyes narrow, giving me a hard glare. "I meant that it's typical to do a post-project review as soon as possible."

I blink, not backing down. "And if Tuesday morning is as soon as possible for our project lead to be in that meeting, then so be it."

Spencer steps between us and says quickly, "I'll be there Monday. There's already a team meeting on the calendar to go over the festival, as well as social media analytics. So no need to argue over useless hypotheticals right now. Save it for your next family dinner."

With that, Spencer spins on her heel and stomps off. Kyleigh follows her, and Toni and Jazmyn disappear to find Steve.

"Dayum, that bitch has sass. She ain't putting up with none of your shit. I like her." Taya clacks her nails together, catching Dad's attention.

He frowns snootily. "And you are?"

I wonder what Dad thinks when he sees Taya. She's dressed outrageously, speaks her mind without filter, and could probably buy and sell the entirety of Americana Land with a single phone call. But I bet he would never consider that, given the way he's looking down on her.

Jayme grabs Taya's arm. "Just leaving," Jayme tells Dad. As she pulls Taya away, she gives me a meaningful look. *Talk to him.*

Somehow, despite being backstage, it's suddenly just the two of us. The entire crew flows around us like we're in a bubble, doing teardown assignments without even pausing to consider our presence. We might as well be completely alone with the uncomfortable awkwardness stretching between Dad and me.

"Today was great," Dad declares formally.

I clench my jaw, waiting for the bomb, but nothing comes. After a moment, I grow restless. "But?"

He sighs heavily, taking his already-clean glasses off to wipe at them mindlessly with a handkerchief. It's a nervous habit when he's thinking of what to say. "But nothing. It was a compliment," he says. Shoving his glasses back on, he adds, "I don't know what to say to you, Carson. It's always wrong, no matter what I do."

I remember what Jayme said, that he doesn't know how to communicate, but that doesn't have to be it for us. I can show him the landmines, even if it means drawing him a map with Xs to mark each and every one. And if he still steps on one, then I can blame him. But now? Maybe he's just ill-prepared.

"You could've said 'good job' when you walked up. That would've been enough. But you called me out in front of my staff, undermining my authority when I was offering a well-earned reward to a project lead." Every word is stiff and forced, and I mostly want to walk away before he has a chance to respond because putting it out there so plainly makes me feel vulnerable in a way that irritates the hell out of me.

He looks as though I punched him square in the nose. "What? That's not what I was doing!" he shakes his head in confusion. "Not what I meant to do. I wanted to have the post-project review because this was amazing! I think the numbers are going to be through the roof."

I stare at him in shock. Never in a million years would I have taken his comment about Spencer not taking Monday off as excitement over a successful project. "What?"

He stares back at me and echoes, "What?"

Shit. I think Jayme was right. Dad's not perfect, but neither am I. And maybe he's not the full-blown asshole I've thought he was. Or at least not this time.

He's just flawed, like we all are.

I swallow my pride, as difficult as it may be. "Thank you. I'll get with the rest of the team on Monday morning, and then maybe we can meet in the afternoon to go over figures?" This is not about a meeting. This is an olive branch and a big step for us. "But Spencer and Kyleigh do deserve a day off."

"I'd like that very much," he says thickly. "And you're right."

I offer a hand, which he shakes solidly. "Good job today, Son."

Maybe we can both learn if given the chance.

CHAPTER 21

JAYME

I'm still in bed, drooling on my pillow, when my phone rings. I think I'm still dreaming about the cotton candy slushie I had yesterday, but maybe dreaming on a mega sugar overload isn't a great plan because the noise startles the hell out of me.

"Wut?" I mutter to my empty room, wiping at my chin.

I shake my head, working the cobwebs loose, and look around for an intruder. Or a giant cotton candy fluff that's going to consume me like the mist in Stephen King's story and melt me into nothingness the way my cotton candy dissolved yesterday.

I find neither. Only my ringing phone.

"Hullo," I groan into it.

"Jayme? Honey? Are you okay? Do I need to call an ambulance? Are you having a stroke?"

"Huh? No, Mom. Um oh-kay."

I can almost hear her judgment. "You don't sound okay. Should I at least call Javier downstairs?"

I blink, forcing my eyes to focus and my brain to work. I swear I can hear the gears creaking and groaning inside my head, but thoughts form into logical, though short, sentences. "I'm fine. It's early."

Mom laughs brightly. "It's ten o'clock. Half the morning's already gone. Why, I've already had coffee and pruned the flower beds with Sasha. Rise and shine, sleepyhead."

185

"I'm awake. Now." The accusation lacks vitriol because I can't seem to muster any with how tired I am. "Went to bed at four."

That's true, though I don't feel like I got six hours of sleep. Maybe the dancing and yelling yesterday got to me more than I thought? Or the go, go, go of helping all day? Either way, I feel like I ran a marathon carrying a twenty-pound weight with zero fuel.

I bet a raccoon weighs twenty pounds, I think nonsensically.

"Ooh, what were you doing? Visiting some hot, new club . . . or on a date . . . or hanging out with Taya?" Mom's ideas of what one can do at four in the morning are pretty sedate, but not nearly as boring as the truth.

"I was working," I confess.

She makes a clucking sound I know well. "Honey, you're always working. Don't overdo it. You're young. You should be out having fun!"

My sigh is underwritten with a groaning noise as I sit up in bed and rearrange the pillows and blankets so I can stay conscious enough to have this conversation. "I know, Mom. And I was having fun. Carson and I were overseeing a music festival. I even danced."

I don't realize what I've said until Mom repeats it back to me. "Music festival? Carson? Who's that?"

Crap.

Mom's good at reading between the lines. She has to be as the mother of five kids, though it was usually one of my brothers trying to pull something over on her. Not me. But there's no 'between the lines' reading needed at all. I threw her that bone, easy and overhanded.

"A client," I answer simply, though he's so much more than that. "Did you say you were pruning the roses with Sasha? How're they coming in?"

Mom isn't fooled for an instant. "Hydrangeas, and fine. Now tell me more about this Carson."

Damn it all, she knows me too well.

"Is that who's been keeping you so busy that you haven't called in weeks?" she continues.

Great, a little guilt trip with my morning wake-up call. I definitely didn't order that.

Though I don't often share too much with them about my job, the good thing is, I can tell my parents anything, even my work details. They are beyond well-versed in keeping things quiet. I could tell them something completely crazy, and they'd nod politely and tell me to be careful and do a good job.

I remember one time I told Mom about a client I was helping get into rehab and managing the image spins that go along with that. He'd wanted one last wild bash before getting sober, and I'd had to sit there with a doctor while he cut out his lines of cocaine. I didn't help him with the drugs, but he was higher than a kite while we figured out how to frame his issues to explain his addiction. It was sad, but he was also hilarious, and along with our work, we'd talked about everything from saving the Amazon rainforest to what makes the best tasting toast.

Avocado and honey was our decision as the winning combination.

But even with all that juicy gossip, Mom and Dad never said a word to anybody. They'd supported me, listened as I worked through processing my feelings, and held me when I cried happy tears as my client emerged from rehab a changed man. All that, and they never so much as whispered or gave me a side-eye.

Though their opinion was that the best toast is cinnamon toast made with fresh, fluffy white bread, cheap margarine, and pre-mixed cinnamon and sugar. Mom even told a story about it being a fancy treat when she was a kid. Dad had laughed and said he'd never had it until Mom made him some after they first got married.

"I'm sorry I haven't called. I've been busy." The apology is easy because I know Mom is just giving me a hard time. Mostly. She does worry when one of us kids doesn't check in regularly, which is probably what prompted this Sunday morning call.

"Mmkay, get to the good stuff." She smells blood in the water. Or at least some good tea.

"Carson is the CMO of Americana Land, the amusement park. He had an . . . incident, and we've been fixing it creatively." I go on to tell her the bare bones about what happened with Abby Burks and then how we've been tackling the issue from all sides, including the Freedom Fest. "It was a day-long event capped off with a young, hot, up and coming star."

187

"So like Woodstock, but electric," she summarizes, not correctly, but also not . . . incorrectly?

I snort unapologetically. "Yeah, sort of."

"I noticed you mentioned this Carson fellow several times, and my Google Image Search says he's quite the looker," Mom hints, though she's transparent as hell.

"You did not Google him while we're talking!"

I can hear her grin as she balks indignantly. "Yes, I did. He's quite the handsome young man."

I don't want to share too much here. Not because Mom won't keep it secret, but because she won't be able to help herself and will get excited about any potential prospect for me.

She's not rushing to marry off her only daughter, but I am the only one of my siblings who's not in a long-term, serious relationship. And given that I'm not even dating and I work so much, Mom worries the way only a mother can.

She doesn't want me to be alone when she dies, though that's hopefully years away.

And as if I'd ever be alone with my brothers and sisters-in-law around.

She's probably hoping for more grandchildren too. And for me to have a partner who makes me happy, of course.

I know where this is going, so I might as well take the onramp to the point. I sigh and admit, "Yes, he is handsome." After a beat, I add, "And smart, has a good heart, and all those other things on your checklist of a potential suitor for me."

"I just worry, honey. I'm not selling you off to the highest—or *only* —bidder."

I gasp, outraged. "Mom!"

She laughs brightly. "Just teasing. Mostly. But . . . uhm . . . do we like him?"

Her interrogation style isn't too harsh, but I fold like a towel anyway. She just sounds so hopeful that I can't bear to burst her dreams. Even if they're not cotton candy fueled.

"We do. A lot. He met Taya. I actually took him to her house but didn't tell him whose it was. He figured it out, though, and never said a word." I don't know why I'm trying to sell Mom on Carson. He doesn't need it.

Neither does Mom. I don't talk about guys, mostly because I haven't dated in ages, so the mere mention of a potential man is exciting to her.

"That's awesome, honey! When do we get to meet him?"

I laugh at her eagerness, but a yawn steals my oxygen. "We'll see."

"Oh, sorry, honey. You sound exhausted. Get some more rest, and make sure you don't stay up too late tonight," Mom recommends, as if I hadn't thought of that.

"Will do." I make a smacking kissy noise as if kissing her goodbye and hang up gratefully.

After I toss my phone to the nightstand, I scoot down in my bed until my head hits the pillow again. I don't want to sleep all day, but a couple more minutes couldn't hurt.

———

THE KNOCK ON MY DOOR IS EASILY IGNORABLE. THE FIRST TIME. AND THE second.

Then my phone rings again.

I peel my eyes open and glare at the offending interrupter. I don't answer, choosing to roll over and go back to sleep. But as soon as I close my eyes again, someone knocks on my door.

I throw the blankets off with a growl. "Can't I have one lazy day? I think I've earned it," I beseech the ceiling.

But because it's nothing more than drywall, it doesn't answer. Stomping to the door, I rip it open with a snarl. "Javier, the building had better be on fire."

Except it's not Javier. Even though he's the only person who knocks on my door on the weekend, and that's usually only if I've had a package delivered.

"Who's Javier?" Carson growls playfully as his eyes trace down my body and then lift to meet my eyes. "And do you always answer the door dressed like that for him?"

I suddenly feel very naked. And awake.

The building might not be on fire, but I sure as hell am with the way Carson's drinking me in. His blue eyes are full of hunger and promise dangerous fun.

I straighten my tank top, knowing my nipples are hard without looking down. I can feel them brushing against the soft fabric. "You know exactly who Javy is. The weekend doorman. And I could answer the door naked as the day I was born and he wouldn't care, though his husband would probably give me shit for it."

I grin even though it's not my best comeback, giving myself credit for the compound sentence since minutes ago, I could barely string two words together. Something else occurs to me. "How'd you get up here?"

He smirks at me devilishly. "Myron was at the door this morning. He said I'd been added to your list of approved visitors. I figured you'd done that?"

When I shake my head, we both realize at the same time. "Taya," we say in unison before Carson adds, "queen of the universe, apparently."

It's her stamp of approval for sure, which is not easy to come by. In fact, I'd say it's exceedingly rare. As far as I know, Taya doesn't like anyone past me, her few close staff, and her manager. The rest of the world, other than her fans, could disappear in a crack in the earth and she'd be fine with it.

"Come on in. I need a coffee IV, STAT." Turning around, I walk to the kitchen, swinging my hips a little extra because I know my sleep shorts leave the bottom of my ass cheeks hanging out. I hear Carson's sharp intake of breath, and then he shuts and locks the door as he comes inside.

I pretend I don't notice him watching me closely as I add water to the coffee maker and pop in a K-Cup. I ignore him as I grab a mug from the highest shelf, the one that requires me to stand on my tippy toes. I look deeply into my fresh coffee as if it holds the secrets of the universe.

"You're killing me," Carson groans. "And you know it."

My lips twitch as I fight a smile, and when I look up, I see that he's leaned back against the kitchen counter with his arms crossed over his chest as he studies me. He's dressed more casually than I've ever seen him, in athletic shorts, an Americana Land T-shirt, and tennis shoes. Carson looks amazing in a suit and sexy in jeans, but I think dressed-down Carson is my new favorite look. His legs look strong, his arms look like they could hold me up easily, and there's a sharp edge to him that says he can not only manage a conference room, but also a ball field.

Wait. That bag wasn't there before. Carson must have brought it with him.

"What's that?" I ask. I set my coffee down, forgotten in favor of what looks like a present.

"That?" Carson repeats, looking sideways at the red, white, and blue bag. "Just a little something I brought for you. I thought you could wear it today."

"You want me to change?" I ask, flirting with everything I've got. If he asked, I'd strip naked right here, right now.

Hell, he wouldn't even have to ask. I'm considering doing it myself and inviting him to christen my countertops with me. His phone dings in his pocket, and he sighs heavily. "I'd give anything to have a few extra minutes right now, but we've got people waiting on us."

"Who's waiting, and where? For what?" I know there is nothing on my calendar today. I double-checked twice before falling into bed last night . . . or this morning, rather. The next appointment I have is the post-project evaluation at Monday's meeting, and the top thing on my to-do list is emailing Patrick at Compass to catch him up on this assignment. Though that's mainly so I can brag a bit and remind him of how lucky he is that I work for him.

"You'll see. Go change." He holds the bag out, one finger hooked through the handles.

I want answers, but given the sober look on Carson's face, I'm only going to get them one way. I hop to it and run for the bag, snatching it and beelining for the bedroom. I reach in and pull out several pieces of Americana Land gear.

As quick as I can, I get dressed. Wearing a special edition Freddy Freebird shirt, athletic shorts, and flip flops printed with a flag design, I look in the mirror and nearly scream. My hair looks like I brushed it with a fork. It's a good thing my other assets were on display because hopefully, they were enough to distract Carson from this mangled nest on my head.

There's no time to wash it now, and if I'm right about Carson's plans, my hair is going to be a bigger mess by the end of the day anyway, so

I grab a ponytailer and twist my hair up into a messy bun. I then rush, furiously brushing my teeth, washing my face, and applying a quick but light bit of makeup, mostly mascara and lip gloss.

"Ready," I say as I walk back into the living room.

Carson is sitting on the couch, typing on his phone, but when he sees me, he drops the device to his lap and stares at me slack-jawed. I grin, posing. "Thank you for the gear."

He finds his tongue and says, "You look gorgeous. Very well-branded." He lifts a dark brow to see if I catch the phrasing.

"Yeah, I'm a walking, talking billboard. I hope I'm not standing on the side of the street, though. I don't think sign spinning is one of my many talents."

He rumbles, "That's okay, you have many, many others." He stands, guiding me toward the door. "I told Toni and the others to go on without us, so we can stay here all day if you want. But . . ."

He drops his eyes, and I freeze, feeling in my gut that he's about to say something important. Or difficult, at least.

"Carson?"

Lifting his eyes to mine, he confesses, "I'm excited to show you the park. To have a real day together, just us. You've done all this work to save it, but you haven't gotten to really experience it beyond the website descriptions. I want to share it with you."

Americana Land is a part of him. It's where he grew up, where he stayed even after becoming an adult, and what he's dedicated himself to. It's his past, present, and future. And he wants to share it with me.

That sounds amazing. And honestly, I can't remember the last time I had a day of relaxing fun.

"I would love that," I tell him seriously, letting him know that I understand how meaningful this is. Brighter, I add, "Let's go! I want to ride the Founding Fathers Carousel first!"

"Starting off easy, huh?" he teases. "I prefer going straight for the coasters."

"Of course you do."

We ride Carson's motorcycle to the park, the trip seeming faster riding behind him instead of in my car. And I notice that he has a helmet just for me now. It's not quite a key to his place, but it means something to me, and I know it means a lot to him. We skip the entrance lines and go straight into the park.

The photographers gathered there politely attack like seagulls at the beach. "Would you like a photo?" Carson looks at me in question, and I nod, so we pose for a couple of shots. The photographer hands us a ticket. "They'll be available after four at the photo booth."

And then the fun begins.

We ride the Founding Fathers Carousel first as I requested, but then we park hop around to hit other attractions. We ride the Twisted Tracks locomotive that reaches speeds of forty miles an hour, which might not seem fast, but when you're surrounded by 'steam' from the hot engine, it feels wildly fast. The Runaway Mine Car has an unexpected dip into darkness before shooting you out of the 'mine' into the bright day as the ride comes to an end with a loud quitting-time bell. We even take a break at the Boston Tea Party snack shop.

"Want a tea slushie, regular tea, or hot tea?" Carson asks without looking at the menu.

"I think I'll take a Georgia Peach Tea Slushie," I answer, scanning the options. "Oh, and a butter cookie. I don't think I've ever had one of those."

Carson orders our food. A moment later, the clerk hands me a small cup with what looks like a brown ICEE in it, except there's a straw with two peach ring candies threaded onto it.

"Oh!" I exclaim, surprised. In contrast to the small cup, the cookie is huge, easily the size of my hand and covered in a yellowy glaze with salt sprinkles. We find a bench in the shade and make quick work of the cookie, sharing the delicious, not-too-sweet treat. In contrast, the tea is super sweet.

"Oh, my God," I groan with the first sip, immediately pressing my hand to my forehead. "Brain freeze and sugar rush all at once."

Carson laughs. "It's the best, right? I started drinking those when I was a toddler. I don't know what my parents were thinking, because I swear they'd make me hear colors, and I remember running around like a maniac until I crashed. They'd chase me all over, and when I got caught, they'd plop me on Dad's shoulders until we got to the next ride."

I laugh at the idea of Carson as a little boy, ducking and diving through the crowds on a sugar-fueled mission to get to the bumper cars that look like miniature fifties classics. "Probably because of the full night's sleep after a sugar crash like that," I suggest.

It's the first time he's said something positive about his childhood, especially a happy memory with both his mom and dad. It reminds me of my phone call with Mom this morning and how I never had to worry about her and Dad. They were busy, but they always made time for us kids when there was something important going on, and I have loads of memories of happy holidays, game nights, and dinners around the kitchen table. Fresh appreciation for them fills my heart.

I take a few more sips of the slushie but leave the majority of the sweet drink to Carson.

"Okay, I think I'm ready for the roller coasters now," I tell him, and he grins happily.

"Let's do it!"

He takes my hand and leads me through the park to the red, white, and blue loop-de-loop monstrosity I saw on the day I first arrived. The sign proclaims it The American Revolution and is decorated with LED light fireworks. Ahead, I can hear riders screaming with each roaring pass of the car.

Nervousness zings through me. "I haven't ridden a roller coaster since my high school swimming team trip to Disney," I confess. "What if I throw up cookie and sugar syrup all over you?"

Carson shrugs. "Let's hope you don't. But if so, I'll grab a new shirt at one of our conveniently located souvenir shops," he answers, sounding like a two A.M. infomercial as he points out the three within viewing distance.

"Don't say I didn't warn you," I caution, but I smile. His light sarcasm feels good, another lens into him and a sign of just how deep we're getting. It's one thing to work together, another to give into sexual chemistry, but to actually enjoy each other's company and have fun doing silly activities and making jokes is a whole different thing. Especially for me. I'm not used to letting people in. In fact, I usually keep my walls solidly fortified, but Carson's burst through them, not like Taya did with a battering ram, but rather, with brutal honesty, an open heart, and hard work.

Carson flashes the same pass he's shown at every ride, and we walk onto the platform for the next ride. The people already loaded are chattering in excitement as they fasten their seatbelts. And then the floor drops out, literally. I reflexively take a step back, but it's only the section under the riders. And with their feet dangling, they disappear through the opening into the sunlight.

Another car shows up and it's our turn.

"You sure? You don't have to do this, Jayme." Carson says, suddenly serious.

This is about more than a ride. It's about trust . . . in him, in me. Hell, in the people who made this crazy-ass ride. If nothing else, Carson has shown me that I can trust him, and I don't do that easily. I'm maybe even more untrusting than Taya, and that's saying something. But where she's loud about it, I'm quiet, just keeping my distance and not letting anyone truly into my heart. But Carson worked his way in there anyway, and this is one way for me to show him that trust.

"I want to. With you." He knows I'm talking about more than this roller coaster too and takes my hand as we step onto the seemingly secure platform.

We sit in the seats, shifting around until the hard plastic is relatively comfortable, and then pull down the shoulder harness. The chest bar locks in place and then fastens between my thighs. Carson holds my hand while the workers do the safety checks. Suddenly, the floor drops out from beneath us. "Oh, fuck!" I instantly feel bad for cursing when there are kids in line and try to cover my mouth, but the harness prevents me from doing so. Thankfully, the kids closest to us seem to have not heard me and the parents are grinning at my surprised outburst.

"We'll be fine," he promises. "Hang on to the handles on the harness." He shows me what he means, and I copy him. The hard metal doesn't give me nearly as much comfort as holding his hand did, though.

But as soon as the car jerks forward, I grip them with all my might.

Carson told me The American Revolution isn't the tallest or the fastest hanging coaster in this part of the country, but it's fast enough for me as it winds around and then jerks to a stop with our feet dangling over a man-made pond area. The track above us clicks and clangs as it pulls us up to the top of a seventeen-story hill, letting the anticipation grow.

"Three, two, one . . ." Carson counts down, obviously having memorized the ride.

"Ahhhhh!" I scream as we drop and my heart jumps up into my throat. It's a steep drop as we accelerate to what I hope is our top speed before whipping into the first and largest loop. There's no chance to recover because it's a double loop, so we continue straight into the second one, and I feel myself lift out of my seat slightly. I grip the handles even tighter. We slide through a section with a few turns and then through a corkscrew.

Next to me, Carson is yelling and laughing in delight, enjoying every second, and his happiness sparks my own, turning my nerves into bubbles as I laugh along with him.

The ride is somehow both an eternity and over in a blip, and as we return to the platform and unload, my balance is completely shot. Staggering with my arm wrapped around Carson's waist for support, I gasp out, "That . . . was . . . amazing!"

His arm around my shoulder tightens. "I know. Let's look at the picture."

"There's a picture?" I ask.

He stops at a kiosk outside the ride's line and points at the television screen there. It's flashing through each car, showing the riders' faces. Some are terrified, some screaming in joy, and even a few look as though they could be chilling on the couch at home. And then our picture pops up.

Carson is smiling happily, but he's looking sideways . . . at me, as though he was making sure that I was enjoying myself. Something about that is very touching. Or maybe he's making sure I'm okay, because my mouth is open in a scream, my eyes so wide that you can see the whites all around my irises. I'm one of the terrified-looking people. But I know I enjoyed the hell out of the ride.

"We'll take that one," Carson tells the worker, and then he pays for the image.

"Here you go, sir," the kid tells Carson, giving him a piece of paper. "Scan this QR code and it'll take you to the website. Put in this code, and the image will be there for you. You can print it yourself, send it to a printing place, or even send it to a smart frame. No need to carry a print with you around the park."

Impressive! That's actually a great idea, I think to myself.

We go for a less intense attraction that mimics riding on a Mississippi river boat on a much smaller scale and then battle it out in a shooting game where you have to hit the target to make your horse win the Kentucky Derby. Carson wins and lets me choose the prize. The adorable stuffed horse is fluffy and soft, so when I see a little girl making goo-goo eyes at it, I gift it to her, hoping she enjoys it.

When we get in line for Bunyan's Breakout, I'm thinking that this might be the best day I've had in a very long time. I'm always head-down working, so doing something strictly for entertainment, with no undercurrent of networking or image repair, is a luxury I don't afford myself. But with the sun shining on my shoulders, a hot dog in my belly, and Carson at my side, I feel like I should indulge like this more often. It's good, old-fashioned fun, and I'm having a blast with Carson.

"Thank you," I say quietly. "For today."

Carson tilts my chin up, his smile gentle and sweet. "No, thank you. For everything."

He presses a soft kiss to my lips, and though some innate part of my brain yells about appearances and public displays of affection, I easily tune it out. I want to be a normal woman on a fun date with a normal guy, enjoying each other's company, and that includes a perfectly acceptable, sweet kiss.

There's a distant roar, and suddenly, we're covered in water, soaked to the bone. I blink, sputtering as water drips from my lashes, nose, and . . . well, everything.

"What the—" I laugh as I blink the water away and see that Carson is equally soaked, his hair swept over to one side haphazardly and droplets stuck in the scruff of his beard.

"Bunyan's Breakout!" a teenager shouts next to us, his arms thrown wide. He shakes his head like a shaggy dog, and water goes flying everywhere.

Carson covers me as if a few more drops are going to make a difference. "I didn't realize we were on the bridge," he explains, though I have no idea what he's talking about. Recognizing my confusion, he points behind us to where the rest of the line has stopped. "The line goes over the bridge, but if you don't want to get soaked, you cross between logs."

Apparently, we didn't cross in time with the ride's logs dropping over the edge and creating a wave of splashing water. Instead, our kiss stopped us right in the water's trajectory.

"Come on!" Carson shouts, grabbing my hand and running for the far side of the bridge. It takes me a second to realize there's another log coming, the kids riding in it already squealing in excitement. On the other side, Carson blocks me again, and I press my face into his wet chest, laughing. "You okay?"

He's worried, thinking I'm maybe upset or crying and not laughing, which just makes me laugh the harder. "I'm melting, *melting*! You've destroyed my beautiful wickedness," I whine, adding a cackle at the end. "What a world, what a world!"

He looks down at me, already smiling at my poorly quoted Wicked Witch impersonation. But then his smile falls and his jaw goes hard. "Shit," he hisses, and then he takes my hand. "Excuse us, please."

He's talking to the people around us in line as he guides me out of the back-and-forth que. "What's wrong?" I ask, confused at his sudden change in demeanor. "Carson?"

"Your shirt."

I look down to see that the white tank top Carson brought me has gone completely sheer, which wouldn't be so bad if my bra weren't also completely see-through. I'm currently dressed as a wet T-shirt contestant except there's no contest! Then I realize that Carson's shirt is sticking to him as well, showcasing the bumps of his abs.

"Uhm, your shorts too," I tell him.

He's still pulling me along, trying to get us out of public view, but that gives him pause. He glances down, seeing what I've already seen . . . the same way my shirt's hugging my breasts, his shorts are highlighting the outline of his dick. And it's apparent that my breasts and maybe that kiss are still having quite an effect on him.

In a flash, my work brain takes over. "We just did damage repair on your reputation. We have to get you out of sight or the next head-line's gonna be 'Carson Steen, pervert flasher,' with a close-up of your dick."

He groans, covering himself with his other hand. "Stop talking about my dick so it'll go down."

I can't help but giggle. "You said 'go down'." Shaking my head, I say more seriously, "Not the time, got it."

"This way," he says, leading me straight into a railing. But then he scoops me up and sets me down carefully on the other side. He hops the railing after me and explains, "There's one of those big dryers on the other side of this line of shrubbery."

The situation hits me fully. We're dripping wet, fully involved in an open and shut case of public indecency, ducking though bushes in the middle of an amusement park, hoping not to be seen. This is not my life. This is the kind of shit I save people from.

But here I am.

And I'm not regretting it. In fact, I'm trying to not laugh at the crazy predicament that all started with something as normal as a kiss on a bridge.

We pop out of the bushes, and thankfully, there's no one in line to use the huge dryer. We step into it, and the machine turns on, nearly blowing me back with its roaringly loud warm air. I peel my tank top from my skin, hoping it'll dry a bit faster that way, and Carson pulls his shorts out so you can't see how much he's tenting them.

Our eyes meet, and then we both burst out laughing. "You think anyone saw us?" I manage to bark out between laughs, hoping the answer's no. "Anyone with a phone, at least?"

Carson looks at me incredulously. "Jayme, *everyone* saw us. But the funny thing is, I don't think anyone cared about who I am. They were just laughing along with us."

"Shit. I'm so getting fired," I tease.

"Maybe next time we go out, we wear something a little less see-through?" he suggests, moving in close to block me from any passer-by's view. "The souvenir shop does offer this stuff in blue."

"Hey! You bought it for me. Maybe this was your grand plan all along?" I joke, knowing full well that he had zero intention of flashing my nipples or his dick to the entirety of Americana Land. Then what he said hits me. "Next time?" I echo with a sly smile, letting my fingers trace over the bumps of his abs that I can still see through his shirt.

"The Americana Land charity event. Would you be my date?" Carson asks formally.

This is more than a simple question. Potentially, Carson won't be my client by the time the event happens in two weeks, so any appearance together would be acceptable. But depending on how the numbers from yesterday's festival pan out, I might still be needed as a PR consultant for Americana Land, which would make a public outing like that a bad idea. Today, running around the park together is one thing, but an event like that will have photographers and media, and we'll be labeled as a couple simply by walking in together. Either that, or they'll imply that Carson is on such a short leash that he can't attend an event without a chaperone to keep him on the right path.

I don't know what to do. Obviously, I want to go with Carson. But I have to put his well-being first. Mine too, though that's secondary at best.

"I don't know what people will say about us," I confess, wanting him to understand that I'm not hesitating because of us, but rather because I'm worried about our images.

"When have I ever given a fuck what they say?" he observes baitingly. "Come on, live dangerously, Jayme. Gamble on me this time."

He makes zero debatable points, but nevertheless, he wins me over easily.

"I would love to."

CHAPTER 22

CARSON

I order in a full celebration spread for our Monday meeting —bagels, muffins, donuts, and even some bacon, egg, and cheese biscuits. Plus high-octane coffee, of course. Even though it's early, everyone rolls in with smiles and excited greetings. They know the Freedom Fest was a rip-roaring success too.

"Please help yourself to breakfast," I offer. "It's a small token of appreciation for all your hard work on the Freedom Fest project. I can't wait to hear everyone's take on how it went."

My team fills their paper plates and finds seats around the conference table, where I'm sitting with Jayme to my right and Spencer to my left, with a blueberry bagel of my own. When Spencer came in this morning, she informed me that she's going to bank the day off I offered, and I immediately agreed. "Thanks for coming this morning. I know it was a long weekend with a lot of mental and physical work, so I'm glad you're here."

There's a murmur of agreement.

"I'm going to turn the floor over to Spencer because she was the one leading the charge from the get-go on this."

I gesture to Spencer, who dips her chin at the recognition. She pushes her blue frames high on her nose and shuffles her notes. "Thanks, Carson. The festival itself went smoothly as far as implementation goes." She runs through a laundry list of items, each with a virtual check mark of success. "So, from set-up to teardown, I felt like it was a solid plan that was workable and manageable."

She glances to Kyleigh, who's sitting slightly behind her and confirms the assessment with an eager nod. Kyleigh's also banking her day off, and I'm proud of her. She's going to learn a lot working with and for Spencer.

"We did have one issue with a nervous artist, but it was resolved and the show began on time. It actually gave us an opportunity to have Toni Steen dance onstage, which was an unexpected bonus that brought an extra touch of that Americana Land family feeling to the festival." She smiles at me, making the near catastrophe sound like a prize toy in a cereal box. "And that section of the show was a complete hit."

I note that she leaves out any mention of Taya and her fierce pep talk, which I appreciate. Taya's see nothing, hear nothing, know nothing proclamation still stands.

"Any feedback on event implementation?" I ask the table.

Stephanie raises her hand the way she always does when she'd like to contribute. "I was on the frontlines with the vloggers I was hosting. The only thing I noticed in particular was the water supply. I think we would've been better off providing free small cups at water stations throughout the park in addition to the water bottles we sold. I understand the profit margin is higher on sodas and bottles, but with the heat and dancing, I think we should consider safety first, and dehydration could be a potential concern. This is something I'd recommend adding to our summer concert series as well, especially given those attendees are . . . uhm . . ." —she clears her throat uncomfortably before finishing carefully— "a potentially more at-risk demographic."

I make a note of that on the yellow pad in front of me because it's a great point. The Freedom Fest attendees were young, but active. The summer concert series guests are usually older, and though they rarely dance, the heat is significantly more serious during those months. "I agree. I'll make sure that gets on their project notes."

Stephanie smiles. "Thank you."

"Okay, well as Maury would say, 'the results are in'. Padma, can you go over the analytics with us?"

She glances down to a yellow Post-It note, and it strikes me as a bit sadistic that my fate, as well as that of Americana Land, can be reduced to a few numbers on a piece of paper that'll end up in the trash. Hopefully, that's not a bad sign.

She rattles off a bunch of metrics about site visits, engagement on social media posts and pictures, clickthrough rates, and hashtag usage. But all that detail obscures the bottom line until Jayme interjects. "Really? Great! What about the user generated content from the festival?"

Padma grins, leaning forward as though she and Jayme are having a private conversation. "I was saving the best for last! We've had so many posts, photos, and videos that we're filtering them into a separate section on the main website, and we added a tab on the blog header specifically for the festival because the video of Jazmyn Starr and King's Krossing . . ." She pauses dramatically, looking around the table to build anticipation. "It went viral!"

"What?" I'm shocked. I got online yesterday before going to Jayme's and saw the positive outpouring of comments about the festival, but I never dreamed any portion of it would go viral. "What does that translate to numerically?"

Padma flips her Post-It note over. "As of an hour ago, the video had seven million views in just over twenty-four hours. 7,200,018, to be exact."

Jayme jumps up and dashes around the table to Padma's side. "Can you pull it up now? What are the real-time numbers?"

Her eyes are bright with excitement as Padma clicks on her laptop to refresh the figures. "An increase of sixty-three thousand in an hour, give or take. Would you like the percentage change?"

I bet Padma could probably do the math on that in her head, or maybe already has, but Jayme shakes her head. "That's okay. Because those numbers are crazy good!" She points at Padma's laptop excitedly. "Any brand recognition or impression stats?"

Xavier clears his throat. "I won't speak to the online portion of that, but I can tell you that I interacted with hundreds of guests on Saturday as I escorted the photographer around. Every single person we talked to was absolutely thrilled to be at Americana Land and called the festival some version of brilliant." He throws his hands wide to encompass all the positive feedback he heard. "If each of those people posted one thing about the festival, the reach and impact for our reputation will be exponential."

"We did it," Jayme says quietly. Looking around the table, she meets everyone's eyes. Just her glance feels like praise and approval when she repeats, "We did it!"

She punches the air over her head, doing a weird shimmy shake of excitement that's accented with a few whispered yes, yes, yeses. Then our eyes lock, and I want to cross the room to hug her. I want to kiss her. I want to tell her thank you by writing the Declaration of Independence on her clit with my tongue, curlicued cursive and all.

But what I say is, "Thank you so much, Jayme. You rescued not just me, but Americana Land with this idea."

I hope she hears the truth, that she's done much more than help restore my reputation after the unfortunate Abby Burks incident. She's made me see myself in new ways, shown me a clearer vision of Dad as a human being, and given me hope for a future that includes her in it.

She clears her throat, sounding on the verge of tears. "It's been my pleasure, Carson, to work with each and every one of you."

She looks around the room once more, and it hits me that in succeeding, she'll be leaving. I'm sure there's someone else fucking up right this moment as we're sitting here, and they'll need Jayme's specialized help, so she'll be off to the next assignment. That's what she does, over and over. Rescue, restore, move on.

The idea makes me sad for her in a way. Always jumping from one crisis to the next, never knowing if the next one is going to be unfixable. Also, the idea of her being on a different assignment soon makes me miss her even though she's still here.

On the other hand, she's been worried about our dating while I'm her client. With the festival and our reputation repair being a complete success, I'll no longer be a client, allowing us to date freely. And that is something I'm very much looking forward to. I want her by my side, publicly and proudly claiming me as I do the same with her.

"I think we'll call this project a complete victory," I say, wrapping up the project review. "Keep an eye on your areas, and let me know of any wins that should be highlighted." I don't even mention potential losses, not wanting to jinx it, especially when there's always someone willing to shit-talk Americana Land.

After wrapping up the team meeting, Jayme and I head straight to Dad's office to catch him up.

"Hi, Boston," I tell Dad's assistant. He's wearing a lime green polka-dot bowtie with a navy vest and slacks today. "Dad around?"

I want to ask him where he gets his unique combinations, but Dad opens his office door as if he was waiting for me to appear. "Hey. We just wrapped up post-project analysis, and I figured you'd want all the details."

"Absolutely," he agrees. We follow him into his office, where he sits down at his large desk. The windows behind him overlook the park, which opened a few minutes ago and is starting to fill with weekday visitors. Jayme and I sit in the chairs opposite Dad, looking out at the rides that fill the blue sky beyond the glass.

I remind myself of what Jayme said about him and steel myself.

Benefit of the doubt. He's coming from a good place. He's a bad communicator, but don't make it even worse by jumping to conclusions and getting butthurt when he doesn't mean it the way you take it.

I'm not going to let anything Dad says knock me off the high I'm on right now, I vow.

It works . . . all through the numbers and statistics, feedback, and blog. He even watches the viral video of Jazmyn Starr and King's Krossing, giving my phone screen a faraway smile. "Toni really is something, isn't she?"

I laugh, realizing he didn't pay the slightest attention to the big star or the popular dance group. All he sees is his little girl all grown up and commanding the stage with her performance.

"Toni's amazing. She really helped save the day, and I think she had a lot of fun yesterday, playing ambassador." It's a new tactic. Normally, I would've taken Dad's compliment of Toni and run with it, assuming he was comparing us and that I was coming out on the unfavorable end. But I can see where that's not what he means at all. He just loves Toni, as he should.

And he loves me. He's just shit at showing it, but he's making an effort and that's all I can ask. And I can return the favor, making an effort of my own.

"Excellent." He hands me back my phone and catches my eye to say seriously, "Good job, Carson."

There he goes, making those efforts again. He did hear me.

To Jayme, he remarks, "Seems like you had a winning idea. I definitely had doubts." He laughs lightly. "But you pulled it off."

"The team did," Jayme corrects. "Carson and I worked hard on getting the talent signed on, but there were a number of people doing the important work of making the festival a success," she adds, claiming credit but also giving it where it's warranted.

Dad leans back in his chair, his elbows on the armrests as he steeples his hands. "I think you'd agree that knowing what a business or person needs" —he gives me a quick glance before refocusing on Jayme— "is a true talent. You were a real asset to the team to spark this idea."

My blood freezes in my veins at Dad's tone—slightly distant, a touch snobby. I've heard it before in business meetings before he cuts someone off at the knees. But why in the world would he do that to Jayme? She's done nothing but help Americana Land! And me.

Though she did call him on his shit, which I'm sure he didn't take well. But is he that angry?

And why is he reducing her contribution down to the initial idea? It's not like she could've made the suggestion and then bailed on us. We wouldn't have been able to do this without her and her connections.

"Dad—" I try to interrupt to prevent him from saying something he'll regret, professionally and personally, because if he hurts Jayme, I'm going to have a hard time stopping myself from lunging over his desk to punch him square in the nose.

He holds up a staying hand. "It's okay, Carson. I have a few talents of my own, one of which is seeing others. And I see something special in you, Ms. Rice. That's why I'd like to offer you a position with Americana Land."

The air is sucked out of the room, and time freezes. It's not Jayme he's blindsiding. It's me.

"What?" I mutter.

"Pardon me?" Jayme asks.

Dad smiles congenially as if he didn't just detonate a bomb with his words. "A position with Americana Land. You're something special. And I think you could take us to a whole new level. You've already shown that you're capable of it. Think of what else you could do here."

Jayme turns her head and looks at me. "Carson, did you know about this?"

I shake my head woodenly, my eyes still locked on Dad.

"I see," Jayme says before making a *harrumph* sound. "Ben, I'm flattered at the offer. Truly, I am. But my talent, as you called it, is in crisis image restoration, and I'm damn good at it." The boast isn't humble in the slightest, but there's no need for it to be. Jayme's claim is backed up with all the facts and figures we went over minutes ago. "I agree that what we've done here has made a major positive impact on your company overall, but you don't need me beyond that. As I've said, you already have an amazing team that can be innovative, bring ideas to fruition, and implement continuous updates to keep Americana Land progressing with the times to be profitable and relevant. And it's led by Carson. You don't need me. You need to let Carson do what he does best."

Once again, Jayme is fighting my battle, saying things I've said to him or have wanted to say. But her filter is nonexistent. Maybe because she does come in, fix things, and go. It must give her a sense of freedom to not be accountable to a boss that way.

Unfortunately, that's not the case for me.

But I'm done biting my tongue.

"Dad, it's grossly inappropriate for you to extend an offer like that without first discussing it with me. Unless your intention is to replace me?" I ask the question with a snarl in my throat.

"What?" he exclaims, managing to look surprised, confused, and horrified all at the same time. "I would never do that! What are you talking about? You two worked well together, so I thought it'd be good for everyone if we kept that dynamic. That's all." He's looking back and forth from Jayme to me as though he suggested something completely logical and we're the weird ones making it sound vastly different. As though he suggested a simple brunch and we heard 'a trip to Mars on flying horses'.

I look to Jayme, who tears her glare from Dad to look back at me.

Is he for real? her eyes ask.

Unfortunately, yes, I answer silently.

I sigh and spell it out slowly for him. "You basically offered her my job with me sitting right here. At minimum, you framed it as job sharing the single role. She's a consultant. She consulted, and now it's time for *us* to continue on as the Americana Land family we are."

I've realized something important through this mess. Dad really does have my best interests at heart. I've been reading so much into his every word and motion for so long that I've made him out to be this villain in my head, but the truth is, he's not. And my making him one needs to stop. No more biting my tongue or assuming he understands what I want or think. I have to speak up, spell it out with hieroglyphics if necessary for us to understand each other.

Actually, maybe that's a good idea. We're two men who've never been good at communicating, so maybe grunts and stick figures are the way to go.

"I didn't mean . . . uh, to offend . . . either of you. I'm sorry." He stumbles to find the words in his confusion, but his apology is simple and sincere, and I believe him, given the way he's continued looking back and forth between us like we're explaining quantum physics and he's stuck on the page-one intro in the textbook.

"It's okay," I tell him. "But it's a definite sign that we've got some work to do." We both know I'm not talking about whatever emails are piling up in our inbox, but rather some personal work to improve our relationship.

Jayme dips her chin at Dad deferentially, offering a polite smile. "Thank you, Ben. It's been a pleasure working with you."

He snorts out a self-deprecating laugh, truthfully stating, "I somehow doubt that."

"You were right about one thing." The tease catches both of their attention. I lock eyes with Jayme, and she lifts a brow, her smirk giving me permission for what I'm about to say. "Jayme and I do work well together."

With that, I drop my arm over her shoulder in a familiar move and she scoots closer to my side.

Dad snaps his fingers and points at us victoriously. "I knew it! Like father, like son. Sometimes, it hits you in strangest places."

A few weeks ago, I would've been murderous for him to say I'm like him in the slightest. Now, begrudgingly, I admit that it's true in more ways than one. And if Jayme and I are half as happy as he and Izzy have been after their taboo workplace romance, we'll be lucky as hell.

"Does that mean we'll see you at the charity event?" Dad inquires curiously.

Jayme grins. "I wouldn't miss it."

CHAPTER 23

JAYME

"*H*ey, Mom!" I say as I answer the door. She's sipping on an iced coffee from Starbucks and holding an extra one for me. I take it gratefully, sucking down a healthy amount in one go.

Mom watches with interest, scanning my face carefully. Probably to see if any checked luggage bags have appeared beneath my eyes yet. "Hi, honey. Up late again?"

She's more curious than accusatory, well aware that my work happens 24/7/365, but always worried that I'm working myself to the bone.

"Up early this time," I correct with a shrug as she follows me into my apartment and makes herself at home on the other end of the couch from me so we can catch up. "Patrick's got a new assignment for me."

"Where are you going this time?" More often than not, Mom knows it all—who I'm working with, where I'm going, and an estimate of how long the assignment will be. Even when I don't tell Mom who I'm working with, she always knows where I'm at when I travel.

"Nowhere. I can do this one long-distance. All done via Zoom and FaceTime. There's a time zone difference, though, hence the early morning."

After updating Patrick about the success of my Americana Land assignment and agreeing that our reputation consultant contract had been fulfilled, I took a few days off to catch up. But before I knew it, I was dealing with another crisis and managing the excitement that comes from figuring out the problem and how best to resolve it. Luckily, other than the early mornings, it's a pretty painless contract.

"Oh, good! Does that mean you can come to dinner next weekend?"

It's a completely straightforward question about a perfectly normal activity. Our family gets together for dinner as often as possible, usually once a month, and whoever can come does. My brothers and I are busy people, though, so if someone can't make it, it's not a big deal. But something about Mom's tone is suspect.

I take another sip of my iced coffee, giving Mom a more thorough assessment. She and I resemble each other—the same height, same size, same facial features, though her eyes are hazel compared to the brown ones that I got from my dad. And luckily, that hopefully means in a few decades I'm still going to be turning heads when I want to the way Mom does.

She's wearing slim-fit jeans, a button-up pink shirt with a popped collar, and designer flats. Her jewelry are all pieces I've seen before, her make-up is classic, and her hair is the same blonde it's been for years. Of course, that's because she gets it colored every four weeks to prevent any grays from popping through.

"Did you get a haircut?" I ask, realizing it's not only styled differently but a few inches shorter.

Mom fusses with the locks at the nape of her neck. "I did! Theresa talked me into trying something a bit edgier. Is it too much?"

She makes it sound as though Theresa hacked into her hair and gave her something trendy like Jazmyn's shaggy mullet. It's nothing like that. It's simple layers that she's currently styled into cute flips. "It looks great!" I reassure her.

"Thanks! I've got to keep up with that handsome stud I'm married to, you know," she teases.

Mom and Dad celebrated their fortieth wedding anniversary last year and are as ridiculously, grotesquely in love with each other as the day they married. Dad would never so much as look at another woman. Hell, I don't think he knows they exist. Even in their sixties, we've caught Dad giving Mom's butt an affectionate pat when she walks by. It's horrifying and adorable, and probably the reason they have five children. That, and Mom wanted to keep trying for a girl.

All in all, my parents set up all of us kids for an uphill battle with relationships because we've seen the real deal and won't settle for anything less.

"Yeah, 'cuz Dad notices your hair so much," I counter. She beams, knowing I'm right. As affectionate as Dad is, checking out Mom's hair is not high on his to-do list.

"What about dinner, though? Between you and me, I think Joel is going to have some big news for us." Her eyes are big with excitement as she baits me into asking for details.

Joel is my brother closest in age to me. He's a research scientist who works in something to do with plastic recycling. I think. Honestly, when he starts talking about his work, it mostly sounds like Charlie Brown's teacher to me—*wah-wah-wah-wah-wah-wah*. He's got a sense of humor, but you have to be pretty high-brow to understand the chemistry puns he throws out as though they're knock-knock jokes.

I wave my hand at her, telling her to spill it because I know she wants to. "Well, since you're twisting my arm," she says dryly, "Joel and Keilah are taking a trip this weekend to the beach."

She gives me a pointed look as though I totally know what that means. I wrinkle my brow. "Uh, good for them?"

Mom's swats at my leg. "Jayme! He's going to ask her to marry him!" she explains as if a beach vacation automatically translates to wedding bells.

Though she's probably right. My brother and Keilah have only been dating for a few months, but they're both analytical and probably decided that marriage made the most sense for their taxes or something logical like that. "You think so? It's pretty quick."

"Sometimes, you know instantly," she says dreamily. "I knew with your father."

I snort, nearly shooting iced coffee out of my nose as I laugh uproariously. "You did not! You've told us the story of how you met him at a party and thought he was a pompous jerk."

It's not a story they've told often, but I've heard it enough times that I know Mom and Dad met at a college party. Dad was the big man on campus, and Mom was a studious library lover. The gregarious business major and the perfect pre-med student . . . not exactly an automatic match made in heaven.

Mom pouts. "Well, he was a bit overconfident. But I knew on our first date when he let me win at mini-golf."

That I do believe. Dad is an expert golfer, and Mom can barely hit the ball.

"Sounds like you were an easy sell," I joke. "What about everyone else?"

Keeping up with my brothers, their wives, and kids is a full-time job. We have a group chat without our parents, but we mostly trade memes and tease each other so I'm not always up to date on the real stuff the way Mom is.

"Well, let's see . . ." She starts at the top with my eldest brother, James, and works her way down through John, Jordan, and she's already told me about Joel. Yes, five kids and five J names. I don't know why my parents tortured us that way. It was a constant roll call until they got the name they actually meant to say.

"James and Yuki bought a small property in Hokkaido. Kent wants to snowboard, and Yuki felt like it would be a good way to spend some time in the winter with her family." I nod along, not wanting to interrupt her, though it's cool that my nephew will get to spend some time on the mountain in Japan.

"John bought a new chef's knife. Something about steel quality and handle grip?" Mom shrugs, which is understandable because when John starts talking about his work tools, I glaze over too. A recipe you want to try out? Bring it on. A restaurant you want to visit? I'll go with you. But discussing the differences pan temperature has on meat, or blade thickness variations, is not exciting dinner conversation. "Sarah and the boys are doing well, mostly focusing on school and lacrosse."

"Jordan's waiting on his bar results. They should be in any day now, but I'm sure it'll be fine," Mom says proudly. She brags on all of us, though, not just those of us with fancy degrees. "He's continuing his clerkship in the meantime, and Drew got a promotion to lead architect."

"And then there's you . . ." Mom trails off, tilting her head in question. Guess it's my turn to fill her in on what I've been so busy with.

"After the music festival, we went over all the stats, and it was a total success. So much so that they actually offered me a job," I tell her with a laugh. "Obviously, I didn't take it."

"Of course not. You've worked hard to get where you are at Compass," she agrees. After a moment, she pries a bit more. "What about the Carson fella you mentioned?"

I smile into my coffee cup. "We're seeing each other."

"Oh!" Mom exclaims happily, clasping her hands. Or she would have if her coffee cup weren't in her way. Instead, she ends up slapping it so hard that the ice rattles wildly. "Oh," she says again, though in a totally different tone. She sets the mostly empty cup on the coaster on my coffee table. "Tell me everything."

It takes me a while to go through it all, from our tumultuous first meeting to the fun day riding coasters. As I do, bits and pieces come back to me, creating fresh smiles with every memory.

"You look happy," Mom summarizes.

"I am." We grin like giggly schoolgirls bonding over a cute boy asking me to the homecoming dance. Actually . . .

"Hey, Mom, you want to help me pick out a dress for a charity event?" I ask.

Mom's eyes widen. "Did you really just ask me that?" And in a flash, she's up and heading for the door. I laugh, not moving, and she prods, "Come on, let's go!"

"I have dresses, Mom. I don't need to go shopping. I meant for you to help me pick from my closet."

She throws me a look of faux-disappointment. "Are you sure you're even my daughter?" she questions dryly. "Not *shopping?*"

I head to my bedroom, knowing she'll be right behind me. "I'm not sure," I joke. "There's not much of a resemblance."

"You look just like me and you know it," she huffs, pushing me out of the way to get at my closet first. By the time I catch up to her, she's already lifting the dry-cleaning bags off my special occasion dresses. I have quite a few from recent years, including one that I wore to the Oscars with a client, though I didn't walk the red carpet. It was strictly behind-the-scenes.

"What about this one?" Holding up the pale lavender gown, I pose for her consideration.

She shakes her head.

"Hmm, what's the event for? That'll help us narrow it down," she asks.

"The local children's hospital. It'll be in the Great Garden at Americana Land, so sort of a garden party?" I flip through a few more dresses, looking for a particular one. "What about a floral one? As a nod to the garden location."

Mom tilts her head back and forth, considering. "Try it on so we can see."

I step out into the bedroom and slip on the dress. It's Wedgwood blue flowers over a cream background, with a hint of a ruffle along the strapless bodice. "I think this might be it. What do you think?"

Mom comes out of the closet holding a garment bag, which she lays on the bed. She twirls her finger in the air, and I spin as instructed. "Good option. Try that one too."

She points at the bag she laid down and then disappears back into the closet. I predict that I'll have to try on every formal dress I own before we narrow this down. Even then, Mom is likely to try to talk me into shopping anyway.

The next option is covered in bronze sequins, and while it's more body consciously fitted, it's also knee-length with cap sleeves. "Option two," I call to Mom.

She doesn't even make it out of the closet doorway before she starts laughing. "Absolutely not. You look like you're going to a political fundraising party and have to dress matronly." She squints her eyes as if that'll help her see me better, though I'm only six feet away. "Uhm, is that a mother of the bride dress, honey? It really looks like it."

"Mom! I like this dress!"

She shrugs. "I didn't say it was ugly. It's perfect for the right event, like your kid's wedding. Maybe I'll take that with me and save it for Joel's wedding?" she suggests as though afraid I might decide to go ahead and wear it to the charity event.

To be clear, I'm never wearing this dress again. Hell, I don't even remember when I bought it or why! But I can't get it off fast enough now. I might have to call Taya to see if I can borrow her flamethrower to give it a proper send-off. I'm pretty sure she has one.

"Go with the floral one," Mom decrees. "It's the right colors for Americana Land, especially if you pair it with a red lip. Festive without being a Betsey Ross costume. And the flowers are perfect for the garden."

"That's what I said thirty minutes ago!" I shout good-naturedly.

Mom doesn't admit that I was right. Instead, she grabs the sequined dress and shoves it back in the garment bag, telling me, "Well, now you know for sure."

CHAPTER 24

CARSON

*S*omewhere, even though there's a friendly rivalry between our amusement parks, there must be a Disney writer looking out for us. It's about the most reasonable explanation for today, which dawned with all of the meteorological perfection that only comes from the pen of a staff writer working in conjunction with the guys at *The Weather Channel*.

I seriously couldn't imagine a better day if I'd ordered it up like a build-it-your-way burger.

Today, the sun was out and the sky was a perfect cornflower blue, with just enough fluffy cotton ball clouds in the sky to break up the sunbeams from time to time. And now, as the sun is starting to sink toward the horizon, there's a light breeze blowing, not enough to be 'windy' but just enough to set the mood for this evening's festivities. Even the thermometer's agreeing, resting at an ideal seventy-three degrees.

Looking out at the crowd that's assembled for tonight's event, I change my mind. I don't think even Disney could have scripted this. No, this is on the level of cheesy Hallmark movie perfection.

The Great Gardens have never looked better. The charity event team definitely took some cues from the success of Freedom Fest, like the chandeliers hanging from the trees in nearly the exact spots the disco balls were. It's not only the chandeliers that give the Garden a special vibe, though. There are white tablecloth covered buffet tables holding candlelit appetizers, a bartender making custom cocktails, and waiters passing glasses of wine.

Tonight is a big night for Americana Land, and we'll most definitely get some great PR from this event. But it's also important for the children's hospital, and we want everything to set the right tone to open people's pockets. That's why we closed the park early and kept all the attention on the Great Garden, which is filled with the richest of the rich from this entire region of the country, all dressed in their swankiest of finery.

"What do you think?" Dad asks from beside me as we both scan the area. "Do people look charitable tonight?"

With a portion of today's park profits and this evening's charity event ticket sales, we've already raised over one million dollars for the children's hospital. And that's before any of the donations our attendees will hand over this evening. That'll add another million easily. Hopefully, the hospital can use the funds to improve the children's stays while they receive treatment, or even pay for the care for those who can't afford it.

"I hope so." Out of the side of my mouth, I whisper, "You think we'd raise as much money if people didn't have to get dressed up and eat tiny bites of fish eggs? Like I'd probably pay to not do that."

Dad chuckles, giving me a look of disbelief as if he were unaware that I have a sense of humor. "That's funny. But unfortunately, no. The process of dressing up, appearing in public, and networking is what opens their wallets." He tilts his head thoughtfully. "Well, that and their accountants telling them they need a tax write-off."

I laugh in return. He's right, but the follow-up to my own cynical joke is a surprise.

We're trying with each other, but old habits are hard to break. Now, we're at least able to have a civil conversation, and if I think he's being an ass, I call him on it. And vice versa. I'd call that progress.

It's not only us who've noticed the difference, either. People around the office are more at ease with us, meetings are smoother and more productive, and Dad and I even had lunch one day without Boston needing to intervene. Major progress.

"Is Jayme coming tonight?" Dad asks, carefully stepping into a touchier topic from the superficial event humor.

I can't contain the smile that steals my face. "She is. She's meeting me here because she knew I needed to be onsite early."

Dad hums agreeably as he takes a sip of wine. We return to overlooking the party in companionable silence. I'll admit that I'm scanning for Jayme, looking for her blonde hair and inviting smile. But that is not who I find.

"Motherfucker."

"What's wrong?" Dad responds quickly, following my line of vision and spying my brother. He sighs heavily, and for the first time, I feel the sadness that resides beneath the disappointment I'd always seen. "Did you invite your brother?"

I glare at Dad incredulously. "Of course not. I'm just getting over an image issue. The last thing I need is to remind people who I'm related to. Or that he's associated with Americana Land."

"I'll take care of it." With a straight back and a clenched jaw that looks vaguely familiar to the one I've seen in the mirror, he takes two steps toward Archer.

I catch up to his side. "We'll take care of this. Together."

Across the garden, Archer is smiling gregariously, looking like the epitome of a rich playboy as he laughs at something Mrs. Stephens, the billion-dollar grand dame heiress, just said. He's wearing a nice suit, though it's gray instead of the standard black, but it at least looks well-fitted.

"Archer. Mrs. Stephens." Dad interrupts their conversation without apology. Before Archer can say something, he smoothly tells Mrs. Stephens, "I believe I saw Delilah Jones over by the bartender getting a gimlet. Have you seen her lately?"

He knows that's a dangling carrot she will not be able to resist. Those two have been frenemies for at least a decade, smiley face to face while clearly trying to one-up each other in terms of fashion extravagance or other ostentatious displays of wealth. Hopefully, that means each of them ponying up huge donations tonight.

"Oh! I haven't seen her in ages!" Mrs. Stephens leans to look around Dad toward the bar. "Ooh! She looks amazing!" she raves. "I need to see what new secrets she's discovered. If you'll excuse me, boys."

She pats Archer's arm to excuse herself and wanders off. While I'm sure that their conversation will be sugary sweet while also laced with arsenic, I know they won't cause a scene.

Personally, I don't think Delilah Jones has done anything other than pull her hair back a bit tighter and had an expert makeup application, but what do I know? Hopefully, she'll share whatever tricks she's got with Mrs. Stephens, or at the least be flattered that she looks so good that people think she's had work done.

Either way, Dad got what he wanted—a moment alone with Archer.

I force a smile to my face, knowing it's more of a feral grimace than anything welcoming. "Archer, what are you doing here?"

He grins easily, taking a healthy swallow of the amber liquid in his glass. Scotch, by the smell of it. Dammit, I should have checked. Most of the permanent Americana Land staff know that Archer Steen is not to be given anything stronger than a Sprite. But he's been out of the picture so long, that lesson might have been ignored or forgotten. "Thought I'd come see what the family's up to. These parties were always so much fun. Remember?"

His eyes cut from Dad to me, measuring the impact of every word, every second. Rather than letting Dad get going, I grunt, "I do remember."

I'm thinking of the time Archer and I were working the party, acting as teenage representatives of Steen Amusements, Americana Land, and Dad, and instead of sticking to the party line of '*watch for the fresh, new rides and fun, Broadway-level shows*', Archer had gone completely off-script . . .

"Great? I guess if you call decades-old, county fair-quality rides 'great', then sure, that's how things are going."

"Archer, tell Mr. Richardson that you're kidding," I say, trying to mitigate the damage my brother can do in one sentence. When Archer's quiet, I speak for him. "He's joking. He just has a bad sense of humor." When he doesn't immediately agree, I bump him with my shoulder, trying to encourage him to get his shit straight.

Meanwhile, Mr. Richardson doesn't look convinced, and Archer smirks at me like the favored child who was gifted a pony for his birthday while I received a plastic horse cowboy toy from the dollar store.

Still trying to undo Archer's work, I add, "Dad's updated our classics, like the Founding Fathers Carousel, because they're the favorites people return to time and time again. Those rides hold their families' history along with the history of Americana Land. But we're also adding new attractions, like the Baked Alaska, our seasonal sledding hill with a firepit and s'mores station at the base. And the upcoming show, 'One If By Land, Two If By Sea'."

I sound like a used car salesman on his first day on the job, but it's the best I can do. I'm just a kid mostly repeating what I've heard at the dinner table. Not the PR department.

"Interesting," Mr. Richardson says dryly before excusing himself. He walks away, and I can almost read his mind and the shade he's going to throw on the park after this. Pissed off, I turn to Archer.

"What the fuck, Archer?" I hiss.

He shrugs as though he's not torpedoing Dad's company. Our company. Or at least what will become our company. Archer's just happy to be here, fucking off with free access to champagne and appetizers.

"It doesn't matter. Dad's never going to turn over the reins of this place to us. It's his baby, the only one he cared about." He snorts, correcting himself. "Other than Toni."

Realization dawns. This is about Toni, who's been sweet and innocent and is still not too sure how she fits in around a house that's probably bigger than the entire apartment building she was living in before things became public. "Are you seriously jealous of your little sister? Is that what this is about?"

"Dad has been putting Izzy and Toni before us for years. We knew it, even when we didn't know why or what he was doing. But we do now," Archer sneers.

Archer has a point, actually. The news of Dad's long-term infidelity and second family is fresh and new and sharply painful. And Archer's been taking Mom's ditching us extra hard, even sitting on Dad's front steps with a backpack, vehemently telling everyone that she's coming for him and that she wouldn't leave him behind.

She never came. And in front of me, I realize that on some level, Archer is still that kid on the porch steps, pouting at being forgotten by one parent and never appreciating the parent who loved him unconditionally, even long after he deserved it.

"Yeah, we used to grab as many desserts as we could and stuff them in our pockets, then we'd sneak champagne by pouring it into the water glasses until they were nearly full to the brim," Archer says as if what we did was always just good, clean fun. "And we'd sit under the carousel, down there with the dirty mechanisms in our penguin suits, and gorge ourselves while we talked about what we'd do to make this place actually fun. Remember that, Carson?"

I'll admit, we did have some fun together as boys, but those weren't the good old days, and Kesha and Macklemore aren't sitting around somewhere singing about us. Archer grew up. And I grew up.

And we definitely grew apart

"I do. I'm actually following through on those plans, making Americana Land better for today and the future," I tell him sternly, my voice a few degrees above freezing only by pure effort. Archer notices and scoffs.

"Making Americana Land bigger, better, wow-er," he mimics in a chiding voice. "You always were a people pleaser, the classic middle child."

It's more of a dig about Toni's existence than any of my personality traits, and we all know it.

"That's enough, Son. I think you've done what you intended tonight, and it'd be best if you leave now," Dad says tightly. He's trying his best to keep his cool, and for once, I'm on Dad's team.

We're not perfect, but after everything I've done to help Americana Land's reputation, I will not let Archer torpedo it again in one drunken outburst. This is bigger than a single, sullen teenage conversation with a donor. This is our charity event, and the hospital is depending on us to fundraise, not make a scene with our family drama.

"Time for you to go, Archer," I growl softly, grabbing his bicep tightly to physically drag him out if need be.

He makes a quick move, breaking my grip at the same time he shouts, "Get your hands off me!"

As he wanted, everyone's eyes turn to us curiously. I can already see heads tilting together as people begin to whisper.

He tugs his jacket down, straightening it as though I mussed him by merely touching him. "Are you saying my donation isn't as good as everyone else's? Think of the children."

His volume is loud enough to draw gasps from multiple people.

"Archer, do not try to manipulate your misbehavior." Dad matches his volume and forceful energy, not putting up with Archer's strategic posturing and very nearly correcting him like the wayward teen he once was. "Your exploits are well-known . . . unfortunately."

Archer's face reddens as he looks around, realizing that the attention he's receiving isn't leaning his way as he expected. Some of the crowd's reaction is due to the fact that Dad is a respected man among them and Archer is the quintessential spoiled brat child that many of them can relate to.

"Hello, gentlemen," a female voice sings from right behind me. I flinch reflexively, but it's Jayme who places her arm around my waist. "Oh! Archer, so nice to meet you. I've heard quite a bit about you. I'm Jayme Rice."

She extends her hand out in greeting, and part of me wants to stop her from shaking his hand. I don't want Archer to even touch her, as if my brother's poison will somehow infect her. But I swallow the growl trying to climb my throat in favor of some vestige of manners.

Archer's confusion is obvious as he looks from Jayme to me and back before he takes her offered hand. "I'm afraid you have me at a disadvantage, as I've heard nothing about you."

He means it to be a dismissive barb, but Jayme's already gotten what she wanted . . . a calmer, quieter exchange between the three Steen men. Everyone's attention is slowly starting to wane now that there's not a fight brewing. She's a fucking miracle worker.

I want to take time to appreciate how beautiful she looks, but with this Archer situation still on a tenuous edge, I can't. But I get a quick impression of a blue on white print dress with a short hem and a floaty train. Mostly, that's because when I glance down, I see that Jayme's tanned, toned legs are visible down to her white strappy heels. Her lips are blood red and smiling at Archer in an ominous way that makes me eager to hear what's about to come out of her mouth. I'm not one to let anyone fight my battles for me, but if there's one thing I've learned, it's that Jayme needs zero help and is particularly skilled in arenas like this. So I let her work her magic while staying very close and watching carefully, ready to jump in if need be.

She laughs as if Archer's told a joke. "Of course you haven't heard a thing about me. Why would Carson or Ben tell you anything? You've been gone for nearly . . . what's it been . . . ten years?"

Archer clenches his jaw, gritting out from behind his teeth, "Five, almost six."

Jayme scans his face, frowning. "Hmm, it looks as though it's been longer."

"You bitch."

In a flash, fury rises in my gut and my fists clench. I'm nanoseconds away from punching my brother in the nose for daring to speak to Jayme like that when she pinches the shit out of my waist where her hand was resting so gently a moment before. "Ouch," I hiss, reflexively jerking the chunk of skin she's got ahold of out of her reach.

And then she steps in front of me. I want to push her behind me protectively, but I realize that in moving between Archer and me, she's effectively protecting me. Not from Archer, but from my own reactions and the repercussions they would have.

Her face flat and no-nonsense, Jayme tells Archer, "What we're not going to do is get in a dick measuring contest here. Because news flash . . . I'll win."

The absolute weirdness of what she just said makes all of us blink, and I remind myself to ask whether she did that on purpose. I wouldn't put it past her because she's too smooth as she continues on. "Not in actual dickage," she clarifies. "I don't have one of those weak, sensitive but fun to play with appendages. I'm talking nature, soul, Archer. You're right, you don't know me, but I know every little thing about you. Even things dear old Dad and your brother over here don't know."

The veil on her threat is damn near as transparent as loose-weave gauze, and Archer raises a brow as he takes Jayme's measure, realizing for the first time that he might've misjudged her. "Who the fuck do you think you are?" he spits out. When Jayme stands stoic and strong, not showing an ounce of fear, nor any sign of answering, Archer turns to the one person he thinks he can manipulate best. "Dad, are you gonna let Carson's latest whore talk to me this way?"

Dad chuckles. "Jayme is many things, but she's no whore. And she's earned the right to speak to you any way she'd like."

Archer definitely didn't expect that. He sputters, eyes wildly clicking from Dad, to Jayme, to me as if he's not sure who to aim at next.

"You should go," Jayme tells him quietly.

As a last-ditch effort, Archer lifts his chin proudly, nose in the air. "What about my donation? If you think I'm giving to the hospital after this treatment, you're dead wrong."

It's Jayme's turn to scoff. "You were never going to donate anything, and we all know it. Hell, I know how much is in your checking account right now." Archer flinches, and even Dad and I side-eye each other behind Jayme. Does she really know that? "Did you have to borrow money to buy a ticket? Consider it refunded."

There's a hint of actual care in the question she asked, and I do wonder what else she knows about my brother's current life. She researched everything else to an obsessive degree, but it never occurred to me that she would dig into my long-lost brother too. He's not an issue or even a thought for me, but Jayme apparently wanted to cover all the bases, including any potential pitfalls. I should've known better. She's nothing if not thorough.

She turns around to Dad and holds out her hand expectantly. Taking the hint, Dad reaches into his pocket and pulls out several hundred-dollar bills. I watch as Archer's eyes widen ever so slightly, as though he's eager to get his grubby hands on that much cash.

Jayme smiles sweetly. "Oh, no, Ben. Charity is for the children who need it, like the ones in the hospital. Archer only needs his ticket refunded, nothing more and nothing less." She keeps three of the bills and tucks the rest in the belt on her dress.

"Here you go, Archer." She holds the bills up, and he snatches them from her hand. Patting her belt, she says, "And this will go into the big Plexiglass box at the front of the Garden. Thanks, Ben."

Dad chuckles as Archer glowers. "This isn't over."

He's trying to save a little face, but it's too late. Jayme's already shown her hand, and it's full of aces, so though she's physically slightly shorter than Archer, she manages to look down her nose at him. When his threats don't get the desired reaction, Archer spins on his heel and stomps out. We all watch until he gets through the gate of the Great Garden and disappears out of sight.

"Holy shit, I thought you two were bad. That one is definitely worse than you combined," Jayme jokes as she turns her attention back to Dad and me.

"Hey!" I retort, but inside I'm smiling a little. I know what she means, and it doesn't sting as much as it used to.

Dad, though, cringes painfully. "I know he's . . . what he is, but Archer is still my son. I'm sad that the choices I made affected him so much, but I'm disappointed that he didn't take control of his life and do better in spite of me."

I've never heard Dad's regret and pain quite so clearly. "Archer isn't your fault, Dad. There are plenty of things you can be blamed for, and I've been doing a fair job of laying those at your feet for years. But he's like that because he wants to be. You can't make him get over his past. Only he can."

I guess Jayme's turned me into Dr. Phil too, or in healing some of my own shit with Dad, I don't want him to blame himself for Archer's failures.

"Thank you," Dad chokes out, fighting down emotions I'm betting will come up again later when we don't have an event to manage. To Jayme, he adds, "And thank you too. Are you sure you won't reconsider that job offer?"

Dad melodramatically winks at me to let me know it's a joke this time, and the three of us laugh.

"Glad things are going better over here," Toni says, walking up. She's holding hands with a guy I've never seen. "With everything going to hell on a speeding train, I figured it couldn't get worse. What better time to introduce you to my date? Dad, Carson . . . this is Topper. Topper, this is my Dad. You can call him Ben. And Carson's . . . friend? Jayme."

Toni's eyebrows lift in question as she tries to suss out what Jayme and I are, and Dad holds out his hand. "Nice to meet you, Topper."

They shake, and then Topper offers a hand to me. It takes me a long second to react because I'm looking from Toni to Topper, trying to figure out the dynamic here. Toni is someone who's never met a stranger and is bold and full of personality. She said that Topper was quiet, but this guy is tall, skinny, with tattooed fingers and hands, and looks like he might shit himself over meeting Dad and me. He's polite, but judging by his rapid breathing and clammy hand, he's also very nearly having a panic attack. "Hi."

Next to me, I can see Jayme's eyes tighten, making me suspect she's going to be running an FBI level background check on Topper by the end of the night. Her protectiveness and thoroughness make me feel better about the situation . . . a little bit.

"You two look amazing," Jayme exclaims after we let go, purposefully warming the mood up instantly. "Your dress is gorge! And your jeans and tux jacket combo is very fashion-forward."

"Uh, thank you?" Topper says uncertainly.

"How did you two meet again?" I ask, hoping my voice doesn't sound like an interrogation and probably failing.

"School," Toni answers. "Topper has Art History across the hall from my World History class. We had lunch on campus and talked about the importance of art in documenting historical time periods."

"Art History, huh?" That tracks, given Topper's shaggy hair, smudged eyeliner-rimmed eyes, and chunky rings and bracelets. He seems like an artist. "Do you paint?"

"Sculpture," he says quietly. "Clay, mostly."

Toni snuggles into Topper's side. "He's really good with his hands."

Dad chokes on the sip of wine he just swallowed. "Excuse me?"

Toni rolls her eyes, even though I know she did it on purpose to give Dad a jolt. "Dad, don't be gross. I meant that Topper's talented. He even did a sculpture inspired by me that was included in a gallery show. Didn't you, babe?"

Topper is staring at Dad as though afraid he might attack over Toni's slipped phrasing. But he does respond politely. "The Moderne Gallery. The piece is called *Journey to the Core*."

Dad smiles tightly, and I give Toni a look of 'seriously?' This poor kid is not doing himself any favors because it absolutely sounds like he made an art sculpture of Toni's vagina and put it on display downtown. Silently, I pray that it was at least sculpted by memory and not an actual mold.

"It sold for one thousand dollars," Toni adds proudly.

Completely oblivious to what Dad and I are thinking, Topper gushes . . . or what I judge to be his level of exuberant gushing, which borders somewhere around that of a faucet on slightly more than dripping. "I custom mixed the clay and water composition to get the right consistency and then used all-natural pigments to hand-paint the dye onto the completed piece. It was important to get accurate color representation and placement of the various shades of red."

"I think I'd like to see this piece," Dad bites out. I don't think he actually does, but he does need to make sure that his daughter isn't posing for anything risqué or full-blown explicit.

Before I can say a word, Jayme takes Toni's available arm, clearly ready to save the situation. "Let's leave these two to prepare their speeches. Come on."

Jayme begins walking away with Toni in tow and Topper holding on to Toni's other side for dear life. I can hear Jayme smoothly making small talk with the two of them. Alone again, Dad looks at me. "She's something else. Jayme, I mean. Though Toni, too." He closes his eyes, muttering almost silently. "She might kill me, but I love that little girl."

I don't have the heart to remind Dad that his 'little girl' is nearly a grown woman now. It definitely doesn't seem like the time either.

"Jayme might even be able to save you from yourself, Archer from us both, or me from . . . anything." His grin is kind, showing the compliment to be sincere, and I laugh lightly. What else am I going to do when Archer shows up uninvited to cause drama, Toni's new boyfriend might be selling replicas of her womanhood, and Jayme somehow smoothly mitigates it all?

"Hopefully, she won't have to," I answer, searching the garden for where Jayme's disappeared to with Toni and Topper. When I find her, she's working the 'room' easily and comfortably, which is definitely more than I can say for the shy, awkward Topper who's now standing on the dance floor unmoving as Toni dances around him. He looks quite a bit like a sculpture himself, but at least he's smiling happily as he lets Toni do her thing. "If you'll excuse me."

Dad makes a sound of agreeability, but I'm already moving toward my target.

Now that there's no impending crisis, I take the time to get my fill of looking at Jayme. She's absolutely breathtaking, her smile sexy and her poise intriguing. Her dress has a tiny ruffle along the bodice that I want to trace with my tongue, but first, I want to tell her how amazed I am with her intelligence and ability to dance her way in and out of uncomfortable situations.

She's everything I've ever wanted, and I realize that Dad was right about something else. When you know, you know. Lightning hits me right in the chest, taking my breath away as it all comes into clear focus.

I'm in love with her.

Jayme worried that her seeing me at my absolute worst would make me want to distance myself from her after the incident resolved. Instead, I find that her acceptance of every part of me, even the ugly things I try to hide, makes me feel that much closer to her. She's in my heart, my soul.

And though this is not the time, nor the place, I need to tell her now. Right now.

"Can I have a word with you?" I rumble in her ear, taking Jayme's elbow and steering her somewhere slightly less in the middle of everything.

CHAPTER 25

JAYME

I'm in the middle of talking with the Fergusons, a couple who've attended the Americana Land charity event for ten years straight, when Carson grabs my arm. His growled request to talk to me privately doesn't bode well for me.

I thought we were okay when I shooed Toni and Topper away, but perhaps not? Maybe I should've left well enough alone with Archer, but he was beginning to make a scene. I might've completed my contract with Americana Land, but I'm not going to stand by and let that absentee asshole waltz in and undo all my hard work. Ben and Carson deserve better than that.

Carson pulls me off to the side of the Great Garden, opposite the bar, which gives us a small degree of privacy since that's where people tend to flock at these events.

"Carson, I'm . . ." I start to say, but he interrupts me.

"Be quiet. I need to say this and I want to say it right," he says in a harsh whisper. That stops my mouth and my brain, and I look up at Carson questioningly. His jaw is tight, his eyes tortured.

Did I fuck up that badly? Have I ruined everything between us?

I can feel the burn behind my eyes, but I blink away any thought of tears and press my lips together to keep from saying anything else. I'm falling apart inside, but I stand straight, throwing my shoulders back in defiance of the weakness I'm feeling.

You knew this was coming, Jayme. You saw him at his worst, and he's seen you jump in every time something goes the least bit awry. The balance is off exactly how you knew it would be. You should've let him handle his brother.

But Carson doesn't say anything. He stares into my eyes deeply, searching as if there's an answer to the meaning of life hiding there. Fuck knows, I don't have any answers. If I did, we wouldn't be in this situation where he's about to ditch me and I want to crawl into his arms and confess that I've developed big, deep feelings for him.

A situation where I still have some important things I need to tell Carson. But not if I've already messed up this badly. I let my gaze drop, my shoulders droop.

"Ah, fuck it," he mumbles. His hands cup my jaw confidently, tilting my face back up, and then he kisses me firmly. His lips claim mine, his tongue demands entrance, and I submit to his every desire.

I want this kiss. Even if it's a kiss goodbye. I match him move for move, our mouths working together to communicate things with this kiss that we won't otherwise say. I can taste the wine he was sipping earlier, but beneath that sweetness, it's passion, raw and powerful. I fall into every second of it, memorizing him as he sears his name into my soul.

I knew better. But I fell for him anyway. I don't regret it. It was a risk I willingly took, thinking I understood the cost. But I was wrong—the loss is so much greater than I ever expected.

Carson pulls back and whispers softly, "Do you understand?"

I understand everything about him, maybe even more than he understands himself. And I know exactly what he said with that kiss.

Goodbye.

Suddenly, I'm airborne. Not figuratively, like Carson's kiss has somehow killed me and turned me into a ghost of my former self. But literally airborne, as arms wrap around my waist from behind and lift me until my feet leave the ground.

Carson's face contorts in murderous rage, and I consider that it might be Archer coming back for another round. And then I realize what my surprise picker-upper is saying. "Hey, Jaybird! Think you can fly?"

No! No, no, no . . .

I can feel my face pale as all the blood rushes to my feet, turning them to lead as I try to kick free. This isn't how this is supposed to happen. Hell, it doesn't need to happen at all if Carson's telling me goodbye.

"Put her down," Carson snaps, moving in closer. He's on the verge of punching my assailant, his hands curled into fists and his rapid breathing causing his chest to rise and fall. The light in his eyes is completely gone. I think if he had a clear shot, he'd have already taken it.

My feet find the grass, though there's no solid ground here now. Not with my brother Joel here now.

"You must be the guy. Carson, right?" My brother holds out his hand, grinning easily and seemingly oblivious to Carson's anger.

I whirl around, pushing at Joel's chest. "What the hell are you doing here?"

Joel answers my hard glare with a laugh, and annoyingly, doesn't move an inch from my push. He's as strong as ever, and pushing him is like pushing a tank.

"Jayme." The single word is laced with enough warning to draw my attention back to Carson. His voice is tight, and he's telling me that I need to step aside or risk being caught in the crossfire when he goes after the guy who just picked me up out of nowhere.

It's almost . . . sweet, in a way? I'm not some damsel in distress who wants to be rescued. Hell, I am the rescuer. But the fact that Carson would risk everything we've worked for with his image over me is . . . sweet.

I sigh, not quite understanding what's going on here, but if I'm one thing, it's adaptable. "Carson, this is my brother, Joel. Joel, this is Carson."

"Your brother?" Carson echoes, the defensiveness beginning to dissipate ever so slowly.

"Her brother, Joel." He's still holding his hand out, but adds a congenial grin to entice Carson. "You passed that test with flying colors too, man."

Reluctantly, Carson shakes Joel's hand. "You test everyone Jayme dates that way to see how they react?" He's still mad, but at least mostly non-violent now.

"Not always me," Joel says easily with a shrug. "There's four of us, so we take turns. I got lucky because it's technically John's turn, but I saw her first. Lucky me." He pats his chest, proud of himself for nearly prompting Carson to beat the shit out of him.

But Carson's not the biggest threat here. I am.

"What are you doing here?" I snap. I dig my nail into the lapel of Joel's tuxedo, forcing him to take a step back, and give him the scowl I patented early in my life as the youngest and only girl in a family of boys.

Joel grins, tempting his fate.

"Speak, or I will wrap your ball sack around your neck and hang you from it like a noose."

My mouthiness is another blessing I received as the youngest child, and my skillful use of threats to the most sensitive of parts is an easy option with brothers. It still comes in handy with clients, though I tend to stick with targeting their pride, ego, and financial solvency over their actual body parts. But this is Joel.

He laughs. "Good one, Jaybird." When I don't laugh back, his brow furrows. "Wait. You didn't know we were coming?"

"Who's we, Joel? Who's here?"

But a sickening feeling is beginning to churn in my belly.

"Jayme, we're all here," he says grimly. "I thought you knew. Mom said—"

"What?" I screech, looking around as though wild, rabid wolves are going to attack us at any second from any side.

"Shit. I should've known, but how could I?" Joel rambles, more to himself than to me. His eyes clearing, he apologizes. "I'm sorry, Sis. Mom said you were raving all about this guy, Carson" —he pauses to look over my shoulder and give Carson a guy-friendly chin lift— "and that it's serious. She mentioned a charity event, and you know how it is, when Mom says get dressed, we put on the penguin suits."

I quit listening somewhere after 'we're all here', even though Joel is still talking.

"You're here. You're all here?" I mutter, hoping . . . wishing . . . praying I misheard.

Joel looks at me as though concerned I might collapse. "Jayme? You okay?"

Eyes wide with horror, I pin Joel in place. "He doesn't know." Joel blinks, but I don't. "*Joel, he doesn't know.*"

Realization dawns on Joel's face, and he looks over my shoulder again, this time giving Carson a pitying look. "Shit."

"Fuck. Motherfucking shit biscuit fart fucks."

"Go. I'll hold them off," Joel vows, spinning me in place and pushing me toward Carson. From behind me, I hear him say, "Nice to meet you. Hope to see you again." He doesn't sound sure that's going to happen, though.

Neither am I.

"Carson, I need to tell you something." I grab his hand, dragging him away from Joel. I need to find someplace private where we can talk. But everywhere we go, people are waving and calling out.

"Carson, the place looks fantastic!"

"Did you hear who's here? Good job, Steen!"

"Heard about that scuffle you had . . . good for you for saving Grandma Barbara."

"Oh! Carson, come meet the Lieutenant Governor."

Nope, nope, nope. We're not stopping. Not even for one of the most powerful men in the state. Because I haven't told Carson my one, biggest secret, and he's about to find out in the worst way.

Publicly.

I need to talk to him, control the narrative of how he finds out. Even if that kiss earlier was a goodbye kiss, he deserves to know the truth.

But Carson pulls on my hand, stopping me. We're near a small bench on the edge of the Great Garden, but I can't sit down. My nerves are too jittery, and my feet need to move as I search for the right words.

"Hey, are you okay?" Carson asks, concern etched in the tiny lines around his eyes as he looks at me carefully. "I don't mind meeting your brothers. I thought you said you were okay with them?"

I nod absently. "I am. We are."

"Then why did we ditch him and run away? What's going on, Jayme?"

If I'm a wild, raging tempest of a sea during a storm, Carson is a still, serene pond. I'm on the edge, about to jump, and he's calmly waiting for me to explain myself and my reaction to seeing my brother here.

"There's something I need to tell you," I confess.

"Okay, you can tell me anything," he answers easily.

If only it were that easy! "Remember when I said my parents are kinda like *Fight Club*? We don't talk about them?" He nods, humming in agreement. "Well, we need to talk about them right now because they're here."

I stop, freezing in place to see his reaction. But he doesn't get it. He couldn't, because he still doesn't know what I'm trying to tell him.

"I'd love to meet them. Unless you're not ready for me to meet them?" He sounds hurt by the very thought, as though he wasn't kissing me goodbye earlier.

Well, you were being a meddling meddler, I remind myself, knowing that Carson has every right to need to step away from me and stand on his own. And this informational nugget is only going to add to that likelihood.

I snort ungraciously, not quite a laugh, though, because this is anything but funny. "If only that were the issue. I'm ready, they're ready, and they already know about you, which is probably why they came. My mom's sort of impatient when it comes to us kids. She wants to see us happy." I say as if that's a bad thing. It's not, at all, but right this minute, I can't even begrudgingly cut Mom slack when she's forcing my hand. *"But you're not ready*. They're . . . they're . . ."

"Jayme! There you are, honey!" Mom's voice rings out from behind me.

My time is up. My chance to tell Carson, my opportunity to prepare him, and most likely, my relationship with him . . . are all gone.

I take a deep breath, apologizing to Carson with my eyes. I spin, putting him behind me as though that'll protect him. Or maybe protect me if he can't see Mom and Dad.

"Hi, Mom. Hi, Dad," I say flatly.

Mom smiles big, her shoulders doing a little shimmy shake of happiness. She leans in, kissing my cheek in greeting. "And you must be Carson," she says to him. "Wow, you are even more handsome than Jayme said!"

"Mom, Dad . . . this is Carson. Carson, these are my parents." Manners and politeness take over automatically, though I have no idea what I'm saying.

Dad looks at me with worry, his mouth turned down into a heavy frown. "Honey?"

Carson takes a big breath, the inhale audible to us all, and then swallows heavily. "You're Jayme's parents?"

Mom doesn't seem to notice the awkwardness and grabs Carson's hand, giving it a friendly shake. Dad extends his, but Carson doesn't take it.

He seems . . . gobsmacked. His eyes are flicking from Mom to Dad and back again, and I can virtually see his brain whirling between his ears. It's not the first time I've seen this reaction to my parents, but it's the first time it hurts like this.

"But you're . . ."

Dad helps as much as he can. "I'm Jameson Brooks, and this is my wife, Leah Brooks. I know Jayme uses her mother's maiden name professionally, so it's sometimes a bit of a shock that she's related to us."

A shock that I'm related to them? That's putting it mildly, Dad.

My parents—well, my Dad—is basically the present-day version of a Kennedy. No, more than that, he's more like Warren Buffet. Richer than God, his face on the cover of magazines proclaiming his financial prediction brilliance, his name on buildings and invitations to dinners at the White House. He's more recognizable than most politicians or celebrities. Hell, he's probably more notable than the Queen of England because while she rules a country, Dad directs and controls the global economy in ways I can't begin to explain.

But to me, he's just Dad.

The man who kissed my boo-boos, taught me to ride a bike, and would listen to me whine about math homework. Later, he was the man who encouraged me to chase my own dreams, step into my own spotlight, and be the captain of my own destiny. All things I was only able to do because he had the foresight, long before James was even born, to decide with Mom that they would keep their children out of the spotlight.

Because though Dad is a hugely known and recognized powerhouse and Mom has been on his arm in countless photos and at hundreds of events, the five of us kids are virtually unknown. Dad wanted it that way, and I've always been grateful for the opportunity at a somewhat normal life that choice gave me.

It's a secret I carry and trust few with. Mostly only Taya, and now . . . Carson.

"Mr. Brooks, Mrs. Brooks . . ." Carson repeats, finally shaking Dad's hand.

He turns his eyes to me, and I don't need my experience at reading people to understand what's lurking in Carson's eyes.

Betrayal.

We've shared so much. But I didn't share this with him. Even after I knew I could trust him, I didn't tell him.

My family is a foundational part of who I am, and I intentionally hid it from him.

I've seen this happen before with my brothers. Both John and Jordan had people react badly when they found out. One of John's exes even went so far as threatening to out our whole family. Seeing how that was handled was my first taste at image management and how things are handled behind the scenes. It's what started my interest in PR.

But I never thought I'd be on this end of an issue. I'm careful, so fucking careful. It's not that Carson isn't trustworthy, it's that I should've already told him, but I didn't. That's my mistake. There's no one to blame but me. No way to spin that or deflect from it. Especially when the proof is staring Carson right in the face.

"Welcome to our charity event this evening, benefitting the children's hospital," Ben says into the microphone at the front of the garden, starting off the formal part of tonight's event. "Maybe if you give him a little encouragement, I can get my son up here to say a few words too. Carson?"

The audience, oblivious to the tornado wrecking through my life and leaving nothing but debris in its wake, claps politely.

"Excuse me," Carson grits out. With a straight back and cold eyes, he simply walks away before anyone can say anything, heading up to the mic. He plasters a fake smile on his lips as he steps onto the small stage next to his dad. "Happy to speak in support of the children, Dad."

"Honey?" Mom whispers.

I turn around and see her and Dad huddled together. They're always a united front, solid and rock steady. A perfect example of a happily married couple, even after forty-plus years. But both of them look worried and confused.

"He didn't know," I intone. "I hadn't told him yet."

"Oh!" Mom exclaims, covering her mouth with both hands. "I didn't realize, Jayme. The way you talked about him . . . I thought . . ."

"I did too, Mom. I did too."

"I'm sorry," Dad adds gently. "But if he can't handle where you come from, who you are, then he's not the right one for you." His words have a bit more backbone to them, not liking anyone who dares to hurt his little girl.

"Thanks. I just thought . . . he was. But that's my mistake." I glance over my shoulder, seeing Carson with the microphone. He's smiling, but it's tight, forced, and he's purposefully not looking in my direction. "If you'll excuse me, I think I'm going to go home."

"Do you want us to do anything?" Mom offers, trying to make amends for overstepping with their uninvited appearance.

Guess I know where I got that trait, too. I'm a chip off the old blocks —both Mom and Dad.

"No, just go. Please. Leave Carson alone." To Dad, I ask, "Please tell the boys to leave him alone too." Dad's the only one my brothers are going to listen to about this. As soon as they find out that Carson flipped shit over finding out about our family, they'll be on him like stink on shit. And neither Carson, nor I, need that.

Especially Carson.

Even now, I want to protect him.

CHAPTER 26

CARSON

I go through my speech to the assembled crowd, thanking them for coming and supporting the children. I know I do because I can see them clapping, but I don't remember a thing I say.

Afterward, I work around the garden, shaking hands and making small talk. I can feel where my cheeks are sore from forcing the fake smile. But I don't register any of that, either.

I'm a zombie, but instead of *brainzzzzz*, my mind keeps repeating *Brooks*.

I feel like I've been blindsided—by Jayme, by information, and even by her parents' unexpected appearance. I don't know what to think.

Why did Jayme hide who she is from me?

We shared so much . . . hell, I shared everything, even my ugly family history and my feelings about it all. I thought she was sharing her soul with me in the same way. But she wasn't. I knew she had secrets, or at least she'd said she didn't discuss her parents. How was I to know, or even guess, that this was why?

Jameson Brooks. Jayme's father.

Are you shitting me?

"Everything's going well, it seems," Dad says, floating up on a cloud of philanthropy with a smile of success.

I blink, forcing my eyes to focus, making myself play the role of the even-keeled, steady, unflappable event host, even with Dad, despite the fire running through my veins. "Yeah, yeah. Going well."

Izzy tilts her head toward Dad's shoulder, looking at me questioningly. Of all people, she's the one not fooled by my act. "Carson, what's wrong?"

That gets Dad's attention, and he peers at me a bit more closely, even dropping his glasses down his nose to get a better look. "You okay? Don't tell me you're still ruminating on Archer? He's my son, and I'll always love him, but . . ." He sighs heavily. "Sometimes, I don't like him very much."

Izzy pats Dad's arm comfortingly. "He's troubled, that's for sure. But at some point, he has to take responsibility for his own shortcomings."

It's virtually the same thing I told Dad earlier, and on some level, I hope Dad can hear that and really let it resonate with whatever he feels about Archer's and my upbringing.

But Archer isn't my issue right now. Hell, I'd forgotten about the earlier incident. My brain's only thinking one thing . . . Jayme Rice is a Brooks.

"Not Archer. Jayme," I mutter. I run my fingers through my hair, tugging at the strands in frustration. "I . . . she . . . I didn't know . . ."

Dad and Izzy look at me in confusion, not understanding what I'm trying to say. A reasonable reaction, considering I don't know what I'm trying to say either.

Izzy guesses, though. "Did you two get into an argument?"

Dad's brows shoot up his forehead when I grunt in answer. "What happened? I saw the look in your eyes when you left me to find her. I know that look. Did she . . . uhm, not feel the same?" he asks gently, stumbling over the question as though he doesn't want to cause me additional pain.

"I didn't tell her. Or at least not in words. But I thought she understood. And then, her brother . . . her parents. It was a secret." I'm rambling, my eyes unseeing as I replay everything. Somehow, one thing does strike me through the noise of it all.

I can't tell Dad and Izzy who Jayme's parents are. I might not understand it, but she hid that purposefully, and I won't tell her secret. It's not mine to tell, anyway.

244

Because she didn't fucking trust me with it.

My initial confusion became something akin to disappointment, which is all too familiar, with years of being the second-rate child, mixed with so long spent being let down by my parents. But now, it's disappointment in Jayme, or maybe it's once again that feeling as though I'm still not enough?

I've dealt with disappointment before, and it quickly turns into anger, the betrayal stinging deep and hot. I want to lash out. I want to demand an explanation from Jayme. Honestly, I want to climb on my motorcycle and speed down a straightaway. Maybe if I go fast enough, I can go back and this will have never happened.

None of it—tonight, Jayme, hell, not even the whole Abby Burks incident that started this mess. Just wipe it all away.

"Her parents are here?" Izzy asks, scanning the dispersing guests. It's creeping up on ten o'clock, and for this crowd, that's a solid hour past their bedtimes, but Izzy would switch the charm on full-throttle for Jayme's parents. I know she would because she can tell how important it is to me. But it's too late.

I shake my head. "Were. They're gone."

I know that much because I looked all over for Jayme, her brother, and her parents during my zombie march. But to no avail. Still, I glance around again anyway, hoping that they'll have magically appeared so I can figure out what the hell's going on.

Shit, I'd even take Joel scooping me up from behind the way he did Jayme, and that's just wrong. But I'm that desperate to talk to her or someone who can explain this to me.

Because I need some answers. Now.

"Carson." Dad's voice is harsh and sharp, making me jump in reaction. I look back at him, and he places his hands on my shoulders, getting right in my face. "I don't know what's going on, but it seems like you need to talk to Jayme. Why don't you go find her and discuss whatever happened tonight? I'll finish up everything here."

"Are you sure?"

Of course, he's sure. It's not as though I'm doing any good here now. I'm distracted and barely going through the motions, which is something we can't afford after I just got done pulling my rep out of a nosedive. Truth be told, I think my righteous anger might be the only thing keeping me vertical at this point.

I nod and turn to go, but Izzy stops me. "Carson, you said, 'It was a secret.' I don't know exactly what you're talking about, but I do know a little bit about secrets and the damage they can do. Open honesty is the only way to be truly happy. You and Jayme both deserve that."

In that moment, I understand more than I ever have about Izzy. I never begrudged her falling in love with my dad or having Toni. And over the years, I've grown to appreciate that she makes Dad happy. I don't need to understand, I only have to respect that. But the beginnings of their relationship, when Dad was trapped in an unhappy marriage and likely making promises to Izzy, was a leap of faith on her part. Being Dad's secret was hard for her, making her feel less than, even when she was the one he loved.

Dad wraps his arm around Izzy's shoulders, pressing a kiss to her temple. "I love you."

Izzy smiles at me, telling me with her eyes, 'you deserve this, so go get it.' I nod, mouthing 'thank you', and take off for the parking lot.

I don't change. Riding my motorcycle in a tuxedo is a first, but it's happening tonight because I need to find Jayme as fast as possible and fix whatever's gotten messed up between us.

I fly toward her place faster than I should, pulling up to the curb and shutting the engine off in record time. Striding up to the door, I greet the doorman, "Hey, Myron. I'm here to see Jayme."

With a hard *thunk* that would be comical under other circumstances, I walk smack into the door.

"Fuck . . . ow!" I groan, rubbing at my nose. "What the hell?"

Myron grunts. "You're not on the list, sir."

I glare at him. "Yes, I am. You've let me in before."

He shrugs casually, but his eyes are flinty steel, daring me to make a go for the door again. Something tells me he'd really enjoy stopping me. "List's been updated."

"What? By whom?"

He lifts a wry brow, not needing to answer, and I basically want to smash his nose the way the door did mine. Though maybe with some actual bloodletting.

"Can you call her and tell her I'm down here?"

He seems to take delight in telling me, "It's after hours. You're not on the after-hours call list either."

I growl, and though his lips don't move, I swear to God, he's smiling at my frustration.

Calm down, man. You're not going to get in like this.

Right. There's got to be another way. I look up at the building, searching for a fire escape. I'm in good shape. I could probably shimmy up a pipe or something like they do in movies. No . . . no, I couldn't. Not that many floors. I'm not a goddamn ninja.

But I am desperate, and though I'm running on adrenalin that makes me think I could scale a building, I've got to use my brain.

"You ever wonder how I got this job?" Myron says conversationally, as though we weren't threatening death and dismemberment with our eyes a moment ago.

I don't even give him a look, pointedly ignoring him as I continue to think.

"I was Secret Service. Security detail, mostly. Investigations weren't my thing," he tells me with a shrug as if that's not impressive as hell. "After I got out, I wanted something easier, but I take my job seriously. This building is secure, no access points unguarded. The doors and windows are bulletproof. Phone lines are impervious to unapproved numbers. Cameras back up to the cloud instantly."

"So you're saying you figured out how to block spam calls?" I retort dryly, focusing on the least impressive thing he said because the rest of it . . . crazy talk.

"I'm telling you that you're not getting in unless she says so."

I realize the bigger picture of what he's telling me. "You're not a doorman, are you?"

He smiles, his teeth bright against his dark skin. "I am a doorman. One of the three best doormen in the city. Me, Javier, and Brad. We're a solid team."

I'm not getting in.

I pull my phone out of my pocket and call Jayme myself. The line rings and then goes to an automated recording. "Leave a message at the tone."

Beep.

"Jayme, I'm sorry. We need to talk. Can you call me, please? I'm downstairs with Myron. He won't let me in." I toss him a glare, though I know it sounds like I'm a toddler tattling on a classmate who didn't share his toys with me. Putting my phone back in my pocket, I tell Myron, "I'm going to be right over there."

I point to my motorcycle, and though he doesn't respond, I know he heard me. Confused, I sit on my motorcycle and stare up at Jayme's window. I can't even tell if the light is on inside. Maybe she's not here? Maybe she went to her parents' house? Would Myron have told me if that were the case?

I consider throwing rocks at her window. Myron said they're bullet-proof, but that doesn't mean she wouldn't hear a rock hitting one. I don't know if I could hit one that high, though. Probably not. I don't think Myron would take too kindly to that idea, either. Probably consider it an attack or something. I wonder if she could hear me if I yelled her name? Though that might get the police called on me for disturbing the peace.

My anger is starting to burn out, leaving only desperation in its wake.

After a few minutes, I get off my bike. It's not the most comfortable thing in the world, so I sit on the curb instead, staring at Myron. Though he's looking straight ahead, I know he's watching me.

I sit there for hours, I think, but finally, I climb back onto my motor-cycle. Myron tilts his head in goodbye, and I wave at him forlornly.

I ride home as the sun's coming up and head straight for the bar when I get inside. I pour myself a bourbon and flop into a chair with a heavy sigh. "Well, fuck."

"Ahh!"

The loud scream comes from the pile of blankets on my couch.

"Jayme?" I scramble to set my drink down and pull the blankets off, but instead of Jayme, I find my sister. "Toni? What are you doing here?"

My hope that it'd been some wild misunderstanding and Jayme was here all along while I was at her place is dashed as Toni wipes at her bleary eyes. I sit back down in my favorite chair, pouting.

"Where've you been?" she mumbles, still half asleep.

248

"Jayme's." Though not technically true, I'm not going to tell her that I've been hanging out on the street all night like some love-struck stalker.

"You made up?" she asks, looking hopeful and considerably more awake.

My eyes narrow. "What do you mean? What do you know?" I don't mean to sound so accusatory, but . . . actually, yes, I do. How does Toni know what's going on with Jayme and me when I don't even know?

Toni rolls her eyes. "Duh, you two are attached at the hip and then suddenly, you're on stage giving a speech and she's nowhere to be found. What'd you do?"

"You assume I did something?" I snap.

Toni drops her chin, frowning at me as if I said one plus one equals pizza or something else equally stupid.

"Fine. I might've overreacted to something she showed me. I mean, told me." I'm not going to out Jayme's secret to anyone, least of all my sister whose version of keeping something on the down low means not posting it to Instagram.

"Showed you? Told you?" Toni echoes, much more interested now. "Are we talking like a third nipple or that she likes her toes sucked? Because really, Carson, you shouldn't kink shame people or give them a hard time for something they can't help."

"What?" I shake my head, trying to make sense of anything Toni just said, but I was focused on how I acted while meeting Jayme's parents. "No, it's not . . . that. What?"

Toni laughs. "Okay, so not kinks. What did you do, really?"

She finally seems more serious. I take a slow swallow of my bourbon, thinking.

"She told me something important, and I was caught off-guard. Really off-guard." I laugh bitterly. "I didn't take it well."

"What'd she tell you? Is she a sleeper Russian spy?" Surprisingly, she's not kidding. Toni's being dead serious.

"No," I sigh. "I can't tell you what it is. It's her business, her story. But she should've told me a long time ago, not let me find out accidentally tonight."

"Or she should've told you whenever she was damn well good and ready. You literally just told me 'it's her story'," she mimics me, apparently thinking I sound like a whiny toddler, "so you don't get to dictate when she tells it. You dick-tator."

I blink in confusion, trying to suss out the actual advice from Toni saying dick repeatedly because now she's singing, "Dick-tator, dick, dick, dick, dick-tator. Hey, do you have any hashbrowns? Potatoes sound good."

She gets up and helps herself to my freezer, shuffling stuff around. There are no hashbrowns there, but I let her look while I mull over what she said. Somewhere in the craziness that my sister spews might actually be some good advice.

I set my bourbon down and let my head fall back, staring at the ceiling. "Fuck! I fucked up bigtime, Toni."

She claps, the sound echoing off the inside of the refrigerator where she's now looking for food. There are no potatoes there either. "At least you realized it fast. Go talk to her. Grovel and beg, maybe throw in that toe sucking and see if it does anything for her, and apologize."

I scrub at my jaw, the stubble getting rough, and ignore the parts Toni adds in for shock value. "I spent all night outside her place, but they won't let me in or even tell me if she's there. I called her, but it went straight to voicemail. I left a message, but she hasn't called back."

Toni sits down on the couch with a bag of chips she found in my pantry. "How desperate are you?" she questions.

I laugh bitterly. "Scale of one to ten? A fifty-seven." Toni looks impressed at my level of desperation. "I love her."

It's the first time I've said it out loud, though I realized it a long time ago, I think. It just took time to come to the forefront of my mind and form into a coherent thought, not only a feeling in my soul.

Toni licks her fingers ungraciously. "Like love-love? Willing to go to the ends of the earth love? Willing to make a fool out of yourself love? That kinda love?"

"Yes," I snap. "But I don't know how to tell her."

"I do." She shrugs casually as if she's not holding the key to my future happiness. "If you're willing to risk it all for her. What do you say, Carson? Are you feeling *lucky*?"

"All right, Dirty Harry. What's this idea of yours?" I ask. I should be careful. Toni comes up with some ridiculous things, but I really am that desperate.

"First, I have one question. Who's Dirty Harry?"

"Feeling lucky?" I repeat, adding a little gruffness to my voice in an attempt at an impersonation.

"Yeah, like the Google search bar thing," she explains, a world away from what I thought she meant.

"Right. Like that." I nod, feeling old. Trying to stay on target, I ask, "Your idea?"

"Let me grab my phone, and then you do what I tell you to. We'll have Jayme back in your arms in no time." Toni lunges for the end table, smushing the chips and grabbing her phone with greasy fingers.

This is who I'm turning to for help.

I think I'm doomed.

CHAPTER 27

JAYME

"*I came in like a breaking wall . . . all I wanted was to wreck your balls . . . all you ever did was bray-ay-ayk me.*"

I sing into my spoon microphone from my kitchen counter stage in Taya's kitchen. So what if I'm getting the lyrics all messed up? Who cares if I'm slurring words and flashing my ass to Taya as she loads the dinner dishes into the dishwasher? And who cares if I sound like two alley cats fucking while I do it?

"Don't quit your day job, bitch. Damn, you cannot sing a lick, and that's coming from someone who appreciates a little autotune when needed." Taya insults me and her own voice, which has never needed a lick of autotune, without missing a beat as she closes the dishwasher door. The slight vibration through the counter tickles my feet, and I dance around. It feels like an Irish Riverdance, but gauging from Taya's slightly amused eyes, it must look more like I'm trying to kill a cockroach and missing with every step.

I sink to the counter, my legs askew and hanging ungracefully off the edge, one toward the counter stool and one foot in the wet sink. "Ew, I have a noodle between my toes." I wiggle the aforementioned foot. "It's icky."

"No, you don't," Taya counters without looking. "I already washed down all the fettucine alfredo you didn't eat."

Taya swivels her head, daring me to argue with her. I can't. I know I didn't leave a single noodle on my plate. Hell, I might've even licked the parmesan cheesiness after I inhaled every noodle. Calories and cheese don't count when you're sad. It's a PR rule. One I taught Taya, and she learned well, given that within minutes of my showing up on her doorstep unannounced and with tears in my eyes, she'd ordered takeout, poured me a mega pint of wine, and helped me out of my formal dress and into an oversized sweatshirt.

I hadn't even known she'd be here. I'd planned to just invade her oceanfront home and wallow in my sadness.

"I fucked up, Taya."

"Duh."

"Hey!" I pout. "You're supposed to say 'no, you didn't' so I feel better."

"You know I keep it real. That's why you love me." She leans back against the island, her arms crossed over her chest as she grins at me.

"Why are you smiling? Can't you see I'm falling apart here?" I grab at my sweatshirt dramatically. Or I try to, but my hands slip drunkenly.

And as my balance is thrown off, so am I. I scrabble to grab the faucet to stop from tipping back off the counter. Thankfully, between my hand wrapping around the gooseneck and Taya firmly grabbing my ankle, I don't bust my head on the tile floor.

Upside down, I see Carlo standing in the doorway and wave at him with my one free hand. "Hi, Carlo."

I forgot he was here, if I'm honest. But he picked me up from the airport and drove me how he always does. Carlo is one of the few freelancers I work with when I need to travel, and he's been with me on countless trips to dozens of locations, though he's based out of Los Angeles. He's much more than a driver, though. He's more like a security-bouncer-assistant-jack of all trades. Plus, he never argues when I want to make a late-night drive-thru stop for greasy fries as long as he gets some too.

He doesn't smile, doesn't react in the slightest. He's the consummate professional. Like me . . . usually.

"What's up?" Taya asks him.

"Just checking in because I heard . . . noises," he answers tactfully. "Shall I call a plumber?"

I flip over, wiggling my way off the counter until my feet touch the tile floor. Lying face down over the counter for support, I tell Carlo, "I was singing."

"Singing?" he repeats doubtfully.

Taya snorts. "That's what she's calling it. We're not telling her that she sounds like a donkey giving birth, who's then been sampled and looped."

She makes an awful braying sound and then does some trick with her voice that makes it sound like a DJ scratching a record. It's eardrum busting. "Hey! I don't sound like that!" I shout.

"Mmhmm," she agrees without agreeing in the slightest. To Carlo, she says, "We're fine. As for Jayme here, I think I'm going to get her in the tub. She's got alfredo sauce on her foot, and now, it's all over my floor."

I twist around, trying to see my foot and Taya's floor. But it makes me dizzy, so I give up and press my cheek to the cool counter. The faint gray swirls in the white are tempting, and I trace one with my fingertip. "I should've told him sooner. I was going to. But Mom and Dad showed up before I had a chance. And he was already mad at me because of Archer."

"Archer?" Carlo echoes, a thread of concern in his voice. He's professional and likely does truly want to be on alert for any security concerns, but he's also not immune to gossip and he's well aware that I was here a short time ago with Carson Steen, so mentioning another man's name is a tempting nugget.

I try to clear my head and speak more carefully. He doesn't know who my parents are, nor does he need to. I gesture to Carlo with a tilt of my head. "Shh," I whisper to Taya, a finger to my lips. "He doesn't know either."

"She's been a bit all over the place," Taya explains, "but Archer is Carson's brother. I think."

"Yes!" I point at her, glad she got my hint about not telling Carlo about my parents. Nodding wildly, I add, "Correctamundo! Get the woman a prize!"

"A prize sounds like a great idea," Taya agrees, taking my hands. "How about a bath, and then you can tell me everything?"

She leads me out of the kitchen, and I'm reasonably sure I'm leaving a trail of footprints from my alfredoed foot.

Taya can deal with that since she told me I didn't put my foot in noodles in the first place, I think bitchily.

"Bye, Carlooo!" I sing, my excellent voice sounding like an angel's as it echoes off the hallway's twelve-foot ceiling. And not at all like a howling wolf. But then, why is he laughing from the living room?

"Ah-Oooooo!" I yell, and that ricochets even better, making me giggle, so I do it again. "Ah-Oooooo! I'm a she-wolf!"

In her bathroom, Taya helps me sit down on the wide edge of her small indoor swimming pool masquerading as a bathtub and starts the water. Her tub is huge and deep, and I can't wait to sink into it and let the water wash away everything that happened. Maybe it can even turn back the clock to last night at the charity event, giving me the opportunity to handle the Archer issue differently and tell Carson my secret. That's not asking for much from a foot and half of hot water and bubbles, is it?

"Okay, strip," Taya orders.

I balk, frowning. "I'm not getting naked in front of you."

Taya barks out a laugh. "You ain't got nothing I ain't seen before. And let's be real, if I wanted your kitty cat, I would've already had it."

"I don't . . . I'm not . . . Taya, we're friends. With *no* benefits." I wave my hands in a classic 'no way' motion in front of my clenched legs.

"Exactly," she explains, slowly grabbing my sweatshirt and working it up as though I might run away. To be clear, I don't think I could run three steps without eating floor. "Which is why I'm helping you. I wouldn't do this for anyone else, Jayme."

There's a bit of tenderness in her voice, and I'm reminded, even through my haze, that Taya isn't a caretaker. She's hard, defensive, and looks out for number one . . . always.

But she's taking care of me. Like a true friend.

"I love you," I gush suddenly, lifting my arms to help her get my sweatshirt the rest of the way off.

"You too, bitch. Now drop yo' drawers and get in the bathtub."

I do as instructed and even let Taya hold my hand as I step into the water so I don't slip and bust my ass. Or my head, which is starting to pound.

I sit down, sinking into the bubbles up to my chin. This feels amazing, and my muscles begin to relax instantly. I lay my head back, lolling over to find Taya. She's sitting backward in the vanity chair in the splash-free zone, her arms resting on the back as she watches me with an amused smirk.

"You look like your video," I tell her.

It's true. After she bought this property, she found an indie filmmaker with a cool style, invited him over, and they spent eight hours filming her singing in various places around the house. The filmmaker turned it into a private peek style music video with some cool overlay effects. Right now, the effects are coming courtesy of red wine, not digital processing, but Taya is sitting the same way she did in the video.

"Want me to sing for you?" she offers.

I shake my head, wincing at the movement.

"Good. Your turn then. Sing like a snitch and tell me everything."

I make a sound of displeasure, thinking I should've told her to sing so she'd leave me alone in my misery. But the water is loosening my tongue too.

"The charity event was amazing. But *Archer* . . ." I sneer his name, even though it's not his fault. It's mine, all mine. I'm the one who stepped into family business when it wasn't exactly warranted, or at least not yet. And I'm the one who didn't tell Carson about my parents. That blame rests solely on my shoulders.

"He showed up. I could see from across the garden that it wasn't going well. I didn't want people to notice, to realize who he was, but he was getting loud." My eyes drift closed, but I keep telling Taya what I remember. "Carson grabbed his arm, handling it himself, but Archer knows what buttons to push, where to aim for maximmmm-mum-mum impact."

I must go quiet because Taya prompts me. "So you stepped in?"

"Yeah, Carson can't afford a scene like that, so I did what I do best. I handled it for him." I snort out a bitter laugh. "Actually stepped between him and his brother and called Archer on his shit. Like I'm some white knight."

I wave my hand around, slinging bubbles everywhere. Taya chose her seat well.

"What did he do?" Taya asks.

"Called me a slut . . . no, wait . . ." I point a finger, trying to remember. "A whore. Yeah, that's it. He called me a whore. As if. My hourly rate is way too high for that."

"He what?" Taya screeches. "I'll kill Carson where he stands, slowly and painfully."

I open my eyes, looking at her in confusion. "Why? Archer's the one that called me a whore."

"Oh," she says, settling.

My eyes drift back closed. "Carson was mad, though. He kissed me. Goodbye." I don't have to be sober to feel the sharp stab of that pain again. The way he looked at me so seriously, like he couldn't believe what I'd done. The passion of the kiss, like he wanted one last memory of something good before walking away. And then . . . "My parents came."

"You finally told him. Good for you," Taya surmises, completely incorrectly.

I shake my head. "Didn't tell. Surprise!" I shout, holding my hands up wide.

Bubbles fling all the way across the room to hit Taya in the face. Taya makes a sound of surprise, and I open my eyes to see her mouth dropped open and her eyes wide, her skin covered with the white foam. I can't help but laugh and hold my fingers up in a frame around her face. Closing one eye, I look through the frame. "Yeah, girl. That's the money shot! Kaching-kaching-kaching!"

Taya laughs, wiping away the bubbles with a nearby towel. "I forgot what a fun drunk you are. But now that you're reminding me, I also remember what an annoying hungover bitch you are." After a minute, or maybe an hour—what do I know—she asks, "He didn't take the parent thing well?"

"Actions speak louder than words. And I didn't tell him. I didn't tell him about my parents," I mumble, drifting off.

I think I snore, or blow bubbles in my sleep, because suddenly, Taya and Carlo are helping me out of the water. I feel a soft robe wrap around me, and I burrow into it, wishing I could hide away from everything in its coziness.

"Bitch is a lightweight with the wine, but fuck if she don't weigh a metric fuckton," Taya grumbles.

I try to argue, but I'm just so tired. They must get me into the bed because the coziness of the robe becomes a cocoon of smushy softness. "I love you," I slur.

"Yeah, yeah. I love you, too," Taya says. If I could open my eyes, I think she'd be rolling hers.

"Not you," I laugh, thinking she's so silly. "Carson. I didn't tell him 'I love you.' And now it's too late." I sigh, giving into sleep now that I'm in such a soft, comfy nest.

I think I hear Taya and Carlo talking, but I might dream it . . .

"Have you been online?" Carlo whispers.

Taya snorts. "No. I've been dealing with her drunk ass. Why? Is the world going down in flames already? And look at me with no fucks to give."

She sounds snarky and carefree, two things she most definitely is not. Taya worries about everything. That's why she's so passionate. Even now, as big as she is and with as much money as she has, she worries it'll all poof! away somehow and she'll be left holding the bag. But she plays the bitchy role to perfection, and most people never suspect that there's a fear of becoming that little girl who was hungry for food and desperate for a hug underneath her barbed, rough exterior.

"The Carson guy. He's going viral."

"What did the asshole do now?"

"He's looking for you," Carlo says. "Come on, I'll show you." The door closes with a soft snick, and I curl into the fetal position.

But that doesn't make any sense at all. Why would Carson be looking for Taya? I mean, her ass is fabulous, and now that he's done with me, I could see why he'd hit her up. But Taya's not gonna hook up with him. She's the bestie of BFFs, and there's a code against shit like that.

"Fuck you! She's my Taya. If anyone gets that ass, it's me," I grouse to the darkness of my mind and the empty room.

CHAPTER 28

CARSON

"*Hey . . . uhm, everyone. I'm not sure how this works, but my sister says you can work miracles, so I need help getting this to Taya.*"

In the background, you can hear Toni whisper, "Keep going."

"*My name is Carson. You might've seen me recently in a viral video. Or maybe with Jazmyn Starr at the Freedom Fest at Americana Land. But those things are not what this video is about.*" *My throat bobs visibly as I swallow.*

"*I'm here because I fell for someone. Hard and fast.*"

The image whirls, refocusing on Toni's grinning face. "No pun intended. He's a dumbass, but not on a Dad-joke level yet."

The video flashes back to me, and trying not to look annoyed and utterly failing, I continue. "As I was saying, this person I fell for, we had . . . have something special, and I need to talk to her to sort some things out—like my feelings for her, what size diamond she wants to wear on her finger, and how many kids she wants. We need to plan out our forever. Taya, if you're seeing this . . . you know what I'm talking about. Who I'm talking about. I can't find her—she won't return my calls, and if she's home, she won't answer her door. Can you help me talk to her? Please."

I meet my own eyes in the video, noting that I look empty and forlorn. No, I look lovesick without Jayme in my arms.

I sigh, putting my phone down.

"This had better work," I tell Toni for the millionth time. I'm still not sure how I let her talk me into this, given how a viral video is what started all this, and Jayme told me that I'd be better served behind the camera rather than in front of it. But here I go again.

Toni doesn't look up from her phone but rather scrolls to the next TikTok video. "Duh, of course it'll work. It's literally blowing up."

When I'm not settled by her reassurance, she comes over to sit on the couch next to me and holds out her phone, letting me see the video I just watched on my own device. "Look, it's been viewed two hundred thousand times in less than twenty-four hours and shared hundreds of times. Taya has been tagged dozens of times, so even if Jayme is avoiding you, Taya won't. She'll either respond to tell you to fuck off or to negotiate a settlement, hostage-style."

"Jayme's not a hostage," I counter.

Toni laughs, pushing at my shoulder. "You are such a dumbass. Of course, she's not. You're Taya's hostage. She's got your dick in a vice, threatening your very future. Or at least your shot at happiness in whatever future you have. And she's a quick draw. Everybody knows that."

"Not helping," I grunt morosely.

Toni posted the video first thing this morning, and it went big pretty quickly with the #helpmeTaya tag she added. I guess the speculation over what I did and just how profoundly I fucked up—because of course I did—is helping push views up too. Toni tells me that there's even a debate going on because some people think my wanting to put a ring on Jayme's finger and a baby in her belly is sexy as hell, and others think it sounds asshole-ish and crude.

I don't care what they think at all.

I care what Jayme thinks. And what she wants. Ring or no ring? I don't care. No baby or a houseful? Whatever. I just need to tell her that I love her and apologize for my shitshow of a family rearing its ugly head again, right when her amazing one showed up for her in a big way. And of course, for my horrible reaction to that in the moment.

I'm still beating myself up for freezing, and then for my lightning-fast flash through every trigger point I have from my own family history. Now, I'm stuck on desperation . . . for Jayme.

I still can't believe her parents are the Brookses, but I've done some reading today. Not the tabloid fodder speculation stuff, but rather the real deal information that's out there. I wasn't surprised by anything I found.

There's very little to nothing about Jayme's brothers, and only Jayme's PR work. And certainly nothing listing any of them as Jameson or Leah Brooks's children. But there's plenty about her mom and dad and their dedication to philanthropy, where they work in the trenches with hands-on help as well as their financial assistance.

Jayme is who she is because of her family. She spoke with love and affection about her brothers, and that's because her whole family appears to be happy, healthy, and well-adjusted. I'm not sure what that's like, given the clusterfuck that mine is, but I can appreciate that they are so close, they're willing to circle the wagons protectively against anyone and anything that threatens them.

I won't let that be me.

It's not me.

I would never do anything to hurt Jayme and will take her family secret to my grave if that's what she wants. Because all I want is her in my arms again.

I sag into the couch, staring out the window blankly.

"Oh my God! Oh my God! Oh . . . my . . . God! Carson!!!" Toni yells from the kitchen, getting louder and louder with each exclamation point. "Look, look, look!"

She runs into the living room, jumping over the back of the couch and landing in a perfect crisscross position next to me with her phone shoved in my face. "We did it!"

"What?"

Toni scrolls up and then back down, restarting the TikTok video. Taya's face fills the screen . . .

"Listen here, you motherfucking bitch boy. You got my girl drunk-singing sad songs, and I don't put up with that kinda shit. Not over some dude who can't get it together for the best thing to ever happen to him."

Taya looks up and down, and though it's through the screen, I feel as though she's scanning me personally and finding me severely lacking.

My heart sinks. She's not going to help me find Jayme. Sure, eventually, Jayme will go back to her apartment, and I could be the guy who stalks the front curb, desperately waiting for her. Or I could go stand outside the gates of her parents' house and beg the security camera or guard I'm sure is stationed there. But by the time I get to plead my case with Jayme face-to-face, it'll be too late. She's already writing me off, I can feel it in my bones.

All I need is a chance to plead my case and apologize, time to explain and vow my silence.

"But for some asinine reason, she thinks you're it. Though I'm not catching that vibe just yet. So I'mma tell you what . . . she ain't home. She's with me."

Taya thumps her chest and lifts her brow to emphasize the words, daring me to not understand what she's saying. But I get it loud and clear. Jayme is at Taya's beach house in Los Angeles, where she took me.

"I need to get to LA right now!" I shout, standing up.

Toni grabs my arm and unceremoniously jerks me back to the couch. "Keep watching," she orders.

"My crew got together with her peoples and set it all up. You do what you did before—like deja vu that shit—and get here by seven o'clock tonight. I'll make sure she's ready. Or sober, at least."

She looks off-screen, her mean-mugging façade dropping for a split second, and I know she's looking at Jayme. Why isn't Jayme saying anything herself? Is this some plan of hers? If so, I'll walk right into the lion's den and play whatever games she wants to play for a chance at fixing this.

"The rest is up to you. You better use that tongue for something more than pussy licking too, boy, because my girl needs a first-class apology before you treat her like the queen that she is."

She licks her lips obscenely, finishing with a smacking noise that leaves her meaning crystal clear, before clacking her now blood-red nails at the camera. And then the video starts over.

"I hope you got all that," Toni tells me. "'Cuz I'm not sure what she's talking about."

"I understand," I reply, nodding impatiently. "I have to get in touch with the private plane company right away to fly to LA." I'm already up and running for my bedroom, throwing socks, underwear, jeans, and a T-shirt in a duffle bag. As I head into the bathroom for my toothbrush and deodorant, Toni stops me.

"Okay, so to the airport, get to Jayme . . . then what?"

"What?" I mutter, considering my razor. I haven't shaved in a couple of days and my scruff is getting a bit prickly. If I'm going to spend some quality time between Jayme's thighs, I don't want to leave her scratched up. Hopefully, I toss it in the bag too.

Toni claps her hands sharply, demanding my attention. "You're going step one to step ten, skipping all the in-between. What are you going to do? How are you going to apologize? What are you going to say?"

I freeze. She's got a good point. But then again . . .

"I'll wing it. Speak from the heart or whatever," I growl, not wanting to slow down. I have to hurry. I glance at my watch.

"How long do you think it'll take me to get to the airport? Plus flight and drive time in LA." I'm trying to add in my head, making sure I can get there by seven o'clock. Did Taya set me up for failure by making an impossible deadline? I wouldn't put it past her.

But I think I can make it.

No, I know I can.

"Yeah, that's done so well for you in the past," Toni says wryly. "Maybe just think about it on the flight? Write some notes on your hand or something," she suggests.

I grab my bag, rushing for the door, but I take the time to do one last thing. "Hey. Thank you," I tell her, pressing a kiss to the top of her head. "Wish me luck?"

Toni's lips lift incrementally. "You won't need it. You've got love on your side."

I hope that's enough.

MY MOTORCYCLE ROARS LOUDLY, ECHOING AGAINST THE METAL OF THE hangars at the airport. I beeline for the one Jayme took me to last time and find a plane sitting on the runway out front. A flight attendant is standing at the steps.

I park quickly and run toward her. "I think you've got me down for a flight to LA?"

"Yes, sir. Please board. We'll be departing momentarily now that all our guests have arrived," she says politely.

All guests?

I climb the handful of steps into the plane and see exactly who the flight attendant was talking about. Jameson and Leah Brooks are sitting side by side, holding hands with stiff backs and straight faces, obviously waiting for me.

Shit.

Toni was right. I should've prepared.

But I'm not letting Jayme's parents get in my way. If Jayme tells me to fuck off, I'll consider it . . . after begging, pleading, and doing anything I can to get her back. But her parents? Nothing they can say or do is going to stop me, short of throwing my body out the door of the plane at ten thousand feet.

"Mr. Brooks. Mrs. Brooks," I greet them, offering a handshake. Maybe next time, it'll include an accompanying smile and some charm, but not now. I'm single-mindedly focused on one thing —Jayme.

Jameson Brooks, the most powerful, richest, most influential man on the face of the planet, looks to his wife. She smiles softly, and only then does he take my hand. There's something intimate and meaningful about that moment between them, and I'm reminded of one of those cheesy sayings about there being a strong woman behind every successful man. I think Leah is that for Jameson.

With a start, I realize that Izzy is that for my dad, too, in a way my mother never was and never could be because they weren't a partnership.

I want Jayme to be that for me, the way she has been through this whole Abby Burks thing and the Freedom Fest. She's taught me so much, saving me from myself and showing me that I can be better, do better without taking stupid risks or turning my back on my family.

Equally as importantly, I want to be that for her. I want to learn all her history, not the edited version she's forced to share to keep her secret safe. I want to make her dinner when she has a hard day and rub her feet while she bitches about some crazy celebrity she's trying to help un-fuck their life. I want to know what she thinks about, dreams about, and more.

I want for us to be each other's support systems, lifting each other up through hard times and celebrating good times together. I want us to be partners in every sense of the word. My strength behind her success, and hers behind mine.

"Carson. It seems we have some things to discuss," he says gruffly, as though he'd rather discuss his last colonoscopy or get right to the no-parachute skydiving on my part.

"Before you get to threatening me or telling me why I'm not good enough for your daughter, I want you to know that I love her. I was about to tell her when you—"

"Oh, no!" Leah gasps in horror, her hands balled in front of her open mouth. "I'm so sorry!"

Jameson sighs, his shoulders dropping from their intimidating, wide-spread position. "Well, that changes things, now, doesn't it?"

I risk a tiny smile. "It does?"

"Have a seat. We're about to take off." He waves at the flight attendant, and she closes the steps to the plane. A moment later, the engines begin to roar and my belly lifts along with the plane.

I'm coming, Jayme. You might've fixed my situation before, but I'm going to fix this deal between you and me. Once and for all.

CHAPTER 29

JAYME

"*F*ix your face. You're sitting over here looking all squishy." Taya smushes up her face with her fingers, pressing her cheeks up and temples down, while adding in a dramatic frown.

"Why? Let me brood in peace," I whine. "You already made me put on clothes just to come sit out here when I could've just as easily sat on the back patio."

Okay, *clothes* is probably pushing it. I changed from a robe into Taya-branded leggings and a fresh sweatshirt. Not exactly high fashion, but I'm only sitting on a blanket on the beach behind Taya's house. The important thing is that I'm here when I could be curled up on the couch watching *The Princess Bride* for the seventy-third time. Or sitting on a pool lounger watching the same thing on the outdoor television.

Sure, sunsets are pretty. But there's no big rush to see this particular one. There'll be another one tomorrow, and maybe I'll be in a better mental space to appreciate it then. Because right now, I wish the sky, which is beginning to fill with oranges and pinks as the sun starts to dip lower, would actually catch fire. That would bring me a little joy because it would reflect what I feel inside.

The wine last night seems to have washed away my sadness, and once the hangover wore off this morning, the only thing remaining is anger.

I gave Carson everything I could and was on the verge of giving him so much more. My truth. Now, however undeservedly, he knows it. I want to think he's trustworthy with it, but I have doubts. And fears.

Fear that he's broken my heart into irreparable shatters.

Fear that he's mad at me for not telling him.

Fear that he'll tell the media about my parents, and this life I've so carefully crafted will fall apart in his wake.

Fear that even now, I wish he'd tell me it was all a stupid dream fueled by anxiety and too many PassionFlix movies.

All that pisses me off. I am not a person who lives by fear or allows it to control me. I follow chosen paths with pre-plotted goals and strategized outcomes in every area of my life, both professional and personal. The one time I go astray, everything goes to hell in one of my mom's Chanel purses without my predicting it.

That's not true. You knew it would go like this.

I sigh, knowing that I'm right, at least on that. I warned myself before I ever gave in to this thing with Carson. I cautioned my own heart about getting too attached because I've had work relationships go full-stop once the job was over. People are finicky and don't like being reminded of their shortcomings or their past bad acts. I'm a walking, talking reminder. I wanted it to be different this time, but . . . it wasn't. And then, adding on the whole family surprise reveal didn't help a bit.

I'm off my game, and I can't have that. I need one of my own classic pep-talks, or maybe one of Taya's no-bullshit ones, so I can get back on the right track. Not whatever wrong way roadway I've been on.

Okay, do what you do best, girl. Let's examine the facts so I can figure out how to best back out of this mangled car wreck I'm calling my life . . .

Carson Steen. A client. A risk-taker who encouraged me to live dangerously. A tortured heart that I helped heal but that couldn't handle my own family drama. A man who made love to me on this beach, just a few hundred feet away.

I look over to that spot . . . the one where he sat back on the sand and I straddled him until we were spent with exhaustion and sore with sand burns. Wistfully, I can almost see us there.

Well, him . . . I can see him there.

Wait.

"What the fuck?" I whisper, blinking and rubbing my eyes. But he's still there . . . no illusion.

"Damn, he's got finesse, I'll give him that. I told him seven on the dot, and man is here at six-fifty-eight," Taya says, tapping her gold watch.

"Huh?" I say dully.

"Girl, that man has been going viral trying to track you down. Best you listen to what he has to say."

Without any explanation, she gets up from our blanket picnic and walks back through the sand toward her place. She calls out over her shoulder, "Yell for Carlo if you need help with the body! I'm sure he knows the tides or whatever shit you gotta know to make Prince Charm-Your-Pants-Off disappear."

That's exactly the kind of thing I should yell at her for saying. Public threats of murder are kinda frowned upon, after all. Or at the least, they're admissible in a court of law. Thankfully, there's no one around to testify against her, given the stretch of beach Taya owns.

Carson is stalking toward me in slow motion. His jeans are rolled up to his knees, and his bare feet are leaving imprints in the sand behind him. He looks dark and thunderous, backlit by the setting sun but also fearful that I might bolt like prey running from a predator.

I am no prey. I'm a predator all my own, with years of experience dealing with assholes who think they know best. Or certainly better than some young, blonde PR consultant bitch. I click into that well inside my core that takes no shit and kills any potential prisoners. Because I won't risk my life for someone unworthy, and Carson proved himself that with his reaction . . . to my dealing with Archer and to my parents.

Just because he's here to take it back doesn't change that.

"Why are you here?" I demand, already planning and considering my possible responses depending on whatever he answers.

"We need to talk. First and foremost, are you okay?" he growls, stopping several feet away from my blanket stronghold.

That is not one of the things I thought he might say. "Yeah?"

He grinds his teeth. "You left the charity event, and I couldn't find you anywhere. I was worried, and then mad. Mostly worried." Quieter, he confesses, "And hurt."

It could be a list of emotions without reference, except that I can see each of them cross his face, with the pain resting there the longest. Plus, I've felt the same way.

"Did you get drunk and sing sad songs?" I ask with the smallest hint of acknowledgement.

He huffs out a wry laugh. "I spent the night with Myron."

"What?"

"I wanted to see you, but he wouldn't let me in or tell me if you were even there. So I waited." He shrugs as if that's no big deal, but I know sitting outside my building while Myron contemplates the different ways he could end your life in ranking of least to most painful is more than most men could withstand.

"Then what?" I ask, suddenly interested in how he went from a Myron hangout session to here on the sandy beach with me.

He takes two steps closer, still standing over me. Not in a looming way, but rather as if he's waiting for me to invite him to sit, letting me control the pace. "Then Toni had the idea to enlist Taya for help. The video of that went viral, which you can yell at me about later, but it worked. She responded, telling me where you were. I don't know if she arranged the flight or if that was your parents." He tilts his head, thinking.

"My parents?" I pat the blanket impatiently, gesturing for him to sit down because this I need to hear.

He approaches slowly, on guard as he lowers down next to me. "They were at the airport. Flew with me to LA so we could talk."

"They're here? What did they tell you?" I ask suspiciously.

"They went back home, just wanted to talk to me." He looks deep into my eyes. "They apologized for 'springing themselves on me', as they called it. They thought I knew. I apologized for being a frozen idiot because I didn't know." He drops his gaze to the blanket. "And then they told me some cute stories about you as a kid. My favorite one was when you tried to go to college with James by enrolling yourself in classes online. That sounded like something you'd do."

I can't help but smile. "That's one of my favorite stories too."

James, as the oldest, was the first of my brothers to leave home, and I was missing him before he was even gone. It only made sense for me to go to school with him. Well, at least it made sense to me. Until Dad found out I'd used his credit card to pay for enrollment and Mom had freaked out about my leaving home, even though it was nearly a decade away at the time.

We're quiet for a moment, and I watch as Carson's fingers dance closer and closer to mine, testing and giving me time to stop him. I should. I know I should. I've already made this mistake.

But I don't want to stop him.

And that's why I do.

I get up from the blanket, shaking my head. "I can't. It's a risk I can't take again. I'm sorry."

I try to run for Taya's house, tears already spilling down my cheeks, but the sand slows me down. I make it as far as the beachy brush before Carson's voice on the slight wind cuts through my raging mind and breaking heart.

"I love you, Jayme."

My feet get caught in the sand, and I stumble, tumbling to the soft ground.

"Shit," Carson hisses, following me down. "Are you okay?" he asks, brushing his thumb over my cheek gently. I think he's asking if the no-big-deal drop to the sand has hurt me, but his eyes scour my face and I realize he's not asking about that at all. He wants to know why I'm running from him.

I scramble to get out from underneath him, needing space, even if it's only a few inches, because my anger is about to explode out. I need to say it and he needs to hear it, but I'm still trying to shield him and get him slightly out of the blast zone. "No. No, I'm not. I got in the middle of you and Archer because that's my job, Carson. It's my job to protect you, your image, and Americana Land. And Archer was purposefully trying to ruin it all and you very nearly let him. He was baiting you." I shake my head vehemently. "I won't apologize for saving you, and if your ego can't handle that, then that's on you."

Carson flinches as if I slapped him, but then a look of confusion wrinkles his brow. "What are you talking about?"

"You came and grabbed me away from the Fergusons. I could tell how mad you were, but you didn't even explain or let me explain. You just kissed me like I've never been kissed before, taking any last bit of myself I had left for your own and then pulling away like it . . .

like I wasn't worth it. I knew what that was—a goodbye kiss. And now, you're telling me you love me? It's too little, too late."

There's a hitch in my voice that I wish wasn't there, but he's broken me, turned me into a puddle of needy longing.

"You didn't understand," he rumbles as he shoves his fingers through his hair, getting sand everywhere. He looks disappointed. In me? Himself? Fuck if I know at this point.

"Carson, obviously, communication isn't a strong point. Can we try it with small words, maybe? See if that helps." It's a bitchy thing to say, way beyond the pale for even how I would speak to a client who needs a bash upside the head to see reason. But I'm so confused, and like Carson confessed to earlier . . . hurt.

"Not mad about Archer. Embarrassed. Not goodbye. I love you." Carson grunts the words out caveman-style without the slightest bit of a smile. In fact, his face is stone cold and flat, giving no hint of the emotion behind his words.

I dissect what he just said in a slow, almost wondering voice. "I thought I overstepped with Archer. But you weren't mad at me for that?"

He shakes his head, one dark brow lifted wryly. "Sexy."

Okay, that is not what I took from the dark looks he was giving me. Could I have been reading him wrong? Was my judgement that clouded by my own worries about overstepping?

"The kiss wasn't a goodbye kiss?" I question.

Instead of answering with his words, he's on me. His weight presses me back into the sand and his mouth covers mine. His lips move over me for a second before I react, and then, when I return the kiss, his tongue demands entry. He claims my mouth, taking my breath away, only to breathe life into me once again.

I realize what he's doing. He's kissing me the way he did at the event, but it seems so very different. It's not a goodbye kiss at all. I can tell that now. He loves me. That I can feel with every press of his body to mine, every glance of his thumb against my jaw, every tender lick of his tongue over mine.

Oh, God! Did I really get it so wrong? Was he saying I love you all along?

But even if that's true, he didn't react well to meeting Mom and Dad.

The thought is a dash of cold water on the passion Carson builds so easily in me, and I push him back, panting for air. "What about after that? My parents."

"Definite shocker," he says nonchalantly, as if my dad isn't who he is. "They seem nice." His eyes are glancing over my face, cataloging every line as I react to his words.

"Wait, what? I'm gonna need more words on that one."

He smiles lazily. "They seem nice. Your mom says there's monthly dinners and we're expected to attend." He relaxes to the sand beside me, seeming wholly unbothered by anything now that we're talking things out in each other's arms.

I look at him incredulously. "You don't care about who my dad is? You damn near froze up like an ice sculpture."

"Well, yeah. It's enough pressure meeting your woman's parents, but to do it unexpectedly like that? Pressure. And then it's Jameson Brooks? Even more pressure." He lays on his back, his arms folded beneath is head as a makeshift pillow. "I didn't understand why you didn't tell me, especially after everything we'd gone through. But your dad explained a bit on the flight. He said your family has worked its collective ass off to stay incognito, and it's like the ultimate and final test, which is understandable. I know I didn't pass with flying colors, but I hope I'm at least passing the re-take." He gives me a blue-eyed wink designed to charm me into agreement.

This is my out.

He wasn't mad about my actions in dealing with Archer. And he understands why I didn't tell him about my parents. I can simply move forward from here and Carson would never know the difference. He'd think that it was all a big misunderstanding that he accepted blame for, and I accepted his apology, and we can simply move forward.

But that's not what I would tell a client to do. I try to encourage people to be honest as much as possible and as often as possible. That doesn't mean being unfiltered or blurting things out, but speaking your truth thoughtfully can be a powerful freedom.

Or so I've told a client or two.

It's time for me to take my own advice.

"I love you too." Carson moves in to kiss me again, his lips upturned into a pleased smile, but this time I do stop him. "Wait. There's more."

He looks worried there's going to be a 'but' after my declaration of love, but that's not it.

"I love you, and I wanted to tell you but I wasn't sure how because I've never felt like this before. And I'm still afraid you won't want me stepping in front of you, but that's what I do. I wanted to tell you about my parents too. But I was nervous and hadn't worked up the guts yet. I know I'm a lot, and if you can't handle it, that's okay. I'll understand if you want something easier."

That's true. I would understand. I'm mouthy with the brains to back it up. I'm bossy with no plans to change. I'm protective because it's how I show that I care. And if I'm too much or push too many of his buttons, he can go. It'll destroy me, but I'll live. I'm scared I'm going to have to, though.

"Fucking badass." He says it as though he's talking about me, but that doesn't make any sense when I'm confessing to all my fears. He lowers his voice, ordering quietly, "Say it one more time."

"I was scared to tell you," I venture. But he shakes his head. It's then that I know exactly what he wants me to say. "I love you."

"Yes," he whispers, as if my words give him actual physical pleasure. Then we're kissing again, and it's different this time. No miscommunications or secrets remain. It's just us, together, the reward finally worth the risk.

"As much as I want to make love to you, I think I've sworn off sandy places as an option. Think Taya would mind if we borrowed one of her guest rooms?" Carson whispers between kisses.

I nod, breaking the kiss. "Come on."

I grab the blanket from the sand, letting the wind shake out the excess grains, and wad it up under my arm. Carson takes it from me, and then, holding hands, we make our way back to the house. We set the blanket outside to keep the sand on Taya's floors at a minimum and go in the back door.

Taya and Carlo are sitting on the couch watching a basketball game. Their eyes don't leave the screen as we come inside, but Taya calls out, "Guest room off the kitchen is all yours. I'll leave pizza in the fridge for you for later."

I see the box of pizza on the coffee table and think that if there's a single slice left, I'll be surprised.

"It's okay. Just taking a shower and getting cleaned up," I reassure her nonsensically because Carson is kissing and nibbling along my neck as he matches me step for step.

In the bedroom, Carson growls, "I want you in a bed where I can feast on you all night, exploring every single inch of your body."

I groan. "*Yes*."

CHAPTER 30

CARSON

I reach out blindly, pure luck letting me flip the lights on as we go into the guest bedroom, thankful that the hallway was long and we're far away from Taya and Carlo because I want to make Jayme scream my name. Honestly, I don't care who hears, though. I want everyone to know I'm the lucky asshole she's chosen.

I reach behind her head and pull gently on the band there, letting her blonde hair fall in a curtain around her shoulders. She shakes her head out with a soft smile as she looks up at me. There's something different in her eyes now. Something more, but also . . . less? There's no filter, no façade between us now. Just pure, full-strength Jayme, and her love shines bright and bold in its power. To be loved by her is something I don't know I'll ever think I deserve, but I will never stop trying to be worthy of her.

"Fuck, you're beautiful," I whisper as I drop to my knees in worship. I lift her sweatshirt up, revealing the flat expanse of her stomach to lay a line of kisses up her flesh as I push the shirt higher and higher, growling against her soft skin, "I love you."

She reaches for the hem of the shirt herself, pulling it over her head. Her breasts drop right into my waiting hands. Cupping and kneading them, I tease her nipples with my thumbs. I nuzzle a hard nub with my nose as I glance up to her, meeting her eyes. Her hands thread into my hair, encouraging me, telling me exactly what she wants.

"I love you," I repeat before flicking her sensitive nipple with my tongue. She moans, and I suck as much of her breast into my mouth as I can, drawing pleasure through every nerve there with continued flicks of my tongue.

I push at the waistband of her leggings, and she wiggles her hips, shimmying them down while still holding me at her breast. I feel her step one foot and then the other, removing the pants completely so when I grab her ass, her bare cheeks fill my hands. "Yes," I hiss, praising her as her hips buck in response to my firm grip. "Is that how you're going to fuck me back when I'm balls deep inside that pussy?"

She whines but finds the strength to say, "Yes. Fuck me."

"I will," I vow. But not yet. I pull back slightly, wanting to draw this out.

Instead, I blow cool air over the bare skin just above her pussy, using my thumbs to spread her lips. "Spread your feet apart," I tell her, and she widens her stance. The beautiful sight of her pussy, pink and gleaming, greets my eyes. She's so wet, there's a string of her honey stretching toward a point high on her inner thigh. "So pretty. So sexy. So wet." I trace my thumb along that crease at the top of her thigh, gathering her juices, and then lick the sweetness from my thumb to taste her. "Delicious."

"Lick me," she demands. There's no begging. She's still hanging on to some thread of control, which is fine . . . for now.

"I love you," I promise, eyes on my prize—Jayme's pretty little pearl of a clit. Holding her thighs apart, I flatten my tongue, lapping at her. I get taste after yummy taste of her honey but focus on driving her higher and higher until the pleasure is causing her to keen loudly.

Her hands wrap around my head, her palms blotting out my hearing, but I wouldn't stop for anything right now. Not when she's bucking against my tongue, holding me against her pussy, and ordering me to make her come. I wrap a tight arm around her waist, wanting to ensure that she doesn't lose her balance when she comes, and drop a hand between her thighs. I slip two fingers inside her effortlessly, the juices coating me and easing my way in. I plunge in and out of her, timing my thrusts with hard sucks to her clit.

Distantly, my cock is painfully throbbing in the tight confines of my jeans, on the verge of coming from her pleasure alone. But I ignore it in favor of getting Jayme there.

I growl against her animalistically, my fingers making a squelching sound as I pound into her. Jayme freezes for a prolonged moment, her entire body going stiff and still, and then she spasms wildly. I fight to hold her securely as her pussy walls clamp and release my fingers in waves, her hips buck, and her upper body folds forward, cocooning me as she holds me to her, still not letting me stop.

As if I would.

I keep licking and sucking, pumping into her deeply and holding my fingers there as I grunt encouragingly. Jayme's cries of pleasure are high-pitched as she falls over the edge and into my arms. I hold her securely, affectionately telling her pussy, "I love you."

She laughs lightly and taps me on the head to get my eyes. "I'm up here," she says, her eyes sparkling as she holds V'd fingers up to them.

"Shh," I whisper with a wink. "I was having a private conversation with my girl down here." I tilt my head as though listening to her pussy tell me a secret and then nod. "Sure thing, babe." As if her pussy requested it, I lick a long line from Jayme's entrance to her clit, sampling her cum. She wiggles, laughing a bit.

The laughter ends with a satisfied sigh that's the best compliment my ego's ever heard. But I'm not done, not by a longshot. Now it's my turn to be bossy.

"Lie down," I command roughly, rubbing my palm over my rock-hard cock. The zipper of my jeans provides just enough painful pleasure to keep me from going insane. Jayme grins girlishly and damn near hops over to the bed to lie down, her head on the pillows and her legs scissoring together as she watches me.

I reach behind my head, pulling my T-shirt over and off. Jayme's eyes follow my hands as I rub my palms over my chest and down my abs. "Show me," she breathes before catching her bottom lip between her teeth.

"You wanna see my cock. See what you've done to me?" I dare.

She nods silently, her eyes wide and hungry. I undo my jeans and push the front of them down, along with my underwear, letting my cock out. I don't need to look at myself to know what Jayme sees. I'm stiff and swollen with desire for her, throbbing and purple with need and leaking pre-cum after experiencing the sexiness of her orgasm. I take myself in hand, giving the base a tight squeeze that makes me hiss as a drop of clear fluid runs over the tip and down my shaft.

"Sexy," she growls. I swear that pride makes another rush of blood go south and I grow even harder. "Let me taste you."

I step closer to the bed, holding my cock in hand. She sits up, leaning on her elbow, and sticks her tongue out. I trace the tip over her lips and then over her tongue. Her mouth closes down around me, and I moan at the heaven that is Jayme's mouth. There's only one thing better . . .

"Just for a second. I'm on edge, and I want your pussy."

She grins with my dick in her mouth, her eyes looking up at me as though I've challenged her. "Jayme, please . . ." I hiss as she sucks my soul through my cock, taking me to the back of her throat over and over, her hands slipping up and down my length as her mouth does. I gather her hair into one fist, keeping it out of her way, and reach down to finger her pussy while she works me.

She takes me closer and closer to the edge, and I feel like I'm dancing with the devil, not sure if I'm going to be able to stop before I come but not willing to stop yet. Too quickly, I feel a tingle in my balls that starts to work its way up my spine, and I jerk away abruptly. "No. I want that pussy. Lie back."

Jayme smirks, knowing she almost had me, but she reclines back to the bed, her head on the pillow and her hair fanned out like an angel. But she's no angel. She's my badass little devil.

As quickly as I can, I shove my jeans and underwear off the rest of the way and climb onto the bed between her bent knees. Sitting back on my heels, I take myself in hand to notch myself at her entrance. Our eyes meet and lock. "Jayme, I love you," I vow, my tone more serious than our sexy talk. "Forever."

"I love you too, Carson," she promises. "You and me against the world."

I know what that means to her. She has people, close friends and family she trusts. But I've been let in even beyond that small, inner circle. I'm not sure how I got so damn lucky, but I won't ever betray her trust in letting me in. She's seen all of me, the good and bad, but still loves me.

And maybe that's what matters. We do see each other, not as some perfect image created by studying impact and statistical likability, but the real deal we hide from everyone else. We see the perfection in each other's flaws and insecurities and don't want the other to change. I want to be there for the successes, celebrations, and smiles, but I also want Jayme's messy moments, her angry outbursts, and her worries because those are all a part of who she is. I'm willing to let her step forward to protect me when she feels it's warranted because I'll do the same for her. We protect each other because we're building a future together.

Starting right now.

I slide into her slowly, wanting to feel Jayme's body surround every inch of me. She stills, letting me fill and stretch her deliciously. "You like that?" I tease.

"More," she pants. The pressure of holding back is building inside her, taking all the control she has left.

With a grunt, I drop my hands to the bed, looming over her. "Hang on."

Jayme puts her hands on my shoulders, gripping me tightly, and wraps her legs over mine for leverage. With no other words needed, I thrust in deeply, fucking her the way she wants me to. The way I want to.

I slam into her hard, the reverberation sending her back down onto my cock again. "Oh!" she cries out. "Yes!"

Each slow and powerful thrust has me bottoming out inside her where I grind, feeling her walls around my tip and her clit against the coarse hair at the base of my cock. I pull back and do it again, over and over, until we're both crazed with need.

I sit back, looping her legs over my arms, the back of her knees over my elbows and her feet flailing wildly through the air as I change the angle of my thrusts, driving into her even more deeply than before. I grip her hips tightly, pulling her onto my cock, and she braces herself against the headboard.

Jayme's eyes meet mine, though hers threaten to roll back in her head. "Yes, yes, yes! Come in me, Carson. I want it," she whines.

"Nuh-uh. You don't ask, and you never have to beg me for anything. You fucking take it. Everything I have, everything I am . . . it's yours. Understand?" I keep fucking her as I correct her, a thrust with every important point.

She nods wildly, any answer lost to her pleasure. I'm on the edge, scrambling to hold onto my last bit of control.

"Then take it. Work that pussy and take my cum. It's yours, all yours," I grit out through clenched teeth. She's already lost to my command, her body taking over and spasming, her walls clenching me in waves of pleasure.

She adjusts her hands on the headboard, leaving one there, and drops the other to her clit. I can watch her rub herself while seeing my cock disappear into her core, and her breasts bounce with every thrust I make. Jayme's head writhes against the pillow, her mouth dropped open in a silent scream.

"Holy fuck," I hiss. I didn't think I could feel any more pleasure. I was wrong. This is the sexiest thing I've ever seen—the most in-control, badass woman I've ever seen giving herself completely over to carnal pleasure at the base of my cock. I have never felt more powerful or in awe.

All thoughts evaporate as pure light surges through me. It starts in my balls and shoots up my spine, and I shudder as jet after jet of my cum pumps into Jayme. I grunt with each spurt, praying it's not the last because I want this ecstasy to go on forever, especially when she starts to spasm harder, cresting on an even bigger orgasm.

Long after my orgasm begins to wane, I keep thrusting into Jayme, prolonging her orgasm and pushing her into another small one by slowly circling her clit with my thumb when her own hand sags.

When she pushes at my hand, only then do I stop. Buried deep inside her body, and her heart, I let her legs drop to the bed and lean over her, supporting myself on my hand once again.

"I love you, Jayme Rice," I say softly.

"I love you, Carson Steen," she replies.

"Aww! Well, I love you both, but you owe me some new bedding after that!" Taya yells through the door.

"What the fuck?" I cry out, eyes darting toward the door behind me. Quieter, I tell Jayme, "If she comes through that door, you're gonna have a new job because the headlines are gonna read *Carson Steen kills Taya after begging her for help in viral video*."

Jayme laughs, but I'm dead serious. "You're harshing my afterglow, bitch!" Jayme yells, seemingly not at all concerned about her friend's potential imminent death, or my bare ass toward the door, or her own nakedness.

"Here, cover up, just in case." I grab at my T-shirt from the edge of the bed where it landed after I took it off.

"Boy, I've seen all her assets and then some. More than you, pro'lly, because there was that one time I did her wax job. Canceled appointment, my ass. You can just tell ole Taya when you want a little looksee." Taya is chattering through the door like this is perfectly normal.

Wait . . .

"She waxed you? Like down there?" I ask, looking pointedly to the bare skin at the apex of her thighs.

Jayme laughs. "Yeah, uh . . . *down there*," she says in a deep voice that's supposed to be me. "What, you think she did my eyebrows? A second ago, you were all 'make your pussy take it' and now you're all 'down there' like a frat bro."

She's right, but I can feel my cheeks go hot. "It's different," I try to argue. But Jayme's eyes are full of laughter.

And she still hasn't put on my shirt.

"What do you want, Taya?" I bark.

"Just thought you'd want to know that the hot tub is on and bubbly, and *The Princess Bride* is queued up. So tick-tock, bitches. I'm going to bed and Carlo is passed out on the couch. I was hoping y'all would be done already because *someone* kept me up late last night. A bitch needs her beauty sleep, ya know?"

I hear her soft footsteps back down the hall.

I fall to the bed next to Jayme, ready to fall into a coma myself. It's been a long day, from refreshing that video over and over, to my mad dash to the airport, flying to LA with Jayme's parents, the scene on the beach, and now the best sex of my life with the woman I love. Before I close my eyes, I look over to Jayme, expecting her to be equally wiped. She's been through a lot today too.

Except her eyes are bright and full of light, her hands are curled beneath her chin, and her smile is wide and toothy. "It's my favorite movie."

I'm such a fucking sap for this woman, but I don't care in the slightest. "Well then, let's go watch *The Princess Bride*. If I pass out in the hot tub, don't let me drown, 'kay?"

"No worries, I'll save you," she promises.

I don't think she realizes that she already has.

CHAPTER 31

JAYME

J'm sprawled out on one of the couches in Taya's living room, my feet in Carson's lap as I eat a bowl full of yogurt and fresh berries. Taya sits opposite us, drinking a Red Bull and champagne cocktail that she calls 'Liquid Cocaine'.

How her heart doesn't explode on the combination is something I'll never understand, except that she dances and works out enough to handle it. Still . . . "Really?"

"Hey, you have coffee. Some people have mimosas. This is just my own mix of alcohol and caffeinated goodness," she argues.

"Is it good?" Toni asks from the television screen where she's video calling us from Carson's condo.

"No." Carson's barked answer overlaps Taya's loud sip of delight.

"Mmmhmm."

Guess it's my job to rally this meeting back to its purpose, as per usual. "Guys, so we need to discuss how best to address the latest social media firestorm you three started."

Taya scoffs. "That's your deal, babe. You tell me where to look and what to say, and I'll do it."

That's a bold-faced lie if ever I've heard one. Taya never does what anyone tells her to do, not even me. Maybe least of all, me. Because she knows we're solid forever. But I can't be too angry at her for lying when she's the one who got Carson here so we could get our stuff figured out.

And oh, we figured some things out last night. On the bed, in the hot tub, and on one of those lounge chairs on the pool deck.

As if he can sense me thinking about him, Carson shifts beneath my feet and I can feel his thickness. I wiggle my foot, rubbing him with my heel subtly.

"If I may say so, Jayme . . . I don't think that's going to help," Toni says, sounding rather adultly professional for a college freshman.

"Oops! Sorry," I tell her. "I kinda forgot you can see us too."

She laughs. "That's how video calls work."

I shake my head. "Right. Videos, that's what we were talking about."

I've watched Carson's viral video asking Taya for help dozens of times, and her answering video half as many times. That's what we have to figure out a response for because people are clamoring for answers.

Who was Carson looking for? Did he find them?

What was Taya talking about with her cryptic answer?

What happened after that? What about the ring and the babies?

These are all questions being posed in stitched videos that are going almost as viral as the originals now.

"What's the issue again?" Taya asks. "Why can't you two just do a lovey-dovey, smooch-fest thing? That's what everyone wants, anyway."

I sigh. She hasn't been listening at all. "Because I'm the behind-the-scenes person. I don't want to be on camera, and it'd torpedo things if I became recognizable, professionally and personally, and you know that. People start digging, and shit hits the fan."

I glare at Taya, not able to say everything I want to because while Carson is trustworthy with my family secret, Toni isn't. It's no fault of her own, she's just young and doesn't understand the risk that comes with a family like mine. She was proud to finally be claimed publicly by Ben Steen when her parents got married, so my wanting to be completely separate from my dad would be a hard pill to swallow for her.

"Oh." She nods. "Yeah, that."

"So, no Jayme," I say, pointing to myself. "But Carson and Taya need to be in the video. He's thanking you, you say no problem."

Toni interrupts, tutting. "People are gonna think they're together if you do that."

Taya snorts so hard that her Liquid Cocaine comes out of her nose. "No, they ain't. Look at us, nobody would think that."

I look from Carson to Taya, both beautiful, smart, wealthy people. Stranger things have happened. I'm glad they didn't.

"Okay, what if I stand behind Carson with my hand on his shoulder but my face off-screen. He can glance up lovingly—"

"Done." Carson agrees easily with that part, making me smile.

"Done." Taya agrees.

"Done." Toni agrees too.

But they're not only agreeing to my hand modeling in the video. They're done with it all.

"Wait, I wasn't finished," I argue, still working out the camera angles and verbiage to ensure it answers the questions but doesn't reveal too much.

"We got this," Carson promises. "I'm like a pro at this now."

I look at him, wryly amused. "Do I need to remind you of why we met?"

"Maybe. But we can do that later when Toni can't see." He licks his lips and gives me a sexy smirk, but then his eyes flick to the side in a quick look of annoyance. "And Taya isn't listening outside the door."

"Good luck with that," she quips, still rubbing her nose a bit after the reverse drink. Yeah, Carson's going to have to learn that side-eye doesn't work with Taya, and she likely took the door comment as a fresh challenge. She'll be hanging out by every door we walk through like a bouncer now, probably singing *Let's Get It On* to serenade us.

A few minutes later, Carson's phone is set up on a tripod and Taya's ring light is angled toward their faces on the couch. I'm standing behind them like we planned.

"Hey, people! Got a little update for you. I helped my man, Carson, find his true love or some shit." Taya tilts her head to Carson like she didn't do anything more than tell him the time.

Carson smiles stiffly, not a natural in front of the camera in the slightest, which is somehow what makes him extra sexy on the screen. "Yeah, uh . . . Taya helped me. And I'd like to say thank you."

He goes quiet, and Taya smacks him before I can press my hand on his shoulder. "Tell 'em you two are in love and shit."

"Oh." Carson lifts his hand, taking mine and pressing a kiss to my knuckles. That was unscripted, but when his eyes lift to meet mine with his lips still against my hand, I forget what we talked about. "We're in love."

Taya smiles at us happily and then turns back to the camera and leans forward, her finger pointing at the lens. "Now don't go thinking I'm in the business of helping out assholes online. This was a one-time deal for a friend, so don't be tagging me in your 'help me get a prom date' business. Mmkay?"

She flops back to the couch, looking at her nails haughtily. "And that's a wrap, bitches."

I run around the couch to press the red button on the screen. "Okay, let me do some editing and then we'll post it. Hopefully, it'll stop the snowball from rolling."

"You do that," Taya tells me. "I gotta get gone now that this situation is straightened out. I bailed on studio time when you needed me, and I think I can go back and trust that you're in good hands." She dips her chin, glaring at Carson.

"Absolutely," he answers. "Very good. And thank you, Taya." He wraps his arms around my waist, pulling me to his side, and squeezes my ass with one of those aforementioned hands.

"Thank you again, Taya," I tell her, lost for words. What she did for me is beyond friendship. She's my sister. I worm my way from Carson's grasp and hug Taya tightly.

"You know I got you." She pats my ass, too, and Carson growls jealously behind me. To me, she whispers, "He's so easy to rile up. Gonna be fun."

"Don't be too mean," I warn her. "I need you both on my team."

At that, they both laugh. "Bitch, we are Team Jayme. You call the plays and we go to *twerk*," Taya replies before dropping to a squat and popping her ass a couple of times.

"Uhm, I'm not sure about . . . that," Carson says slowly. "Think I might start another scandal if I did that."

"I'll teach you sometime," Taya threatens.

———————

After Taya leaves, it feels weird to be here, like this is a special place for Carson and me, a protective bubble away from the real world. But I want to get back to the real world, with us side by side.

Carlo makes the arrangements and drives us back to the airport and the waiting plane. The flight is easy, and before I know it, we're landing again. As we walk down the steps of the plane, I realize something. "Oh, I don't have a car here. I had Javier drive me."

Carson smirks devilishly. "I've got my motorcycle right over there. You want to go for a ride?"

I think back to the first time I rode his motorcycle with him and how exciting and terrifying it was. I felt unsure with Carson, wild and untethered, with the wind rushing past me and honestly uncertain whether I could help him as a client.

Things are so different now.

I feel grounded and sure of not only myself in deeper ways, but of Carson. I've learned what's really important and that trust can be worth the risk. Carson certainly is. He's the biggest risk I've ever taken and my most valued reward.

"I would love to," I answer. "But no risky business. I want us to get home in one piece."

"Me too, Jayme." Carson slips my helmet over my head, adjusting the clip beneath my chin. With the face shield still up, he ducks in for a quick kiss before grabbing his own helmet. "Make sure you hang on tight. It's gonna be a hell of a ride."

I wouldn't have it any other way. We roar off into the night, and I'm not sure if we're going to my place or his. I don't care as long as I fall asleep in his arms.

EPILOGUE

ONE YEAR LATER - CARSON

"*H*ey, man, you still going to be able to get those tickets for me?" Myron asks, looking nervous.

I grin, patting his thick shoulder. I won't call him a buddy, but we're simpatico now. "Of course. Though I couldn't get the front row ones I promised."

Myron's face falls, but he rallies quickly. "No worries, no problem. General admission is fine," he says hopefully.

I can't hold a straight face much longer. Myron's too good of a guy. Despite looking like he could beat the shit out of you with one punch, I've learned that Myron is a real softie like Jayme said. Case in point, he looks out for the widow and daughter of one of the guys he served with, and when we announced that Jazmyn Starr is coming back to headline the second annual Freedom Fest this spring, he asked if I could help him get tickets.

Of course, I said yes.

"Yeah, I could only get VIP Access ones. I hope she won't mind being part of the on-stage group instead of in the crowd." I let the mic drop on that, waiting for it to hit the floor of Myron's mind.

"Holy shit, man! Are you for real?" He shakes my hand so hard that my teeth rattle in my head. "Thanks a lot!"

"No problem. Glad I could help," I tell him. "I'll bring them home as soon as the lanyards come in."

Myron goes to grab the door and then whispers, "She has no idea."

"I know," I reply, excited for what's happening tonight and impressed with myself for being able to plan something right under Jayme's nose without her realizing a thing. "We'll go up top at five o'clock sharp."

Myron nods. "I'll call if there's any delay."

Upstairs in our apartment, I find Jayme sitting at the dining table, stacks of contracts surrounding her and her laptop glowing brightly. She usually works in her office down the hall, but sometimes, she prefers the windows out here as a change of scenery. She waves at me with a distracted smile, talking sharply into her headset, "I'm glad you agree with me that the priority here is accessibility. Your client comes off as out-of-touch, quite frankly, and that's concerning beyond the scope of this current issue. He needs to adjust more than his tie to make that happen."

She's quiet, listening thoughtfully, and then hammers right back. "If that's all you're looking for, Patrick can assign you a different consultant from within the Compass family. That's not what I do and not what I recommend. If you want the best, that's me. If you want results, you'll do what I say. And so will the client."

Fuck, she is sexy as hell when she's in boss mode.

Thankfully, she hasn't had to save my ass again. Once Jayme worked her magic with her initial suggestions and the first Freedom Fest, both my reputation and Americana Land's image were restored. There was a small blip with the video of me asking for help, but the duet with Taya proclaiming success was equally viral and settled everything down . . . after a bit. At first, people wanted more answers . . . especially who I'd fallen for and what was going to happen next. People even started an online petition for us to have a live streamed wedding ceremony!

But time passed and people forgot about it in favor of the latest media storm. And since then, Americana Land and I have had nothing but positive scores on every analysis Jayme runs.

She nods, her mind on her new client and the firestorm she'll have to put out, apparently. "Sounds good. I'll see you then."

Jayme taps a button on her earpiece and then smiles as though she didn't just cut some suited, power hungry asshole down to size. "Hey, babe, how was work?"

"Not as good as yours, I'd bet. You get the Rollins deal straightened out?"

She wrinkles her face cutely. "Yeah, kinda wish he'd decided to let Patrick send someone else, though. It's going to be a pain in the ass."

I press a kiss to the top of her head. "People want the best, and like you said, that's you." I take both of her hands, pulling her up from the chair, and take her earpiece out, laying it on the table. "We have dinner plans with your parents tonight, remember? We need to leave by five."

She groans. "Can we stay home and order out? We can get Korean barbecue, and you have that new bourbon to open."

She's negotiating hard, dangling all my favorites in front of me . . . her, barbecue, and liquor. But not tonight. Instead, I spin her in place so that I can't see the pout on her lips or the disappointment in her eyes and push her toward our bedroom. "Nope. Go get ready. Maybe wear that new dress you bought?"

She peeks back over her shoulder coyly. "You like that dress?"

The dress is a backless, swoopy sundress that falls to her ankles. It also comes completely undone with a quick release of a single tie at the waist that lets me open the dress like wrapping paper on the best present I've ever received—Jayme.

I let my eyes trace down over her back to her ass, imagining her in the new dress instead of the still-hot pencil skirt and blouse she has on from her meetings this morning. "Fucking love it. I'll fuck you in it when we get back. Just that dress and—" I freeze, knowing I almost spoiled the surprise I've been working on for weeks.

"And?" she prompts. I lift a wry brow and she smirks. "Can't blame a girl for trying, can ya?"

I pop her ass with a solid smack, and she whoops out in laughter as she scampers toward our bedroom to get ready.

WE TAKE THE ELEVATOR UP TO THE ROOF LEVEL AT FOUR FIFTY-EIGHT. I heard the rotors of the helicopter several minutes ago as it landed and had hurried Jayme along, mostly so we actually made it out of the house with her in that dress. I shift from my right foot to my left, trying to get my cock to relax. But damn, she looks good in that dress. I stare at the numbers instead of Jayme, gritting my teeth. Dinner is going to be torture.

When the elevator doors open, we step into a safety area until we get the all-clear. The co-pilot holds open the helicopter door and waves us forward. I hold Jayme's hand, helping her, and then I step up into a luxurious cabin that's clearly designed not only for comfort but also to impress—the dark leather seats, each of them embossed with a scripted *B*, the wood accents, even the soundproofing that reduces the roar enough that I don't have to scramble to yank the headset down over my ears just to preserve my eardrums—all of it subtle nods to the wealth and power at the fingertips of the Brooks family.

"Welcome aboard," the pilot says through our headsets. "Beautiful flying tonight. Should reach our destination shortly."

I reach over and take Jayme's hand, tracing the length of her fingers, especially her empty ring finger. If everything goes to plan, it won't be naked much longer.

"Do you know who all's coming tonight?" Jayme asks me.

We've done the monthly dinners at her parents' numerous times now, but it's always a bit hit-or-miss on who's there, depending on travel schedules, work, kids' bedtimes, and more. But not this time.

Tonight, the whole Brooks family is going to be there.

I shrug. "Who knows? Hell, your dad might be skipping out in favor of work."

Jayme laughs, knowing Jameson Brooks would never do such a thing. He looks forward to the monthly dinners as much as Leah does.

The flight is smooth and the landing gentle, with barely a bounce. We tell the pilot thank you and take our headsets off. The co-pilot opens the doors for us once the rotors stop, and we exit the helicopter.

I don't think I'll ever get used to coming to the Brooks home. Or imagining Jayme growing up here.

The property is a deep green valley surrounded by the giant protective natural barrier of the mountains on two sides. Forests of trees spread for miles in every direction, only broken by a peek at the stark white of the fencing surrounding the homestead area, which is still nearly fifty acres. The bright beacon of the Brooks home stands tall and proud in the center of it all. It's truly more of an American-style castle, large and with so many wings and floors that you can get lost inside. Or at least, I have . . . several times.

The whole property is like a paradise on earth, with everything you can imagine—a movie theater, bowling, horses, pools, a lake, ball courts, and more. Being a teenager here would've been amazing.

Though growing up at Americana Land with roller coasters wasn't too bad either, I think with a smile.

Dad and I are doing much better now too, at work and as a family. We haven't heard another peep from Archer since his unexpected showing at the charity event, and I agree with Jayme that it was intended as some sort of shakedown for money. When that didn't work, he crawled back under whatever rock he lives under.

But along with these Brooks family dinners, Jayme and I have started having dinner with Dad, Izzy, and Toni regularly too. Dad still tries to get Jayme to come work for Americana Land, but I think it's more of a joke or habit now. He couldn't afford her full-time consultant rate, anyway. Sometimes, even Topper comes, though I've yet to hear him string together more than seven words at a time. Toni says he writes her poetry, though, so I guess there's that.

We walk through the side door of the house, the entry closest to the private helipad, and Jayme calls out, "We're here!"

From deep in the house, in the direction of the family room, an echoing cheer sounds out. "In here!"

Jayme takes my hand, pulling me in the direction of all the voices, and I let her go in before me. "Oh, my God! You're all here!" she shouts, looking around the room. "This is amazing!"

This is the first of my surprises, and honestly, the hardest one. Getting all the Brookses together at the same time can quite literally require an act of legislation, or at least a threat of death from Momma Brooks.

James, Yuri, and their son, Kent.

John, Sarah, and their boys, who I can never tell apart, but one is Grayson and one is Hunter.

Jordan and Drew.

Joel, Keilah, and their new baby girl, Norah.

And of course, Jameson and Leah.

All stand to greet us. "The gang's all here," Jameson says with a hearty laugh.

"I'm so happy," Leah chokes out, tearing up.

We work our way around the room, hugging and shaking hands with each other, and I realize that though Jayme talks about her brothers as though she's seen them recently, for some of them, they haven't seen each other in over a year. Especially James and Yuri since they moved to Japan. They stay in touch with phone calls and texts, but this is different.

I stand back, taking it all in.

"You sure you haven't changed your mind?" Jameson whispers to me from behind his scotch glass.

"Not a chance."

He smiles, giving me a proud nod. "Can I make a suggestion then?"

He waits for me to disagree, which I'm definitely not going to do because my heart is racing, my stomach is flip-flopping like I'm on the loop-de-loops of our The American Revolution roller coaster, and my feet are drumming on the wood floor like I've taken up tap dancing.

"Do it now. Get it over with before anyone has to leave. There's going to be a crisis somewhere, or a diaper that needs to be changed, or something. Right now, everyone's here. Do it."

Oh, shit. That's what this whole night is for, but I thought I'd have a chance to build up my guts. Maybe slip it into conversation at dinner or something. But Jameson is right.

I clear my throat and step forward.

"Uhm, everyone . . . if I could have your attention for a second, please?"

The chatter of various Brookses talking over each other dies out as all eyes turn to me. "Carson?" Jayme whispers. "You okay?"

I cover the few feet between us and take Jayme's hand in mine, meeting her eyes. "Yeah. I'm more than okay." I take a big breath, trying to remember the words I practiced, but they're gone, simply lost to the static in my head. I decide to speak from the heart and hope it's enough. "Jayme, the first time I met you, I thought you were a smug bitch, and you called me an arrogant asshole."

One of her brothers let out a small chuckle, and someone whispers, "She can be."

"We've come a long way since then, learning and growing, both together and apart, supporting each other and taking some really fun and rewarding risks. There is no one I'd rather spend the rest of my life with. So, Jayme Brooks Rice . . ."

I drop to my knee in front of her, pulling a black velvet box from my pocket. I open the box, hoping she likes the ring I had custom-made for her. It's a sapphire, not a diamond, but the stone and setting felt like Jayme—unique and bold, delicate and strong.

She gasps, covering her mouth with her free hand as tears spring to her eyes. "Oh, Carson!"

"Will you do me the honor of being my wife? Will you marry me?" I ask, fighting off tears of my own.

Jayme nods wildly as the tears fall down her cheeks. "Yes! Yes, I'll marry you!"

She holds her hand out, and I push the ring onto her finger. It fits perfectly, but I don't think she's even looking at it. Her eyes are locked on me and filled with joy. I scoop her into my arms, spinning her around in her parents' family room as I kiss the hell out of her. I don't want to stop. I don't want to ever stop, but after a moment, Jameson clears his throat and reluctantly, I set Jayme down.

Still only a breath apart, I tell her, "I love you, and I'm going to spend forever making you happy."

She smiles. "You already have. I love you too."

One of the kids—Grayson, maybe, or Hunter?—says, totally unimpressed by what just went down, "Does that mean we can eat now?"

Jayme laughs through her tears, looking at her nephew. "Yeah, we can eat. And then I'm gonna beat you at snooker."

John chuckles, telling his son, "No way. We'll play teams, you and me against Jayme and Carson."

I put my arm around Jayme's shoulders, keeping her right at my side. "I'll take that action. I'd bet on Jayme anytime," I tell John confidently, though I know all the Brookses are skilled snooker players because Jameson enjoys the game quite a bit and has taught them all.

"Hmmph." Jayme snorts. "I'd bet on us. Show me the money! No risk, all reward, baby!" And then she holds up her hand for a high-five.

I don't smack her hand, though. I grab it in mine and kiss the back of it, just above her new engagement ring. I look up at her with a smirk designed to remind her of some of our riskier endeavors. "Well, maybe some risks are worth it."

ABOUT THE AUTHOR

Truth Or Dare Series:
The Dare | | The Truth

Big Fat Fake Series:
My Big Fat Fake Wedding | | My Big Fat Fake Engagement | | My Big Fat Fake Honeymoon

Standalones:
Drop Dead Gorgeous | | The Dare | | The Blind Date

Bennett Boys Ranch:
Buck Wild | | Riding Hard | | Racing Hearts

The Tannen Boys:
Rough Love | | Rough Edge | | Rough Country

Dirty Fairy Tales:
Beauty and the Billionaire | | Not So Prince Charming | | Happily Never After

Get Dirty:
Dirty Talk | | Dirty Laundry | | Dirty Deeds | | Dirty Secrets

Printed in Great Britain
by Amazon

84728243R00174